THE IMAGE OF YOU

NEW YORK TIMES AND USA TODAY BESTSELLING AUTHOR

MELANIE MORELAND

The Image Of You by Melanie Moreland
Copyright © 2022 Moreland Books Inc.
Copyright #1193846
Paperback 978-1-990803-04-8
All rights reserved

MORELAND
BOOKS INC.

Edited by Lisa Hollett of Silently Correcting Your Grammar
Proofread by Carissa Riggs of Carissa's Books n Coffee
Cover design by Karen Hulseman of Feed Your Dreams Designs
Cover Photography and Model by Stuart Reardon
Cover content is for illustrative purposes only and any person depicted on
the cover is a model.

Dear Reader,

Thank you for selecting The Image of You to read. Be sure to sign up for my newsletter for up to date information on new releases, exclusive content and sales. You can find the form here: https://bit.ly/MMorelandNewsletter

Before you sign up, add melanie@melaniemoreland.com to your contacts to make sure the email comes right to your inbox! **Always fun - never spam!**

My books are available in paperback and audiobook! You can see all my books available and upcoming preorders at my website.

The Perfect Recipe For **LOVE**

xoxo,

Melanie

DEDICATION

Love endures.
For those who truly love—you will never be alone.

and

For those who know the meaning of friendship and
giving.
Your fierceness is noted.
Appreciated.
Returned.

CONTENTS

PROLOGUE
ADAM

Present Day

I YANKED IMPATIENTLY at the silk of the tie I was attempting to get into place. I cursed through gritted teeth as I looked at the skewed knot and, once again, tore it off. Taking a deep breath in, trying to calm myself, I started over. A memory stirred of the last time I'd worn one of these godforsaken things.

She held the length of silk in her small hands, her touch confident as she twisted and tugged, smiling while she patted the perfect Windsor knot in place. Standing on her tiptoes, she stretched up to smooth my shirt collar, and I ducked down to help her reach. She slid her fingers along the collar as she pulled and adjusted, her voice low and teasing. "Considering the magic your hands can create with so many other things, you would think you could figure out a tie, Adam."

Growling, I lifted her off the floor easily, holding her to my chest. "I'll show you magic later, my girl. My big wand and all."

Her giggle made me happy, her kiss was filled with warmth, her touch love personified. She was mine.

I shook my head to clear it as I looked in the mirror, my face angry now as I yanked the knot too tight. I didn't have her touch anymore.

He did.

Grabbing my rarely used suit jacket, I thrust my arms into the sleeves then added my press credentials and phone to the right-hand pocket. I frowned when my fingers brushed something in the bottom of the pocket, and I pulled out the item, stopping when I saw the piece of pink paper. She always wrote me notes on pink paper.

Thank you for doing this. I love you.
~Your Nightingale

Her writing. Her words. Her love.

Lifting the paper to my nose, I could still smell the faint scent of her on it. Light, airy, floral. She always smelled so good to me. Like home.

I looked at the words again and swallowed the painful lump. I had worn this jacket to have dinner with her parents, Sarah and Ronald—a dinner neither they, nor I, wanted to be at, but I did it for her. Back when she was mine.

Mine.

She wasn't mine anymore.

Tossing the note onto the table, I picked up my camera, although I didn't plan on using it tonight. It was the prop to get me in. The only way I could think to come face-to-face with a past that haunted me. To get answers to the questions that echoed in my head daily. To stop the ache that burned in my chest every waking moment. Maybe once I did, I could move on.

I ignored the voice in my head telling me moving on was something that would never happen.

———

The ballroom was crowded. Overflowing with people dressed in gowns, tuxes, and jewels. Too many voices, too many faces; all laughing, moving, talking. I swallowed heavily, trying to stay in control. How different this was for her. There was a time she would have hated this sort of event as much as I did. The entire over-the-top fake glamour would've made her shudder, and she never would have wanted to be the center of attention. However, it would seem, things had changed.

She had changed.

She was here somewhere. I could *feel* it. I hadn't been this close to her in months. And now that I was here, I wasn't leaving without seeing her. I wanted to know *why*.

Why was I so easy to throw away?

Why had she stopped loving me so abruptly?

She owed me that, at least.

Getting in was simple. I was known well enough, most of the hotel security just let me walk through. The one time I was stopped, I used my charm, a sly wink, as if we were sharing a secret, flashed my pass, and explained the bride-to-be wanted some special photos taken for her groom, and I was doing it on the down-low. The idiot let me in without another thought.

I moved around the perimeter, scanning the crowd, keeping my eyes open for her mother and Ronald. If they saw me, I would be escorted out immediately. I sidled up to one of the many bars and ordered a scotch, knocking it back quickly for added courage. I ordered a second and stood in the shadows as I watched.

Looking. Seeking. For one person.

And then I saw her.

Across the room.

Surrounded by the sorts of people she once claimed to dislike—fake, loud, brazen.

Seeing her felt like a hard punch to the gut. My stomach twisted, the acid burning its way up my throat as I observed her. She was still perfect. Small. Even in heels, she was tiny enough she would fit under my arm as though she was made to go there. Her vivid hair glowed under the light, twisted up in some sort of elaborate style on top of her head, not a strand out of place. Her gown—long, black, tight, and elegant—encased her petite frame. It wasn't the sort of dress she would have chosen. She always liked flowing, loose clothing that "let her move." She always liked to wear my clothes.

"You ever gonna give me back that shirt, Ally?" I grinned at her across the room. "I might want to wear it myself one day."

"Nope," she giggled, popping the last part of the word loudly. "I like it."

I crossed the room, leaning down, my hands resting on the arms of the chair she was curled up in. The one I'd had made for her so she could be comfortable in this sparse space where I lived. I brought my face close to hers. "I like it too." I ran my lips down the column of her neck, my teeth pulling on the neckline of the shirt teasingly. "I like it far better on the floor, though."

Which was where it ended up a few seconds later.

We were never able to keep our hands off each other.

I blinked, bringing myself back to the present. My eyes focused on her, staring, following her every move as she mingled, talking to people, often smiling as she listened to whatever they were saying. It took everything in me not to cross the room and grab her. I curled one hand tight around the glass I was holding, while I twisted the other one in the strap of my camera, anger building as I watched on in silence.

Her smile was still her—shy, sweet. Her posture still spoke of uncertainty, as though she wasn't entirely comfortable with the spectacle playing out around her. Maybe she hadn't changed completely.

I narrowed my eyes, studying her. Something else was different—her usual poise was absent, and there was a slight limp to her gait. A twisted ankle, perhaps? Except, from the way she walked, it was as if the slight list wasn't a temporary injury, but part of her now.

My gaze intensified, and I willed her to look my way.

To see me.

I stared, my eyes never wavering, and then it happened. Her wide, too-big-for-her-face eyes met mine. Deep, flat blue met angry, confused brown. She blinked and stared, frozen in place. I glared and fumed, trapped in a haze of memories at the way her eyes used to look at me.

Warm and caring. Filled with desire. Flashing with anger. Flooded with tears. Overflowing with love. Always so emotional. So easy to read. Constantly changing in their beautiful hue, reflecting her mood and emotion—I'd seen them brilliant blue when she was happy, a soft mossy green when tired or sad, and a deep slate gray on the rare occasion when she was angry. I'd never witnessed eyes like that—I'd captured them all on camera. I knew their shades by heart—I could always read her. But now, they were different, staring at me with an expression I didn't recognize, a dullness I had never seen in them. They were always filled with life when she was with me.

Not confused and blank as they regarded me, and then she frowned and glanced away.

Dismissing me.

I tightened my fist on my glass, my hand shaking so hard, I was sure the glass would shatter at any moment, spraying scotch all over me and causing blood to drip down my hand.

The way my heart was dripping blood inside my chest at her indifference to seeing me after all this time.

"Adam?"

I turned to the shocked voice beside me. "What the hell are you doing here?" Emma demanded, narrowing her dark eyes. "How did you get in?"

I smirked at Ally's best friend, taking a swallow of my scotch, letting the burn settle the tight muscles of my throat. "I came to wish the happy couple congratulations. Capture the moment for posterity." I indicated the camera I had slung over my shoulder.

"You can't be here. You have no right."

"*I* have no right?" I sneered.

She stepped forward. "You chose to walk away. You can't do this to her. Leave."

I gaped at her.

I chose to walk away?

What the fuck was she talking about?

She grabbed my arm. "Please, Adam. If you ever had any feelings for her, leave. Leave now. I'm begging you."

"I want to talk to her."

"Why?" she hissed.

"I want some fucking answers."

She shook her head. "She can't give them to you. Nothing has changed. Don't you understand?"

I wanted to laugh at her statement. *Nothing has changed?*

My whole life had blown up, and I still didn't understand why.

"No, Emma. No, I don't. I don't understand a thing about this entire situation."

She stared at me, puzzled. She looked past my shoulder, her eyes widening, but before she could speak, I heard it behind me. The voice that had flooded my memories in the day and haunted me in my restless sleep. It was a voice that used to soothe me but now caused a vortex of emotion: anger and frustration, mixed with need and want.

Her voice.

My Nightingale.

"Emma? Is there a problem?"

I turned, nudging Emma to the side. *She* stood there, a mere three feet from me, staring at me with a frown on her face. Her blue eyes, the ones I loved to capture with my lens, were confused and unblinking. I stepped forward, my entire body shaking, fighting the urge to start yelling and demanding answers. The logical part of me knew that would only get me thrown out, and I needed to remain calm.

"Not a problem," I rasped, keeping my voice steady. "We were just talking." I exhaled hard, knowing I had to get her somewhere private so we could talk. "Hello, *Ally.*"

She grimaced, her hand flying to her forehead, where her fingers restlessly rubbed the skin as though she were in pain. Her fathomless eyes stared at me, her brow furrowed.

I realized in that one moment something was terribly wrong.

"I apologize," she spoke, sounding formal. "You have me at a disadvantage." Her hand rose in greeting. "I'm Alexandra Robbins…and you are?"

I stared at her hand and then her beautiful face.

The woman I had loved passionately—desperately—and still loved to this day.

My former fiancée…who was looking at me with no recognition.

As if I were a stranger to her.

And then it hit me as I took in the emptiness in her eyes.

I was.

ONE

ADAM

I SWUNG myself up onto the ledge, cursing Sean silently as I shifted and balanced. Tonight, of all nights, was when he had his boats out, and he wanted this picture. He rarely asked me for anything outside of work, so I couldn't refuse him. It had rained earlier, and now all the surfaces in the city were covered with a thin layer of ice after the temperature dropped suddenly—an unexpected thing in April. The angle was wrong from the ground, however, and I needed this extra height to give me the right depth for the shot.

I lifted my shoulder to distribute the weight of the rucksack. I should've shucked it off before getting on the ledge, but my assistant, Tommy, had been a no-show. The roof was covered in half-frozen puddles, the gravel and sand accumulating with leftover snow in small piles. I didn't want the bag to get wet or stolen; the contents were far too valuable. I wasn't the only one out on this night enjoying the view. Several people were milling around on the large rooftop, although I was sure I would be the only one climbing the ledge. At least it was a cold, clear night—perfect for what Sean wanted—with no wind to hamper me. The cold, I could handle. The wind was just a bitch, so I was grateful for its absence.

Another few inches—that was all I needed for the perfect shot. I slid my foot carefully along the ice as I balanced myself and the camera, the view coming into perfect focus, the water smooth and reflective. The shutter clicked as I got shot after shot of the illuminated boats anchored in the harbor. I only needed a couple more, then I was done. A sudden shout and a hand on my leg caused me to start, my foot to slip, the bag on my shoulder to shift, and me to lurch sideways. I heard another shout, felt the sharp tug on my coat that threw me backward, followed by a nasty pain in my head...

...and then the world went black.

My eyes flew open, my entire body in panic mode. The space around me was dim, unfamiliar, and unfocused.

Where the hell was I?

Someone was bending over me, the weight of their body on my chest feeling peculiar and not welcome. My head ached and throbbed, and there was something wet and cold in my eyes. My arms felt heavy, as if they were restricted when I pushed on the weight, which only seemed to increase, and I started struggling in earnest, cursing and striking out blindly.

"Get off him!" A voice broke through my panic. "You're frightening him."

"He needs to be restrained. He's been fighting us the whole way here."

"He needs to be looked after, and his head is bleeding again. Back off, Hank. *Now!*"

Gentle hands touched my face as I turned my head, trying desperately to focus and figure out where I was. A female voice, close to my ear, spoke. "Hey, it's okay. You're safe. Please stop thrashing, you're making the bleeding worse."

Blood? I was bleeding? Is that what was in my eyes?

I shuddered, and a wave of nausea washed over me.

God, I couldn't stand the sight of blood—especially my own. It was one of the few things I couldn't handle.

Somehow, the quiet timbre of her voice helped to calm me down, and I drew in a deep breath, pulling in the needed oxygen.

"Good. That's good," she soothed. "More deep breaths, Adam. Good."

I turned my head toward the sound of the voice. "Where am I?" I rasped.

"You're at Toronto General. You fell. Do you remember?"

I frowned, searching my brain, and then it all came back.

The shot.

The ice.

The hand grabbing me and the shout.

Tommy.

That little fucker had startled me.

I tried to sit up, struggling against the sheet and whatever machines they had hooked up to me. "My camera. Where's my stuff?"

Hands on my chest eased me back. "Stay still, or I'll call Hank back. Let me flush your eyes and finish cleaning your wound. The butterfly bandages they put on it didn't hold."

"My camera?" I insisted.

"You should be more worried about your head than your camera." She chided me.

"My camera is worth more," I quipped.

I heard a sigh, then felt the weight of my camera in my searching hands. "Your stuff is fine—somehow your camera hit your bag not the rooftop. Your equipment and clothes are right here. Now, will you settle down?" There was a pause, and her voice became more teasing. "Or I'll get Hank back. Your choice."

I ran my fingers over the metal and plastic, checking for cracks, grateful it seemed to be fine. "I'll behave," I grumbled. "No need to get the fucker back."

"Language," she admonished.

Cold hit my forehead with a stinging sensation, and I jerked.

"Sorry. I need to clean the gash. All your thrashing has made it reopen."

"You better be a doctor," I growled. I didn't want some med student messing with my eyes.

"I'm a nurse. I went to school for it and everything. Will that do?"

I huffed at her annoyed tone. "For now."

"I can let you keep bleeding if you want to wait for the doctor."

Right. Blood.

"No, carry on," I said grudgingly.

"Fine. Then I'll get to work."

"Why am I in a damn gown?" I snarled, fingering the scratchy cotton. "Is my coat in that bag?"

"You were bleeding, and we had to examine you," she explained patiently. "Your coat is with your clothes in the bag under your bed. You fell into a nasty slush puddle, so your things are wet. Soon as we're done and you're all cleaned up, I'll give you a set of scrubs to change into."

"Fine."

I ran my hand along my arm, relieved to feel the familiar heavy links and leather on my wrist.

"We didn't have to remove your bracelets."

Bracelets? Jesus, women wore bracelets.

"*Bands*," I corrected. "They're called wristbands."

"Whatever you want to call them. I suppose wristbands sounds more masculine for you, so okay."

My lips twitched, but I didn't say anything. She had me there, and her sass was amusing.

"Do you want me to get your friend?" she asked, working away at my head.

"Friend?"

"I think he said his name was Tommy?"

"No," I hissed, shifting my torso. "It's his damn fault I fell. Tell him to go to—"

"Adam," she warned. "I asked you to stay still."

"How do you know my name, anyway?" I demanded.

"You're at the hospital. The paramedics got your information from Tommy, and we checked your wallet."

That made sense.

"Why do I have an IV? Is it really necessary for a fucking bump on the head? Seems unnecessary to me."

"It's standard procedure. Once the doctor examines you and okays it, I can take it out." She paused with a sigh. "We're only trying to help you."

Then her voice sounded teasing again. "If you're good, I'll give you a sucker."

I grunted in annoyance. Did I look like a kid who could be bribed with sweets?

I did like suckers, though.

"What kind?"

"Grape."

Those were my favorite flavor, and since I really had no choice, I decided to cut her some slack.

Who was she anyway?

"I think it's only fair I know your name since you know mine."

"Are you always this grumpy and demanding?" she countered.

She had me there. I *was* being difficult. I knew I was being an ass, but I hated this feeling of helplessness. I wasn't used to it, and it pissed me off.

"Only when I hit my head and can't see for shit. I need to see. My whole life revolves around me being able to see."

The bed tipped back, and gentle hands touched my face then brushed along my hairline. "This won't take long. I'm going to clean your eyes now. You have some blood, plus sand and dirt, in them. Once I flush them, you'll be able to see. Okay?" She paused. "And my name is Alex."

"Okay, Alex." I cleared my throat, feeling embarrassed by my demands. She was right—she was trying to help. "Thanks."

She worked quietly for a few moments. She was close enough that her soft fragrance overrode the antiseptic smell of the hospital, and I inhaled the scent deeply. The deluge of liquid in my eyes was warm, and the burning eased. She patted my arm and raised the bed.

"Okay, Adam, open your eyes. They may be a little blurry because I put in some antibiotic ointment to prevent infection. The blurriness will clear soon. They might be sore, but I have the lights low to help you focus."

I blinked, feeling as if my eyes were coated in sandpaper, but I could see, although things farther away were somewhat fuzzy.

"Hello."

My gaze flew to the sound of the voice. The only light in the room was the one over the bed. Alex was bent low and close, her kind smile the first thing to greet me. Time seemed to stand still as I looked into a pair of eyes so blue, deep, and fathomless, they took my breath away. A small shock ran down my spine as I stared into their depths.

"How are the eyes?"

I cleared my throat, breaking my stare. "Good. Yeah, ah, I can see. They're still blurry and sore." I frowned. "So is my fu—" Remembering her chiding, I paused and reworded my statement. "Um…my head."

"I'm sure it is. You hit it hard, judging from the bruises and how bad this cut is. I'll finish cleaning it, and then the doctor will come in to see you and discuss the results of the CT scan." I relaxed into my pillow as she tended the cut on my head, trying not to wince at the pain. It hurt like a bitch.

"Sorry," she murmured. "It's a deep one, and I think you need stitches." Drawing back, she glared at me. "*What* were you thinking, standing on the ledge of that building? Do you realize what would have happened if you'd fallen forward, not sideways and back? A bad gash and a headache would've been the least of your troubles. You could have been killed."

Her lecture took me back, but then I chuckled at her statement and her bossiness. I couldn't help but study her with my photographer's eye, something I did without thinking. I took in many details about her appearance, even with the discomfort that lingered with my vision. She was a little thing, with hair that could only be described with one color. It wasn't auburn or chestnut. It was *red*. It glowed under the light, a shimmering, bright copper. It was pulled back into a ponytail, and I could only imagine how striking it would be loose and flowing over her shoulders. Her eyes were amazing—huge, with long, dark lashes. Her ivory cheeks were rounded and smooth, covered in hundreds of freckles—small flecks of hammered gold embedded under her skin, enhancing her unique beauty. Even as she frowned at me, I could see the indent of dimples beside her full lips. The dimples added a mischievous look to her pretty face. Her hands were on her hips as she lectured me, a stance I was sure she thought made her look tough and serious, but it didn't work.

"I wasn't standing, I was crouching," I teased, unsure as to why I was trying to defend myself or wanting to reassure her. I wasn't used to anyone taking notice of what I did, so her worried frown and gentle reprimanding were oddly touching.

"You shouldn't have been on that ledge. That was dangerous!"

I shrugged dismissively. "I needed the shot. It was the right angle."

Her brow furrowed as she gathered up her used supplies. "You'd risk your life? For a picture?"

I smirked, wondering if she lectured all her patients like this. I had to admit, I liked her spunk. But crouching on the wide ledge of a building was hardly dangerous stuff for me.

"Here. Look." I held up my camera, squinting as I flipped through the last few shots, and showing her the viewfinder. All the sailboats lit up in the darkness, their lights reflecting mirror images on the flat water, were fantastic. "I wanted *this* shot."

She gazed at the photo. "It's lovely. But not worth risking your life."

"My life was never at risk. I was perfectly safe. I should've removed the bag from my shoulder—it knocked me off-balance. I wouldn't have fallen over the edge." I frowned. "And I wouldn't have fallen at all if Tommy hadn't startled me."

"He feels very bad about what happened."

"Good."

She shook her head. "Between the cut, all the bruises, and the concussion you may have, I hope it was worth it. You're going to feel it for a few days."

"Good thing I have you to look after me then, isn't it?" I grinned and lowered my voice, reaching out and squeezing her hand. "My very own Florence Nightingale."

Looking down at our hands, she blushed.

Blushed.

The color flooded her full cheeks.

I couldn't remember the last time I saw a woman blush. It was soft and feminine, and it seemed at odds with her sassiness, but it suited her. There was something about her. Something that drew me in and made me want to be closer to her.

Without thinking, I raised my camera and started clicking. Her gaze flew up, and I captured her startled expression and flushed cheeks to perfection.

Leaning forward, she grabbed it out of my hand. "Stop that."

"The camera loves you."

Her cheeks darkened even further. My fingers itched to capture that. They itched to touch her. I stuck my hand back out, to introduce myself. "Adam Kincaid."

"I know. I saw your chart, remember?"

I chuckled at her tone. "Just wanted to do it properly. Your full name? Or should I just call you Nurse Nightingale?"

She shook my hand, rolling her eyes. "Alex Robbins."

I held her hand tighter. "Robin? Another lovely bird. A pleasure, Ms. Robin."

"Robbins," she corrected.

I winked at her, knowing full well the correct name. But I wanted to tease her—I liked her sassing me back. "Robbins. Got it."

I coughed, my throat feeling dry. "May I have some water?"

She poured me a glass, and I drank the cool beverage. "Better?"

"My mouth tastes like sh— Um, awful."

She rummaged in her pocket and brought out a small tin. "I have Altoids. Want one?"

"That would be great."

She pressed a small disk to my lip, and for some reason, I wanted to capture the end of her finger and nibble on it, but I resisted. My strange reaction to this woman mystified me.

"Okay now?"

The rich taste of cinnamon filled my mouth, banishing the wet wool taste that had been there since I'd woken up. "Thanks."

She popped one too. "I'm addicted to these." She turned to leave. "I'll get the doctor and tell him you're awake."

"You'll come back, right?"

"Yes."

"Okay, I'll wait right here," I deadpanned, enjoying the banter with her.

"Good plan," she stated dryly.

But she was smiling when she left the room.

———

"You have a concussion. I'd like you to stay overnight for observation," Dr. Nash informed me after his examination and looking over the CT scan.

I stifled my groan. Was he kidding me with this shit? It wasn't as though this was my first concussion. I could look after myself. "I don't need to stay. I'll be fine."

Across the room, Alex chuckled. "He's a stubborn one, Doc."

The doctor frowned. "You said you live alone. You need to be woken up every couple of hours, and your eyes should be flushed a few more times. The wards are full, but you can stay here, and Alexandra can check on you and clean your eyes."

Suddenly, going home to my empty loft was no longer appealing. Not with the chance of spending more time with the sweet little nurse. I held up my hands in supplication. "If you insist, Doc."

He nodded. "Alexandra can stitch you up, if you're okay with that? She's got a light touch."

I bet she did.

"Sure, I'm good with that." Glancing over, I saw her watching us warily, and I winked at her. Her gaze skittered away to a spot on the wall, and I tried not to snicker as I looked down.

I liked her reactions to me. A lot.

Dr. Nash spoke quietly with Alex, patted her shoulder, and left, muttering something about my chart and instructions. I followed his retreating form with narrowed eyes, and then I watched as Alex opened cupboards and drawers, looking for whatever she needed to stitch me up. If I had to stay, at least I'd get to talk to her more. I wanted to know more about her. A lot more.

"Why does he call you Alexandra?" I asked as she laid out supplies on the table.

"He's my boss, and that's my name."

"You said it was Alex."

She smiled at me, the sweetness of it warming my chest.

"My friends call me Alex. He's more formal, and he prefers Alexandra, which is fine."

Her friends. She introduced herself to me as Alex, as if I was her friend. I liked being thought of as her friend.

"I need a couple of other needles. I'll go get them, and we'll get started."

Needles—they ranked up there with my dislike for blood. I looked down, not wanting her to see yet another weakness. I was losing all sorts of checks on my man card tonight. "Yeah, not big on those," I mumbled.

She patted my hand in comfort. "Most people aren't. I can use a topical freezing cream on your head first. You won't even feel me stitching you up. Promise."

I tried to make light of my discomfort, offering her my most charming smile. "Do I get my sucker afterward?"

With a grin, she pulled one out of her pocket. "There's another one when I'm done if you're good for me."

I took the sucker, ripped off the plastic wrapper, and stuck it into my mouth. "Deal. Make it quick, okay?"

Alex chuckled.

"What?"

"You're cute when you're squeamish." She winked as she left the room. "I'll be gentle."

I crunched my sucker.

She thought I was cute. Very few people would ever describe me as cute. Yet …

I was okay with it.

———

She did have a light touch, and she was done quicker than I expected. She chatted as she worked away, no doubt to distract me, but her closeness was enough of a distraction already. I rested my hand on her hip while she worked. When she raised her eyebrow at me quizzically, I told her it was to keep her steady. Her eye rolling made me smile.

Everything about this petite woman seemed to make me smile.

After applying a bandage, she stepped back. "Okay. Let's get you comfortable, and I'll give you some painkillers and you can rest. I sent your friend home."

I had forgotten about Tommy. I'd text him later.

"Fine." I shifted in the uncomfortable bed. "I, ah, I need to, um—"

"What?"

"Um—" I indicated the door behind her, and I was

shocked at my inability to say it out loud. I huffed. "I need to hit the head."

"Oh, of course." She nudged the cart out of the way and lowered the bed. "You may be dizzy. Stand up slowly."

Swinging my legs out of the bed, I stood, surprised to find she was right. The floor tilted, and I reached out. Alex's arm came around me, and I leaned heavily into her, blinking for a moment to clear the white spots flashing across my eyes and get my equilibrium back. "Whoa," I breathed out.

She looked up at me from my side. "Are you always this stubborn?"

I grinned down at her. She was like a pixie, tucked perfectly under my arm. I hadn't realized just *how* tiny she was until I stood beside her. "You're just a little thing, aren't you?"

"Pfft," she scoffed. "I'm big enough to take on the likes of you, buddy."

Buddy?

I chuckled all the way to the can. I kept chuckling as she handed me a set of scrubs to change into, asking me briskly if I needed help. I let her off the hook, finished up, and got dressed myself, gingerly brushing my hair away, wincing at the sight of my bruised forehead in the mirror. Another scar to add to the collection. My longer, wavy dark-brown hair was matted in places with blood and bits of gravel, the random shots of silver showing in the bright light. I could see the bruise was going to extend down, the color already forming around my eye socket. My eyes were bloodshot and sore, the eyelids heavy. The golden brown of my irises were barely visible, and I looked exhausted. I splashed some cold water on my face, the temperature feeling good on my cheeks. I ignored the rest of the mess—it would have to wait until I could go home and shower.

I faked being dizzy so I could put my arm around Alex again on the way back to the bed. I liked how she felt next to me.

"Can the IV come out now?"

"Yes. Sit down, and I'll take it out."

She helped me sit on the bed, and I noticed her looking at the ink that ran up and down my arms. Her eyes were wide as she took in all the tattoos revealed on my skin. The whole time she removed the IV, her eyes kept drifting toward the images. I was puzzled at the feeling of wanting to share this part of myself with her. I was usually more reserved.

"You can touch them if you want," I offered, when she finished securing a small square of plastic covering the injection site.

She stepped closer, transfixed, as she traced the various designs with her fingers. Her touch was gentle, almost reverent, as she traced the swirls and patterns.

"Do you like them?" I asked curiously.

She nodded. "Do they mean something?"

I shrugged. "Yes and no. They're all symbols of legends and myths." I traced the dragon's tail. "My father used to read to me a lot," I explained. "Medieval stories." I pointed to the sword. "King Arthur, dragon slayers, that sort of thing. I got my first one at eighteen." I grinned at her. "They are rather addictive."

"So I've heard. The work is beautiful."

So was she.

"But you don't like needles?" She sounded puzzled.

"Tattoos are different. The hum of the machine, the slight bite of the ink—it's not the same as a sharp jab of a normal needle. Hard to explain, but it doesn't bother me." I winked. "And I never look until it's done and the blood is wiped away."

"Ah."

"Do you have any ink, Nightingale?"

"No," she whispered. "I'd like one someday. But it would have to be hidden."

"Hospital policies?"

"That's one reason."

I was curious about her other reasons, but I let it go. "What would you like to get?"

She shrugged. "I don't know—something significant. But what, I haven't decided yet."

I studied her bare arms. The skin was pale, dotted with more freckles, making me want to know if those sexy little dots of gold were all over her body.

"Don't mar your lovely skin until you're sure. You'll wear it the rest of your life."

The door opened, breaking the bubble that seemed to have descended around us. "Alex! We need you!"

It was only when she stepped back I realized how close we had been.

She handed me some pills and a glass of water. "This will help with the pain. Take them, please."

"You'll be back?" I asked, doing as she asked.

She smiled. "Yes." She glanced at the clock. "I'll check on you after my break."

"See you soon, Ally."

"Alex," she corrected me. "My friends call me Alex."

I shook my head. "I like Ally. Or Nightingale."

She pushed the call button into my hand. "I have the feeling there isn't any point in arguing with you. Use that if you need it."

I grinned at her retreating figure. I certainly intended to.

CHAPTER
TWO

THE SLIGHT CREAK of the door made the edges of my lips twitch, knowing what was coming next. Ally had checked on me every two hours. I'd hear the quiet footfalls of her feet as they came closer, the rubber soles of her shoes making a distinctive squeak on the worn linoleum floor. Then she would lean in, her floral scent surrounding me, and lay her hand on my arm, murmuring my name to wake me up, her voice a gentle balm to my ears. When I didn't respond, she would shake my arm, then run her fingers over my head, calling my name louder.

Keeping up the charade, I'd blink and slowly open my eyes, offering her a small grin. "Hey, my Nightingale."

She'd given up correcting me and only smiled at her nickname. I'd ply her with questions as she checked my vitals, inventing excuses to have her stay longer. Somehow, when she'd bend over to flush out my eyes, my hand always found its way to her hip. I held back my amusement at her muttered comment about "handsy patients."

I knew her shift was over soon, so this was my last chance. This time, I planned on asking for her number, and to see her privately; tonight, if she'd agree. I wanted more time with her. A lot more time. I relaxed into the pillows, waiting for her touch.

But the footfalls were wrong, and the heavy hand on my shoulder jostling me made my eyes fly open. A tall, older woman was standing over me, my chart in her hand. "Wake up, Mr. Kincaid."

"Where's Ally?"

She frowned at me. "*Alex's* shift is over. She went home. I'm Vivian."

Disappointment spiked, and anger hummed down my spine.

She left? Without saying goodbye? I felt a flash of disappointment in my chest. Was I the only one who had felt that strange connection between us?

I sat up, ignoring the small burst of pain as my gaze flew to the clock. "It's only five. She said she worked until six," I insisted.

Vivian's eyebrows shot up. "I wasn't aware you knew Alex—or her schedule."

"Yeah, we're, ah, friends. Well, acquaintances. *Good ones.*" I stressed, hoping she'd give me some more information if she thought we were friends. But her response was short.

"Hmm. I've known her for a while now, and she's never mentioned you."

"She will soon."

She crossed her arms. "Well, you can speak with her another time. I sent her home early."

"That was kind of you." It was, but I was still bothered by her leaving.

She didn't respond, and I knew there was no point in asking her for Ally's number. Flinging back the scratchy blanket, I swung my legs over the edge of the bed.

"What are you doing?"

I stood slowly. "Going home."

She stared, shocked. "I can't let you leave until the doctor sees you."

"Nope. *Now*. I'll sign whatever form you want."

"Mr. Kincaid—"

I winced a little, bending down to grab my bag from under the bed. "I'm leaving." I smirked. "Are you planning on standing there while I drop these scrubs, or are you gonna get me those forms?"

She glared at me. "I heard you were stubborn."

I had to laugh; I knew who she had heard that from.

"Ally was right." I reached behind my head, beginning to pull off the loose smock, and arched my eyebrow. "Am I getting those forms?"

"Don't you dare leave until I get back."

"Hurry up, then."

I wanted out of here.

———

Half an hour later, I was standing outside the hospital, cursing Tommy again for startling me last night. My head was pounding nonstop. I put up a good front to the staff, refusing help, agitating Vivian to no end, and finally walking out with her fuming at me for refusing to listen to her advice.

But now, leaning back on the cold brick wall outside, I could see why they wanted me to stay.

My head hurt like a bitch. Between the pain and lack of sleep, I was unsteady on my feet.

And pissed no one would give me Ally's information.

I had to find her. I needed to know if she felt the same connection with me, or if it was all my imagination.

As soon as I got home, showered this hospital smell off me, and slept for a while, I would try to find her. I had friends who knew people; someone would be able to help me. Or I could take up residence in the hospital lobby and see her when she came back for her next shift. Vivian had let it slip when that would be. I didn't want to wait for days, though.

A hand on my arm, and the gentle voice I recognized, made me start. "Adam, what are you doing out here?"

I lifted my head off the bricks, a smile already curving my lips as I opened my eyes and stared down at Ally. Her hair was even brighter in the natural light, her eyes shimmering. "Waiting for you."

She frowned at my answer. "Why are you out here? You can't have been released already."

"I checked myself out."

"*What*? Are you crazy?"

I shrugged, noting the concern in her eyes. I liked it. "I only stayed because you were there. You left, so there was no point in hanging around." I narrowed my eyes. "You left without saying goodbye," I added.

Her cheeks colored, fusing with a deep pink that heightened her pretty face. "Vivian ordered me to go home. I had already had too much overtime."

"Then why are you still here?"

"I had coffee with another nurse. I was leaving, and I saw you standing here, holding up the wall. Or is it holding you up?" She shot back.

I ignored her remark.

"You could have come to tell me you were leaving."

She crossed her arms. "No, I couldn't, Adam. We aren't supposed to fraternize with the patients, and I wouldn't risk my job. I *was* going to call you later and see how you were, though."

I itched to touch her cheek. I wanted to know if her blush warmed her skin. Her words, however, grabbed my attention.

"You were going to call me?" I asked, surprised. "How'd you get my number?"

"Off your file," she admitted.

"I was gonna give it to you. And ask for yours," I

murmured and gave in to the feeling, cupping one of her cheeks as I stroked it with my thumb. Her skin was incredible—silky, smooth, and yes, so very warm.

She didn't back away from my caress. Our eyes met and held. So many emotions were in her wide, expressive gaze that looked more green than blue in the dim light. I could make out shadows of exhaustion under them, and the sudden need to care for her hit me. I blinked at the sensation—I had never once in my life experienced anything like it. I stepped back, my sudden movement making me dizzy, and I leaned back into the wall for support.

"You need to go home, Adam. You should have stayed until they released you," she admonished.

"Yeah, this head thing is messing me up." I huffed in frustration, unused to feeling so weak. "I need to grab a cab."

"I'll drive you."

I looked at her in surprise. "Yeah? You sure?"

"You're not a serial killer, are you?"

I arched my eyebrow. "As if I'd admit that when you were falling into my trap so easily?"

She grinned, her dimples deep. "Well, 6B drove me crazy all night. Maybe you could take out your homicidal tendencies on them instead."

I laughed at her humor. "I'll try to resist." Then I frowned. "Wait, what room was I in?"

Her grin widened, and I knew who had driven her crazy. I grinned back, liking her teasing.

"Okay. My car is right there." She pointed to an older, but still nice Lexus parked at the curb. "Do you need help?"

I couldn't resist the chance to touch her. "Maybe just your hand."

She let me enfold her hand in mine. I liked how it felt enclosed in my larger palm. As if it belonged there.

I wondered if my recent head injury was causing these strange emotions.

Except, I had a feeling it was something much more tangible.

Something much more real.

———

Ally faltered when we arrived at my building. Conversation had been limited in the car, aside from directions. I had slumped down, closing my eyes and fighting the pain as she drove. Her car smelled like her, and I breathed in the scent, holding the air in my lungs, filling myself up with her essence. Now I could see she was torn, unsure of the next step.

I turned to her with an apologetic grin. "Can I ask another favor?"

"Sure. What do you need?"

"I'm starving." I indicated a small, hole-in-the-wall restaurant across the street. "That's Alvin's. They make the best breakfast sandwich in town. Would you come have breakfast with me?" When she hesitated, I said the one thing I already knew she couldn't resist. It hadn't taken me long to figure out how much of a caregiver this woman was, and I took advantage of her giving nature. "I don't think I can get there and back on my own."

She unclipped her seat belt. "Of course. I could use something to eat, too."

She slipped an arm around my waist, and we walked across the street slowly. I liked how it felt having her close, even if she was acting like a nurse. It was early, so Al wasn't busy yet, and we grabbed a table at the back. I leaned forward conspiratorially. "I recommend the sandwich, but I would stay clear of the coffee. You may be awake for days."

"Good to know."

She only ordered toast, nibbling on it while I devoured two thick bacon sandwiches and some hash browns. She lifted her eyebrows at my full plate. "It's feed a cold, not a concussion."

God, she was cute. And funny. I arched my eyebrow back at her. "Bacon fixes everything. It's a fact."

"Hmm. I'll have to consult some other medical professionals. I don't think that's a well-known fact around the hospital."

I smiled, taking another large bite. After her playful remarks, we were mostly silent, but I found the quiet soothing. I didn't feel the need to fill in the silence with inane chatter, and Ally didn't seem to be the type to need it either. It was a trait I found refreshing, and I enjoyed her peaceful companionship—especially given the fact that my brain felt sluggish.

After I paid the bill, we went back across the street to the door of my building. We had an awkward moment when she stopped, and I saw she was unsure of what to do.

"If you could just help me upstairs, I'd appreciate it." I wanted to spend more time with her and talk. Not as caregiver and patient, but two people getting to know each other.

Once inside, she took in the expansive space I lived in. I looked around, knowing what she was seeing, and for the first time, I wished the space were different.

The loft was large and open; it was also utterly bleak. In one corner was my bed. The huge, plush mattress set was comfortable enough, but I had never bothered buying a bed frame, so it just sat on the floor, the sheets rumpled and messy. A makeshift cupboard was shoved against the wall, the door open, a towel draped over it, hardly any clothes inside. On the floor was my sizable duffel bag I used when traveling, which also served as a dresser for me.

A single chair sat in the middle of the room, an ottoman in front with a small table and lamp beside it.

The kitchen ran against the far wall, a tall, polished cement counter separating the areas. One hard wooden stool was tucked under the edge.

The opposite corner was my work area. A huge glass-topped desk with a variety of computer monitors sat along one wall. Large steel shelves held my equipment, and a fireproof safe kept my work protected. A tall display case exhibited a few items and my older cameras—ones that held sentimental value to me. They had belonged to my mother and were some of the few things I had that meant something to me.

The entire space was stark and empty. There was nothing personal in the loft—no pictures or knickknacks anywhere. There was a flat-screen TV and a set of Sonos wireless speakers for my music—the one thing I was passionate about besides photography. The walls were either rough brick or plain concrete, the ceiling open with exposed beams and lots of light coming in from the skylights and the huge windows that graced two of the walls. It was a place to sleep, to work, and be alone.

She was quiet as we walked over to the lone chair, and she gently nudged me down into the seat. "Did they give you some painkillers?"

"No. I told them I didn't need any."

"Of course you did," she replied sarcastically.

"But I do have some in the cabinet from my last, ah, *mishap*. I didn't use many, so I'll take them if needed."

She stood over me with a sigh of frustration. "Adam, using painkillers is not a sign of weakness. By staying ahead of your pain, that helps you to heal faster. Stop being so stubborn."

She was rather sexy with her hand on her hip as she lectured me. I gave in since her words did make sense.

"Okay."

"I'll get them."

I pointed to the door. "They're in the bathroom."

She disappeared, and I leaned my head back, closing my eyes. At least that room was decent. I had a large walk-in shower and all new tiling and fixtures. The bathroom and the kitchen had been done after I moved in. The rest of the space had never mattered—at least until this moment.

"Here."

She held out two pills and a glass of water. I swallowed them, watching her walk to the kitchen, opening the cupboards and the fridge, pulling a few things out.

"Hey, what are you doing?"

"Making sure you have a sandwich for later before I go."

"You don't—"

She interrupted me. "I am, so be quiet. Your head is going to be sore the rest of the day. You need to rest, and you'll want something to eat later."

I settled my head back on the chair. "You're really bossy, Ally. Has anyone ever told you that?"

She laughed as she bustled around. "You're one to talk, mister."

I listened to the sounds of her moving around. It seemed odd to have another person in my space. I liked my privacy, and with all my traveling, I wasn't around much to have company.

I was grateful I had been to the store and gotten some groceries in the cupboards. Usually, I just ate a lot of takeout. The sounds coming from my rarely used kitchen made me grin, and I relaxed, letting the pills do their work. I drifted a little, my contentment lingering at the sound of her quiet humming as she puttered.

A touch to my face startled me, and I realized I had dozed off. Ally was sitting on the ottoman, smiling.

"You need to get to bed and rest," she instructed affectionately. "I left a plate of sandwiches in the refrigerator for later."

"Thank you."

She nodded and stood. "You said you wanted a shower. Why don't you do that before I go home? I'll wait and make sure you're okay. I'll tape some plastic to cover your dressing so it doesn't get wet."

I didn't want her to go. I wanted some more time with her, but she looked weary after her long shift, and I knew she had to leave. I shuffled over to my cupboard, pulling out fresh clothes and disappearing into the bathroom.

I enjoyed the heat of the shower and felt better after having washed off the antiseptic smell. After dressing, I walked into the main room, noticing that my bed was straightened up, the covers pulled back, with the pillows fluffed and welcoming. Ally was waiting, and I was so tired I didn't argue, slipping between the sheets to my usual spot in the middle of the bed and sighing in relief at the ice pack she wrapped around my aching shoulder.

"You have a few of these," she observed with a touch of humor, perching on the edge of the mattress.

"I'm getting old. Holding a camera makes my arms ache sometimes."

"Thirty-three is hardly old."

I snorted. "Invasion of privacy again? Tsk-tsk. Only fair I get to know how old you are."

"Twenty-five."

I knew she was younger, although it was more due to appearance than to actions. Eight years younger than me didn't seem like such a vast difference.

She ran her fingers through my hair. I had to stifle a groan at the sensation. Like most men, I loved having my hair stroked.

"How's the head?"

"Okay." I reached out, touching her hand, wishing I could find an excuse to get her to stay. "How can I thank you?"

"No thanks are needed."

"Dinner," I said. "Please have dinner with me."

She bit her lip, worrying the plump flesh as she hesitated. I knew it was fast, but I wanted to see her again. I had never felt such a strong connection to someone.

"Please, Ally. It would mean a lot to me." I grimaced as I tried to lift my head.

"Okay. But first, you need to stay still and give yourself a chance to recover. You need to sleep."

"I need your number," I mumbled, trying to fight off the drowsiness pressing down on me.

"I'll leave it," she promised.

The mattress shifted as I rolled closer to her and wrapped my hand around hers. "Just a few minutes. Stay for a few minutes."

Something warm, light, and soft touched my head. "I'm right here, Adam."

With those comforting words, I let the darkness claim me.

CHAPTER
THREE

CONSCIOUSNESS CAME GRADUALLY. I was warm, comfortable, and my pillow smelled good. Better than good. It smelled amazing. Like the scent you get when walking past a garden in full bloom in the summer, a mixture of many soft floral scents blending into one spectacular inhale of fragrance. Clutching it tighter, I breathed in deep again. My pillow was unusually soft as well…and slightly ticklish. With great effort, I opened my eyes, frowning when I saw my pillow was bright coppery red.

Blinking, I realized it wasn't my pillow I was clutching, but thick, rich, soft hair. Pulling back a little, I was shocked to find Ally lying beside me.

No, not lying. She was curled up, much like a contented kitten, nestled into me with her head under my chin. She had one hand clutching my shirt and the other tucked under her own chin. Her hair had come out of its ponytail and was spread out around her—at least the tresses that weren't locked in my fist. I pulled back a little farther, unsure how she got there. I knew she'd been stroking my head when I fell asleep. I remembered how tired she looked; she must have fallen asleep as well and ended up in my bed.

Not that I was complaining.

I couldn't remember the last time I had woken up with anyone in my arms. I also couldn't remember ever feeling this happy when I did—or this content. I wondered, though, how she was going to feel when she woke up.

As if sensing my thoughts, she moved, and I held my breath waiting to see what she would do. She was nestled so tight against me, my arms holding her closer than I had ever held another human being, and I was worried she would freak out when she woke up.

I had to bite back the laughter as she stretched—her legs bending and flexing, toes pointing out. Her hand holding my shirt loosened, lifting and curling, only to go right back into the same position. She tucked up her legs even tighter and she burrowed back into my chest with a little sigh, relaxing once again into sleep, looking more like a kitten than before.

Unable to resist, I loosened my hold on her hair and ran my hand through the curls, resting my cheek on her head, breathing her in. I knew she'd probably wake up in a few minutes and there was a good chance she'd be upset with herself, and even me, but until then, I could hold her. I'd wanted to do that all night.

She inhaled with a low sigh, shifted a little, then tensed up. I knew she was awake and trying to figure out what was happening.

"Relax, Ally."

"Wh-what am I doing here?"

I tugged on her hair gently so her head tilted back. "Well, until a few minutes ago, you were asleep."

"But… But…how?"

I grinned at her. "Usually a person closes their eyes and unwinds. Sleep finds them."

Her gaze flew around, panicked, and she struggled to sit up. "I have to go."

"Relax, Nightingale. Relax. Nothing happened. You fell asleep, that's all."

"What time is it?"

I glanced at the clock. "Almost one."

"One? I'm supposed to meet my mother. She'll be so angry I'm late!"

I frowned. "You worked all night. Vivian said you worked extra hours too. Your mother will understand."

She shook her head frantically. "No, she won't. She'll be disappointed. She's always disappointed in me."

She was off the bed and heading toward the door, grabbing her purse and keys as she hurried away. Reaching into her pocket, she pulled out a tin of her cinnamon candies, struggling to open the container. She uttered a mild curse as she dropped the container, bending down to pick it up and taking one before she stood back up. I launched out of the bed, ignoring the pounding of my head caused by the abrupt action, and in a flash, I was behind her, drawing her back to me, wrapping my arms around her.

"Hey, Ally, calm down. You can't leave like this. You're trembling."

"I have to go."

I tightened my hold. "When you've calmed down. I'm not letting you leave when you're shaking so hard that you can't drive safely."

Her shoulders slumped, and I spun her around, holding her tight. "It's just lunch."

"You don't understand."

"I want to."

She tilted her head back. "Why?"

I ran my fingers over her cheeks, cupping her face. "Because of this."

I stared into her lovely eyes. Never breaking her gaze, I covered her mouth with mine. Softly, our lips met, parted and joined again. Brushed gently, touching lightly. I drew her bottom lip into my mouth, stroking the plump flesh with my tongue.

She whimpered, a breathy little sigh that I felt in my soul. With a groan, I slipped my hands into her hair, pulling her to me. In this very moment, nothing else existed. Only her warmth, her sounds, and her sweet, cinnamon-flavored mouth. Our tongues touched, stroked, and teased. She grasped my shoulders, then she flung her arms around my neck, holding me close. I wrapped an arm around her, crushing her to my chest. I wanted to take her back to my bed, lay her down, and kiss her until she forgot about everything else but me—but us.

I knew, however, I couldn't do that—not yet. Slowly, I tempered the kisses, until they were gentle nuzzles of my lips against hers. I drew back, setting her feet on the floor, and enfolding her in my arms. "I want to understand everything."

"It's complicated. You might find me a lot of work."

"I think you'll be worth any effort."

She only shrugged.

I lifted her chin. "Go see your mother. Take care of what you need to do, then come back to me."

"Tonight?"

I shrugged. "If you're done in an hour, come back then. If it's tonight, then it's tonight. I'll be here. You promised me dinner."

"I need to get some more sleep after I see my mother." She grimaced. "If I can."

"You can sleep here. I'd watch over you."

Her inhale of air was fast. "Adam."

I dropped another kiss on her sweet mouth and slid her purse over her shoulder. "Whatever you need, Ally. I'm here."

She shook her head and turned to go, then she glanced back, with a nervous expression on her face.

"I'll be here. Right here."

"Okay," she breathed.

Then she was gone, leaving me alone in a space that suddenly felt far too empty without her.

———

I grabbed another shower, frowning at the sight of my face in the mirror. The bruises were dark and nasty-looking. I popped some more painkillers and sat down to work on the photographs I took from last night.

I studied the laptop screen, flipping through the images. Sean was going to be pleased. The pictures were sharp, clear, and exactly what he had wanted. I rubbed my aching temples. He'd better like them. A night in the hospital had been a high price to pay for these pictures. Except, I couldn't find it in me to be too upset. I had met Ally, and with any luck, I would see her again soon. I paused as the images I snapped of her came on to the screen. Not my best work, but I had been right. The camera loved her. The images showed how expressive her eyes were—in the few frames I had taken, she was irritated, amused, and frustrated.

And beautiful. She was so beautiful. My body tightened as I studied the image of her on my screen.

I looked forward to taking many more pictures of her. Getting to know her more. I wanted to know if the pull I felt with her was real or simply a result of feeling vulnerable after my fall. I had never reacted to another person the way I did to her. I was certain that she felt it as well, but the only way to tell was to spend more time with her. I just had to figure how out to get her to want the same thing.

———

By eight o'clock, I'd almost given up. I was sure she wasn't going to show. Maybe I had pushed too hard or come across too needy. Maybe staying with me earlier was too much. But the intensity I felt when she was close threw common sense to the wind. I wanted her here.

Finally, a timid knock sounded at my door. I flung it open, visibly relaxing when I saw her on the other side. "I didn't know if you were coming."

"I wasn't sure I should."

I heard her apprehension and worry. I slid my hand up her arm, over her shoulder and neck, to her face, cupping her smooth cheek. "But you're here."

"I had to make sure you were okay."

I didn't point out she could have done that with a phone call. I was too happy she was here.

"I'm fine." Leaning over, I shut the door behind her and flipped the lock. "You're staying." I paused. "Right?"

She hesitated, then nodded. "For a little while."

I kissed the top of her head and led her to the counter, helping her onto the stool, then sitting beside her. I poured the wine I had opened earlier, placing the glass in her hand. She shifted on the stool with a curious frown.

"These are new. They weren't here when I left."

I patted the leather. "I wasn't sure you'd want to sit in my lap all night, and I saw them while I was out."

After I was done working, I had ventured out into the neighborhood to pick up some supplies.

When I'd bought the building, the area around it was run-down, with mostly empty storefronts and buildings, but beginning a slow transformation. Four years later, it was rejuvenated, with lots of shops, businesses, and eclectic stores. The main floor of my building was completely rented out, adding a good profit to my portfolio.

I had noticed these stools in the window of a trendy furniture store while I was out and had them delivered right away. The thickly padded, chocolate-brown leather tops were far more comfortable than my old wooden stool.

"You were okay to go out? How's your head?" she asked anxiously.

"Nothing I can't handle. I'm fine. The drugs have helped, and my head feels better. I think your humming fixed it all."

She shook her head. "Stop it."

"I mean it. You have a lovely voice."

She ignored my words. "You shouldn't overdo it for a few days," she reminded me. "Give yourself time to heal."

"I'm sure you'll monitor me closely."

Her gaze skittered away, and the blush I liked stained her skin. I enjoyed seeing it.

I got up and began to pull out some of the food. "Hungry?"

"I don't want to bother—"

I shook my head, interrupting her. "You aren't a bother, Ally. I'm not a great cook, but I picked up a few things, instead of ordering in."

"Okay. That would be lovely."

"Good." I set down a couple of plates of snacks I had bought—cheeses and dips, some bread, and other munchies. "I didn't know what you liked, so I grabbed a variety."

"This is great. Thank you."

As we ate, I studied her. The only word that came to my head was weary. She looked weary. "Did you run around all day with your mother?"

"Yes."

I waited for her to say more, and when she didn't, I prompted her.

"How was your mother?"

"Annoyed."

I heard the frustration in her voice. There was an underlying edge as well. Hurt, perhaps? I was right thinking her mother was the source.

"I don't understand."

She paused, her wineglass inches from her lips. The lips I'd wanted to kiss since she walked back in my door. "There are…*expectations*. When I don't live up to them, my mother isn't happy. Not only was I late, apparently I was distracted and not as involved as I should have been…" Her voice trailed off, and she shrugged.

"You overslept because you were here with me, right? I threw off your schedule?"

She met my eyes. "Yes. But that part I enjoyed. Don't even think to apologize."

I grinned at her tone. I wanted to tease her and ask what had been distracting her all afternoon, but I resisted.

"You just got off working nights. She must understand that."

She sighed, crumbling a cracker over her plate. "My mother only understands what she wants to understand. I worked five nights in a row. My shifts are normally four nights on, three nights off. But I had to work an extra one because one of the girls was sick."

"Then why can't she understand you needed sleep? She's your mother, for fuck's sake."

She cast a look at me over my language, but I ignored her.

"It's complicated. She's always annoyed with me, no matter what I do."

That puzzled me, and I studied her guarded expression. "If you think that will scare me off, you can think again."

She pushed her plate away in exasperation. "Why is it so important for you to know all this?"

I picked up a small piece of cheese, placing it on a

cracker. I held it to her lips. "You've hardly eaten anything. Open up."

I waited patiently until her lips parted, and I slipped the morsel in.

"I want to know all about you." I tore a slice of bread and dragged it through the olive oil and balsamic vinegar I had mixed on a plate. I waited until she swallowed and held it up for her, smiling in satisfaction as she accepted it. I would happily feed her all night if that was what it took to make sure she ate.

"I may be far more trouble than I'm worth."

Those words made me frown.

"I doubt that."

"I shouldn't be here," she said, then paused. "I wasn't going to come back."

"I figured that out, but you did." I took a deep swallow of my wine. I needed to know. "Why?"

"I couldn't–I couldn't stay away," she admitted. "I tried, but I couldn't stop thinking about you. I swore I'd only check on you and then leave."

I stood, cradling her face between my hands and kissing her, unable to bear one more moment without doing so. "I don't want you to stay away," I murmured against her lips. I didn't understand the draw I had to her, but it was there. I was certain she felt it as well, but she was fighting it.

She shivered, the smallest breath of a sigh escaping her mouth as I kissed her. I rained light whispers of kisses on her mouth, her cheeks, the tip of her nose, finally nuzzling her forehead. I wrapped her up close and rocked us for a minute, before helping her off the stool and guiding her over to the chair. Once she was sitting, I fetched our freshly topped-off glasses of wine, pulled up the ottoman, and situated myself in front of her.

"Talk to me."

She hesitated, so I gathered up her hands, kissing the soft knuckles. "Tell me your story."

"My dad died when I was eight."

"I'm sorry."

"I don't remember a lot, but I remember his hugs, his laugh, and the way I felt so safe when he was around. He was larger-than-life." She tugged on her hair, smiling ruefully. "I got his hair."

I curled my finger around the silky texture of her long tresses. "I like it."

"I think my mother would prefer it to be like hers."

"Why? It's gorgeous."

"It stands out. She prefers it if I blend in."

I rolled my eyes. "You are too special to blend in. She needs to open her eyes and see that fact."

"Thank you." She frowned. "Adam, we barely know each other. Are you sure you want to hear this? It's not your usual let's get to know each other conversation. It's… personal and not exactly pleasant."

I studied her nervous posture. She was right; this wasn't the sort of conversation I would have with someone I had just met. But Ally was different—how or why, I still didn't understand, but she was. I wanted her, and in order to have her, I had to hear this.

I pressed a kiss to her lips. "I'm sure. I want to know. Hot getting-to-know-each-other sex will be far more enjoyable, I guarantee you that…but we'll tackle this first."

That made her smile, then once again, she became lost to the memories she was sharing.

"My mom remarried a year later, an older man by the name of Ronald. He was—is—very rich. My life changed. Ronald was very strict. I was expected to act a certain way, always be a little lady. My mother—she was never loving and open, like my dad, but she was still my mom, you know? I thought she loved me."

She pulled on the sleeves of her shirt. I stilled her fingers, holding her hands in mine.

"Of course she did."

She shrugged. "Not necessarily. I guess when my dad died, it left us in financial trouble, and marrying Ronald solved that problem. She became detached. She was exactly what he wanted: a trophy wife. Younger than him and beautiful—completely at his beck and call. She rarely spent much time with me. She was *his* first."

"Yours second?"

She shook her head. "A distant third, maybe fourth. Whatever Ronald deemed important became important to her too. Image, her place in society, Ronald's reputation— those were always upmost in her mind."

"Sounds rather cold."

She took a sip of her wine, her expression desolate. "Ronald had a son. He was six years older than me. He carried Ronald's surname, his blood. He was more significant than I was. I was made aware of that fact, right from the start."

I narrowed my eyes in irritation at such a fucked-up statement. This was going to be more intense than I expected.

"I take it you didn't get along with Prince Charming?"

"No, actually, I adored him, and he, me. He hated the fact that he was doted on and I wasn't. He used to call me 'Princess' and said I should be treated like one."

I pulled her hands away from her pant leg that she was gripping tightly. She was clutching the material so hard, I was certain she would tear the fabric. I was fast discovering one of her nervous traits. Clothing destruction.

"Do you still get on well?"

Her eyes grew larger in her pale face, then damp as she swallowed and cleared her throat, shaking her head again.

"No. He died."

I TOUCHED my wineglass to Ally's lips. She'd been silent, and I let her be so she could gather her thoughts. After she took a small sip, I tipped back the glass and swallowed a large mouthful. Given her last statement, I had a feeling I was going to need it. This was an intense conversation, and it had only just started. Still, I wanted to hear it.

"What happened?"

Her voice was quiet when she spoke. "I was eleven, and Oliver was seventeen. I called him Ollie. He called me Princess. Ronald hated that, he and my mother hate nicknames. Whereas Ronald was strict and exacting, Ollie was so different—happy and laid-back. The two of them had been arguing a lot. Ollie had been, ah, in trouble a fair bit—drinking, acting out at school, that sort of thing—I think it was his way of getting back at Ronald's demands.

He was grounded and lost his car, except to go to school." She sighed sadly. "Poor Ollie had to listen to lecture after lecture from him about his behavior." A ghost of a smile curled her lips. "He did such a wicked imitation of Ronald. It was so funny. He'd come to my room, flop on my bed, and tell me how much trouble he'd gotten into that day." She shook her head. "He was so tired of hearing how he had to be responsible and uphold the Givens name. Tired of trying to live up to an image his father had of him."

"Wait," I interrupted, "I thought you said your last name is Robbins."

"It is. Ronald never adopted me, so my name was never changed. He didn't believe in giving his name to someone who wasn't 'really family.'"

I suppressed my urge to swear aloud. What a callous bastard. From what she had said so far, I had a feeling I'd never like either of the two people Ally called her parents once I met them. They seemed to treat her terribly. I had heard of Ronald Givens. He was a well-known investment broker, and he was said to be shrewd and unbending. And with what I was finding out, I would add cruel to the list.

"One night, I was at another girl's house for a sleepover. I didn't want to go, but Arlene was the daughter of one of Ronald's powerful friends, and he insisted. She wasn't very well-liked at school and didn't have many friends, so they made me go. I wasn't feeling well, and it got worse. I called home to ask my mother to come get me. But they had gone out with some associates of Ronald's, so Ollie said he'd come get me. I told him he couldn't because he wasn't supposed to drive and Ronald would be furious, but he said he didn't care. I was more important than his dad's stupid punishment."

Her hands began to fidget again, her gaze flying around the room. She drew her legs up to her chest in a defensive manner, and I rubbed her calves, trying not to notice how her smooth skin felt under my hands. I pushed aside the physical reaction I felt to her and concentrated on her words.

"What happened?"

"I was feeling sick to my stomach. Ollie pulled into a gas station to get a ginger ale for me."

"And?"

She inhaled, a long, shaky breath. Her fingers tore at her sleeves, and I reached up to still them.

"I'm right here. It's a memory—it can't hurt you."

She nodded and continued. "Ollie went inside. He was taking a long time, and I followed. I was afraid if I stayed in the car, I'd be sick. He was standing with his back to the door, and there were two men inside plus the clerk and Ollie —they seemed to be arguing." She swallowed several times, her pale face now ashen. "When I opened the door, there was a huge commotion. Ollie was screaming for me to run and I heard some loud noises, then I was on the floor, Ollie on top of me. He was bleeding, and when I looked up, I saw one man had a gun. He had shot Ollie, who had jumped in front of me."

"Jesus—"

I was horrified listening to her story. Ally kept talking, tears running down her cheeks as she spoke.

"Then the clerk pulled out a gun and shot the robbers. One crumpled to the floor in front of me, dead. The one who shot Ollie was hurt, but he survived."

I already knew the answer, but I asked her anyway. "Ollie?"

"The clerk called 9-1-1, and I tried to help him. But he died before they arrived."

I shut my eyes at her pain. I could only imagine what she had witnessed. The boy she loved as a brother dying in front of her and another man shot dead, too.

"There was so much blood." Her voice shook. "I felt as if I was swimming in it. I kept pressing on his chest to stop it. His last words to me were 'I'm sorry, Princess.'"

"Ally—"

She kept speaking, almost as if I weren't there. "The police arrived, and they got hold of Ronald and my mother. They came to the hospital. Ronald had to identify Ollie's body, and I told the police what I saw. I heard them say it was a miracle the other bullets from the gun hadn't hit me. I don't know how long we were there—I think I was in shock."

"Of course you were. You had just witnessed two men die."

She could have been dead too.

"They took me home, but nobody said anything to me. I

was sent to my room and told to clean up." Her voice dropped. "I had thrown up and had Ollie's blood all over me, and some from the other man too. One of the nurses was very kind and tried to clean me up, but I was still a mess."

"Your mother didn't help you? Didn't comfort you?"

"No."

The one word said so much. I reached for her hand, holding it to my face.

"Were you hurt?"

"I had bruises and I was sick and scared, but no, not hurt."

"You were traumatized, though."

"I survived, Adam." She clutched her shirt, whispering.

I frowned at her tone. Her words were saturated in guilt—but why?

"Thank God." She'd experienced something horrific, and I had the feeling it was something she never talked about. Something she wasn't *allowed* to talk about.

"It was my fault."

I gaped at her. "What? How the *fuck* can you say that?"

"It was all my fault. I never should have called and asked Ollie to pick me up. I shouldn't have asked for the ginger ale. He wouldn't have left the house that night if it weren't for me."

"No, Ally—that is so wrong. You can't *possibly* blame yourself for what happened."

"Ronald told me repeatedly it was my fault. He blames

me to this day. Because of me, *his* son was dead. My mother agreed with him."

"He was wrong," I insisted, tamping down my anger at her unfeeling parents. They had heaped this burden on her for all these years? Took a horrible situation and blamed her to the point she accepted that responsibility? It was inconceivable to me.

"It wasn't your fault. You were a child. You were sick and wanted to go home. The only decent person in this whole scenario was Ollie—he came to get you."

"And died because of it."

"You didn't pull the trigger. There is no fucking way you could have predicted what was going to happen. Nobody could."

She looked at me, pain flowing from her eyes. "The day of Ollie's funeral, Ronald told me he wished it had been me."

Fucking hell. What kind of monster said that to a child? He knew she would carry those cruel words with her the rest of her life.

"The man who shot Ollie—was he convicted?"

"Yes, he went to jail, but he died there."

"Ally, you have to know what happened was *not* your fault. Surely now, after all these years, you realize that."

Didn't she?

She shrugged, her voice almost robotic. "That's not what I've been told for fourteen years. My phone call made him leave the house—it was my fault. I asked to stop for the soda. I've been trying to atone for fourteen years."

"You can't atone for this."

"Exactly."

"No. That's not what I fucking mean. You can't atone because there is *nothing* to atone for." I stared, aghast. "I think you actually believe they're right." I leaned close, my voice firm. "They. Are. Wrong."

"That's not what I've heard all this time, Adam. What I've been trying to make up for since the day he died."

Make up for? Jesus, on some level, she still believed it. She believed she was at fault. How was that possible?

"What do you mean?"

Her voice became bitter. "Ronald had no problem telling me it was my fault. He *still* reminds me. My selfishness cost him his only child. He said I owed him."

"And how exactly did he collect on this *debt*?"

"By controlling my life. The behavior he expected from Ollie was now on me. I had to be perfect. I was only allowed A's on my report card. There were no parties or dances or going to the movies. He sold the house, and we moved into a condo in town, and I went to a new school where I didn't know anyone. My time was spent volunteering at places approved by Ronald. The only after-school activities I could be part of were ones he chose." Once more, her voice became distraught. "Dance, language clubs, tennis—things to help make me better, in his eyes, not that it ever helped. I needed to be more graceful, a better athlete, smarter—" She stopped abruptly, shutting her eyes. Then she sighed. "My weekends were spent studying. If I went out, it was with them. The only people I associated with were those approved by Ronald. And there weren't many friends. If—" She cleared her throat. "If I ever showed any feelings for someone, Ronald removed that person from my life." Her tone became wistful. "I tried so hard to be what they wanted —to get them to love me. But I was never enough."

Her pain was palpable. "You lived a solitary life."

"Yes. I still do."

I sat back in surprise. The person she was describing was different from the woman I thought her to be. The caring, lively person I saw at the hospital and last night. It was as if she lived two different lives, trying to please her parents—to have their love. An effort I already knew would never work, yet she couldn't accept.

"What the hell did your mother think? Didn't she try to stop this?"

"No. She became even more distant. She told me I was lucky Ronald hadn't shipped me off to boarding school, or worse, divorced her. She was upset I almost cost her the lavish lifestyle she enjoyed."

Rage tore through me at the callous indifference she'd experienced. Her parents should have been grateful she hadn't been taken from them as well—not punished her for surviving it.

"Tell me you had some counseling."

"No. Ronald didn't believe in talking to strangers. Once I went to school, I was busy. I thought I had moved past it. I'd handled it—nothing was going to change at that point."

Of course not. If she'd had counseling, she'd know all of this was bullshit, and his true nature would be revealed. She was wrong, though—she hadn't handled anything. The past still held her in its grip.

I gazed at her, realizing how much she needed someone in her life to support and care for her. Someone on her side.

She needed *me*.

And given my reaction to her company, I needed her. We were meant for each other.

"How did you endure it all? End up where you are today?"

"I had a guardian angel."

"Sorry?"

She was quiet for a moment, her gaze unfocused as she gathered her thoughts. "The one who gave me her car. An aunt of Ronald's, Elena—Ollie's godmother, actually. She's the matriarch of the family, I suppose. One of the most cantankerous, grumpiest old women you'd ever want to meet—unless you truly know her. Ollie adored her, and I do too. She thought Ronald's behavior was terrible and cruel. She was the only person I could talk to. But she never let him know how she felt or how fond of me she honestly was. She was the only one who told me what happened wasn't my fault."

"But you didn't believe her?"

She shrugged. "I only saw her on occasion when permitted. I heard it from *them* every day. Sometimes it easier to believe the bad, you know?"

I wondered if she would ever fully believe the truth.

"Tell me more about Elena."

"She used to have me come and stay with her. She'd tell them it was so she could be sure to keep an eye on me for their sake." She smiled fondly at some memory. "I always had such a good time with her. We'd eat junk food, go shopping, watch TV, and talk about Ollie. I loved going there, but I never let them know it. I let them think it was like a punishment to me. She played Ronald so well. She'd say and do things, drop hints and make him think he was making a decision about me, when, in fact, she'd put the idea in his head.

"I knew I wanted to be a nurse, to help people. The kindness the nurses had shown me the night Ollie died had always stayed with me. As I grew up, I also knew if Ronald realized I wanted something, he'd make sure I didn't get it. Elena knew how much I wanted to be a nurse, how I longed to get out of that place and be on my own. She, ah, made it her mission to make sure I got both those things."

"How?"

For the first time since we started talking, a glimmer of mischief appeared in her eyes. "Oh, she's crafty. One night at dinner, she demanded to know what my plans were for the future or if I was going to continue to sponge off Ronald. She went on about some gossip she had heard about another family and their daughter—how content she was to do nothing. Ronald hated gossip."

"You need to choose a career," she had insisted. "Something honorable, like nursing. That's a good profession."

Ally smiled. "She told Ronald they needed to discuss it further. So, I got what I wanted, thanks to her."

"I like her."

"She'd like you too."

"Tell me what happened next."

"Elena told Ronald it would be good for me to learn responsibility, so I moved out of their house and into a small place close to the university. I had to work to pay for expenses."

My hands tightened in anger. "You had to work *and* go to school? Your stepfather is a wealthy man."

"My tuition was paid, as a loan." She shook her head and sighed. "I was given an allowance and a place to live, but it wasn't enough for all my expenses—books, food, and personal needs. The rest I had to cover by working. Ronald felt it would help build character."

"Selfish, tight-fisted bastard," I hissed. Not only was he cruel, he wanted to control her and make her miserable.

She shook her head. "No, it was worth it. I liked working, and I had some freedom. I came and went as I pleased. I could eat what I wanted and sleep in if I felt like it. I made sure to keep my grades up, attend every social function my parents expected me to, and tell anyone who asked how Ronald was generously paying for my education."

"So, what happened after you graduated?"

She frowned for a minute, chewing on her bottom lip. "Elena insisted they have a graduation party for me. Ronald surprised me with the keys to a condo, close to the hospital. He made a big speech in front of all their friends about helping me start my life." She exhaled heavily. "It was all for show—everyone there was part of their circle, and again, the gift was only to make him look good. I didn't want either one. But he had me exactly where he wanted me. I had to repay him for the years at school, and the places I could afford were pretty bad, given how expensive Toronto is to live, so I accepted his 'gift.'"

"It's not a fucking gift. It's emotional blackmail."

"I know, but it's not forever. Another few years, my debt will be paid, and I can move on. I've managed to carve out my own life in between their demands."

I shot her a quizzical look.

"I work at a job I love, and I live a quiet life. I attend the functions my parents support, have lunch with my mother, no matter how exhausted I am, and have brunch on Sundays with them at their exclusive club. Everyone sees us, the well-adjusted family, eating together. Ronald the benefactor, who forgave his stepdaughter for her role in the death of his son and has supported all her endeavors." She sighed and closed her eyes for a moment. "I hate that part of my life—the parties and required functions. All the fake people."

"Why do you still do it? You're on your own now."

She pushed her hair back off her shoulder. "Nursing

jobs are difficult to find. Full-time ones especially, with all the cutbacks to health care here. When I graduated, I could only find part-time shifts. I finally got this position, and even it is only considered permanent part time. There are no benefits, no retirement plan, nothing like that. But I was happy to get it, because it was steady." She sighed. "Not long after I started, Ronald became a member of the board and made a large donation to the hospital. He became a benefactor."

I knew instantly it wasn't due to his boundless generosity—he was still controlling her life. "So, he's a silent threat?"

She shrugged. "I know he keeps an eye on me. I let him think I dislike the night shift, and I keep a low profile at work and do my job."

"And you never make friends at work."

"I keep my relationships private."

As I suspected, she did that so he wouldn't try to interfere. If he thought she was happy, he would do something about it. I couldn't help but practically growl. "He's a fucking asshole."

"I know. I keep my eye open for other jobs. I haven't had any luck yet, but I keep looking." Then she shrugged. "And as for the other part, I do it because of whatever charity it benefits. Ollie was always huge on giving back—he hated his father's extravagant way of life. In my own way, I do it to honor Ollie. The rest I do to get along…for now."

I grabbed the wine and refilled my glass as I thought about what she had told me, trying not to sound curt when I spoke. "How long do you think you have to atone for something that wasn't your fault?"

She looked at me, frowning in thought. "I will never atone. My monetary debt will be paid in a few years."

I shook my head, frustration building. "There is no debt. They've drummed this into your head for so long, you really believe it. What you should be doing is telling them to fuck off."

"You sound like Elena."

"She sounds like a smart woman."

"So, I do that, and what? Lose my apartment, risk my job, and have to ask someone else for help? It will be done soon enough, and I can move on."

I shook my head in frustration. I couldn't understand how she allowed this, but then, I didn't have years of bullshit drummed into my head. This was Ally's reality. "You shouldn't *have* to be doing any of this."

She crossed her arms, beginning to look angry. "It's my life and my choice. Nothing's going to change it."

"I want to help you change it," I retorted. The protective feeling I had when it came to her was unexpected. The desire to have her in my life was paramount, and I wanted her to feel the same way.

"You can't. This is how it is for me—at least for now." She shifted, beginning to push herself out of the chair. "I shouldn't have come here, and I shouldn't have burdened you with all this. I'm sorry, Adam. I need to go."

I tugged her back down. I knew if she walked out my

door, it was over before it started. She would overthink and make a decision based on even more guilt, instead of going with what *she* wanted. "No, I don't want you to."

"Don't you get it? I'm still tied to them. Soon, I won't be. I just have to wait, and then I can move on with nothing holding me back."

I gaped at her. "You can't put your life—your happiness—on hold. *Jesus*, Ally, life moves so fast. You can't waste it."

"My mother and Ronald would *never* approve of you. They would make my life miserable. They would make *your* life miserable. I'm not worth that aggravation."

I snorted. "Why don't you let me be the judge of that."

"You don't know how crazy this all is. They constantly push the 'right' sort of men my way. Ones they approve of."

And no doubt, ones who were totally unsuitable to her, I thought in anger, but suited *them*. It was something else she allowed because she didn't have the strength to fight them.

But I did.

"And I wouldn't fall into that category? Because I don't wear a suit and tie, and I have tattoos? Because I'm not a member of their 'exclusive club'?" I huffed in exasperation, knowing my voice was edging toward antagonistic.

"Yes."

"I can hold my own, Ally. I'm not in the same league as your parents, but I assure you, my stock portfolio is impressive. I own this building, my bank account is sizable, and I'm well-known and respected in my world."

"You're missing the point—you're not part of *their* world."

I laughed without humor. I despised elitism. "I'm common, you mean?"

"Worse." She softened the word with a smile. "You're a wild card."

"I am. I like being a wild card." I ran a finger over her cheek. "I don't care what they think of me, I care what *you* think of me. Do you feel the same draw I do?"

"Yes," she whispered.

"Then don't shut me out."

"They'd never allow me to have you, and starting a relationship with you is unfair."

I leaned forward, rubbing her thighs with my hands. "I'm not fucking asking for their permission."

She started to speak, but I laid a finger on her lips. I wanted her to give us a chance.

"Don't brush me aside because of them. If you don't want this, that's one thing, but not because of them or anyone else."

I drew in a deep breath. "I'm not easy to take on. I'm moody, blunt, and demanding."

"*Really.*" She held back a grin. "I hadn't noticed."

I chuckled. "I speak my mind, and I go after what I want. I travel a lot—I'm gone for weeks at a time at the drop of a hat. I live out of a suitcase most of the time."

"You mentioned you travel a lot last night. Why?"

"I specialize in photographing natural disasters. I travel

all around the world, often in very remote areas, and I can be out of touch for days, sometimes weeks. I do some freelance stuff, but I also work for *Nature's Edge* magazine."

Her eyes widened. "I've seen your work. *A.M. Kincaid.* I didn't know that was you—I never put it together."

I wasn't surprised. I had suspected as much, and it didn't matter to me.

"What does the M stand for?" she asked.

"Martin."

"You're so talented, Adam." Then she frowned. "So, what you do, is it dangerous?"

"Sometimes," I answered honestly. "But I'm careful, and a professional, and the people I work with are as well. But if you thought me being on a building ledge taking some pictures of boats on the water was dangerous—" I shook my head and gave her a pointed look "—that was tame compared to what I normally do on a shoot."

"Have you been hurt before?"

I thought of the bluffs I'd fallen over, the precipices I'd dangled from, and the occasions I'd been knocked out by flying debris. "A few times, but nothing I couldn't handle."

"Is this something you're going to do for the rest of your life?" she asked, concern woven into her words.

"No. I'll move on to something else. No one can keep up this pace forever. I'm at the top of my game, and it's not something I want to give up—yet. One day, I will." I curled my hands around hers. "Is it something that would stop you from exploring this—whatever *this* is—with me?"

Her answer was a quiet hum in the air. "No."

"Your parents don't scare me. I don't care about what they think, I care about what you think. Can you handle that? Can you handle me?"

"I want to find out."

Relief swelled in my chest. "Why don't we take it one step at a time? You already live two separate lives—let me be part of the one that makes you happy," I said. "I'm not anxious to meet your parents, to be honest."

"I'd like that."

"So would I. I know it's fast, but I feel a connection with you, and I want to explore it." I ran my knuckles down her cheek, resting my hand on her neck, feeling her pulse pick up. "I want to explore *you.*"

Leaning forward, I brushed my mouth against hers—easy, gentle touches of our lips. She sighed into my mouth, her eyes fluttering shut as I slipped my hand around the back of her neck, burying my fingers in her hair, and deepened the kiss. She curled her hands on my shoulders, and I pulled her close, lifting her to my lap. I caressed her tongue with mine—long, sensuous strokes that teased and promised more. I relaxed, content right now just to hold her. She snuggled into my chest, her head fitting perfectly under my chin. I felt her yawn, her entire body shivering as she did so. I nuzzled the top of her head regretfully; I knew she had to be exhausted.

"Will you go somewhere with me tomorrow?" I asked.

"Yes," she replied without hesitation.

I held her closer. "Good."

"I should go, but I don't want to," she murmured.

I frowned. "Are you all right to drive?"

She tilted her head. "I'm fine, but if I stay much longer, I won't be."

"Just for a little while."

She agreed easily, curling tighter to my chest. I enjoyed the simple pleasure of having her in my arms.

I felt it when she fell asleep, the way her body relaxed, her breathing evening out. I looked down at her, pleased at the trust she showed me. I frowned, thinking of her story and what she had lived through. The callous treatment from the two adults she called parents. They didn't deserve that title. I planned on being the person who helped her break from the chains they had her in.

Carefully, I stood and went over to the bed, lying down, taking her with me. She barely moved, instead burrowing closer, the way she had the night before. I drew a blanket around us.

I would just hold her for a while.

CHAPTER
FIVE

WHEN I OPENED my eyes again, the early morning light was flooding the loft and Ally was gone, her scent still lingering on the pillow. On the counter was a note on pink paper she had left me. It had her number and a brief message.

> *You snore.*
> *And I love the way you hold me.*
> *Your Ally*

My Ally. I liked that.

I stayed busy, and I called her mid-morning. She sounded pleased to hear from me and laughed when I told her we were going shopping.

"Shopping?" she repeated.

"I'll text you the address. Meet me in an hour."

"All right," she agreed.

I grabbed a cab and met her outside the store. She got out of her car. Her hair was pulled into a thick braid, and she was sexy as hell in her leggings and long-sleeved shirt. She'd been on my mind since she'd left earlier. I wanted to push her against the side of her car and fuck her. My cock was in full agreement. Instead, I pressed a long kiss to her full mouth, trailing my tongue along her bottom lip.

"Mmm. Cherry."

She reached up, wiping my mouth. "It suits you."

I pulled her in for a hug, needing to feel her close. "You suit me."

"How's your head?"

"It feels pretty good. Not dizzy, no headache." I ran my fingers over the bandage. "It hurts to touch it, though."

"Stop touching it, then."

"Ha-ha."

"Can I look?"

"Sure."

She was careful as she peeled back the bandage, pursing her lips as she inspected the wound. I felt her featherlight touch, then the bandage being resecured. "It looks good. It'll hurt for a few days, but it's healing well."

"I had a great nurse."

She smiled, and I took her hand as we walked into the large store.

"What are we doing here?"

"I told you—shopping."

"Duh."

"I want some housewares shit. Sheets, towels. I know nothing about it, so I need your help."

"Any reason for this sudden nesting?" she teased.

I yanked her to my chest. "You."

"Oh."

"Maybe I can convince you to spend more time at my place if it's comfortable." I snaked my arm around her waist. "More time in my bed. I liked you sleeping beside me."

"I liked it too." She touched my cheek. "Maybe I don't need that. Maybe all I need is for you to be there."

I groaned and covered her mouth with mine. I stroked her tongue, losing myself in her taste, only breaking away when someone walked beside me, reminding me we weren't alone. I eased back, dropping another fast kiss to her inviting mouth.

Smirking, I pulled at her braid. "We need to move before I throw you down on one of these displays. I'm pretty sure what I want to do to you on that bed would get us kicked out of the store and most likely arrested."

"Probably."

"Stop distracting me. Come and help me pick something out."

I gaped at what seemed like hundreds of sheet sets—all various sizes, colors, and patterns.

"What do you like?" Ally asked, running her fingers over a sample.

"Plain. No flowery shit or lace." I shuddered at the thought.

She chuckled. "Okay. White?"

"Whatever color you want. Except girly colors."

Laughing, she strolled away, looking at the vast selection.

Leaving her to browse, I walked to the end of the aisle and found what I was looking for. I zoned in on one bed. It was a massive frame, leather, tufted and thick. The curved headboard and footboard were joined with padded runners, and it looked like a giant sleigh. It was heavy and masculine. The color shone a deep, dark espresso, and inspecting the piece, I could tell it was well-made—the craftsmanship was amazing. It would look great in the loft. I ran my hand over the rich wood, the surface smooth as satin under my touch. For the first time since moving in, I wanted to add to the place. Make it more comfortable. And the reason for it confounded me.

There was only one reason. My little Nightingale.

The past years had been spent chasing images—moving from one project to another with no contemplation of anything but the next great shot. Now, in just a couple of days, Ally had taken over most of my thoughts. This morning, I had noticed how threadbare and rough my sheets were. I didn't give much of a shit, but I had a feeling she would. I wanted to spend time with her—as much as she would give me—so it made sense to have her come and choose what she liked. As long as she was there, I was good. It was the first time in my life I wanted to care for someone

—to protect them. It was also the first time I wanted someone to care for me in return.

"Do you like that?"

I met the gaze of an older man.

"Yes. Is it for sale?"

"It will be once I finish setting it up. I designed it."

I reached out my hand to shake his. "No need. Consider it sold."

Ally appeared beside me, frowning as she listened.

"Do you want to know how much it is?"

"No. Can you deliver it soon?" Then I had an idea. "Do you design other furniture?"

"Yes, I do."

After making arrangements for him to bring the bed to the loft the following week, along with his sketches for a chair I wanted made, I turned around to find Ally staring at me.

"Are you always this demanding?"

"When I want something—yes."

"And you want that bed so much?"

"Yes."

I bent lower, brushing her ear. "I want you, as well."

Cue her blush. Chuckling, I ran my fingers along her smooth cheek. "Have you picked some sheets?"

"No."

"You can't find anything?"

"I wanted to make sure you liked what I found."

I held out my hand, not wanting to tell her I didn't care

about the color, as long as she'd be resting between them. "Show me."

I had never been one to enjoy shopping. My clothing was necessary for work, and I went to the same place to purchase the rugged pieces I used when traveling. I had some suits but rarely wore them. Most things, I ordered online or made as brief a stop as required.

But shopping with Ally was surprisingly fun. Picking towels, sheets, and other items she deemed needed. Dishes and glasses were apparently a requirement and the two chipped mugs I had in the cupboard not acceptable.

I tackled her onto a bed in the back as she studied a fluffy duvet. I kissed her until she was breathless. Until I was hard and aching for her and ready to hide under the duvet and have her, regardless of where we were. She rolled out from under me, standing by the bed, flushed and disheveled, her hand on her hip. "You're going to get us kicked out."

I grinned, lying back, not worried. "With the money I'm spending here, I doubt that, Nightingale."

She rolled her eyes.

I patted the luxurious material, then swung myself off the bed. "But we're buying the duvet."

It took two trips to her car, and it was packed by the time we finished. We'd spent a shit-ton of money on stuff I didn't really care about, but it seemed to make her happy. I liked making her happy—another first for me.

I gave her directions to my favorite pizza place, once again enjoying the quiet with her. I took her hand as we crossed the street, smiling as she slipped her palm along mine.

I smiled at her across the table. I sipped a beer, but she ordered tonic water again. Her eyes were huge when the pizza was placed on the table.

"How do you expect two of us to eat a pizza this size?"

I laughed. "I usually eat one by myself."

She shook her head in disbelief. I watched her eat, fascinated. She sliced a bite of pizza with her knife and fork, chewing it slowly. I'd demolished over half the pizza, and she was barely starting on her second slice. She ate with precision, almost meticulously, each bite disappearing at an unhurried pace. She sipped her tonic water the same way. Small, delicate little sips, the level in the glass lowering only a fraction with her swallows.

She looked up, embarrassed, when she realized I was watching her.

"What are you looking at now?"

I ran a finger over my lips, studying her. "You're very sexy. It's artless. You don't understand how much you turn me on, watching you."

"I think you need another CT scan. Your head is really messed up."

I laughed at her deflection. She had no idea how she affected me.

She rolled her eyes, indicating the remaining pizza sitting between us. "You should have another slice."

"I already ate more than half."

"This will be it for me."

I sat back, frowning. "Is there anything you need to tell me? Do you not like food, or do you just eat really slowly?" I narrowed my eyes, remembering the way she nibbled her toast and barely ate any of the snacks I had put out for her. I wondered if she had some sort of eating disorder. She was certainly tiny enough. "Or something else?"

She frowned and shook her head. "I was taught a girl eats like a lady. I never eat very much, I suppose out of habit."

"Habit?"

"My portions were controlled. When I was younger, Ronald felt I was too pudgy. That was unacceptable."

I held back my curse. What was *unacceptable* was his attitude.

"So, you mean it's fine I stuff my face and you don't?"

She shrugged.

I slid another piece onto her plate. "Nope, not happening. Be yourself with me." I took the last slice and folded it in half, taking a huge bite, chewing and swallowing. "And by the way, *this* is how you eat pizza."

She giggled, and I leaned forward, holding out the piece. "C'mon, Ally. Be a rebel. Take a bite—no utensils."

I quirked my eyebrow in a silent challenge. My laughter couldn't be contained when she took the slice from my hand and awkwardly bit into it, sauce and cheese spilling over onto her chin. She handed me back the slice, chewing and wiping her face with the napkin as she tried not to laugh with her mouth full.

"Tastes better, yeah?"

She rolled her eyes as she picked up her glass.

I winked.

"Suck it back, my girl. A big, long, hard swallow. It's good practice."

Her eyes grew round, with her lips wrapped around the straw, her cheeks growing redder every second.

I burst out laughing. She was so easy to tease. Her eyes were very expressive, and I could read every emotion she was feeling in them. I was determined to start taking her picture this afternoon. I wanted to capture every expression I could.

She glared and swallowed the liquid, setting her glass down with a thump. I struggled to stop laughing, grabbing for her hand again. "I'm sorry. I'll behave."

"Can you?"

I slid out of the booth and slipped in beside her. Before she could ask what I was doing, I kissed her. I plunged my hands into her hair, fisting it tight as I claimed her mouth. She whimpered, clutching my shirt in her hands as I kissed her until we were breathless.

Leaning my forehead to hers, I tried to catch my breath. "You do this to me. You make me want to tease you. Get you to laugh. Laugh with you." I confessed. "Sean tells me all the time I'm too serious and I don't laugh enough, yet with you, I find myself doing it all the time."

"Oh," she breathed out.

Slipping my fingers under her chin and caressing the silky skin, I kissed her lips. "You make me feel things I can't explain. You make me want to buy sheets so I know you're comfortable. Want things I've never wanted before."

"You hardly know me," she whispered. "How could I affect you like that? How do you know you want all those things with me?"

I shook my head. "I only met you a couple of days ago, Ally, but I've been waiting for you all my life. Waiting for you to find me."

"*Adam.*"

She stared at me, her eyes glistening under the lights.

"Am I scaring you?"

"No," she replied, her lips quivering, eyes watery. "That's the part that does scare me. I feel—I feel the same way."

"Good."

I slid back over to my side of the table. I knew if I stayed beside her, I would just keep kissing her, and I wanted her to eat her lunch. All of it.

I ordered coffee and sipped at it while she resumed eating. Although she was still slow, she did at least pick up the pizza with her fingers. It was progress.

"So, you go back to work Monday night?"

"Yes."

"Your schedule is set?"

"For now. This is the first time I've had entire weekends off. Next change, I'll have Sunday to Tuesday off."

"Do you have plans?"

She frowned. "No, I was hoping to see Emma, but she canceled her trip. That happens a lot these days."

"Emma?"

"She's my best friend. She got married a few months ago, and they moved to Ottawa. She designs clothing and owns a boutique here and one there, so she goes back and forth. I see her when she's in town, and I visit when I can."

"You miss her."

"She was the first friend I made when I went to school. She lived in the same building, and I met her when I was doing laundry. We started talking and have been friends ever since." She smiled wistfully. "I adore her husband, Alan, and they're great together, but yes, I miss her. She's so busy now. And Elena is away, so I can't see her either."

"You see her a lot?"

"I try to. I can just be me when I'm with her. We have sleepovers, which are always fun."

"Should I ask what those entail? I assume there're no pillow fights happening."

Ally snorted and covered her mouth. I chuckled at the very unladylike sound.

"That's just a male fantasy, Adam. We don't really do that sort of thing."

I shook my head. "Don't destroy the illusions. We men, as a whole, cling to them."

"Elena and I make martinis and finger food. We play cards or Scrabble, and she fills me in on all the gossip. I love spending time with her."

"Why don't you live with her?"

"The place she lives in is age-restricted. It's very elegant, very expensive. She has a circle of friends and her life. I can stay the night on occasion, but I can't live there."

I nodded. I knew the type of place she was talking about.

"What about other friends?"

"I'm friendly with a few of the nurses at the hospital." She shrugged. "Working nights, it's hard to maintain a lot of friendships. I'm asleep while they're awake, and vice versa. But we do sporadic get-togethers."

She wiped her fingers. "What about you?" she asked.

I sighed. "My lifestyle is even less conducive to friends. I never know when I'm going to be in town, and often when I am, I'm busy working on the last shoot or planning a job I got hired for. Like you, I'm friendly with a few people I work with. My boss, Sean, is probably my closest friend. And to be honest, we're both so busy, we rarely see each other outside the office."

"Ah."

"Do you keep in touch with Emma via social media? Facebook and such? Do you save pictures of cats and share funny stories?"

"No, I'm not one for all that stuff. Not much point since I know so few people, and they all live in town. I don't even have an account. Emma doesn't either. At least, not a personal one. She has a business page, but her assistant handles it. We both prefer to talk or text. Are you a big social media guy?"

"I have a presence on most of the platforms, but they're all business-related too. My people handle all that. Much like you, my circle of friends is small, and I prefer to talk rather than use Facebook to connect." I brushed a finger down her cheek. "I guess we're both private people."

She smiled. "I guess so."

"So, you work until Thursday, and Friday is lunch. Can I take you out on Saturday?"

She started to nod again but then froze. Panic flared in her eyes, and I frowned.

"What?"

She put down her pizza, wiping her fingers. "I'm done."

"Forget the pizza. What's wrong?"

"I can't go out with you on Saturday."

"Why?"

"There's a charity event I have to attend."

"Another command performance?" I tried to keep the sarcasm out of my voice and failed.

"Yes," she answered in a whisper.

"What else?"

She didn't say anything, and she didn't look at me.

"Ally, look at me. Now."

Slowly, her gaze met mine. "What else?"

"I have—" she cleared her throat "—a date."

I clenched my hands, forming fists as I struggled to stay calm. "Cancel."

"I can't."

"Why?"

"It's complicated."

There was that word again. I was beginning to hate it.

"Then uncomplicate it," I growled.

"I, ah, sort of have a boyfriend."

I felt as though I'd been sucker-punched. "What the fuck?" I hissed. "You didn't think to mention that before now? Maybe when we were shopping for sheets together?"

"It's not what you think. If you want to calm down, we can talk about it somewhere private."

I inhaled and counted to ten. I pulled some money out of my wallet and flung it on the table. "Fine. Let's go and talk at the loft."

I stood and held out my hand. "Now, Ally."

She got up and went in front of me, ignoring my hand. But she didn't argue when I plucked the keys from her hand and opened the passenger door for her. Not a word about my head, not driving, or anything else.

We remained silent the entire trip home.

But this time, it wasn't a comfortable one.

She sat on the stool, watching me pace. Twice, she opened her mouth to speak, but I held up my hand. Finally, I stood in front of her. Her teeth were buried in her bottom lip, and she was paler than normal, the dark circles under her eyes standing out against the pallor. I cursed myself for dragging her out shopping when she should have been resting, and then I remembered why I took her shopping in the first place, and my anger burned a little hotter.

"You sort of have a boyfriend, like someone is sort of pregnant? Is that it?"

"No. It's not like that. I shouldn't have said boyfriend."

"Well, you did. After we spent the morning picking out sheets for you to sleep on when you're here *in my bed*. You dropped that line."

She cupped my cheek, and with a groan, I leaned into her tender touch. Her caress calmed me.

"Explain it to me."

"I told you my parents were constantly pushing suitable men, ones they approve of, on me."

"He's one of them?"

"Bradley's my friend. He's a doctor—a surgeon. A good one."

I didn't want to hear a list of this asshole's attributes. "Well, bully for him."

"His dad and Ronald are business associates. They've been trying to match us up since Bradley moved back here after medical school. He's older than me. We were constantly thrown together, and we went out on a few dates. He's a great guy."

"This isn't helping."

"Listen to me, Adam. He's a wonderful man. But he isn't the man for me. We're good friends. That's all."

"Then why did you call him your boyfriend?"

"Bradley and I let them think we're closer than we are. It gets them off our backs, and we use each other for dates for these events or any dinners we attend where our families are going to be."

I narrowed my eyes, finding it difficult to believe any man would want to be only friends with her.

"It's true. Bradley isn't interested in settling down right now. He uses me as a cover, and he dates other women—" she chuckled mischievously "—*lots* of other women, he tells me. He just does it quietly."

I couldn't wrap my head around the fact that he didn't want Ally. It didn't seem possible. "He has no romantic interest in you?"

"No."

"Or you him?"

"I love him the way I loved Ollie. Like a brother. Nothing more."

"And you're seeing him on Saturday?"

"Yes. He'll pick me up, we'll make an appearance for a while, and once that's done, he'll drop me home."

"No one ever gets suspicious?"

"We talk and text sometimes so we know what each other is doing. Then if we're asked, it sounds like we're seeing each other. Sometimes, he'll come up, and we watch a movie or talk. A couple of times, he's taken me to a bar or dinner, and we purposely take our picture and he posts it on Facebook where he knows it'll be seen."

"Have you kissed him?"

She sighed. "Yes. I told you we dated."

"Did you like it?"

She shook her head. "There was nothing there—no spark." She took in a deep breath. "I didn't feel the way I do when you kiss me."

"Which is?"

"Like I never want you to stop."

"Good answer," I huffed, still annoyed, yet finding my anger dissipating in the face of her explanation.

"How long ago did you start going out?"

"About seven months ago."

"So, you've been fake dating him for seven months?"

She shook her head, peering up at me with an impish grin. "No, I played hard to get, so we've only 'fake dated' for about four months."

My lips twitched. She wanted me to laugh with her and see how simple this was. Two friends helping each other.

"Was this your idea?"

"No, he suggested it. I thought it was a bad idea, which is why it took a while for me to agree. But he was right. My mother, Ronald, and his dad backed off. It's made things easier for me."

"Why him? Because he's a doctor? The *right* kind of people?" I sneered.

"He comes from old money, yes. Just like Ronald. His

father is well-known and respected." She sighed. "It's the sort of match he approves of."

"In other words, he gets something out of it too."

"Yes."

"I don't like it. I get it…but I don't like it."

"I'm sorry."

"Why do they want you married off so badly?"

"Then I'm not their responsibility anymore. They know there's a good chance Bradley will move to another city at some point—he has his sights set to go out west. They can ignore me completely then because I'll be someone else's problem." She shrugged. "Out of sight, out of mind. Any embarrassment I cause, they can blame on someone else. It's all about image with them. If it weren't, Ronald would have turned his back a long time ago."

It was also about control and punishing her, but I kept my thoughts to myself.

I crushed her to me, holding her tight. "You're not a problem or something to be given away. Stop thinking like that."

She clung to my waist. "Not to you."

I held her for a long time. When I pulled back, I stroked her cheek. "Friday night, then? Or better yet, would you come here after your lunch?"

"I'll probably sleep."

"That's fine. I can watch you sleep."

"Pervert," she mouthed with a grin.

"When it comes to you, definitely." I caressed the back

of her neck, kneading the tense muscles. "But I don't want to wait until Friday to see you again."

"Really?"

"Really. I'm not sure I can wait until tomorrow."

"How will—"

I shook my head, interrupting her. "We'll figure it out, as long as you want it."

"I do."

"You don't have to go, do you?"

"I have things I need to do," she murmured, not sounding convinced.

"I know, but you could stay a little longer?" I asked quietly, running my finger along her jawline and down her neck, making her shiver. "Maybe go for a walk or have a little nap?"

I helped her off the stool, surprised when she wrapped her arms around me, staring up at me beseechingly. "Bradley is just a friend, Adam. Please don't be upset with me."

"Ally, I'm not." I barked out a humorless laugh. "Even if he weren't, I have no right to tell you who you can or can't see. We've only just met." I fisted her long braid, feeling the softness of her hair on my skin. "As much as I want to have that right, I know it's too soon. I acted like a jerk. I'm sorry."

"I'll cancel."

"No. You have to go, and I assume he does too. So, you go together, the way you planned—" I pulled her flush to my chest "—as friends." I dropped a kiss onto her head. "Do you have any other dates planned?"

"There are a couple of events coming up."

"And then?"

"I'll have to look. I'm sure there is something on the schedule. We'll probably see each other for coffee or dinner at some point."

I didn't want her seeing him at all.

I rested my forehead to hers, trying to figure out when I had become this jealous caveman. I had never felt possessive about anything in my life until I met her.

Still, I didn't make any demands. I didn't tell her she couldn't help her friend. I resisted the urge to tell her she was mine now and the only person she could date—fake or otherwise—was me. She already had enough people in her life telling her what she should or shouldn't do.

"Can we discuss this again before then?"

She tilted her head back. "Yes."

"Thank you."

"I don't really feel like going for a walk."

"No?"

She shook her head. "I'm kinda tired."

"Is that so?"

"Yeah."

I drew her closer, my lips hovering over hers. "Maybe just the nap, then?"

"Yeah, that'd be good."

"Indeed."

CHAPTER
SIX

I PULLED my mouth away from hers with a groan. Kissing Ally was highly addictive. The way she whispered my name and tugged at my hair with her fingers drove me crazy. The smoothness of her skin as I slipped my hands under her shirt was a tease of something still forbidden. Having her body pressed into mine was torture, because I wanted more—even if it was too soon. What was supposed to be a nap was now dangerously close to becoming me tearing her clothes off and fucking her deep into my mattress. I rolled off the bed, breathing hard. "Naptime is over," I stated.

She eyed my evident erection with a small grin. "Obviously."

I stomped over to the kitchen. "Keep looking at me like that, and you'll be sorry."

She shook her head as she passed by. "I doubt sorry is the right word."

I smirked, liking the fact that I affected her too. But we knew it was too fast.

After I handed her a cup of coffee, she walked around the loft, spending a lot of time looking at my cameras and asking questions.

"You don't have any of your photos displayed."

"No, I keep it simple. I don't want to look at my own work most of the time."

When she studied my display case, I sat at the desk behind her.

"These are special to you."

"They belonged to my parents. After they died, my uncle Jack saved them all for me."

"They were both photographers?"

"My mother was a professional photographer. My dad was a historian and an author. The books are his. Ones he wrote and his journals. They loved to travel the world. They took me with them as often as possible." I scratched the back of my neck, unused to sharing personal information with someone. "I didn't exactly have the usual upbringing. I was absent from school more than I was there."

"But what an education you must have had, regardless."

"Yeah, my parents insisted I bring schoolbooks with me, and they taught me, too. I saw so much of the world and experienced life differently from the classmates I would eventually be with. I never fit in."

"When did they die?"

I swallowed around the emotion building in my throat. "I was thirteen, and I broke my leg. We had a trip planned to Brazil, but I couldn't go. I stayed with some friends of theirs, and they went—it was only supposed to be a short trip, but there was an accident. The bus they were riding in crashed in the mountains." I traced the edge of the desk, not looking at her. "There were no survivors."

I pointed to the top shelf, and the camera with the cracked lens and broken case. "That is the only camera my mom had with her, and somehow my uncle got it back. I keep it because I know she touched it. Morbid, I suppose."

Ally stroked my shoulder. "No, not morbid. It makes you feel close to her."

"Yes." Usually, I didn't like to talk about my feelings, but with Ally, it felt right.

"I keep an old book of Ollie's. No one knows I have it. It was his favorite, and sometimes I hold it, just remembering how he used to read it constantly."

"Which book is it?

"*Peter Pan.* He loved that story."

I pulled her to my lap, kissing the top of her head. "Then you understand."

"Yes."

I fingered the metal around my wrist. "This was my dad's. My mom gave it to him. One of the links had broken, so he hadn't taken it with him. My uncle had it fixed for me. I never take it off."

She traced her finger over the silver, the heavy links scarred from years of wear and abuse.

"And these, ah, leather *bands*?" she asked with a twinkle in her eye.

I chuckled, remembering her teasing in the hospital. "Those are because I like them. I'm cool that way."

"Yes, you are."

She ran her fingers through my hair. "I love your hair."

"Yeah?"

"Yes."

"Not too long for your taste?"

"I love the waves and how silky it feels." She made another pass with her hand.

I smiled. "I love how it feels when you do that."

I squeezed her close, and we sat silently for a moment, lost in memories. I enjoyed the gentle, repeated caresses of her fingers through my hair. Her touch soothed and relaxed me.

"What happened to you after your parents died?"

"I went to live with my uncle and his family."

"Were they good to you?"

I let my head fall back with a long exhale of air. "They tried. Uncle Jack was my father's brother. They were as different as night and day. Their life was the complete opposite of what I was used to. I was so out of my element. I had to stay in one place, attend school—I had a schedule like their other kids. I didn't cope well, and I was angry. I was angry at my parents for dying. For leaving me alone. I was angry at my uncle for not being like my father. I hated everything and everyone."

"What happened?"

"My uncle gave me my mother's equipment and enrolled me in some photography classes. It was the lifeline I needed. I started working in a photography shop part time, and it helped settle me down. As long as I kept up my grades, my uncle gave me a lot of freedom. He knew I didn't fit in, and he tried to make my life as easy as he could. I owe him a lot."

"Do you still see them?"

"I left when I was seventeen. But I went on good terms. I visit on occasion, attend family weddings, that sort of thing. Every year, I send the entire family on a two-week vacation to the destination of their choice." I grinned. "They like Florida. They go there a lot."

"Not what your first choice would be?"

"Not in my top ten. But they love it, and they enjoy resorts. If it makes them happy, then I'm fine with it. They're good people. Quiet, steady. They have their life, and I have mine. But I'm fond of them, and they did the best they could with me."

"I guess you don't use your mother's cameras anymore?"

"I do on occasion. I like the old-school way at times. I have a place I can still get film, and I use the closet over there—" I indicated the door with a tilt of my head "—as a darkroom, and I develop the images myself, but I don't do it a lot."

"You have a lot of equipment." She ran a finger over one of the large monitors on the desk.

"I do all my own work. I don't trust others with my images, unless I have to send the files back in a hurry."

"Smart and talented. The more I get to know you, the more you amaze me."

"You amaze *me*, Nightingale. I just told you more about myself than I have ever told anyone. I never talk about my past."

"You never sit around after a day of chasing storms and spill your guts?"

I snickered at her words. "No, we're usually too tired after braiding each other's hair."

She chuckled, then became serious. "I'm glad you feel you can. You can talk to me about anything."

I kissed her hard. "Good. Tell me more about you."

"What about me?"

"Tell me your hopes. Your fears. Your secrets," I added, lifting her hand to my mouth and kissing it.

"I hope to be a good nurse. I hate thunderstorms and spiders. I'm terrified of snakes. I love chocolate, and I keep some in my purse all the time. My locker at work too."

"More," I said.

She laughed. "Once, when I was little, my dad took me ice-skating. He loved to skate. He brought a chair I could push until I found my balance, except I never did. I was really awful at it."

"Did you ever learn?" I asked drowsily.

"No. But I excelled at tobogganing."

I chuckled.

She glanced at the clock. "I have to go," she said, sounding regretful.

I kissed her again and walked her to the door. I hated to see her leave, even though I knew she had to. But I planned to see as much of her as possible.

Over the next few days, we talked, texted, and I dropped by the hospital to see her. I liked being able to stay around and see Ally.

There were moments she was too busy for coffee, but I enjoyed watching her in action. She had no shyness or hesitation when she was at work, in her element. She was Alex—the nurse I met who was in charge, confident, with no sign of the girl so plagued by guilt she couldn't break free of her chains.

When the ER wasn't as busy, I could steal her away for a few moments. We snuck into the staff room, where I was free to kiss and hold her. I had to hide my smirk when she would walk away from me, patting her hair back into place, attempting to look professional and failing. Her lips were swollen, her eyes bright, and her smile too wide.

It was a great look on her.

I hated seeing how she looked after her fake-date with

Bradley and brunch with her parents. The light in her eyes dimmed, and she withdrew into herself. I looked forward to the day she no longer had to pretend for any of them.

Then reality intruded and I was gone, my world once again focused through the lens of my camera. It was the first time I ever resented getting that call.

It wouldn't be the last time.

———

Days later, I walked around a lavish ballroom at a charity dinner and auction, gazing at the overdone opulence, which included heavy, expensive linens and delicate china on the tables. The scent of the hothouse flowers that adorned the center of each of them hung heavy in the air. Trays of extravagant delicacies were being carried around by waiters in tuxedos, then scanned and refused by too-thin women and men far more interested in the contents of their drink glasses. I examined the huge auction table laden with overpriced, decadent items not needed by a single person in this room, yet knowing each one would be bid on zealously, only to be forgotten once it was acquired.

It was all done in the name of charity.

I skirted the room, knowing I shouldn't be here, but I couldn't stay away. It was a new feeling for me—missing someone. Ally had been on my mind constantly the entire time I was gone, another first. Usually, I was so involved with my work, nothing else filtered in. But images, thoughts, and memories of her laughter, how she felt in my arms, would seep into my mind, breaking my concentration. I longed for her.

It felt like forever since I had seen her, and I was aching for a glimpse of her sweet face. I had sent a text saying I had been called away but had no time to go and see her. I couldn't leave town without letting her know.

I spent days capturing the devastation of the small villages hardest hit by the disaster. Most of the areas were still inaccessible, but the ones Tommy and I had been to had been heartbreaking to witness.

I flew back today, arriving in town only a few hours ago. My only contact with her had been the occasional text when I was somewhere I could get access to the internet, which was rare. There was always a short message waiting for me when I was successful. Simple ones: *Take care—I miss you. Thinking of you. Stay safe.* The small words meant so much.

I went home, got cleaned up, and came to this event, hoping to see her, even if it was a mere glimpse. The ticket had been hard to come by, but I had told my business manager to do whatever it took to get it for me, and he had come through. I wasn't usually this irrational or demanding when it came to my emotions, but with Ally, control seemed to fly out the window.

Seeing the money spent on the decor alone made me shake my head. The money could've been used so desperately for *real* needs. Thinking of what I had just seen—the suffering and devastation I had witnessed, knowing how little relief those people would receive—made me angry.

Grabbing a double scotch and dodging around the overdone women and the men all looking as if they'd rather be anywhere else but here, I found her.

I stood in the shadows and drank her in. Small and delicate, she looked so out of place; it made me adore her more than I already did. Standing among the black-and-beige palette around her, she was like a burst of sunshine amid a dark storm. She wore a dress that seemed to float around her, in the colors of a sunset. It left her shoulders bare and swirled about her as she moved. Her hair hung down her back, gleaming and bright under the lights. I wanted to bury my hands in it while I kissed her perfect mouth. Beside her was a woman who was, no doubt, her mother. She was an older, taller version of Ally, without her warmth. More than once, I saw her reprimand her daughter, and not once did she smile at her with any fondness. I had the feeling Ally's choice of gown didn't please her since, often, she glanced down at her dress. The more her mother spoke, the more uncomfortable Ally appeared to become.

Her husband, Ronald, was equally as dour. Even the fake pleasant expressions when they would greet other people seemed strained.

I had used the internet and done a little research on

Ally's family. I found a ton of information on Ronald and his business, and Sarah spent a lot of time on charity work. I found a few articles on the incident that killed Oliver. It was interesting to me how Ronald had used the exposure to further his own agenda, using Oliver's memory, building it to the point he made him sound like a saint. He never mentioned Ally—ever.

All the pictures of them I could find online were stiff and posed. I wondered what would happen if either of them truly smiled.

I assumed their faces would crack.

Mrs. Givens said something else to Ally, and her shoulders fell in defeat. I was about done with this bullshit. I knew she didn't know I was here and striding over there and pulling her away from the cold people she referred to as her parents was going to cause her more grief, but I couldn't stand the way she was folding in on herself. I wanted to yank her into my arms and kiss her until she smiled the way she did in my loft.

I set down my glass and started to move forward, coming to a halt when a tall blond man appeared in front of Ally. Her relief was obvious when she accepted his embrace with ease and smiled when he spoke to her.

I gripped the back of the chair as I saw the familiar way he cupped her cheek, kissing it.

I could only assume the infamous great-guy-who-is-just-a-friend Dr. Bradley had just shown up.

He shook Ronald's hand, air-kissed her mother's cheek,

then wrapped his arm around Ally's waist, holding court in their small circle.

I narrowed my eyes, watching the way he held her possessively, his claim on her obvious to anyone looking.

Just a friend.

My ass.

I glowered through the entire dinner. The people at my table gave up trying to include me in any conversation and left me alone. I could see Ally's table and watched the interactions the entire time. She was virtually ignored, even by her so-called boyfriend. Rarely was she included in the conversations, and if she was, her answers were short, mostly due to the fact that someone—usually Ronald or another man—would interrupt and talk over her.

I wanted to go over and tell them all to shut the hell up and let her speak. She seemed so small and vulnerable among the stiff bodies surrounding her. More than once, I saw her hand press to her collarbone in what I thought must be a defensive gesture. She hardly ate—her gaze often focused on her plate, and throughout the entire meal, she wore a distant smile.

I clenched my hands, watching her. She was a ghost to all of them. Did they not see what a special, wonderful woman was sitting in their midst? She wasn't a cookie-cutter, younger version of all other women around her. She was unique and special.

I hated seeing her like that. I had witnessed her confidence at the hospital. When she was with me, she was warm and open. She smiled and laughed easily, and I found her clever. Here, among the people she had known most of her life, she folded into herself, trying so hard to be accepted, she lost what made her so special.

She lost herself.

I had done some research on survivor guilt. Ally fit into the syndrome well. I wasn't a doctor, but it seemed to me that if she had received counseling and support, she would have been able to move past the horror of what happened. Instead, she was forced to relive it, the events on a constant loop in her mind. She was made to feel so guilty that it became part of who she was, and she hadn't been able to break free from it. Even her training as a nurse hadn't made her see how wrong they were. She could help other people, but she couldn't help herself. I wanted to help her, and I hoped she would let me.

Bradley leaned back, his arm draped casually around the back of her chair as he focused his attention on the man beside him instead of her. He was deep in discussion, but his fingers played with the skin of Ally's bare shoulder. I saw her shift away more than once, obviously not wanting his touch. I smirked to myself. When I caressed her skin, she leaned into my touch, not away.

I couldn't take it another second. I pulled out my phone and texted her, hoping she had her phone with her.

Hello, my Nightingale.

I watched her head bow, and she fumbled with her purse, pulling out her cell phone. She tapped away fast.

Hello, my daredevil. Are you somewhere safe?

Her first instinct was to make sure I was all right. I wanted to kiss her.

Yes. Perfectly safe. Back to the land of communication. No more daredeviling right now.
No suckers needed this time?

I grinned.

Nope. How's your evening?
Boring.

I smirked as I typed a reply.

Can I do anything?
You're too far away. I miss you. When are you coming back?

My breath caught in my throat. I needed to get her alone.

You don't have to miss me anymore. You look beautiful.

Her head flew up, her gaze scanning the room, and for the first time in days, our eyes met. Her hand flew to her collarbone again, and as the light glinted off the chain, I realized she wasn't just doing it as a reflex.

She was wearing my necklace.

I had found it the first day I was in Indonesia, waiting for transport. I had spotted it as I wandered through the market, the significance of the nightingale bird hanging from the silver links too perfect to pass up. The tiny sapphire in its chest was the best part—the clear blue reminded me of her eyes. I sent it to her via courier, paying an exorbitant fee to get it to her fast, wanting her to have a reminder of me while I was gone.

She kept clutching it because I had sent it to her, and she was seeking our connection, even when we were apart. I was correct. She needed me as well.

One word came back to me.

Please.

I stood, typing as I left, heading for the terrace at the back of the room. I knew she was watching me.

Tell them you have a headache. Go get some fresh air. Come to me.

I was anxious, waiting on the terrace for her to join me. Time seemed to drag on, but when I checked my watch, I saw it had only been five minutes.

I heard the door open behind me and turned, relief flooding through me at seeing her. She looked around, hesitating. I stepped away from the shadows, and seconds later, she was in my arms. Holding her, I moved behind the decorative shrubs.

"You're safe." She pressed her lips to my neck. "Thank God, you're safe."

I kissed her head. "I'm fine. I'm right here."

"Your head?"

"Fully recovered." I didn't tell her I removed the stitches myself. I didn't need a doctor to do that.

"Good. But why are you here tonight?"

"I missed you. I couldn't wait."

"I missed you too. So much, Adam."

I held her close, overwhelmed by the feelings coursing through me.

"I want you alone. I want you at my place."

She gripped me tighter. "I'd like that."

"How did you settle into my heart so fast, Ally?" I murmured into her hair.

She tilted her head back, her eyes bright. "You did the same."

Light caught the heavy silver of the chain around her neck. "You got my gift."

Her finger caressed the metal. "I love it."

I ghosted my fingers along hers on the surface of the chain. "I saw you touching it tonight."

"Yes, because I knew your hand was on it. It made me feel closer to you."

I inhaled sharply. "I need to kiss you."

"Yes, please."

My mouth covered her full lips. She tasted of the red wine I'd watched her sip and cinnamon. She always tasted like cinnamon. I groaned as our tongues slid together, exploring and reacquainting themselves. Her hands clutched my waist, and when she shivered, I opened my jacket, wrapping her inside, never breaking away from her lips. I was like a dying man in the desert, and her mouth was the sweet nectar of lifesaving water. Deeper and deeper, we drowned, lost to the world around us. It was only the click of the door opening that startled us out of our haze. I stepped farther back into the shadows, taking her with me, cradling her face into my chest.

"Shh," I whispered into her ear.

"Alexandra?" a male voice called out.

She stiffened in my arms, pressing herself closer to my chest, tightening her hands on my waist.

A few seconds passed, and I heard the door close again. I looked down at her, the moment passing, our bubble broken.

"Your date is looking for you," I griped, stating the obvious.

"He thinks I'm unwell. He'd want to check on me."

I didn't care what he thought or what he wanted. I knew what I wanted.

"I want you to come home with me. Now."

"Adam—"

Bitterness tinged my voice. "I know. He's your *friend.*"

She pulled back, frowning. "Yes, he is. I told Bradley I had a headache. I'm sure he'll take me home early."

I scoffed. "I'm sure he'd be happy to."

"What?"

"Your *friend* wants you, Ally."

"It's not like that with Bradley. I told you."

"Maybe not for you, but he's not telling you how he *really* feels. It's so obvious, even you should see it."

"What do you mean by that?"

"The way he looks at you—touches you. He thinks you're his."

"He's only doing it—"

I interrupted her. "He's doing it because that's what he wants. He wants more than friendship with you." I blew out a breath and gritted my teeth. "I know. I saw it with my own eyes."

She shook her head. "You're wrong."

"No, I'm not," I growled, unable to help myself.

She rubbed her temples, her eyes narrowed in frustration. "Stop this."

"What? Stop telling you the truth? You're in denial over his true intentions."

A chime ran out from her purse, and we stared at each other in the dimness.

"Your boyfriend, I presume."

"He's not…" She sighed, her frustration evident. "I have to go."

I clenched my fists, feeling angry and distraught. This wasn't how I planned on our reunion going. "Of course you do."

"Adam, please. Don't do this."

I yanked her back into my arms, brushing my lips over her head. "I'm sorry. I'm tired, jealous, and I shouldn't have come here. I wanted to see you so much I couldn't wait." I inhaled her sweet scent. "I didn't think how seeing you with him would affect me." I dropped another kiss to her skin. "Go inside before you get cold. I'll go in a few minutes."

"You're leaving?"

"It's for the best. I'm sorry."

She huffed. "You're wrong about how he feels. We're only friends helping each other."

I leaned my forehead to hers. I knew I was being a possessive dick when it came to her, but I couldn't help myself. "I hate seeing him touch you."

"It means nothing to me."

"I still don't like it."

She clutched my arm. "Do you still want me to come to your place?"

I cradled her face, claiming her mouth, hard and demanding.

"Yes, of course I do," I insisted. "I'm an ass, but I still want you to come to me."

"I will. I'll get there as soon as I can."

"Will you stay the night? Just let me hold you."

"Yes."

"Okay. I'll be waiting."

CHAPTER
SEVEN

I PACED THE FLOOR, unable to relax or sit. It had been two hours since I'd left Ally at the benefit, and I hadn't heard a word from her.

I ran my hands through my hair in vexation. I had sent her back inside, then slipped in through another set of doors, in case anyone was watching. I saw her easily in the crowd, the dress she was wearing catching my eye. She was talking to Bradley, gesturing toward the door, and I had assumed she was asking him to take her home.

Then she could come here—to me.

But I was still waiting.

Had he convinced her to stay? Had she thought about it and decided I was out of line with my jealous behavior and she wasn't coming? Never one to overreact, I seemed to lose control when it came to her. I couldn't think straight.

I glanced at my silent phone. Would she at least let me know?

My gaze fell to the new bed that had been assembled in the corner—my thick, comfortable mattress now set into the rich leather form. I had been meeting with the designer when I'd gotten the call to leave town, and he'd not only set up the massive bed, he'd left the sketches of the chair I asked him to create.

The sheets and towels were still in bags on the floor, not yet unpacked to put on the bed. Ally had lectured me thoroughly about the chemicals in new sheets and towels and how they had to be washed before being used. She told me horror stories about allergic reactions of people who had ignored the labels and warnings. By the time she finished, I swore I wouldn't sleep on them until they'd been laundered. I didn't tell her I'd never bothered before now. For tonight, the old sheets would have to do.

I wanted to see her in my bed, her hair spread across the pillows as she slept. I wanted to be able to smell her on those sheets.

A quiet knock had me racing to the door and flinging it open, startling Ally with the quickness. She stepped back, her hand flying to her throat. I lunged forward, dragged her inside, and slammed the door behind her. I lifted her into my arms, burying my face in her neck, holding her close. Her arms wrapped around my neck, and she ran her fingers through my hair.

"I was afraid you weren't coming."

"I was delayed. My cell phone died after your texts," she said. "I forgot to plug it in, and I didn't think I should use Bradley's to send you a text," she added lightly.

I walked over to the kitchen, still holding her in my arms, and set her on the counter. "Afraid of what I'd do if I got his number?"

She shook her head, all teasing gone. "No, I didn't want him to have yours. I–I don't want any of them to bother you."

Her words eased some of my tension. She was trying to take care of me.

"I'm a big boy, I can look after myself."

"I know."

I fingered the silk of her dress. "Have you not been home?"

"No. I went to Bradley's to talk, then I came here."

I swallowed the instant flame of jealousy I felt at the thought of her being in his place with him, alone. My voice was tight when I spoke. "He drove you here?"

"No, I took a cab. I was hoping you'd still be up."

"I said I'd wait for you." I stroked my thumbs under her eyes, not liking the faint shadows that seemed to be there all the time. "Did you get any rest today?"

"A couple hours."

"You're sleeping in tomorrow." If she wasn't going to look after herself, I fucking would.

"I have brunch with my parents."

"Cancel."

"I—"

"You need your sleep." I hated the fact that she always seemed to put herself, and her needs, last.

"I can't sleep all day, Adam."

"You could if you stayed here."

"I have to work tomorrow night."

"Why?"

"I traded shifts."

"You can stay here until you have to go."

She picked up the skirt of her gown, letting it fall back down in waves of brilliant orange and gold. "And go to work in this?"

I lifted her off the counter. "Let me get you some clothes, and we'll go to bed. You can plug in your phone and call to say you're not coming. I'll take you home early enough you can change before work."

"I have to go. Especially after tonight."

I scowled as I searched the cupboard, grabbing her a T-shirt and some boxers that were too small on me now. At least they wouldn't fall off her when she moved—not that I'd object to that.

"Are you in that much trouble for wearing a pretty gown? Do they object to you looking different from all the bland women who were there this evening?" I complained. "It was like a fucking Stepford wife meeting."

I thought she'd agree, maybe laugh at my assessment. What I didn't expect were the words that came out of her mouth.

"No. I have to go and talk to them. I want them to hear the news from me."

"What news?"

She drew in a deep breath, taking the clothes from my hands. "I told Bradley I couldn't do this anymore. I—I broke up with my fake boyfriend."

Then she disappeared into the bathroom, leaving me stunned.

———

I paced as I waited, anxious. I needed to know why she "broke up" with Bradley.

Everything in me prayed it was because she had the same intense draw to me as I had to her—that she didn't want anyone in her life except me, fake or otherwise.

She came out of the bathroom, looking adorable in my old shirt. It was torn and tattered, the material thin, showing off her curves.

"I can give you a better shirt."

She stroked the material. "No, this one is soft. I like it."

I liked the way it hung around her shoulders with the ragged, wide neck, and the way it showed off her milky thighs. My body hardened at the simple beauty that shone from her. I wanted her.

I patted the bed next to me, lifting the covers so she could be warm as we talked. I wrapped my hand around hers. "Tell me."

It was a minute before she spoke. Her eyes were trained on our hands, her fingers tracing over my bruised knuckles which happened when I slipped on some wet rocks. She bent down, brushing her lips to the discolored flesh.

"I can't do it anymore. The constant demands and the disappointment I see on their faces. Nothing I do is right or good enough, and I'm tired of trying." She sighed in resignation. "I knew my dress wasn't what my mother would want me to wear, but I thought it was so pretty."

"You were beautiful."

She tilted back her head, meeting my eyes. I saw the sadness swimming in the blue depths, her irises cast in gray. "You're the only person who said that."

I lifted our hands and kissed the thin skin inside her wrist. "You should always wear what you want. Act the way you want to. Do what makes *you* happy."

"When I'm on my own, I do. My mother hates the way I dress, but I like to be comfortable. I find it hard to conform to their vision of what is right all the time. I wore it because I loved it. The last dress I wore, Bradley told me I looked like an old woman and my mother said it was dreadful. So this time, I wore what *I* liked. But once again, it was wrong."

"No. *They're* wrong."

"How can you be so sure?"

"Because you're perfect—just the way you are."

She shook her head, frustration in her voice when she spoke. "I'm *not* perfect, Adam. I don't want to be put on a pedestal by you. I've had to be perfect for so long. I'm just me."

I held her hand to my face. "I know you're not a perfect person. But all your little imperfections, all the things you think you have to change, make you perfect for me."

She drew in a shaky breath. "Thank you."

"What did great-guy Bradley think about being fake dumped?" I queried, interested in his reaction.

No matter what the bastard told her, he wasn't faking anything. He wanted her—and he wanted to control her the same way her parents did. He just covered it better.

"He wanted to talk, so that's why I went to his place. I felt I owed him that at least."

"What did you tell him?"

"The truth. I told him I realized it didn't matter what I did, it was never going to be enough. I was tired of living for everyone else and trying to make up for something I could never make up for—no matter how long or hard I tried. And using him only made me feel worse. We were both lying." She took in a deep breath. "He asked me if there was someone else."

"And?" I tensed as I waited for her reply.

"I told him yes. I'd met someone, and I wanted to explore it."

"He didn't like that, did he?"

Her gaze flittered around, and she didn't answer.

I cupped her cheek, turning her face to mine.

"Did he do anything?" I paused. "Tell me the truth."

"No, he didn't touch me."

"He said something?"

"He didn't like it and said he didn't understand why I didn't see you secretly until I made sure it was going to work out, and then we could discuss ending things. He seemed to think whoever I was interested in wouldn't stay interested in me very long."

"Well, the bastard is wrong. Did you tell him about me?"

"No, it's none of his business."

I liked the no-nonsense tone of her answer. I wished she'd use it on her parents, but I knew that would take time.

"He dropped it but asked me a favor."

"What?"

"There's a benefit on Thursday. His father and my parents are going to be there. He asked me to go with him, so I switched my shifts and go to work tomorrow and have that night off."

I tamped down my irrational possessiveness. "I see."

"I'm going to tell my parents tomorrow that we've decided to be only friends, but I'm going on Thursday to show my support—as his friend."

She smiled. "Besides, Elena will be back from her latest trip. I haven't seen her in a month."

"Will she sit at your table?"

"No. She doesn't like Bradley. She'll sit at another table." She chuckled. "Or, I should say, hold court at another table. She's very, um, entertaining."

I liked that woman more and more with everything I heard about her.

"Brunch won't be pleasant, but I have to do it."

"Will you let them change your mind?"

"No," she stated firmly. "I've thought about this the whole time you were gone. You were right. They're going to be disappointed no matter what."

"Then what?"

She looked at me, her gaze all at once tender and determined. "Then I start living my life—for me."

"Can I be a part of that life, Nightingale?"

"Yes," she breathed. "I missed you so much while you were gone. It felt like a part of me was missing."

"I felt the same."

"I'm glad you're home."

I gathered her close, wrapping myself around her as I slid down in the bed. Our mouths met in a series of long, deep kisses. My tongue sought out her sweetness, reveling in her taste. My cock hardened as she arched against me. A long shudder racked her small frame, and I pulled back from her mouth, dragging my lips over her skin to her ear. "I'll always come home to you."

"Adam," she whimpered.

"You're mine now."

"Yes, I am."

Her admission exhilarated me, and as much as I wanted to have her, I could feel her exhaustion in the heaviness of her limbs. "Sleep now."

"I want to know all about what happened when you were gone."

"I'll tell you everything tomorrow."

"Even where you got those bruises?"

I brushed a kiss to her head. "Yes."

"Were you in danger?"

"No."

"Were you careful?"

"Go to sleep."

"Were you?"

"Yes, Ms. Bossy. I was careful."

"Good."

I smiled at her protectiveness. "I have extra reason to be careful now."

She nodded, her eyes serious. "Yes."

"I liked your texts."

"I didn't like not being able to talk to you," she admitted in a quiet tone. "Why don't you have a satellite phone?"

"Tommy had it—my track record with one isn't good. They have a habit of going over cliffs or getting forgotten on the top of the truck and I drive over them." I stared at the ceiling, thinking. "To be honest, I never thought about it. I'm not used to having someone worry about me. Or think about calling someone while I'm gone. I'll get better at staying in touch."

"I don't expect daily calls, just let me know you're okay. A fast text. Something. That's all I'm asking."

"I will. I missed you, and I thought about you a lot."

"I thought about you all the time."

She yawned, and I pulled the blankets tighter around her. "Sleep now."

Like a kitten, she curled up, tucking her hand under her cheek.

"Ally—"

"Hmm?"

"This benefit, what's it for?"

"To raise money for more equipment for the pediatric ward at the hospital. Why?"

"Just asking."

She nestled closer, her head on my chest. I ran my hand up and down her back, long, slow strokes meant to relax her. She sighed, the hand clutching my shirt loosened, and her breathing leveled out. My mind was too full to sleep yet.

An idea was forming.

I was well-known. My photographs drew a lot of attention and commanded a tidy sum. It was a worthwhile cause. A very worthwhile one.

Perhaps I should get in touch with the organizing committee. Offer something as an auction piece. Be there at the event to autograph it—personally.

I could meet a few people. Introduce myself.

I thought of Ally's parents and their bored, cynical expressions earlier this evening. I knew they wouldn't approve of me, despite the fact that I was well-off and successful. How I earned my money, and my lifestyle, were not up to their standards. Not to mention the ink that covered my skin—Ally had told me how much they disapproved of body art or anyone who didn't conform to their narrow-minded world.

I was also blunt, outspoken, disliked them for the way they treated my girl, and I didn't care about their opinion.

Wait until they got an eyeful of me.

We were going to hate each other, but they were going to have to get used to me.

Because I wasn't going anywhere.

As far as I was concerned, if they walked away from Ally, her life could only get better.

And if they stayed, they were going to have to deal with me when they treated her badly. I was putting an end to that shit.

They were going to have to learn respect was a two-way street.

She needed someone to protect her.

That someone was me.

CHAPTER
EIGHT

"STOP TAKING MY PICTURE."

I smirked but set down the camera on the table and picked up my coffee cup. "Stop being so fucking sexy when you sleep, then."

She sat up, her hair a bright burst of color around her face. She glared at me drowsily, then she dragged the loose shirt back up her arm. "I highly doubt my drooling is sexy."

"Your snoring is, though."

"I don't snore!" she gasped. "You're the snorer in this relationship."

I winked, liking the thought of being in a relationship with her. "I'll never tell."

"What time is it?"

"Relax. It's barely eight. You have lots of time."

Her shoulders loosened. "Okay."

"I still think you should cancel."

"No. I want to tell them today."

"Why is it so important to do it today?"

"You might think less of me if I tell you."

I opened my arms. "Come here, Ally."

She scrambled out of the bed, dragging the blanket with her. When she coiled around me, she was warm and perfect. Her softness molded into my hardness, meshing perfectly. She felt right in my arms, and I wanted to be able to explore it. Explore her.

"Why today?" I asked again.

"Appearance is everything to them. We'll be in public," she confessed quietly.

Understanding dawned on me. "They won't make a scene."

"They'll express their displeasure and let me know how much I've let them down, but it will all be done very civilly." She shrugged. "Then once they've discussed it, they'll summon me to let me know in private how disappointed they are in me."

I shook my head in frustration. "They shouldn't be disappointed. All you're doing is what is best for you. Your life. Not theirs. I wish—" I stopped myself from finishing that statement.

"You wish what?"

"I wish they would get the fuck out of your life."

She was resigned. "They will soon enough."

I could make it happen faster—pay her monetary debt

and help her exorcise her mental responsibility, but I held my tongue. It was too soon for that.

"Good," I muttered instead.

"I know you don't understand, Adam, but she's my mother."

I stroked her cheek, tamping down my irritation. "You're right. I don't understand. Because she shouldn't treat you like this. She should support you." I murmured. "You should never have been made to feel as though you had to do this in the first place."

Turning her face, she kissed my palm.

"Why did you think I'd think less of you?"

"Because I'm taking the easy way out. Or at least, delaying the inevitable."

"I think you're brave and wonderful. I also think you're finally getting to the point you need to do this—it's time you live for you." I paused. "I didn't know Ollie, but I think he'd want that for you."

She curled into me, her head burrowed in my chest, and I held her tight, knowing she needed my closeness and support.

She'd needed that for a long time. I'd give it to her freely and without question.

Before I drove her home, she helped me wash the sheets and make up the bed. Watching her effortlessly stuff a king-sized duvet into the cover and smooth it out without breaking a sweat was amazing. She laughed as she watched me try to imitate the way she tucked the sheets in place and fluffed the duvet on the end of the bed, standing back and admiring her handiwork. She made me move the bed twice until she was satisfied it was "in the right place." I didn't care; I liked her bossing me around.

I had to admit it looked good—and very inviting. So inviting, I tackled her onto the smooth sheets and kissed her passionately as we rolled around the large mattress, messing it up. When she finally escaped my clutches, her eyes were twinkling as she looked at the bed, scolding me and shaking her finger, trying to sound serious.

I propped myself up on my elbow, leering at her. "I like it better like this."

"Why?"

I picked up a pillow and inhaled. "The sheets smell like you now. I imagine this is how the bed will look after we make love. Rumpled and messy." I arched my eyebrow. "And smelling like *us*."

Her eyes widened, and she hurried to the bathroom, leaving me laughing at her reaction.

When she emerged, damp and clean, her hair neatly plaited into a long braid down her back, she was wearing my T-shirt and a pair of sweats I found for her.

She was quiet as I drove her to her place. The closer we got, the tenser she became. When we pulled up outside, I turned to her, ghosting my finger down her cheek. "Do you want me to come with you?"

"No!"

"I will."

Her expression softened. "I know you would. But I have to do this on my own."

"Will you call me when you're done?"

"Yes."

I leaned over and held her face between my hands. "If you need me, text or call. I'll come get you, no matter what."

"Thank you."

I brushed my lips to hers. "Anything, Ally."

She slipped out of the car, her brilliant gown clutched in her arms, wearing my clothes and a pair of high heels. She looked odd and utterly perfect.

I hated to see her walk away.

By the time I got home, I had a return call about the benefit on Thursday. They were beyond ecstatic for my last-minute contribution to the live auction segment of the evening and were thrilled to have me be part of the event. They were more than happy to accommodate my request for two tickets and to make sure I was seated at the same table as Elena Ames. I decided I wanted to meet the one person who seemed to care about Ally. The other ticket was for a table far away from me, just as I requested.

Then I got to work on the item I'd be donating. As I skimmed through my photos, I paused on one I had taken of Ally this morning. She was nestled against the headboard on her side, her hair fanned out all around her, her face not visible. The ragged neckline of my T-shirt had fallen away, exposing the curve of her shoulder, and the hint of her rounded breast. The pose and the coloring were an erotic visual. High on her shoulder were seven dark freckles in the shape of a *V* that stood out in vivid detail against the ivory of her skin, adding another element of sexiness. The sun was just rising, the rays of light highlighting her hair.

Remembering one of my favorite photos I had taken last year, an idea struck, and for the next while, I worked, layering and highlighting until it was exactly the way I envisioned it in my head. When it was done, it was the perfect symmetry of the two. A photo of sunset over the ocean, the waves rushing to the shore, with the washed-out, barely seen image of Ally drifting through the sky, the bright waves of her hair dipping into the ocean, diffused stars scattered around her. The layered effect of the clouds had captured my eye the night I had taken the picture, and now they were like the blankets that covered her. With a few more touches, I brought out the freckles in the shimmering light my lens had captured.

I called it *Sleeping Angel.*

It would bring a high price—I'd make sure of it.

I stopped working only once, when Ally called. Her voice was drained; although she assured me she was fine. Brunch, she told me, had gone exactly as she thought it would. They were disappointed in her selfish actions and made sure she knew their feelings. But I was proud she hadn't given in to their displeasure.

I wanted to go and get her, but she refused. I stopped arguing, deciding she'd probably been doing nothing but arguing for the past few hours, and I told her I would call her tomorrow.

However, I was there when she left for work, waiting outside her building, needing to reassure myself she was all right. The way she flung herself into my embrace let me know my decision was a good one. She held a small bag, and as we were driving, I asked her what it was for.

"The people above me started renovations today. I barely got any sleep, so I'm going to crash in the on-call room tomorrow. At least I'll get a few hours of sleep in."

My brow furrowed. "How long will this go on for?"

"They said a week to ten days."

"You can't get by on a few hours that long."

"Well, I don't want to go to my parents'. I'll crash on Elena's couch when she gets back."

I pulled up in front of the hospital. "I have a better idea. Stay with me. I'll pick you up in the morning."

"Then I'll interrupt your day."

"No. I have some work to do. The loft is quiet, and you can sleep."

"I'd like that, but are you sure?"

I wrapped my hand around hers, kissing the knuckles. "I want to make sure you're okay. Please let me do this."

"I'm not used to anyone looking after me."

"I want you to get used to me doing it." I studied her. "Does this bother you?"

"Bother me?"

I placed my hand on her neck, stroking her skin. "This

need I have—to take care of you. It's so important to me. I'm worried I may overwhelm you."

"Does it overwhelm you?" she asked.

I stared at the dashboard, thinking. "At times. I'm not used to thinking about someone else. I'm afraid I'm going to scare you away."

"Adam…" she began, waiting until I met her gaze. "Aside from Ollie or Elena, no one *has* cared for me. Once my dad died, I was alone. It doesn't scare me. I understand it, because I feel the same way about you. I want to be with you when you're here." Her voice caught. "I know when you leave again, I'm going to miss you even more."

There was nothing else to be said. I kissed her and watched her walk into the hospital, her words ringing in my head.

Had anyone missed me before she came into my life?

I was certain the answer was no.

The next morning, I picked her up, taking her to my place, parking underground. Her eyes grew large as she stared at the gleaming black motorcycle parked beside my deep blue Audi RS 7.

"Is that yours?"

"Yep." I ran my hand over the shiny metal. "You like to ride, Ally?"

"I've never been on one." She eyed the bike with trepidation. "What kind is it? It looks powerful."

I slung my arm around her shoulders as we walked toward the private elevator. "It's a Harley. It is powerful, but

I'm careful. I'll take it out soon. We'll get you some gear, and you can come with me, if you want."

"I would."

"Good."

I stayed busy during the day while she slept. I had hung my old sheets in the windows by the bed, hoping to at least dim the sunlight so she could rest.

It began raining midmorning, a fast-moving storm blowing through. She became restless, her body tense, her hands clenched. When she whimpered my name, I was done. Recalling her confession of hating storms, I lay beside her, drawing her into my arms, murmuring to her, assuring her she wasn't alone.

"Adam," she breathed out again, still asleep but on the verge of waking. But the tone had changed, and the sheer relief in her voice made me hold her close.

"I have you, Ally. You're safe," I crooned as she nestled closer.

"It's just a little storm," I whispered, pressing a kiss to her head. "Nothing to fear. The storm will end, but we won't. You'll never be alone again, Nightingale. I have you," I repeated, smiling as she relaxed and drifted back to sleep. "I'll always have you now."

I liked her reaction to my closeness. I calmed her much the way she helped to center me. We were good for each other.

I held her, talking quietly about nonsensical things until the thunder stopped and I knew she could rest.

I was furious how often her phone rang. I grabbed it, lowering the volume so it wouldn't disturb her. My mood got darker with every occurrence. Bradley and her mother were the two persistent callers.

They knew she worked all night, the selfish fuckers.

I worked on the computer, stepping into the hall when I needed to make calls, planning a few more changes in the loft.

I didn't question my motives now. I wanted to look after her. It was important to me, because she was fast becoming the most important thing in my life.

When she woke up, we spent some time talking.

"What do you do when you're not nursing people back to health?"

"I like to read, and I go to a lot of movies."

"On your own?" I asked, even though I knew it was none of my business.

"Usually, yes. Sometimes with a friend."

I resisted asking if that friend was female.

"Ah. And any other interests?"

"I do some volunteer work, go to yoga, that sort of thing." She shrugged. "I like to cook and bake, and I take things into work to share. I'm a bit of an introvert."

"I can relate to that."

Her eyebrows rose. "Really?"

"Does that surprise you?"

She pursed her lips. "It does, actually. You seem too energetic to sit at home much."

I found that an interesting choice of words. I certainly felt energetic around her. "Energetic?"

"You're larger-than-life."

"Does that scare you?" I asked, curious.

"No, I find you fascinating."

"I feel the same way about you."

She made omelets, teasing me about my dwindling supplies and having to be inventive.

"I was busy today," I laughed, picking up the somewhat dry toast. I did have to get to the store and purchase some groceries.

"Do you ever keep much food here?"

"No. I never know when I'll be called away, and it spoils. Takeout is easier."

"I guess that makes sense."

"Now that I have you, I can get a few more things. You could always come and stay here if I was away."

Our gazes locked.

"I could," she murmured.

"I'll go grocery shopping tomorrow."

She laughed, slipped off her stool, and went to get ready for work.

I drove her again, already filled with plans for my night. At the hospital, she turned to me. "I slept so well today. Thank you."

I ran my finger down her cheek. "I'll be here in the morning."

"I could drive myself."

"I'd like to come get you, if you'd let me," I added, unable to explain the yearning I felt when it came to her. I needed to be close to her as much as possible and I didn't question it

Her lips were warm on my cheek. "I would."

I stayed up most of the night installing the blinds I had ordered and picked up. I wasn't much of a handyman, but they looked damn good when I was done and would be useful.

When I arrived at the hospital, she was waiting. She slipped into the car, immediately leaning over for my kiss. I held the back of her head securely, enjoying the feel of her mouth.

"You look tired," she observed.

"I was awake most of the night." I grinned. "Busy." I lifted her hand, kissing the knuckles. "I plan on sleeping beside you today."

"Oh." That was the only word she uttered, but her smile was bright.

It was even brighter when she saw the blinds, and she seemed surprised.

"Why?"

"For you. So you can sleep."

"I can't sleep here every day," she reminded me gently.

I tucked another item into her hand I had picked up. She looked down at the shiny keys in her palm, and her gaze flew to mine.

"Anytime, Nightingale. Whether I'm here or not." I had been home for a couple of days now, and I never knew when I would have to head out again. "You're welcome to be here. Day or night."

"Adam—"

I shook my head. "Anytime. The larger one is the front door —at least for the times the lock isn't broken—the other one is for the loft." I added another item to her palm. "This pass is for the garage. You can park in there beside me—you'll be safer. Use the private elevator. You know the pass code already."

I closed her hand around the keys and pass, silently begging her with my eyes to accept them. Accept me.

She lifted them, giggling at the little key chain that had a camera on it. I showed her how it worked as a flashlight if she needed extra light to see the keyholes. I was thrilled when she slipped it into her purse after grazing my cheek with her lips. I handed her another T-shirt, apologizing for the threadbare condition. I winked when I told her I'd been too busy to wash the other one since she'd bought me too many damned sheets to wash.

We moved around, quietly comfortable with each other. She nibbled at the toast I made her, talking about some of the happenings in the ER the night before, making me laugh with her imitations of a groaner who, it seemed, never stopped.

"All for a splinter." She shook her head and snickered. "You'd think we were cutting off his arm."

She smirked at me over her shoulder as she walked away. "He was worse than you."

I laughed at her teasing. I was an awful patient—I knew that, but it had gotten me her. Well worth it, I'd say.

She paused by the side of the bed and turned to me.

My breath caught in my throat. Standing there in the morning sun, she was an incredible vision. The light behind her highlighted the curves beneath my shirt, the thin material showing the faint outline of her nipples straining against the fabric. As she lifted her arms, gathering her hair into a ponytail, the shirt rose, exposing her hips. Tiny straps sat low across the bones and a red triangle nestled between her legs—small, lacy scraps of material that passed as underwear.

A hiss escaped my mouth, and my cock hardened at the sight of her sensual beauty.

She froze as I pushed off the stool and stalked toward her. I stood in front of her, so close our chests were touching, her nipples hardening into pebbles as I pressed nearer. "You're so sexy," I murmured. "Standing here in the light, in my clothes, beside my bed." I ran my fingers up her bare thigh. "I want you, Ally."

Her breath began to come out in small gasps as I edged my fingers higher, barely brushing the lace I had seen. "I've never seen anything sexier than you are, right here, right now."

"You think I'm sexy?"

"Maddeningly so." I wrapped my arm around her waist, pulling her to me, letting her feel what she did to me. Her eyes widened, and she tightened her fist on the material of my shirt.

"I'm not a virgin," she blurted out.

I laughed low in my throat. "I'd hardly expect you to be." I rubbed my nose along hers affectionately. "I'm not either," I murmured, dragging my lips across her cheek to her ear.

"I don't have a lot of experience, though."

"We can work on that." I tugged on her soft lobe, smiling as she moaned. "You just have to tell me what you like. Show me how to please you."

"That's the problem, Adam."

I leaned back, frowning. "I don't understand."

She drew in a deep breath and let it out slowly. "When I say I don't have a lot of experience, I mean with any of it. I can't tell you what pleases me because…"

She paused. "I don't know what pleases me."

"WHAT ARE YOU SAYING, ALLY?"

She shrugged, looking shy. "How can I tell you what I like when I don't know? I've only had two short relationships, and I only had sex with one of them."

I blinked. This beautiful, sexy woman had only had sex with one man?

"Impossible," I breathed.

Her cheeks flushed. Not the soft blush I was used to seeing on her cheeks when I would tease her or kiss her unexpectedly. This was the color of embarrassment—Ally's embarrassment.

"You know how sheltered my teens were. I didn't have a real boyfriend until I was at university."

"That's not a big deal, a lot of people start late."

"Did you?"

I shifted uncomfortably. "No, I didn't. Trust me, if I

could, I'd go back and change some of my behavior, but I can't." I ran my hand along the back of my neck. "Besides, we aren't discussing me. We were talking about you."

"My first time, with my boyfriend Ben, wasn't enjoyable."

"I don't think any woman's first time is," I agreed. I tried to keep my voice even. I hated, *loathed*, the thought of her with anyone else, but I had to ask. "But you tried again?"

She crossed her arms over her chest. "We did. We tried a few days later. But I think he was so afraid of hurting me that he treated me like spun glass—as if I would shatter any second. It hardly felt as though he was touching me, and I wasn't, ah, ready…and, yeah, it wasn't good. And we broke up not long after. He said it wasn't anything to do with what happened, but I'm not stupid. Who wants to be in a relationship with someone who doesn't respond to you sexually?"

I could hear the mortification in her voice. Between the way her parents second-guessed every decision she made, criticized her, and how her jackass of a boyfriend had treated her, she had no confidence in this area of her life. Not to mention the "fake" relationship she'd had with Bradley. She had no idea how truly sexy she was.

"Nightingale," I called quietly. When she didn't respond, I tried again. "Ally—look at me."

I waited until she looked up to speak. "Your so-called boyfriend was an idiot," I stated flatly. "Obviously, he had no idea how to please you, and instead of manning up and doing something about it, he walked," I insisted. "He probably had as much experience as you did and didn't want to say that out loud."

She frowned. "He had other girlfriends."

"Was he your first boyfriend?"

"No. I had one other in high school. It wasn't much of a relationship—not at that age. I was too young and naïve for that, and with the restrictions I had, well, it never had a chance." She shrugged self-consciously.

"So *Ben,* he was the first man you slept with?"

"Yes. I wasn't ready before." She sighed. "I don't think I was ready then either. But he kept at me."

"Maybe it was the same for him."

Her eyes widened. "I never thought of that. He never said—he kept pushing…"

"He wouldn't, would he? He wanted you to think he was experienced." I smiled knowingly. "Of course he kept pushing. I mean, look at you."

"What?"

"He wanted you. The same way Bradley does."

She shook her head. "Bradley has never tried anything like that with me. I just assumed…"

"You assumed wrong. He was just playing the game, hoping to wear you down. Trust me, he wants you."

I moved closer. "I want you. I want you so fucking much, I ache with it." I sucked in a deep breath. "You're right—you weren't ready. He wasn't the right man for you. Neither was Bradley."

"And you are?"

"Yes," I stated with conviction. "I am."

"What if I disappoint you?"

"Impossible. We'll learn together. I'll teach you."

"I don't…"

"Don't what? Tell me," I demanded.

"I don't want to be treated like glass all the time."

I laughed, the low sound rumbling in my chest as I shook my head. "I don't plan on it. When I make you mine, you're going to feel it—I promise you that."

A small whimper escaped her lips. Her chest was moving rapidly, her skin flushing the pretty petal color I loved. It tinted her cheeks and swept down her neck, covering her chest. I wanted to know how far down that color went—if her skin was warm when my tongue dragged across the surface. If I could make the color deepen the way her eyes were darkening as she looked at me.

"There are so many things I want to do with you," I assured her and licked my lips as I stared at her, my voice husky. "To you."

"Tell me," she implored, curling her fingers into fists at her sides.

I stepped behind her, wrapping my arm around her waist and pulling her to my chest. I smoothed my fingers up her arm, trailing them along her skin. Small goose bumps broke out, pebbling the surface as I dropped my head down into her neck, kissing and swirling my tongue. "I'm going to explore you—everywhere. I'll touch and discover every part of you. I want to know what makes you gasp, what drives you to distraction. I'll find out what I can do to make you groan and beg me to take you. I'll know your body better than you do." I drew her skin between my teeth, biting and sucking. "I want to kiss you…taste you everywhere." I slipped my hands under her shirt, teasing the softness of her stomach and side, stroking upward until I cupped her breast lightly in my hand. "I bet you taste different all over. Sweet some places—" I dropped my hand down, running it along the edge of her waistband "—musky and tangy others."

She moaned and clasped the back of my neck, tugging on my hair. Her back arched, pushing her breast into my palm, the nipple puckering as I kneaded and teased the firm flesh, and she breathed my name, the sound raspy in her throat.

I lowered my hand to between her legs, listening to her breathing pick up as I cupped her warmth. I could feel the blazing heat of her through the thin fabric—the dampness telling me without a doubt how right I was for her. I grazed my lips over her ear. "I want to lick you until you scream my name, Ally." I caressed her with my finger. "And you will scream."

"Oh God…"

"No, God won't be there," I growled. "But I will." I pressed my finger against her harder. "I want my face between your legs. I want to fuck you with my mouth. I want you to come all over me, riding my fingers and my tongue." I bit down on the skin by her shoulder, knowing I would leave a mark. My mark.

"Then," I promised her, releasing her flesh with a small flick of my tongue, "I'll drive into you so hard you'll see stars. I'm going to fuck you so passionately—we'll end up on the floor. I want you to take me, take all of me, and when you're finally done—when I've fucked you so much you can't take it anymore…I'll keep going until *I'm* done."

I stepped back, pulling my hands away. She stumbled forward, and I caught her around the waist, bringing her back to my chest. She was trembling, her body shaking, her breath coming out in small gasps. My cock was hard and aching, my body tense with the desire to do all those things I told her, to feel her molded to me, to taste her. She moved back, both of us groaning as I surged up against her ass. "That is what I'm going to do to you." I dropped a heavy kiss onto her head. "I promise you—the first time. Every time. You'll know who you belong to."

I spun her around so she was facing me. Her eyes were wide, with so many emotions swirling in their depths.

"I can be gentle too," I vowed. "I want to lay you on my bed and make love to you until you forget everything but us. I want to bury myself inside you for hours and watch you come."

Her eyes softened, melting into pools of blue water.

"We're going to be amazing together. Whether you want me to take you hard or make love to you in the slowest way possible, I *am* the right man for you."

I dropped another kiss on her mouth. "When you're ready, my Nightingale. When you're ready."

I moved away, the physical act of separating from her painful. I made it a few feet when she whispered my name. "Adam."

I turned, forcing a smile to my face.

"I'm on the pill," she said quietly.

I nodded in understanding. "I'm clean. It's been a long time for me. When you're ready, we're good."

In a move I didn't expect, she launched herself at me, and I caught her, stumbling back to the bed, holding her tight to my body.

"*Now*," she pleaded. "I want you now. Teach me, Adam."

We sank to the mattress, our mouths fused together.

She *was* ready.

Thank God.

I tore off her shirt, the material ripping under my hands easily. Between us, the rest of our clothing disappeared, some pieces pulled off intact, others torn and thrown away —littering the room around us.

Her skin was as soft as I knew it would be. It tasted sweeter than I imagined. I stroked and caressed her, fanning the flames until they ignited into an inferno within her. I trailed my fingers over her body, following them with my mouth. I relished her gasps, soothed her shudders, and learned how to make her quiver and beg for me.

I laid myself out for her, watching with hooded eyes as

she explored and learned my body. I encouraged her explorations, pleading for her touch, which grew bolder as we lost ourselves in the vortex of lust between us. Her hot mouth tugged on my nipples, her hands stroked my aching cock, and her body shook with passion as she watched my reactions. Sitting up, I pulled her back to my mouth, praising her, whispering how much I wanted her, how sexy she was. I lowered her down and explored her again, parting her thighs and finally sinking between them, tasting her for the first time.

She arched as I closed my mouth around her, gasping when I used my tongue, swirling and lapping at the tender flesh. She wrapped her hands in my hair, pulling on the strands, as she whimpered and undulated under my mouth. I growled, her reactions as much of a turn-on as the act itself, and slipped two fingers inside her, massaging and stroking until she began to pant and cry out.

"Come for me, baby. Let yourself go…"

She stiffened, her muscles clamping down, and cried out my name. I gentled my mouth, riding out her orgasm, slowly trailing kisses over her skin as she calmed. Sitting back on my heels, I pulled her forward, gripping her hips with my hands, brushing the heat of her with my aching cock.

"*Now*, Ally. I'm going to make you mine now."

Brilliant, yearning blue met my intense gaze. Desire raged in her eyes.

"Yes."

I buried myself in her.

Fast. Hard. Deep.

We both cried out.

I stilled, our gazes locked at the overwhelming intensity of the moment. "I told you I wasn't going to treat you like glass."

She whimpered, her hands grasping for me.

I withdrew and slammed back into her. She tightened her legs. I thrust again, and she shut her eyes, her back arching. Her breasts jutted out, her nipples stiff and still red from my mouth. I groaned her name and surged forward, everything else around me ceasing to exist but how she felt. Her tight, wet warmth gripped my cock as I thrust, fucking her—loving her—showing her how right we were together. I took her the way I told her I would— powerfully and completely, forever marking her as mine. The room spun, sweat dripped down my back as I hovered over her, my body telling her everything I hadn't said with words. Her orgasm was beautiful to watch—the utter bliss on her face as she sobbed my name, her voice hoarse and needy. Her pussy contracted around my cock, her nails digging into my shoulders, as she shuddered and quaked around me.

I buried my face into her neck as my balls tightened with my impending orgasm. I gripped her hips as I continued to move, strong and fast, cursing as I exploded. I emptied myself inside her, ecstasy pounding through my body until I collapsed beside her, my breathing ragged. Unable to bear being separated from her, I wrapped her up in my arms, kissing and nuzzling her soft hair, whispering her name.

Gradually, we calmed. I never stopped caressing her—she never released the way she clutched me. When she shivered, I drew the blanket around us, pulling her close again. I felt her sink into me, her body growing relaxed with sleep.

"Mine," I whispered, my breath blowing over her cooling skin.

"Yours," she replied.

Nothing, and no one, was going to change that.

Ever.

We slept. Wrapped around each other, neither of us could let go. Even when I woke up, the afternoon sun high in the sky, my need for her building again, I refused to move or disturb her. Instead, I watched her sleep, felt her light breath on my skin, and savored her closeness.

I couldn't be without her anymore.

Slowly, she woke, blinking, soft and sweet. Her gaze was shy but filled with so much tenderness, I ducked my head and covered her mouth with mine, kissing her deeply. She wound her hands into my hair, pulling me close, and within seconds, we were lost—the world outside disappearing.

There was only my Nightingale and me.

We didn't have a breath of air between our bodies as our kisses became deeper. Longer. More. Hard, pumping heat rushed through me. Everything became magnified. The feel of her skin on mine as our chests slid together. The erotic noises she made as we moved. Her wetness that teased my aching cock.

I found her rapid pulse beating erratically at the base of her throat, and I bit down, hissing in satisfaction at her low moan. Her fingers clawed at my back, pulling me closer. I slipped into her warmth and stilled at the powerful pleasure of being buried inside her. Our gazes locked and held, and an intense tenderness flooded my chest. I moved with long, deep thrusts that made her whimper and arch under me. I couldn't pull my lips from hers, my tongue needing to be in her mouth. We shared oxygen, our united touch more important than air.

My orgasm rolled through my body, gathering strength and erupting fiercely. I held her close, rocking as she shuddered, my name a muffled sound between us.

Reluctantly, we moved apart, separating back into two halves, both of us knowing we'd only ever be whole again with each other.

I tucked her into my side, breathing her in, every sense attuned to her. It was as if my entire world was contained in my arms.

It was too soon and too fast. I knew it. But I had seen how quickly life changed, moved, and was gone. So I said it anyway.

"I love you, Ally."

Her mouth pressed on my chest. "I love you too, Adam."

———

I woke, meeting Ally's contented gaze.

She was sitting in the chair, holding a cup of coffee and watching me with a grin. "You're very sexy when you sleep, even with the snores."

I moved, letting the sheet fall, resting over my hips. "Is that so?"

"I love your tattoos."

I glanced at the swirls of ink on my body. "I'm thinking of a new one."

"Oh?"

I tapped my finger over my heart—one of the few bare areas on my chest—knowing she'd understand. "I think I've found the perfect design."

I'd wear her on my heart. I'd etch her into my skin, because she was already under it, living within me.

I sat up, swinging my legs over the mattress. They hit the floor with a dull thud, the sheet slipping lower. "What are you doing all the way over there?"

"I needed coffee."

I eyed the cup in her hand. "You gonna share, Ally?"

In silent offering, she held out the mug, and I stood, the sheet slipping to the floor. I stretched, her eyes following every muscle as it bunched and moved, lingering on the heavy erection already growing as I looked at her. Her long red hair flowed around her bare shoulders, her blue eyes lit with desire as she watched me. The color of the duvet set off her creamy skin. Skin I knew was smooth under my tongue and tasted sweet, like her. A tiny purple mark stood out on her shoulder from my teeth. I liked seeing it. I sat down on the ottoman, taking the cup and drinking deeply. The hot beverage was laced with her favorite flavor, cinnamon, and I liked it. With a grin, I drained the mug and placed it beside her.

"I said I'd share."

"Yep."

"You drank it all," she pouted.

"I'll get you more after."

"After?"

She gasped as I reached under the duvet and grabbed her hips, pulling her out of the chair and flush to my chest. I wrapped the duvet around us and kissed her fiercely, my tongue seeking the warmth of her mouth. I lifted her, pushing the ottoman out of the way and lowering us to the floor, covering her with my body. She wrapped her legs around me. I groaned at the slickness of her.

"So ready for me, baby."

"*Adam*," she gasped as I surged into her, pleasure rippling through my body. We fit together perfectly—she was made only for me. And I was equally hers. Only hers.

"Told you," I groaned, tugging on her earlobe.

"Told me what?"

I smiled into her neck. "We'd end up on the floor."

A short while later, we cuddled in the chair, wrapped in the duvet, and talked.

I told her stories from different places I'd been. Some of the things I'd seen—both beautiful and tragic. There were images I knew I'd never forget and would never share with her, while others I could speak of with fond memories. She listened raptly, her eyes focused on my face as I spoke. After a while, she asked more about me.

"How did you end up here?"

"I came into a trust fund from my parents when I was twenty-one, and I had already been earning good money, so I decided it was time to buy something. I lived in a small place for a while, and when I found this building, I bought it. It was a great investment."

"Do you see yourself staying here?"

"As a home base? I think so."

She was quiet for a minute, and when she spoke, her voice was nervous. "But you still have the travel bug. The need to move—not stay in one place."

I cupped her cheek, stroking the smooth skin with my thumb. "Until now, I had no reason to."

"But now?"

"You're my reason, Nightingale. You're what I've been looking for. My anchor."

"Adam—"

"I'm not giving up my career. You have to understand that. I love what I do."

"It's dangerous."

"At times. But I'm careful, and it's not forever. One day, soon enough, I'll stop doing it."

"Can you?"

"Yes. When the time is right. There are other things I want to take pictures of—people and places. Beautiful parts of this world some people can only experience through photographs." I drew in a breath. "Maybe, one day, you'd come with me while I visit those places?"

I wanted to show her the world—to give her everything she had never seen. I wanted her to be a part of my world.

"That would be amazing."

I pulled her close, my mouth hovering over hers, wanting to say the words again. Needing to hear them.

"I love you," I murmured against her softness.

"Oh, Adam," she breathed. "So much. I love you so much."

"We'll figure out our life together."

"I know." She sighed. "But, for now, I have to go."

I hated that we had to return to reality, but I knew she was right.

"I'll drive you to work and pick you up in the morning."

"I have to go back to my place."

"I know."

"I start my days off again after tonight."

"Will you spend them here, with me? I want more time with you." My need for her was overwhelming. I couldn't explain it, but I felt it and I refused to deny it.

"I'd like that."

I nuzzled her head. "So would I."

HAVING SLEPT on and off most of the day, I was restless all night. I worked on some photos and sketched out some ideas for changing the layout of the loft, giving the sleeping area some privacy with added walls. I wanted Ally to feel at home here. Then to pass the time, I worked on my expense report and sent it off to Sean. Barely five minutes passed when he replied.

What the hell are you doing sending me an expense report at 4 in the morning? Don't you have pictures to take somewhere?

I grinned as I replied.

My boss is slacking, not sending me anywhere. Stuck with paperwork, instead. Why are you up so early?

I read his reply and laughed.

Some idiot sent me a message and woke me up.

I knew he was lying since he was in the office before five daily.

I'll make it up with coffee this week.

Lunch, and it's a deal.

Done.

I signed off and went for a shower so I could be ready to drive Ally to her place.

We were quiet when I picked her up and drove in the opposite direction of my loft. I pulled up in front of the small building where she lived, leaving the engine idling, at a loss for what to do next. She surprised me when she hesitantly asked if I would come upstairs with her. I shut off the car and went to her door, offering her my hand.

Inside, she punched in a code to open the security door. Then she quoted the code for me. "If you come over, you don't have to wait to be buzzed up. And there are visitor spots around back."

I followed her to the elevator and wrapped my arm around her waist as we rode up.

Inside, I looked around curiously. It was small, neat, and tidy. Everything was precise and in order. It didn't feel like her. It felt empty. Like a stage.

She shrugged, knowing what I was thinking. "It's not my place. It belongs to Ronald. I live here, but only until I don't have to anymore. I'll be finished paying off my debt to him soon, and I'll find a place I like to live."

I withheld the urge to tell her again that I would pay him whatever monetary debt there was so she could be free of him right now. I knew she wouldn't accept it, and this was something she insisted on doing herself.

Wandering over to her desk, I picked up a frame and studied the picture. Ally as a child, looking happy, held by a man with red hair and a friendly face.

"My dad," she murmured sadly.

I picked up another picture, a teenage boy with his arm around her, laughing.

"Ollie?"

"Yes. That was about a week before he died. Elena took it while we were visiting her."

There were only two other photos. One was Ally and Ollie with Elena. She was an older woman—tall, regal-looking, with brilliant white hair, sparkling green eyes, and she had her arms wrapped around them.

The other photo was set off to the side, and I glanced at it, recognizing her mother and Ronald. It was obviously a staged photo, looking very proper, their expressions lacking in any real emotion.

I shook my head as I turned away from the desk. They were missing so much of life. Missing out on knowing a wonderful woman who, despite everything, still wanted to be loved by them.

Ally was watching me closely.

"Do you want to give me some things I can take home with me for this weekend?"

"That's a good idea. I can take a cab to your place after the event." She grinned. "You don't have to wait up—I have a key."

I chuckled. As if I wouldn't wait up for her. "Go get what you need. I'll wait."

She chatted as she got her things together, reappearing quickly.

I decided not to tell her I would be there tonight. She would worry about it all day. I glanced upward, listening to the renovation noise overhead. I wasn't sure she'd get any sleep as it was, and I didn't want to add to the problem.

I knew I couldn't sit beside her, hold her hand, and show the world she was mine—yet. But I could be in the same room, and hopefully she would draw strength from my presence. I knew her first instinct would be to protect me, tell me to stay away, but I couldn't.

So, I remained quiet, took her small bag, kissed her

deeply, and promised to see her later. We had plans for the entire weekend together.

I could only hope they would still be in place when she saw me and my donation piece tonight.

———

Later that evening, people were milling around everywhere. I tried not to fiddle with the collar of my shirt, failing miserably at times. The suit felt so constrictive, the tie heavy around my neck. I wasn't used to dressing up, but I knew it was expected.

It was less decadent than the last dinner I attended—more about the cause it was for and not for show. Still elegant, but the flowers were simple, the settings held fewer glasses and cutlery. The room was brighter, and there were lots of pictures of the children from the ward and their stories. I made a mental note to ask Sean if there was a favor he could call in from a friend and have a story done about the work they did. I'd be happy to provide new images.

Striding up to the bar and ordering a scotch, I did my best to ignore the looks I was getting from many of the women in the room. There was a time I would have met their stares with my own, perhaps deciding, long before the evening was over, which one would accompany me to a hotel when the event was over. But those days were past me, and now there was only one set of eyes I longed to meet and have their approval. I made my way back over to where my donation was on display, playing the part required, answering questions, feigning interest in their comments about the piece. There was only one opinion I cared about.

Then she walked into the room—a vision in a deep blue dress that swirled around her legs, showing off her shapely calves. Her hair was swept up off her neck, curls escaping around her face.

I knew what that hair felt like wrapped in my fist. How her neck tasted under my tongue and how those legs felt wrapped around me. I wanted to feel it all again.

She was alone, her parents already present. They had stopped briefly, offering fake interest as they looked at the photo, their expressions blank. They had no idea what they were looking at. One of the committee members was standing with me and introduced us. I was offered a cool handshake and an even cooler smile. It was only the fact that the committee member droned on about my success and generosity that I was deemed passable enough for polite conversation. Because they were told I was important, I became such in their eyes.

I met their impassive gazes with one of my own, acknowledged the praise with a tilt of my head, as if it was my just due. Stood tall and proud in my designer suit and expensive watch, both of which spoke of the only thing they understood—money.

I answered their inane questions with a wealth of technical phrases I knew they wouldn't understand. Smirked arrogantly as other people came forward, crowding around the piece, listening to their words.

Erotic.

Stimulating.

A masterpiece.

I accepted them all.

Because with Ally in the picture, they were all correct. But it was she who made it that way. Their praise was for her—they simply didn't know it.

I narrowed my eyes as Bradley appeared behind Ally, wrapping his hand around her elbow. I felt a simmering anger in my chest.

No one should be touching her but me.

Someone approached them, and Ally turned, greeting an older woman I recognized as Elena. They began to talk, and Bradley moved away and grabbed a drink from the bar. As he approached, I tensed up, wanting to reach out and punch him. There was no reason to, aside from the fact that I wanted to feel his flesh give way under my fist. Instead, I observed him in silence as he looked at the picture, congratulating myself on my restraint.

"Interesting," he commented. "Not my cup of tea."

I smirked. The idiot had no idea. "No?"

He waved his hand dismissively. "I'm not much for…*art.*"

I nodded, keeping my face blank.

He took another pull on his drink. "Good of you to donate it, though."

"It's a worthy cause. Very close to the heart of someone I care deeply for."

"Excellent." He stuck out his hand, surprising me. "Dr. Bradley Bennett. I'm part of the committee for the event."

For a brief second, I looked at his hand and then clasped it in mine, giving it a firm shake. I could be generous. After all, Ally was mine now. "Adam Kincaid."

"Thank you for this."

"I hope it does well."

He tilted his head and moved on.

I drained my glass and set it on the table close to me. Then I heard a small gasp I'd know anywhere and turned to face Ally.

Up close, she was more stunning than ever. But her beautiful eyes were wide and confused, her gaze bouncing between me and the picture. Standing beside her, Elena took us in, her steady gaze shrewd. She tilted her head, studying the image, then she smirked and brushed a kiss to Ally's cheek.

"I'm going to the table. These old legs need to sit down. I'll see you after dinner, child." Then she looked at me. "I understand you're at my table, Mr. Kincaid. You'll sit beside me."

It was a command, not a request.

"My pleasure, ma'am," I murmured, not taking my eyes off Ally.

Elena chuckled and swept away. "We'll see about that, boy."

My lips quirked at her tone and the name she'd bestowed on me.

My Nightingale looked at me and then again at the picture. I wanted to pull her into my arms and kiss her until she couldn't breathe. I needed to touch her, but I knew I couldn't.

"No one knows it's you. I promise."

"Elena knew… *I know*."

"Are you angry?"

"I'm overwhelmed." She gestured toward the image. "When?"

I inched forward, needing to be closer. "After you left for brunch."

Her fathomless eyes met mine, her exhaustion making them dull in the dim light. "Why, Adam? Why are you here?"-

"I wanted to be here tonight. Be close to you." Unable to resist, I flicked my fingers out, touching her wrist. "I was afraid if I told you, you'd tell me not to come."

She moved, seemingly to get closer to the photo. I startled when her fingers slipped into my hand, squeezing tight before withdrawing. "Thank you."

"You're so beautiful."

She offered me a smile, a warm one filled with her light. "You clean up well, Mr. Kincaid."

"Your dress is lovely. It looks spectacular on you." I lowered my voice. "It's going to look even better on the floor beside our bed."

Her hand flew to her neck, where my nightingale pendant rested. "Adam…" she breathed out.

"I need you alone."

"You'll have it later."

"I'm not sure I'll last until then."

"*Try*, Adam," she teased. "It's only a few hours. At least make it through dinner."

I smirked. "I can do that. No doubt Elena will keep me on my toes."

She hummed in agreement. "I'd hate to see this work of art not get auctioned off if you misbehaved and got dragged out."

"Do you hate it?" I asked, indicating the photo.

"No." She shook her head. "I think it's one of the most beautiful things I've ever seen. I wish I could afford to buy it."

"I might be able to help with that."

She hummed. "Somehow, I'm not surprised."

Bradley appeared suddenly, and she took a step back. He looked between us, and only then did I realize how close we were standing. I moved back as well.

"Alexandra, we need to move to our table."

She smiled at me. "Thank you again for your explanation. Your photo is mesmerizing."

"You're welcome, Ms. Robbins." I returned her smile. "Enjoy your dinner."

"I will."

I watched her walk away, moving in front of Bradley so he didn't touch her.

Then I dragged in a deep breath of air, making a silent promise to both of us.

It was the last time she'd have to walk without me.

CHAPTER
ELEVEN

DINNER WAS a cat-and-mouse game with Elena. Ally was correct when she'd stated Elena would preside over the table. The old woman was a powerhouse—shrewd, sharp, and blunt. She was also catty and snarky when she felt like it —which, it seemed, was a lot this evening. Her jibes were laced with the sweetest of smiles, her sharp words spiked with kindness. She didn't suffer fools easily, and this table was full of them. I would have gone mad without her presence.

I liked her a lot.

My view of Ally was perfect. More than once, our gazes met, lingering far too long, and I had to tear my glance away. Hundreds of words passed between us without a sound. Lifetimes of promises made with the lift of an eyebrow. The intense closeness I felt to Ally was uncanny— unlike anything I had ever experienced until her. More than once, Elena caught our stares, her all-seeing eyes studying us as if she knew what was occurring.

I tuned out a great deal of the conversation, covertly making sure Bradley didn't get too handsy and Ally wasn't picked on by her mother every moment. She was stuck between them again, but tonight, she didn't seem as drawn in on herself. Her shoulders were back, the light glinting off her pendant. Her face was almost serene, and I knew I'd made the right decision coming here. She needed me as much as I needed her.

Elena cleared her throat, and I realized I'd been staring far too long at Ally. She shifted in her chair, turning to face me. Most of our table had gotten up to look over the auction items one last time, leaving us to talk.

She regarded me astutely and leaned close. "I know who you are, boy."

I arched an eyebrow. "Do you now?"

She was direct. "You're the reason Alexandra is glowing this evening."

"You think?"

"Don't play dumb with me."

I sipped my scotch. "I have no idea what you're talking about."

"You don't want to take credit for making her happy?"

My expression gave me away. "It's Ally's news to share."

She took my glass, then sipped at the golden liquid. "For the money they charge for these things, they could bring in a better vintage." Then she chuckled. "Ally? That's going to go over well with Sarah and Ronald. They dislike nicknames."

I narrowed my eyes, taking back my glass. She was right about the scotch, but it was better than nothing. "I don't much give a fuck about Sarah and Ronald."

She surprised me by clapping her hands in delight. "Oh, I'm going to like you, boy."

I smiled—the first real one of the night I'd bestowed other than to Ally. "That's a good thing. I'm already fond of you."

She pursed her lips. "You're older than she is."

"Eight years isn't a lot."

"I think you've crammed a lot of living into those years." With a sly grin, she ruffled my hair. "I see the evidence here."

"Ally should be grateful I don't take after my father. He was as bald as a billiard ball at thirty. I can live with some silver."

"It suits you."

I winked at her teasing. "Like what you see, woman?"

She sniffed and turned her head, but her lips curled into a grin.

"That's a rather risqué picture you've donated."

"It's a work of art. Something I created."

She shook her head impatiently. "Alexandra has spent many afternoons in my pool." This time, it was her eyebrow that arched knowingly. "I recognize those freckles."

A grin broke out on my face. "Enchanting, aren't they?"

"You made a huge mistake, though."

"Oh? Do tell."

"Someone is going to walk out of here with that picture. That lovely, *enchanting* picture—the *subject,* who obviously means so much to you." She narrowed her eyes. "And you have to sign it for them, I believe."

I lifted her hand and brushed a kiss along the paper-thin skin. "Madame, you underestimate me."

She shrugged as people returned to their seats to start the bidding. "We'll see, boy. We'll see."

I watched the action around me during the auction. Most of the items hit high numbers, but I knew mine would blow them all out of the water. I didn't like everyone ogling the image of Ally in my photograph. I knew they had no idea who it was, but it didn't matter. No one would ever see it again after tonight.

Except me.

My item came up for auction, and I sat back, relaxed. Her parents had walked past it, barely sparing it a glance. Bradley had looked at it, not knowing what he saw, proving to me he didn't know her intimately at all. Ally had stared, her eyes wide, shocked. She knew.

And the brilliant, all-knowing Elena knew.

The bidding started at five thousand. It jumped to ten fast. I remained relaxed as it continued to escalate. When it hit twenty-five thousand, I smiled benignly and sipped my scotch.

"I hope you're ready to sign your name soon." Elena

frowned.

"Not a problem."

Thirty.

Forty.

I tapped one word on my phone.

Now.

"One hundred thousand!" a voice shouted from across the room.

There were gasps of disbelief, a round of applause, and just like that, it was done.

Elena shook her head, then grinned. "You are good," she mused.

I snickered into my glass. Thanks to my business manager, John Reynolds, I had bought my own piece.

"She's so worth it."

She sighed and offered me a smile. A rich, honest smile.

"Finally," she murmured. "She *finally* has someone real."

I nodded. "She has. And no matter what anyone else thinks, I'm here to stay."

"I like you, boy. I want you to come for tea."

"Make it coffee and scotch, and I'll bring the scotch."

She laughed, a boisterous sound loud in the quiet hum of the room.

"Soon," she insisted.

"Done."

After the last few auction items were sold, people began

to mill around. I stood, once again kissing Elena's hand. "I'm going to go and mingle. I look forward to coffee."

Her gaze drifted over the table where Ally sat with Bradley and her parents. "Watch yourself, boy. They bite."

I took off my jacket, hanging it over the back of my chair. I released my hair from the tight knot I'd had it in and let it fall around my ears. Slowly, I rolled up my sleeves, exposing my ink-covered forearms. I grinned down at her as I flexed my muscles. "So do I."

She eyed my hair and arms, her eyebrows high and her eyes glowing. One shaky finger trailed along a long black line of ink. "My husband had a tattoo. I found it rather *sexy*."

"Really," I drawled with a grin.

She winked at me, her expression saucy. I could imagine her in her youth, mischievous and bright with life.

"It was in a more, ah, private place. Only he and I ever saw it."

I winked back. "*Scandalous*."

"It was. And I saw it—a lot." She indicated the table I was anxious to visit. "Go get 'em."

Smoothly, I moved through the crowd, accepting some handshakes and explaining to a few people that, no, I didn't do private photo sessions for portraits. I managed to keep my temper until I got to the table and saw Ally. She was still stuck between her mother and Bradley, and they were talking. I wasn't sure if it was at her or to her, but she was now uncomfortable, her hands twisting together on the table. I straightened my shoulders and stepped forward.

"Ally."

Three sets of eyes met my gaze. Two displeased, and one startled, soft, and so blue I wanted to drown in them.

"Adam," she breathed out.

Bradley stood, his hand on her shoulder. It took all my inner strength not to knock it off and tell him to keep his fucking hands off my girl.

Ally reached up, brushing away his grip.

"Can we help you?" Sarah demanded, her cold eyes widening as they took in my longer hair and the artwork now displayed on my arms. Disapproval colored her tone.

"Mother, this is Adam Kincaid. He contributed the piece that fetched such a large donation. He's very well-known."

"Ah. Yes. We met earlier. It was an *interesting* piece."

I tilted my head in acknowledgment of her "praise."

"I had an exceptional muse."

Ally's cheeks colored and her eyes glowed.

"I was wondering if I might borrow Ally for a moment."

"Her name is Alexandra," Bradley interrupted, frowning.

"And how do you know my daughter, Mr. Kincaid?"

"I was fortunate enough to meet her after a small work-related mishap. She took very good care of me." I gave Ally a huge grin before turning back to her mother. "When I heard about the benefit for the children's ward, I remembered her kindness and wanted to give back. You must be so proud of your daughter, Mrs. Givens. Such a caring, gifted nurse and a truly remarkable woman."

She cleared her throat, her disdain for my opinion evident. "Yes, of course."

Ronald appeared, a drink in hand, and I reintroduced myself, shaking his hand firmly and meeting his eyes. I wasn't going to back down in front of these people. Ally needed to know I was there for her.

"I've seen your work," he acknowledged grudgingly. "You're very good, I hear. Several of the men at the bar were discussing your last shoot in the Amazon."

"I hold my own."

He eyed my hair and arms distastefully. "Dangerous work. Almost reckless."

His tone said the word he didn't speak—*unacceptable*.

"I'm careful." I glanced in Ally's direction. "I get into far more trouble close to home. Thank God for nurses with a healing touch. It'll come in handy if I have an accident with my bike."

Sarah's voice became more displeased. "You drive a motorcycle?"

"When weather permits."

She eyed me in silence, and I watched as I was effectively dismissed. Without the cover of the suit and the safe veneer of respectability surrounding me, she saw me for what I was—at least in her eyes.

I was everything they wouldn't tolerate: free, reckless,

blunt, open, strong, covered in ink—with a motorcycle waiting to whisk Ally away—making me dangerous as well, and rich or not, I was *not* acceptable.

Nor was I afraid of them.

Bradley made a displeased noise, then turned and stomped over to the nearest bar. Ally tensed as her mother spoke again. "How long have you been *acquaintances*?"

"Oh, that's *not* the word I'd use, Mrs. Givens," I assured her. "But I still plan on getting to know her much better."

Her voice was like ice. "I see."

I held out my hand. "Will you walk with me, Ally?"

She gazed at me as my eyes beseeched her to accept. She could refuse and convince her parents I was some crazy artist she had no interest in. She could be polite and turn me away in a gentle manner.

Or she could be brave and let me claim her. Leave this table and the judgment they had laid on her so many years ago, and come with me, knowing she'd never be subjected to that again in her life.

She stood, clutching her small bag. "Good evening, Mother."

Sarah didn't move, but her lips thinned out in warning.

Ally slipped her hand into mine, allowing me to pull her closer. I dipped my head in victory. "Have a pleasant night."

Elena smirked as we went by.

I stopped and dropped a kiss on her downy cheek as I grabbed my jacket. "If I hadn't met Ally first, I'd so go for you."

Her laughter followed us out of the room.

I pulled Ally into the closest alcove and wrapped my arms around her.

"I can't believe you did that," she whispered into my neck.

"If you're furious, I'll drive you home," I murmured.

She lifted her face to me, her eyes filled with wonder. "How can I be furious? You stood up to my mother and Ronald. In a way I've never seen anyone stand up to them before. You did it on their level." She shook her head. "In a room full of their peers, you…*claimed* me."

"I can work a room."

"You're shameless."

"No. I'm in love with you. I want everyone to know you're mine. They can either accept it or get the fuck out of the way."

"They'll never accept it."

Slipping my fingers under her chin, I dropped a kiss on her sweet mouth. "I know this is going to explode around us. I only wanted to come tonight and let them see I exist. I didn't plan the whole pissing contest with your mother."

"What changed?"

"Seeing you. You weren't beside me. I couldn't touch you. He could, and I hated it. He can talk to you, act like you belong to him, but you don't." I slid my hands down her arms, pulling her closer. "You're mine, Ally. You belong with me."

"Yes, I do."

"You're not angry?"

"No. I'll be summoned soon, though."

"I'll go with you. You don't have to face them alone."

"You'd do that?"

"I'd do anything for you."

I held her tight. "We'll do this together." I snorted. "Or I can call Elena. She'll set them straight in a fucking heartbeat."

"Elena adored you. I could see her talking to you."

"I like her. She's *wicked*. She likes my ink." I winked. "I think the old gal fancies me a little."

Ally giggled. "I don't blame her. You're pretty hot stuff, Mr. Kincaid."

"Can I take you home?"

"Yes."

"My home?"

"Can I use my key?"

I tucked her under my arm. "Yes."

"Could we—could we stop and get a pizza?"

I had seen how little she ate at dinner.

I nestled her closer. "Absolutely. Extra cheese?"

"Yes."

"No utensils," I bargained.

"I might get messy."

I lowered my head, my lips brushing her ear. "I'll lick it off you."

She shivered. "No utensils," she agreed.

"Okay. Let's go."

CHAPTER
TWELVE

ALLY'S PHONE CHIMED AGAIN, but this time, it was a different sound than usual. Bradley and her mother had tried several times to reach her since we'd left the gala last night, but she ignored them all. She glanced over from her spot in my arms, frowning.

"You need that?"

"That's Vivian. She may need me to cover a shift."

Reluctantly, I handed it to her. I didn't want her going in, but I knew I had no voice in the matter. She read the screen and rolled her eyes.

"What?"

"She's reminding me about my lieu time."

"What about it?"

"The fact that I need to take some."

"Oh yeah?"

"Yes. This happens every year, but my old boss let it slip. Vivian insists on me taking time off. She was horrified at the amount of time I had accumulated when she took over as head of the ER."

"Why don't you take your time?"

She sat up, looking out the window. "There never seems to be any point. I don't have the money to travel or anyone to travel with. I went with Elena once on a brief trip to New York, but she likes her own kind of thing." She sighed. "Mostly playing cards and gossiping with her cronies. I hated sitting around the apartment. I take a few days every so often when Vivian demands, and I play tourist here, but that's about it."

I sat up, running my fingers along her arm. I leaned in and kissed her V of freckles. "Take some time then—now. With me."

She looked over, puzzled. "What?"

"Take a week off. We can take some road trips on the bike, sleep in, eat out, and get some time with each other."

"What about your job?"

I grinned. I'd had another stretch of time here—something rare, but I was pleased to extend it. "I'll shock the hell out of Sean and tell him I'm taking some time off. If anything happens, he can get someone else."

Excitement lit up her eyes. "Really? They can do that?"

"Yes. Can they get someone to cover for you?"

She clutched her phone. "I'll ask."

———

We had days of nothing but us. Rides on the bike. Sleeping in. Late meals. Making love. Talking. Ally's smiles were bright and contagious. I took endless photos of her. Smiling, laughing, sleeping, even crying while we watched some terrible chick flick she insisted we needed to see. I had captured all her emotions and the way her brilliant eyes projected them. The hues transformed all the time, and I wanted to catalog the changes.

Today, we were having a picnic. She had cooked all morning, while I attempted to help. I was kicked out of the kitchen, after being told in no uncertain terms that trying to fuck her on the counter did not constitute "help."

I did it anyway.

She was too sexy, wearing one of my shirts, with her hair piled on her head, and her bare feet thumping on the floor as she moved around, humming softly to herself. Around her ankle was one of my leather wristbands. I had slipped it on while she slept, the caveman in me liking how she now had a piece of me on her body. When she woke up, she had lifted her leg, the black of the leather a dark stripe on her ivory skin, and studied it, running her fingers around the thin circlet, then she smiled. She knew what it meant to me to see it on her.

Watching her hips move in time to the music as she stirred something in a bowl was too much to resist. My shirt ended up on the floor. She ended up on the counter, and my face ended up between her legs.

She did scream my name—twice.

Once while I fucked her with my tongue, and once when I buried myself deep inside and took her hard and fast.

The way I told her I would.

Even now, looking at her across the blanket from me, I wanted her. I glanced around at the trees—they were thick and plentiful, and the place mostly deserted this time of day. We were in a private little area we'd found on the edge of the park.

I could pull her onto my lap and bury myself inside her. She was even wearing a skirt.

How convenient.

"I know what you're thinking," she sang out as she popped a grape into her mouth.

"Mind reader now, are you?"

"No." She indicated my lap and the prominent bulge I was sporting—a constant state, it seemed, when she was around. "Body language." She shook her head. "Is that all you think of?"

"Not my fault you're so fucking sexy." I patted my knee, leering at her. "Why don't you come over here, and we can talk about whatever…pops up?"

She started to giggle. The giggling became laughter, and she clapped a hand over her mouth, trying to hold in her mirth.

I began to laugh with her. I loved seeing her like this.

She was rested and relaxed, the dark circles under her eyes vanished and the worried look gone. She had cut off all communication with her parents and Bradley, refusing to listen to their objections or to see them until her break was over. It had done her a world of good.

She said I had done her a world of good.

I pushed off the tree, lunging and catching her around the waist, pinning her underneath me.

"You think that's funny? You find my cock funny, Ally?" I growled and thrust forward.

Her eyes widened, all the laughter ceasing as she felt how hard I was for her. A small moan escaped her lips.

I ran my tongue up her neck and pulled her earlobe into my mouth, swirling and teasing. "You like that, don't you? Feeling how hard you make me."

"*Yes...*"

"You want me? You want me to fuck you outside, knowing someone might see us?" I bit down on her neck gently, sucking the skin between my teeth and rolling it. "*Tell me*, my wild girl. Tell me what you want."

I slipped my hands under her shirt, ghosting up her torso and tracing her lace-covered nipples with my thumbs.

"My hands? You want my hands on you?"

I tickled her skin with my lips, dipping between her breasts and nuzzling.

"My tongue? Is that what you want?"

I sat back and pulled her against me, my cock hitting her heat. "Or my cock?"

She whimpered, the sound making me harder. I stroked her leg, inching my hands higher until they reached the satin of her panties. Her very small, very damp panties.

"Oh, my girl is ready," I crooned, slipping my fingers inside and stroking. "So ready."

"Please, Adam," she pleaded.

"Tell me what you want, and I'll give it to you."

I loved hearing the dirty words she only ever said to me fall from those sweet lips. She thrashed her head as I flexed my fingers, stroking that spot that drove her crazy.

"I'll give you everything. Just say it."

She arched, forcing my fingers deeper. "Oh God… Adam… *I want*… I want you to *fuck* me."

"With?" I demanded.

"Your *cock*… I want your cock."

I moved her panties aside, tugged my jeans down, and lifted her onto my lap, sinking in deep. "Good answer, baby."

I held her tight, her face buried in my neck as she rolled her hips, pressing down as I thrust into her. She whimpered and moaned, her breath hot on my skin. She fisted my shirt as she rode me hard. The feel of her teeth biting down into my skin as she quivered sent me over the edge, and I groaned as I climaxed.

We stilled, wrapped around each other. I wove my hands in her hair and lifted her face to mine, covering her skin with kisses, murmuring endearments as I brushed my lips against hers.

"God, I love you, Ally. I love you so fucking much I think I'll burst."

She hummed in agreement.

"You're everything to me, baby. *Everything.* I can't imagine life without you anymore."

She drew back, her expression radiant.

"You'll never have to."

All levity left me as I gripped her face between my palms. "Promise me."

Her hands covered mine. "I promise. I'll never leave you, Adam."

I clutched her to me, overwhelmed at the strange emotion. "Thank God."

———

"You both look well rested." Elena smirked at us.

I leaned back in my chair, holding a glass of scotch. We'd been given the nonnegotiable invitation to appear for lunch. I brought the promised scotch and the biggest bouquet of orchids and roses the florist could create.

Somehow, I knew extravagant was the way to go with Elena. Nothing less would be right.

She accepted both as if it was her due, as well as the kiss I bestowed on her soft cheek.

"I convinced Ally to take some time off."

"Well, that's a first."

I winked. "There've been many firsts, Elena."

Ally slapped me on my arm. "Adam!"

I grinned. "What?" I asked innocently. "You rode my…*bike* for the first time, didn't you?"

Elena scoffed as Ally's cheeks darkened. Chuckling, I brushed a kiss to her heated skin.

"Behave," she admonished quietly.

"I'll try."

Elena clapped her hands. "No! I like seeing the two of you like this. It's like a breath of fresh air." She sighed as she picked up her glass. "My Theo and I couldn't keep our hands off each other. We—what is that phrase you young ones use nowadays—we fucked like rabbits all the time. I remember getting kicked out of the country club for inappropriate behavior on the golf course." She paused dramatically. "Now, it wasn't the first time. The only difference was we got caught. That man knew his way around my putting green, let me tell you."

Ally sputtered into her glass as I threw my head back and laughed. "I bet you got kicked out of a few places didn't you, you minx, you."

"A few. He was a very physical man." She chuckled. "Thank God. So many of the men I'd met before him were dreadful, boring people. As if they had sticks up their asses—like that Bradley. What a tool."

I promptly decided I was arranging for flowers to be sent to this woman weekly. I adored her.

She turned to Ally. "I like this one. Sassy *and* good-looking."

Ally rolled her eyes. "Don't encourage him. Stroking his ego only makes it bigger."

"That's not what you said this morning when you were stroking my big...*ego*," I deadpanned.

Ally dropped her head in her hands, laughing. Elena chuckled.

"I can't do anything with him," Ally groaned.

"Do you want to?" Elena asked, tilting her head.

"No. I love him just the way he is," Ally admitted with a smile.

Elena leaned forward and patted my hand. "I'm glad she found you, boy."

Lifting Ally's hand, I kissed her knuckles. "So am I."

Ally excused herself to clean up from lunch. I watched her walk away with a grin, loving the sway of her hips as she moved.

Elena cleared her throat, and I dragged my gaze back to her.

"You have it bad."

"It's terminal."

"I want to see lots of you, boy."

"Ditto. On one condition."

"Oh—negotiations. Excellent. Let's begin."

"Only one."

"Name it."

I leaned forward, earnest. "I get called away a lot. Promise me when I do, you'll watch out for Ally."

"Keep the monsters at bay, such as it were?" she asked with a wry grin.

"They know exactly how to destroy her. I've never seen anything like it."

She narrowed her eyes at me. "How serious are you about my girl?"

I met her gaze unwaveringly. "She's my world now. She feels the same about me. Her parents, though—"

"Hate you," she finished.

"I'm not *acceptable*."

She scoffed. "Ronald. There's another tool. My brother, Randall, was younger and spoiled rotten. Grew up to be the biggest snob that ever lived, and he passed that along to his son. My nephew is so worried about keeping up appearances, he forgets to actually *look* and see anything. He's built Ollie up into a saint in his own mind. He will never forgive Alexandra for his death."

I nodded, having figured that out. "I'm worried what they'll do and say to her when I'm not around."

"They'll try. But I'll say this, boy. I've never seen Alexandra look at anyone the way she looks at you. It won't matter what they say or do. For the first time in her life, she's made up her mind about what she wants. And she wants you." She patted my arm. "But I'll keep an eye out. Now, I have a request for you—two, actually."

"Name them."

"I know what you do is dangerous. Promise you'll be careful and come home to her."

"Always."

She hesitated, her eyes becoming distant for a moment.

"Ollie was a gift to me. I never understood how two such uptight people had a son like him. He was pure sunshine. I adored him." She looked at me purposely. "And he adored your Ally. She's paid an unnecessary price for his death. He would have hated his father for it."

"Ally loved him as well. She still misses him."

She frowned. "They drummed so much guilt into her head for so long, she believed it. I've only ever been able to do so much." She gazed into space for a moment. "Ronald has always been rigid. Always in control and demanding. His first wife was much the same as Sarah. She did whatever he told her to do. When he lost Oliver, it was as if he snapped. His bitterness was so strong it twisted him, and he needed to punish someone."

"And he chose to punish a defenseless child who did nothing wrong."

"And a mother who did nothing to stop it. I wanted to take her away. I spoke to my lawyer, but he told me it was a lost cause since her natural mother was alive and in her life. He told me if I tried, I would probably never see her again, and I couldn't take that risk. So, I played his game to stay close. I knew if I showed her affection, he would send her off to some boarding school as far away as possible. I've always had to hide my fondness for her. It's only been lately I've been able to be more open with her, but it's still not enough."

I held her frail hand. "She knows, Elena. Believe me. She calls you her 'guardian angel.'"

She shook her head. "Some guardian. I wanted to pay for her education and an apartment for her, but Ronald insisted he would. I had no idea of the terms until it slipped out one night after Ronald had a few too many drinks in him. But Alexandra refuses to let me pay him on her behalf, even now. It took me forever, it seemed, to talk her into accepting a used car I could no longer drive."

"She's stubborn." I agreed. "She won't let me pay him off either."

We'd had our first argument when I had made the offer to pay off the so-called debt.

"It's my debt." Ally's eyes flashed with a spark of anger.

"An unnecessary one. I can pay it, and you'll be free."

"Money won't free me from the guilt."

"There should be no guilt. It wasn't your fault. Stop letting them make you think it was!"

"Stop telling me how to feel!" she snapped back, her rare temper showing. "That's no better than what they do!"

I held up my hands, shocked by her vehemence, yet pleased at the way she spoke her mind. It showed the strength she had inside. "Sorry. I only want to help. I hate seeing you struggle."

Her face softened. "I have to do this my way. I need you to understand that, the same way you need me to understand your need to travel and capture the kinds of images you do."

I pulled her into my arms, knowing I had to accept it. "Okay, Nightingale. I hate it, but okay."

Elena's voice pulled me back to the present. "She still suffers with guilt."

"Unnecessary guilt."

"True. But it's been shoved down her throat so long, she believes it. But I hope soon she can break free of all that. I think perhaps you may be the key."

"I want to look after her."

"That's my second favor."

"What?"

"I'm old, dear boy. Getting older by the day, and I'm getting tired. I miss Theo. One day, in the not-too-distant future, I'll be gone. I want you to promise you'll look after her. If I know she's all right, then it will bring me some peace."

I swallowed the thickness in my throat. "You have my word. But please, Elena. Stick around. Ally loves you, and I think you're fucking amazing. I want to spend years getting to know you. Not months."

She smiled at me—a wide, beaming smile that made me smile back.

"You remind me of my Theo, dirty mouth and all. God, I loved that man. I'll do my best, boy. We'll each keep our end of the bargain, yes?"

"Yes."

"All right. I hope you brought some cash, young man. I feel like playing poker, and I don't take candy."

I chuckled and dug into my pocket for the rolls of coins. Ally had warned me—Elena liked to play poker. She donated all the money to an animal shelter and expected her guests to do the same.

"You're on, old woman. But I warn you, I play to win."

"That is exactly why I like you."

I nodded, smirking. I liked her too.

Those flowers were going to start arriving this week.

CHAPTER
THIRTEEN

I SIGHED as I slid into the car, exhausted from holding in my temper. Ally reached over and squeezed my hand. "No more dinners."

"Was I that bad?"

It had been another disastrous attempt at getting Ronald and Sarah to like me. Their contempt never lessened; in fact, it only grew deeper every time I was in their company. Ronald like to talk down to me, and Sarah barely spoke, instead casting disapproving glances and barely concealed disdain.

I did like to goad them. They pissed me off so much with their attitude.

Ally shook her head. "No, they were. I won't let them taunt or talk down to you anymore."

I loosened my tie, pulling at it gratefully. I hated wearing one. "I do it for you. I'll keep doing it until they crack."

"They won't crack. And frankly, I don't care if they do anymore. I tried. You tried."

I loved hearing her say those words. To know their opinion was becoming less important. The thought of not having to spend another evening in their stiff company filled me with relief. "You sure?"

"Yes. When you're home and there's a benefit, I'd like it if you came with me, though."

"Absolutely."

She shifted in the seat. "Then that's that."

"We should celebrate."

She laughed. "The end of your torture?"

"Something like that."

"What did you have in mind?"

I had the sudden desire to hold her in my arms. "I know a place—great drinks, music, dancing. Can I interest you?"

"I'd love that!"

"Me too."

For someone who claimed to be clumsy, on the dance floor, Ally came alive. She was perfect in my arms as we glided around the floor. She shimmied and moved to the faster beats like she was born with rhythm in her soul. I loved watching her and regretted not having a camera with me. I used my phone and got a few shots to satisfy my need.

At one point, we swayed to the sultry sound, her pressed close to me.

"I love dancing with you," she murmured, trailing her fingers over my neck, making me tighten with want.

"They say dancing is like making love upright," I replied, tightening my hold. "With the right person anyway."

She tilted back her head. "Am I the right person?"

I kissed her deeply, exploring her sweetness, needing her cinnamon-scented breath inside my mouth. "Yes."

"Good. You're mine too, Adam."

We stumbled into the loft at two o'clock in the morning, after dancing for hours, leaving the tension of the night behind us. I'd left the car parked at the club, and we took a cab home. We made out all the way home in the back seat and in the elevator up to the loft. I could hardly wait to get her naked.

Pieces of our clothes were strewn around the floor as we made our way to the bed. I growled low as I saw the lacy blue lingerie she was wearing under her pretty dress. I planned on peeling it off her smooth skin—with my teeth.

She giggled and I grinned, realizing I'd said that out loud. Then I did exactly that.

I hummed against her breasts, capturing a plump nipple in my mouth. She arched up with a low moan, making me hiss as her movement dragged her wetness along my cock, coating me with her want.

"Fuck. What you do to me," I groaned as I slid through her heat. I stilled at the completeness of being buried inside her. Every time was like the first, a feeling I never wanted to lose.

She flexed, her body surrounding me.

I thrust slowly, deeply, taking my time with her. These moments were so perfect—joined with her in the most intimate of ways. I rocked leisurely, our bodies melded, skin against skin, never apart. A long shiver ran down my spine at her closeness.

I took her mouth, our tongues sliding, mimicking our bodies. Languid, fluid, deep, and sensuous. I stayed locked inside her intimate embrace until we both shook with the force of release. Until she was limp and sated in my arms. She rested against my chest, idly tracing her finger over my skin.

"Did I tell you Emma called?"

"Oh?"

"She's in town, so we're going to have lunch. You want to join us?"

"How about I drop you off and have coffee, then leave you to it?"

"Are you sure?"

I dropped a kiss on her head. "You haven't seen her in a while. You two need to catch up. I'm not overly interested in girl talk."

She laughed. "Okay, but I know she wants to meet you. She's heard lots about you."

I grinned. "Bragging, are you? How sexy I am, how good in bed, my incredible looks?"

She huffed, the air drifting over my skin. "More like how bossy you are, the fact that you can't find the laundry basket, and you have no idea what a towel rack is for."

Laughter rumbled through my chest, and I pressed a kiss to her head. "Whatever, Ally. You know you can't resist me."

"Just keeping it real."

"That's my girl. Now, go to sleep."

"See? Bossy," she mumbled sleepily.

I grinned against her head. She was right.

———

Emma Jones was tall with intelligent dark eyes, and her fondness for my girl was evident. We sized each other up, both cautious, then she smiled.

"Nice to finally meet you, Adam."

"Same here," I replied, shaking her hand.

"Ally said you were hot."

I grinned, leaning back. "Did she now?"

Ally groaned. "Not you too. Elena already fills his head with compliments."

I bent close to her ear. "Already talking about my filled head, Ally? You're making me blush."

Emma burst out laughing, and I had to chuckle. Ally tried to ignore me.

"I have some news," Emma announced. "I'm selling my stores."

"Why?" gasped Ally.

"The offer is too good to pass up. They'll still carry my clothes, but they'll run them, and I can concentrate on my designs. With Alan's new job, he's traveling a lot, I'm traveling—we never see each other. This is a good compromise." She took a sip of her coffee. "Life is too short to be apart that much."

I felt Ally tense beside me. I knew she was already thinking of the next time I would be called away and dreading it. I hadn't told her Sean had texted while she was in the shower, warning me about a massive weather system being tracked. If it continued inland, I'd be leaving tonight. I needed to check with him, then break the news to my girl.

I stood. "Ladies, I'm going to go do some errands and leave you to catch up."

Ally frowned. "You don't have to go. You could eat with us."

I leaned down, kissing her forehead. "But I do. I saw the girly shit on the menu for lunch. No tofu for me." At her chuckle, I brushed a finger down her cheek. "Besides, I know you're dying to brag more about my, ah, *head*." I winked. "Have some time with your friend."

Emma grinned. "I'll drop her off when we're done."

"Sounds good."

"Nice to meet you, Adam. Keep up the good work. I've never seen Alex look so happy."

I smiled as I shook her hand, already knowing Ally wouldn't look so happy in a few hours.

And I hated it.

———

"D49." The attendant handed me the keys. I located the car and threw my stuff into the back, anxious to get on the road. I'd been away for over a week, and when the plane for the last leg of the trip was delayed due to mechanical failure, I decided I couldn't wait another whole day before seeing Ally, so I rented a car, planning on driving the final six hours to get home. It was far better than pacing around a hotel room or the airport.

The miles passed as I mulled over thoughts of Ally and the far-too-frequent times I left her.

I had always enjoyed my career; I liked the travel and adventure, and yes, I liked the dangerous aspect of it. But now when my phone rang with Sean's ringtone, instead of the thrill of the next great shoot came the dread of saying goodbye to the woman I'd lost my heart to. The pain of leaving her behind each time grew more intense with each parting. I loathed being away from her. And lately, I'd been gone far too often.

Her little love notes written on pink paper, the grape suckers she would tuck into my bag, and her sweet texts kept me close to the life she led while I was away and made the time bearable, but only just. Our farewells saddened us both and although she was nothing but supportive, I knew it weighed on Ally.

When I would get back, Ally loved to sit and pore over the photographs I'd taken. She saw my work through different eyes, always finding moments of beauty in the images—the light amid the dark— people helping others, a rare smile when a person would find some precious article they thought was lost forever, or my camera would be clicking away at the perfect moment when the sun shone just right across a field of grass or lowered into the ocean. Her good eye and quiet praise made me proud. I found myself experiencing more emotion to the desolation I saw. It was as if Ally had opened up that part of me and it was reflected in my work.

Elena kept her promise and made sure to check in with Ally all the time. Even though her parents still dictated too much of her life, Ally was getting stronger, saying no more often, and standing up to them. We both saw the changes in her and how their hold was slowly being eroded.

When I was in town, I lost a lot of money to Elena's cheating ways at poker. And I loved every minute of the time we would spend with her—sipping scotch, playing cards, and listening to her stories. I sought out different scotches in every country I went to, bringing Elena back some rare, exotic bottle to try. I also made it my mission to find Ally something and send it. More times than not, it had a nightingale theme. A beautifully carved wooden box I found in Thailand. A silver pendant with an oval disk—the nightingale form carved out of the gleaming metal—that I saw in Japan. In Hawaii, I found a delicate gold and enamel necklace. I sent other things—a pretty porcelain tile and an exquisite pair of diamond earrings I had purchased on a layover in Brussels—but I knew how much the symbols of my name for her meant to each of us, and I loved seeing her wear them.

They were small tokens, feeble attempts to make up for the fact that I wasn't there with her.

Flowers and presents. They were all I could give her, until I was able to give her what she truly wanted—a life with me, home, beside her. Not chasing images around the globe.

I was waiting for her when she walked out of the hospital, the sky overcast and drizzling. Her head was down, her shoulders hunched against the weather when I called out to her. "*Nightingale.*"

She looked up, her face transforming, as she flung herself into my open arms. I held her tight, lifting her feet off the ground. Her face was buried in my neck, and I felt the wetness of her tears.

"Hey, what's this?" I asked quietly. "I'm fine. You know that."

"I missed you so much."

I kissed her head, inhaling her comforting scent. "I missed you. Can I take you home? Do you need anything from your place?"

She tilted her head back. "I stayed at the loft a few times. I have some things there."

"I'd like it if you stayed all the time."

She cupped my face. "You look so tired."

"I drove all night to get to you."

"Adam," she whispered.

I crushed her to me, burying my face into her neck. "I couldn't wait to get back to you. I need to take you home to our bed. I want to fall asleep in your arms. Wake up beside you. I *need* that—I need you. Please tell me I can have it. Tell me everyone else can fuck off and I can have you today."

"Yes."

"They'll come pick up the rental later. Will you follow me home?"

Her voice was like music to my ears. "I'll follow you anywhere."

My need was so great we barely got in the door, and I had her in my arms. We made it to the bed, discarding our clothes as we went. She stiffened as my fingers slipped below her waistband, tugging on the material to get her pants off. I needed to be buried inside her, deep inside her, and I needed it *now*. I frowned when I felt the edges of a bandage, and I gently pulled down the fabric. A bandage covered the area below her hip bone.

"You're hurt?" I traced the edge of the bandage. "What happened, baby?"

"I'm not hurt."

I looked up at her quizzically.

"You came home early. I was going to surprise you. I got a tattoo."

My eyes widened. "You got a tattoo?" I repeated.

She nodded. "I thought the bandage would be off and you'd see it…"

I shook my head. "No. This is good—let me take it off."

I peeled back the bandage, revealing her ink. Low on her hip, where only I would ever see it, was a small camera etched out over a swirl design. As I traced the design with my fingers, I realized my initials were woven into the swirls, over and again. She had marked herself with my name and the love I had of photography.

"Ally," I breathed out.

"Do you like it?"

Bending low, I nuzzled the tender skin. "Yes."

"I was too scared to get it on my chest. I was so worried it would hurt too much and I wouldn't be able to finish it."

"No, I like it here. Only I'll see it. It's mine." I met her gaze. "You're mine."

"I am," she whispered.

"Who did it?"

"I found a business card on your desk. I called the guy and he said he did all your tattoos, so I went there."

I nodded. "Rod is great—his artwork of all my favorite legends is incredible. He worked on the designs for weeks. I'm glad you found his card."

"I told him what I wanted, and he drew it up and did it." She tapped my cheek. "He said he'd been working on a design for you, but he wouldn't say what it was."

I lowered my mouth to hers. "Trust me, Nightingale. You'll like it. When it's done, there'll be no doubt who I belong to as well."

I tugged her to the mattress, kissing her deeply. Then, with a grin, I rolled over so she was straddling me. My cock slid along her heat, aching to be joined with her. "You need to be on top. We won't rub the tattoo, and I get to watch you move with my mark on you."

With a low moan, she slid down, taking me inside. She stilled, our eyes locking at the intensity of our connection. It was there every single time, a living, breathing thing that surrounded us.

"Part of me is missing when I'm away from you," I confessed.

"I long for you, Adam. I'm lost without you."

"Show me, baby. Show me how much."

I groaned as she started to move, my eyes never leaving the tattoo.

It was the sexiest thing I'd ever seen.

I gripped her hips, guiding her over me, my thumb never far away from the ink she now wore. The need I felt for her was acute, alive and burning within me. Ally was feeling it as well. There was nothing slow or gentle about her today. Bowing back, she grabbed my thighs, her breasts jutting out and heaving with her deep inhalations. Her wild hair shimmered in the light, a fiery explosion that drifted across my skin like silk. She moaned and bucked, slamming herself down, her heat engulfing me.

"Ally," I groaned. "You need to slow the fuck down."

"No," she panted. "*Now*, Adam. I need you now."

She clutched me harder, her head thrown back. She cried out, and I rose, wrapping her in my arms, crushing her to my chest as she orgasmed. I buried my face into her neck and gripped her as I heaved and throbbed, lost in the moment. Lost in her. My world narrowed, funneled into one powerful pinpoint of pleasure. I rode it out, breathing her name, the intensity of my release exploding behind my eyes in sharp ribbons of ecstasy.

With a quiet murmur, I lowered us to the mattress, our bodies still joined. Ally lay on my chest, her breathing ragged and warm on my skin.

"Welcome home, Adam."

CHAPTER
FOURTEEN

MY THOUGHTS RAN rampant as I gazed outside the window of Sean's office. I hadn't been able to relax since arriving home yesterday. The images I had seen had shaken me to the core, and my camera had captured the darkness of the event.

He made approving noises as he scanned the pictures on the iPad. "These are brilliant, Adam. Horrific, but brilliant."

"It was a brutal trip," I stated, not turning away from the window. Below me, the streets bustled with people coming and going—living their lives, safe and unharmed.

"Are you all right?"

I didn't answer for a moment.

I didn't know how to explain it to him. My priorities had changed, because of Ally. The excitement I used to feel was gone. Now I dreaded his phone calls.

The longing I felt when I was away from Ally grew every trip, and I knew she was suffering as well. I felt the devastation around me more as I would capture the images with my lens. She lost some of her strength when I was away. I experienced the sensation of knowing how short life was—how time slipped away. She longed for the time to pass so I would come home to her.

I didn't want to be halfway around the world and away from her. I wanted to build a life *with* her, and I knew she wanted that as well. I wanted our walls covered in memories we had created together. I wanted to watch the wonder on her face as she discovered the beauty of the places I'd talked about. I wanted to share the world with her—not be parted by it.

I turned to face him, crossing my arms, deciding to lay it on the table. "I'm done, Sean."

"*What?*" he asked, laying down the iPad.

"I need to walk away before this consumes me."

And Ally. She was always emotional, gripping me tightly and unrestful in her sleep when I first got back. When I left for this last trip, she had sobbed when I walked away. I had turned around to wave, only to see her leaning on the car, her head in her hands as her shoulders shook with the force of her tears. Seeing what my leaving did to her when she thought I wasn't looking had shaken me. I stepped back, observing her as she cried. Then she pushed off the car and slid into the driver's seat, slow to drive away. That image stayed with me my whole trip.

"What I want from life has changed. I can't do this anymore. It's not just about me any longer."

"I'd hate to lose you."

I shrugged. "We both know it'll happen sooner rather than later. You have other photographers younger than me wanting to do this stuff."

Sean nodded, leaning his head back on the chair. "Businesswise, I hate it. Personally, I'm happy for you. You're certain?"

"I am. I don't want to leave you in the lurch, so tell me what I can do to make us both happy."

He indicated the chair across from him, and I sat, watching him think. He steepled his fingers, his lips pursed. His silver hair, combed to perfection as usual, gleamed under the lights, and his dark eyes were contemplative.

"I admit, I thought this might happen. I've seen a change in you."

I lifted one shoulder. The change was obvious to both of us.

"What do you think about Chris? He's itching for a shot."

"He's got a good eye. A little green, but he'll learn."

"Would you consider taking him under your wing for the next while—give me some more time before you do this? Share your experience?"

I eyed him knowingly. "You want me to teach him the ropes?"

He nodded, not at all ashamed of his plans. "I need you.

I need you to pass on your knowledge and help Chris—which, in turn, helps me."

I thought about it. "I'll give you six weeks."

"Fair enough." He paused, stroking his chin. "I have one other favor. I want you to do a feature edition with a writer on staff before you go."

"Of?"

"I have a friend—a doctor. Peter Conrad."

"And?

"He went to Africa with Doctors Without Borders over two years ago. He hasn't come back. He opened a clinic and an orphanage which he runs with his wife. He's constantly trying to get supplies and help. He's desperate to garner more attention. I thought I'd send a team in to do a story—stay with them for a while and see how they do it. I was going to devote an entire issue to it. Your photos would be an amazing addition to the piece."

"When?"

"I'll arrange it for right after your time with Chris."

I thought about it for a minute—it would be a different experience, capturing images that maybe would make a real difference.

"How long?"

"A week, maybe two. Give me eight weeks."

I mulled it over. Eight weeks. If I told Ally my decision, perhaps that would help her worry less. Knowing the end was in sight for the dangerous aspect of my job, she could relax a little.

"Okay. Six weeks with Chris and a couple to do your story. Then I'm done."

He held out his hand. "Done. Do this for me and move on with your plans. Maybe travel with Alex. I am always looking for destination photos as well. I know yours would be amazing."

Then he grinned. "And once you're around more, I get to meet this incredible lady of yours. I know Abby would like to meet her, too."

I nodded. I knew I was selfish, but the short spans of time I was around, I never wanted to share Ally, so she hadn't met Sean or his wife, Abby. I needed to introduce them.

I wondered if I could convince Ally to take a couple months off and travel with me. I wanted to show her the world, take lots of beautiful pictures, and create good memories for us. Then we could come back and settle into a life together. Briefly, I pondered asking her to go to Africa with me but decided not to. I would be working, and when that happened, I immersed myself, and I would worry about her too much to be able to do my job properly. When we traveled together, I wanted to concentrate on her.

I slipped my hand inside my pocket, feeling the small box I carried in it. I'd had it for over a month. I'd seen it in an antique shop in London as I wandered around, my flight not leaving until that evening. As soon as I saw it, I had to have it. It was delicate, set in white and rose gold, and it would be perfect for her small hand. Hand-tooled with filigree and a unique design, the ring held small, round diamonds that caught the light and reflected their brilliance. It wasn't your standard engagement ring, nor was it big and flashy. She would love it because it was special, like her.

I would love to see her wear it, too. I wanted to mark her as mine and marry her.

I shook his hand. "Eight weeks."

———

I picked up Ally and took her to lunch. After we were done, we returned to the loft, and I sat her down and told her my decision. Ally stared at me, shaking her head.

"I can't ask you to do that, Adam."

"You're not asking. I'm the one who's making this choice."

She stood, pacing the room, stopping by the window. "Based on the fact that you think I'm upset when you leave."

The sunlight poured in behind her, highlighting the red in her hair. She was wearing one of my T-shirts again, the light showing the curves of her form underneath the thin material. She was fuller, slightly more rounded than the day I met her. She looked healthier. Now I wanted her happier —all the time.

I moved toward her, taking her hand in mine. "Are you denying it?" I looked into her eyes. "I saw you, Ally. I saw you leaning on the car, crying last time I left. It almost killed me, knowing I was leaving you like that."

"Yes," she admitted. "I cry. I always cry. But I knew what being involved with you meant, right from the start. You were very honest about it. You can't give up something you love because I'm sad."

"You're not the only one, though. I used to get the call and be on the next plane without a thought. But now, as soon as I leave, I'm anxious to be back. I miss you so fucking much it hurts." Cupping her soft cheek, I stroked the skin with my thumb. "I had nothing to anchor me here. But I have you now. I want to move forward. I'm ready for a different life." I drew in a deep breath. "One with you."

Her eyes widened. "What are you saying?"

"I want you to take some time off work and travel with me. Let me show you the world. I'll take you places you've only ever dreamed of. We can discover new ones together."

"But your work—"

I shook my head. "Sean is going to have me work with Chris. He's a young guy eager for the next adventure, like I was—and he has a good eye. It's his turn to do this. I want to start taking pictures so full of beauty they'll help rid my mind of all the darkness I've been capturing for so long. The same way you've banished the darkness out of my heart and filled it with light."

"Adam—"

I hadn't planned this here and now. But the moment was right. I bent down on one knee, pulled the box out of my pocket, and slipped it into her palm, closing her fingers around the tiny leather case. "Come away with me, Ally. You can pick the time and place, and we'll get married. Anywhere you want. On a beach in Greece with the sun setting behind us, at dawn in Scotland. A small chapel in England. Anything you want."

Tears filled her expressive eyes, shining an intense blue as she looked between our hands and my eyes.

"Marry me. Start a new life with me. One with no rules or demands. Where the only thing expected of you is to be *you*. Because you are *perfect* the way you are."

Standing, I opened her palm and lifted the lid on the small box. She gasped as she looked at the ring, the diamonds sparkling in the bright sun. "Accept this as a symbol of my love. Wear it, and show the world you're mine."

"I—I don't know what to say."

"Say yes. Say yes to a life of love with me. Say yes to finally knowing you *are* enough. You're everything to me. I want to travel with you and fill our heads with memories. Then we can come back here, or go wherever you want, and make a life for ourselves. Have a family and grow old together."

"Your photography?"

"I'll take Sean up on his offer and capture some other types of photos when I feel like it. You won't have to work. You can travel with me if you want." I stepped closer, cupping her face in my hands.

"You honestly want this?"

"More than anything." I brushed her lips with mine. "Marry me, *please.*"

"Yes."

————

I splayed my cards and snorted. Looking over at Elena, I cocked my eyebrow. "Nice, woman. Do you ever not cheat?"

She shook her head, feigning indignance. "I have no idea what you're talking about, boy. I dealt the cards, fair and square. You watched me shuffle them."

I shook my head. "Then you sent me to fetch you more ice for your scotch. Which in itself is a travesty, I might add, watering down this bloody amazing scotch. You switched decks while I was gone." I flipped my fingers between us menacingly. "I'm onto you, old woman."

She did this every time. Stacked the deck, added cards, sent me to fetch something from the kitchen—whatever it took for her to win. And I let her, since I knew she donated all the winnings. But I loved teasing her and watching her get all blustery and snotty at me. It amused me to no end.

Beside me, Ally snickered; I looked over at her and rolled my eyes. She was the worst poker player in the history of poker. Ever. She didn't understand the game at all, only playing with us because Elena enjoyed it so much. But when she got an apparent good hand, her tells were so obvious it was hilarious. Her eyes would widen, she'd smirk and bite her lip, all while holding the cards up in front of her face as if no one would notice her expression. Often, she giggled as well, trying to cover up the sound with a little fake cough. Between Elena's blatant cheating and Ally's bad card-playing, the games were only pathetic excuses to sit around drinking scotch and talking smack.

I enjoyed every single moment of it, because I loved these women so damned much it was shocking.

I tossed four quarters into the pot and smirked at them both. "Let's go, ladies."

Ten minutes later, I was desperately trying not to laugh at the silliness of playing with the two of them. I threw down my cards in mock disgust.

"I fold."

Ally crowed as she took the pile, flinging her cards on the table, showing her flush. Elena always let her win a few hands before she went in for the kill. The only time I won anything was when I shuffled the cards, but Elena always insisted her house, her rules, and she liked to deal. Her code word for cheat. Neither of us walked out of here with any of our money. We never would—and I was fine with that.

I grinned and sipped the scotch, rolling the deep, almost smoky flavor around on my tongue. I liked this one.

"Maybe you should start a new business," Elena mused as she watched me shuffle the cards and deal them properly.

I arched my eyebrow. "A new business?"

She nodded as she arranged her hand, throwing two cards back. "Hit me."

I chuckled and looked at Ally. She was frowning and moving her fingers across the cards, which meant she had nothing and was trying to figure out what to do. Sure enough, she laid her cards down.

"I fold."

I shook my head. I could never get her to understand how to create a decent hand, and I had given up trying.

"What kind of new business?" I asked, dealing myself a couple of new cards.

"Maybe one of those boudoir photo-shoot places."

I almost choked on my drink, the scotch burning my throat. "The only woman I'm interested in taking boudoir shots of is Ally, Elena. But thanks for the idea."

"No, you'd do great," she insisted. "With those killer looks, sexy tattoos, and smoldering eyes, you'd pack them in. Toss that dark mane of yours a lot—like a lion. They'd love it."

Ally laughed, and I shot her a look.

"Not happening."

Elena poked at her hair and batted her eyelashes at me. "If I were twenty years younger, I'd let you do a spread of me."

I caught Ally's gaze and winked. Leaning forward, I brushed Elena's cheek with my lips. "If you were twenty years younger and I were single, I'd take you up on that offer, you minx. It wouldn't be my shutter snapping open in that spread either."

They started to laugh, and I grinned. I loved making them laugh.

Elena dropped her cards. "I'm tired. No more cards."

Ally gathered up the cards, the action making her ring glint in the light. I had misjudged just how small her fingers were. It was too big for her, but she had wanted to show it to Elena and share our news. She had wrapped tape around it to keep it on, saying even after a few hours her finger felt wrong without it. We planned to take it to the jewelers and have it sized.

She'd been so excited to show it to Elena, who had studied it carefully, then kissed us both, wishing us a lifetime of happiness together. She was even more pleased when I told her of my plans.

I smiled as I lifted Ally's hand to my mouth and kissed her fingers.

Elena beamed. "When are you going on this grand adventure?"

"I promised Sean I'd do this feature for him. He thinks it'll happen in about six weeks. He's working on all the documents and arrangements now. I should only be gone two weeks, then I'm done."

Elena fixed me with a look. "So, eight weeks and my girl can stop her constant worrying?"

"Elena!" Ally admonished quietly.

"It's fine," I assured her. "Yes, Elena. She can stop worrying. You both can."

Elena sniffed. "I never said I worried about you, boy."

I winked. "I know you do, you miserable old bat. You love me."

She rolled her eyes. "You think too much of yourself." Then she chortled. "I can hardly wait to see the look on Sarah's and Ronald's faces when the two of you announce your engagement." She clapped her hands. "I have to be there."

I shrugged. "Sorry, only those who love me can be present to witness that showdown."

Ally chuckled, as Elena shot me a frown.

"Alexandra, my dear," she announced haughtily, "I need some tea."

I watched Ally leave, smiling as she glanced back toward me then wiggled her fingers, admiring her ring.

"You made two of the best decisions of your life today, Adam."

I smirked. "My job and marrying Ally, you mean?"

She snorted. "No, playing poker with me and choosing that scotch. Of course I meant that, you dolt."

Laughing, I shook my head. "I know."

She leaned forward, suddenly earnest, clasping my hand tight. "Life's too short, boy. Stop taking sad pictures and grab this opportunity. Marry her and take her away—show her the world. Make sure she knows what she means to you. Make lots of babies and memories."

I squeezed her fragile bones carefully. "I will."

"Your decision of a career change is a good one. You can still do what you love and be close. She needs you here—she suffers when you're gone, more than you know."

"How?"

"Not only does she miss you terribly every time you leave, and worries herself sick, but Sarah and Ronald use every excuse to try to cause trouble for you. They smother her in darkness when you're gone. Use guilt on her every time you're absent. She needs you here with her. Get her away from them, or they'll control her forever."

I had suspected everything she told me, but Ally had never breathed a word. I felt the stirrings of anger in my gut. "Why can't she break free?" I growled. "I'll take care of her. She knows that."

Elena shook her head. "Adam, she was a child when the accident happened. A child already unsure of her place in life, given the way she was treated. It's been drummed into her head all these years that she isn't enough, that what happened *was* her fault, and she had to make amends by being perfect." She sighed. "An impossible task for anyone, but she's tried so hard all her life. It will take her time to finally accept it's okay for her to be happy. To think of herself, to think *for* herself." She patted my hand. "Be patient and keep loving her. She needs to be loved—openly. It's what she's always needed."

"She'll have it forever." I leaned closer, worried. "I'll get called away again before this is over. I promised Sean."

She nodded. "I'll watch her. But promise me, as soon as your final commitment is done, you'll take her away."

I hummed in agreement. I was already planning a trip to Fiji. I wanted Ally to see the beauty of the island, sleep the mornings away with her every day, and dance on the sand under the stars until late into the night. I wanted her to lie by the pool and see her pale skin kissed by the sun and watch the stress leave her body.

And marry her.

"Come with us."

Elena looked startled. "What?"

"Come with us. I'm taking her to Fiji. It's beautiful, and the villa I plan on renting is huge. You can have your own suite."

"You don't want an old lady there," she scoffed, but I saw the flicker of delight in her eyes.

With a grin, I lifted her hand and kissed it. "No, we want you. Ally would love it. You can stay for a week or a month—whatever you want."

"You want to see me in a bikini."

I threw my head back, laughing. "You got me."

"I won't go with you, but I'll come visit for a few days."

"At least a week. Two would be better."

"On one condition."

I grinned. "Negotiations? Excellent."

She grinned back. "I want to be there when you tell Sarah and Ronald."

"You'll have to say it," I teased.

She leaned forward, cupping my face in her hands. They were as soft as powder, the skin thin and pale, her veins a map of bruised purple under the skin. Her rings were cold on my cheeks, but her expression was filled with affection.

"I love you, boy. You and your Ally. The two of you are my heart."

I held the gaze of a woman I had come to love dearly. She was blunt, honest, and snarky—and underneath all the bluster was the sweetest woman I'd ever known, aside from my girl. We loved spending time with her.

I kissed her cheek. "Front and center, Elena."

She beamed back at me.

Ally walked in, carrying a tray, smiling at us.

My phone rang.

She stopped smiling.

I shared a look with Elena. She dipped her chin, telling me silently she would watch closely.

I stood to answer, moving past Ally. She gave me a brave nod, but I saw the worry in her eyes already taking hold. I stopped beside her, brushing her lips with mine. "Soon," I promised. I hit *accept* to stop the ringing, already looking forward to the day it was silent forever.

CHAPTER
FIFTEEN

WIND TORE THROUGH MY HAIR, the fierceness of it stinging my eyes. Debris flew around, and I ducked and bobbed, trying to avoid being hit as the storm raged.

This time, I was closer to home. The phone call from Sean had been to tell me about a huge hurricane blowing toward the Atlantic coast, and Chris and I flew out to capture the images as it hit and the aftermath. We'd been watching it roll in, capturing the violence and the beauty as it came inland. It was immense in its fury.

I hit the ground as a huge piece of debris barely missed my head, and I knew it was time to retreat. We needed to hunker down until we knew it was safe to return and capture the aftermath of the storm.

When it was safe, we ventured out into the weak morning light, staring at the path of destruction. Grimly, I glanced at Chris. "Time to get to work."

Hours later, I returned to the motel, exhausted. I hadn't slept in three days, going on adrenaline and caffeine when I could grab it. Wearily, I sat on the edge of the old bed, powering on the satellite phone. There was no other way of getting hold of Ally and I knew she'd be worried, so I needed to talk to her before I tried sleeping. I dialed Ally's cell phone, thinking I would catch her before she went to work. When she answered, her voice was thick and raspy. When she heard my voice, she began to weep.

I stood and started to pace when I heard her deep sobs. "Ally, what is it? What's wrong?"

There were more cries—heart-wrenching, pain-filled cries that were frightening. "Baby," I pleaded. "Tell me what's wrong. Are you hurt? Ill?"

"No," she gasped out.

"Take a deep breath. I need you to calm down and tell me."

Her voice was so rough, I knew she'd been crying for hours. "Elena," she whimpered.

My heart sank. "Elena?" I repeated in a low voice.

"She—she died, Adam."

———

I had to fight, bribe, and plead my way home. There were no flights leaving the storm-ravaged coast. Chris stayed behind to keep working, and with Sean's help, I found a car.

I drove as fast as I could, finally getting to a major city, and flew back to Toronto and my brokenhearted girl.

Ally was finally able to tell me that Elena had suffered a stroke.

"I couldn't save her," she'd sobbed into the phone.

I had to tamp down my grief and use everything at my disposal to get to her. Elena had died two days prior, and the funeral was happening today. Ally had been alone and dealing with her grief, unable to get in touch with me.

When the plane landed, it was already past two, and I had missed the service. I knew they would be at the cemetery, so I instructed the cabbie to take me straight there.

I was a mess—still wearing the same clothes from the previous day, my dark jeans and T-shirt wrinkled and worn. My hair was wild, and I hadn't shaved in days. My ink was on display, and I looked rough and haggard—Elena would have loved it.

I stood at the back of the mourners, finding Ally in the crowd. She was standing to the side, right at the front. Dressed in black, her hair pulled back off her face, she was pale, her skin dull and white against the black of her attire. She had her arms wrapped around her torso, as if she were holding herself in. I wanted to go over and draw her into my arms, but I knew it would cause a scene, and out of respect for Elena, I remained apart from Ally, waiting for the right time. Her mother and Ronald stood near, neither showing any emotion nor attempting to comfort Ally. Hovering close was Bradley. More than once, I saw his hand reach for hers, but she shook him off each time, moving to avoid his contact. Carefully, I circled the group, coming up across from them, lowering my head in reverence to the woman we were saying goodbye to. I kept my eyes on Ally, hoping when she finally looked up, she would see me. When the service ended and people started to disperse, I focused all my attention on her, willing her to see me.

I moved closer, ignoring the fact that Sarah had spotted me and grabbed Ally's elbow, attempting to pull her away. Her plan backfired as Ally glanced over to see what Sarah was frowning about and, with a gasp, ran straight into my open arms.

I held her close, engulfing her tiny frame completely. She gripped my neck tightly, sobbing into my chest as I nuzzled her head, whispering words of comfort to her while I rocked her from side to side. Looking up, I met the baleful stare of the good doctor Bradley, who frowned before turning around and walking away.

"I'm here, Ally," I murmured. "I'm so sorry, baby."

"Adam—" she sobbed, sounding shattered.

Sarah approached us. "Alexandra, control yourself. We need to go to the club. There's a luncheon, and we can't be late."

I gaped at her. Her daughter was on the brink of a breakdown, sobbing openly in my arms and trembling so hard I was holding her up, and she was worried about being late for a *lunch*?

I shook my head. "We're not going to a *luncheon*."

The bitch sneered at me.

"You, Mr. Kincaid, were not invited. You're hardly dressed suitably for such things. I'm surprised you managed to pull yourself away from your hobby to make an appearance—as inappropriate as it is."

I narrowed my eyes, ignoring her jibe about my work and my place here. "I've been in a place with no power or amenities for the past while, Mrs. Givens. I've spent the past thirty hours trying to get back here to be with your daughter. I don't think how I'm dressed matters."

"Really, well—"

I cut her off. "What matters is the fact that Ally is distraught and exhausted."

"What matters," she hissed back, "is that Alexandra stops this emotional grandstanding and pulls herself together. We will present a united front at the club. She can give in to these ridiculous dramatics later in private." She reached out, attempting to grab Ally's arm. "And you have no idea what matters here. Nor do you have any say."

I stepped back, taking Ally with me, and glared. "I believe I do have a say. She isn't going anywhere with you. We're going home."

Sarah glanced behind her, and I shook my head in disgust. Her daughter was an emotional wreck, and all she was worried about was what people would see, what they would think or say about our interaction.

"Don't worry, *Sarah*," I sneered. "All people see is me

holding your daughter and us having a perfectly civilized conversation. Although, if you don't back off, *right the fuck now*, they'll get a show none of you will ever forget. I promise you that."

Our gazes locked.

"Do you want to go to this lunch, Ally?" I asked quietly, not taking my eyes off Sarah. I'd go with her if that was what she wanted.

She shook her head against my chest, lifting her ravaged face to her mother. "I'm staying with Adam," she rasped. "You go without me."

"Your place is with us," Sarah insisted. "Remember your duty."

I rolled my eyes at her statement. I'd had enough of her "duty" when it came to Ally.

"My place is with Adam."

"You're disrespecting Elena's memory, Alexandra. This is for her."

I couldn't help the snort that escaped. Elena wouldn't have cared less. "You, lady, have no idea what respect is. Your daughter doesn't want to go, so she isn't going. She's staying with me."

"My daughter is coming with me—where she belongs."

A sudden breeze stirred the branches of the trees around us, causing the picture of Elena on the easel to thump loudly on the metal bars. I recognized the photo—I had taken it myself one night during a poker game. Elena was glancing at the camera, laughing hard at something Ally had said, the warmth so few people knew radiating from her. It was my favorite photograph of her, and a smaller copy was in my loft. No doubt Ally had supplied the picture for the service.

I almost started to laugh at the timing and knew this was the moment I'd been waiting for.

It was time to give Elena her last wish. She was waiting —impatiently—and had given me the sign.

Front and center, I'd promised her.

"Ally is staying with me," I stated clearly, drawing in a deep breath. "My *fiancée* is exhausted and overwrought and will *not* be joining you at the lunch. She's going home—with me. *That* is where she belongs."

Sarah's face became ghostly white as her eyes widened. "What did you say?"

I grinned at the horror in her voice. "You heard me, *Mom.* Ally and I are engaged. So, I think I *do* have a say in the matter. And I say she belongs with me."

"You lie."

Ally turned in my arms. "*Don't* speak to him like that, Mother. He *isn't* lying. He asked me to marry him, and I accepted."

I lifted my arm with a smirk. "Want to give me a hug and welcome me to the family?"

Sarah's lips thinned, a deep scowl now marring her face. Strangely, it made her look the most human I'd ever seen. "We'll be discussing this when you're calmer."

I shook my head. "No thanks. We've already decided on

a small, intimate ceremony in a place of our own choosing. We don't require any *discussions*."

"I won't allow it."

Before I could say anything, Ally spoke. "You have no say in it. I'm an adult and it's my decision. I'm marrying Adam. I love him, and he loves me."

I pulled her closer and kissed the top of her head, smiling at her declaration.

"He'll be the ruin of you."

"No, he showed me what life is about. He loves me for me. He makes me happy." She placed a hand on her mother's rigid arm. "Can't you be pleased for me? Adam's the best thing that's ever happened to me. Give him a chance, please." She squeezed her mother's arm beseechingly. "Please…Mom."

For one brief second, I thought she had succeeded. There was a small flash of something in Sarah's eyes at the word *Mom*, but they quickly became cold again.

"You've been nothing but a disappointment. You do this, and I wash my hands of you."

Ally sagged into me at the harshness of her mother's words, her hand dropping in defeat.

"You coldhearted bitch," I seethed. "How could you say that to her? You'll turn your back on your own daughter because she wants to be happy?" I shook my head. "Of course you would. You turned your back on her when you chose that prick of a husband over her. I shouldn't be surprised. You don't deserve her."

With those words, I lifted Ally into my arms, cradling her next to my chest. "We're staying here for a while, and then I'm taking her home. Unless you want that scene, I suggest you step aside." I indicated the small groups, still hovering around, now watching us with interest. "I'm sure your counterparts would love a good show to talk about at your *lunch*."

With a glare, Sarah turned on her heel and stormed away. Ignoring everything and everyone around us, I walked over to Elena's grave and sat down on the stone bench that was close, holding Ally.

We needed some time with Elena—alone.

"I tried to save her."

"I know, Nightingale."

"I talked to her at lunch, and she was fine. When I got there for dinner, I knocked, but she didn't answer. I used my key and found her on the kitchen floor. I called the ambulance and started CPR. She wouldn't wake up. I tried," she repeated, her voice plaintive. "But she stopped breathing, and she was gone."

I drew back, concerned, looking down at her. I had seen her strong and capable. Happy and laughing. Weary and tired. I had also seen the effect her mother and Ronald had on her, destroying anything positive and making her feel less than she was, but right now, she sounded so lost and vulnerable—almost broken.

"I'm sorry you found her like that, but I'm sure she knew you were there with her."

"I hope so." She exhaled a shaky breath. "I miss her already."

I looked over at the fresh grave, blinking away the moisture that gathered in my eyes. "So do I."

She tilted up her head. "She loved you, Adam."

"I loved her." I traced a finger down her cheek. "I'm sorry I wasn't here for either of you."

"You're here now."

"Too late to say goodbye."

"Elena hated goodbyes. She always said 'Until next time.'"

I lifted my hand and blew a kiss in the direction of the sky. "Until next time, you minx." A tear slid down my cheek. Another followed in its path.

Ally cupped my cheek. "Let it out," she whispered.

I pulled her to me, burying my face into her neck as the emotion crested. I mourned for Elena and for the future she would never see. I had wanted her to see us married. To hold our first child in her arms and know, beyond any doubt, her girl was safe and cared for and would be for the rest of her life. I had wanted to hear more of her stories and tease her so she'd laugh. Share another hundred different scotches with her. Let her take my money and give it to whatever charity she wanted. Send her flowers every week for another twenty years.

Kiss her wrinkled cheek and hear her call me boy.

I had only known her a short time, but she meant as much to me as Ally did. She had become my family, and her death hit me hard.

I felt Ally's shoulders shaking again, and she held me fiercely.

Together, we mourned the loss of someone we loved.

———

Two days later, we were present at the reading of Elena's will.

"Impossible!" Ronald shouted, standing abruptly when the lawyer finished. "I'll contest!"

Elena's lawyer, Andrew, shook his head. "You'll lose."

Elena had left me a million dollars and a note. When I opened the envelope, her spidery writing filled the elegant stationery.

> ***When the time comes,***
> ***you'll know what to do with this.***
> ***Remember your promise.***
> ***Look after my girl. I trust you, boy. I love you.***
> ***~ Elena***

Always with the last word. I refolded the paper—I had

no idea what she wanted, but I'd invest the money and figure it out. And I would look after Ally the rest of my life.

She left some money to Ronald. A large chunk to Ally. The rest went to a fund that would benefit the local animal shelters for a very long time.

I wasn't sure what Ronald was objecting to the most. He didn't need the money. I had a feeling it was the money she left Ally and me—combined—and what it essentially meant.

Her final act had been to do what she couldn't do while she was alive.

Set Ally free.

My Nightingale was no longer beholden to Ronald. She could walk away from the condo she disliked, pay him back the money he said she owed him, and be done. She didn't have to accept anyone's help to do so. All her "debts" would be paid.

As I observed him, I realized that was it. He didn't give a crap that Elena had left me something or that most of it went to helping animals.

His power over Ally was gone, and he hated it. He could no longer make her pay for a crime he felt she committed. One she was never guilty of in the first place.

I lowered my head so he didn't see my smirk.

Silently, I sent a thank-you to the minx.

She got him in the end.

CHAPTER
SIXTEEN

DAYS PASSED, and we remained mostly in solitude. We went for walks; I took Ally out for a few rides on the bike, and we stayed close. She was quieter than normal, rarely starting a conversation, but when I engaged her, she would respond. The first time she laughed, she stopped, her eyes widening and her hand covering her mouth. Gently, I pulled it away.

"Don't. Elena loved to hear you laugh. She'd want you to. She wanted you to be happy." I stroked her cheek. "She wouldn't want us to mourn her—she'd want us to keep going and do everything we talked about."

Ally only nodded, but it was her suggestion to go for a picnic the next day. But when we woke up, the day was dark and rainy so we improvised and had a picnic in the loft. I picked up Chinese food, making her laugh when I refused plates, instead feeding her bites from my fingers. I insisted the sticky chicken and spicy plum sauce tasted better that way. I twirled the noodles on chopsticks and fed her bites, licking the sauce from her chin and kissing her every chance I got.

After we cleaned up, I leaned back against the bed and simply looked at her—lying on the pile of pillows we'd made, with her bright hair spread around her. Her eyes were shut, one arm tucked behind her head; she looked the most peaceful I'd seen her since I got home. Unable to resist, I lifted my phone, capturing her with my lens. My collection of images of her was large. I loved catching her different moods and expressions. Her eyes said so much when she looked at me—warm and filled with love, even when I pissed her off.

Like I was doing now, taking her picture.

She cracked one eye open. "Put the camera away. You have enough pictures of me."

"Never."

"I look a mess today. I have no makeup on, and I'm in your shirt and a pair of sweatpants—hardly attractive."

"I disagree," I informed her. "You're beautiful to me no matter what you're wearing."

She sat up, her face serious. "You think that, don't you? You really think I'm beautiful."

I lowered my phone. "I don't think it—I know it. You're the most beautiful woman I've ever seen. With or without makeup."

I held out my hand, pulling her onto my lap. Brushing

her hair away from her face, I ran my fingers over her silky skin. "I love you, Nightingale."

"I love you," she whispered. "So much, Adam."

Music played in the background, and for once, the gathering storm outside didn't cause her the usual distress. She was more focused on us. I stood, tugging her up off the floor.

"Dance with me," I murmured.

We swayed to the rhythm and I held her close, enjoying the feel of her against me. We moved around the loft, not talking, simply touching. I loved holding her, feeling her move in time with the music. Be able to touch her hair, nuzzle her neck. Hear her whisper my name before I'd drop my head to kiss her. I felt our connection wrap around us, binding us together.

Eventually, we ended up back on the pillows, and I fed her some strawberries I had picked up, choosing the sweetest, juiciest ones to give her, eating the part closest to the stalk. She was so sexy, licking her lips, moaning at the taste. I gathered her close, taking her mouth. Her mouth was pliant underneath mine, molding beneath the pressure. I swept my tongue across her bottom lip and slipped inside, tasting her sweetness. Her warm breath filled my mouth, her low sigh igniting my passion that had been dormant the past few days. She wrapped her arms around my neck, holding tight, returning my desire. Our tongues danced and stroked, the kiss becoming deeper and profound. Gentle became powerful. Our caressing hands became fists as we tugged, *ridding* ourselves of the thin barrier of clothing that kept us apart.

I sat up, with Ally wrapped around me, her body welcoming my aching, needy cock. Her supple breasts rubbed along my chest as she started to move over me. She buried her hands into my hair as our kisses became frantic. Her sounds escalated as we moved faster, our bodies coming together in perfect rhythm. Long, hard thrusts. Deep, wet, needy kisses. Our hips moved, mouths fused, and damp skin rubbed together in the most erotic way.

The floor creaked as I guided her hips, the wood hard under me but I didn't care. All I cared about was this moment—reconnecting with the woman I loved so passionately, I burned with the feeling. Pleasure so intense it made me groan loudly rushed through me as we lost ourselves to each other.

She surrounded me. Her scent, her sounds, the feeling of completion only she brought out in me. The push and pull of her body as it tightened was powerful. Her breaths became small pants in my mouth. Every thrust made me groan as her muscles contracted around me, milking me. Small whimpers made me clutch her tighter. Every ripple of ecstasy down my spine intensified as my release threatened. Long shivers ran through her, her hold on my hair tightening to the point it was almost painful. She arched back, her mouth leaving mine, crying out in her release. *"Adam!"*

I surged into her, burying my face in her neck. My

hands tensed on her hips, slamming her down as I spilled deep inside her, my orgasm burning through my body like a trail of wildfire.

"*Fuck…Ally…*" I groaned into her damp skin, my teeth clamping down as the sensations became too great and I rode them out, cursing and moaning. Never had I experienced this extreme emotional connection with someone. Never had another person overwhelmed me the way she did.

Every. Single. Time.

She shuddered, falling against me heavily. I held her briefly, then leaned over and grabbed my shirt, pulling it back over her head. "I don't want you cold," I murmured. "And I love how you look in my clothes." I kissed the end of her nose. "Although taking you out of them is one of my favorite things to do."

"What are your other favorites?" She nuzzled into my chest.

"Listening to your laugh. Seeing you. Hearing you say you love me." I sighed, running my hand through her hair. "Anything to do with you is my favorite."

She played with the hair on the back of my neck. "I feel the same about you."

I shifted and she chuckled. "We're messy."

"I like being messy with you." I stood, lifting her into my arms. "But I love getting you clean and doing it all over again even more."

She shivered with desire, and I carried her to the

bathroom, turning on the water and letting it heat. I lifted her into the shower, kissing her endlessly and pressing her against the tile as I took her unhurriedly, showing her with my body how much I loved her. Our mouths never separated, our groans and whispers of pleasure kept between us. She shook as she came around me, setting off an orgasm that seemed to stretch on, and I gripped her close as I lost myself to the sensation. To her.

After, I made her coffee, and she sat in her chair, reading. She loved the new chair and always looked so right curled up in it. I tucked a blanket around her, kissing her head, and sat in the other chair, wanting to stay close. She dozed, and I watched her sleep, ignoring the book I had open. She was far more fascinating.

From the counter, my phone rang, the noise shrill and loud in the silence that surrounded us. She woke, instantly tense, her eyes wide with worry and disappointment.

Sean hadn't bothered me since I'd come home in such a rush, but I knew that wouldn't last very long.

"Do you have to?" she whispered.

"I promised. The sooner I go back and fulfill my word, the sooner I'm done."

"You'll be careful?"

I let the call go to voice mail. Holding her face between my hands, I nodded. "Yes."

"Vivian wants me to go back to work as well."

"We have to move forward. Get through the next few

weeks and then we can start our new life together. We can do this, right?"

She nodded, although her eyes were sad. "Right."

———

Weeks later, her eyes were more than sad. For the first time ever, the words I had dreaded ever hearing were spoken out loud.

"Don't go," she pleaded. "*Please*, Adam, don't go."

I stilled in the task of packing my equipment, shutting my eyes at the level of desperation in her voice. I couldn't bring myself to look at her. She had never asked me not to leave. Not once.

"It's the last time."

"That's what you said before—and the time before that."

I turned to face her.

She was right.

The trip to Africa had been postponed while details were worked out and paperwork procured. Now, two weeks past the time I should have been returning, I was just leaving. In addition, I was going for an extra week. Massive storms had torn through the entire country, setting off wildfires and causing devastation everywhere. Sean wanted as much of it documented as we could get. Chris and Tommy were coming with me, and then we would meet with Larry, the man writing the article, and do the feature.

It was my last assignment. But with the additional time waiting and the strange weather around the world, I had barely been home since Elena's passing. Ally and I would reconnect for a short interval, then once again, I'd be gone, leaving her behind. Each time, it got harder.

She tried to be brave and strong, but I knew it was getting too much for her. She missed Elena terribly, her grief overwhelming her at times. She cried a lot, and she was too thin. Our time together was permeated in sadness, and we were both argumentative and tense.

"This is it. I promise. I'll finish this and come home to you." I stepped forward, holding out my hand in supplication. "Then I'm done."

"Are you?"

I frowned. "Yes. You know that."

"No, I don't. You keep finding excuses to leave."

Excuses?

"I can't help the weather conditions, Ally," I said, beginning to feel impatient. "You knew what I did when we started—what my life was like. You know this is the last assignment. What the hell is going on?"

"Are you really ready to give this up, Adam? Are you regretting your decision?"

I stared at her, aghast. That was what she thought? She was doubting me? Doubting *us?*

"No," I snapped. "I don't regret anything, except your lack of faith. I said I would go, and I'm sorry for the extra time, but I gave my word."

Her voice became angry, her eyes flashing. "What about your word to me? To Elena? You said you'd stop!"

"I will. I know the schedule got fucked up, but it's almost done, Ally. What the hell else can I do?"

"I don't know if I believe you! You keep leaving me alone, Adam." Her voice rose. "I *hate* it!"

Shock and disbelief coursed through me. I had never heard her raise her voice or speak with so much venom. Ever.

What the fuck was happening?

I drew in a deep breath, trying to keep calm. I spoke in a firm voice. "I've *never* lied to you. Exactly what are you accusing me of?"

"I'm not accusing you of anything."

"Sounds like you are," I bit out, angry and defensive.

She didn't back down. "I don't think you lied knowingly. But I'm not sure you're ready to close the door on that part of your life. I'm not sure you *want* to stop."

I counted to ten before I spoke.

"*I do.* I want to move on to a different life with you. I've been away a lot—way more than I wanted to be gone. I know you're still mourning Elena, and without her here or Emma around, you're lonely." I also knew her parents still made things difficult for her every chance they had. "I hate being away from you as much as you hate me going. But I gave Sean my word, and I *will* follow through on it. I owe him that."

"What about what you owe me?"

Her words threw me. Her entire demeanor was wrong. Everything about this was wrong. We were both tired, stressed, and on edge. We hadn't made love when we went to bed last night, an unusual occurrence, both of us silent and still, an invisible barrier keeping us apart. I didn't understand what had brought this on. Had she reached the end of her rope? Was this grief talking? Had Sarah managed to plant a seed of doubt when they'd had lunch the day before?

"What did your mother say to you yesterday?" I demanded.

"Nothing."

I narrowed my eyes. "Now who's lying? She must have said something to make you act like this."

"Stop blaming my mother for everything. This is about you leaving, not her stupid remarks!"

"Bullshit. I think one has a lot to do with the other. She knows exactly how to get to you." I tossed a lens into my bag. "Stay busy while I'm gone. Go see Emma. Avoid your mother."

"Right. Emma's not been available, in case you haven't noticed that either. She couldn't even come for the funeral. She's been sick and busy, so I'm not going to bother her." She tossed her hair. "Maybe I'll have coffee with Bradley. At least *he's* around."

I tightened my hand on my case. I knew they occasionally bumped into each other; she had never hidden the fact. She was always upfront and honest. I knew she was goading me now, because she had never taken him up on his coffee invitations.

"That's low," I seethed, now really pissed. "Are you fucking trying to hurt me? Or do you really want to start a war here?"

She shrugged, the action dismissive. "No. It's just coffee." She glared at me. "You don't own me, Adam. I can have coffee with a friend. Or do you not trust me?"

"Of course I do. It's *him* I don't trust."

"If I thought he was going to do something, I wouldn't see him. He's just a friend. Stop acting like I can't look after myself."

"Yeah," I spat. "You've done a great job of that so far."

Her eyes widened, and she held up her hands. "Wow. I think we need to stop before this gets even uglier. You need to pack. Your plane leaves in a few hours. Can't have you missing that," she added, then started to walk away, but I grabbed her arm.

"Don't ask me to leave without us resolving this. I don't want to go knowing you're angry and upset."

And planning on spending time with Bradley.

"And I don't want you to go. I guess neither one of us is going to get what we want."

My anger reached its limits, and I shouted. "What do you want from me, Ally? I'm fucking being pulled in every direction here! I don't want to go, but I have to because I promised Sean I would. There's an entire crew waiting for me. I have obligations!"

"Fuck your obligations!" she hissed, shaking my hand off her arm.

"*Fuck my obligations?*" I snarled back to her. I pulled my hands through my hair in vexation. "You're one to talk. You know all about obligations, *Alexandra*. You let them rule your life," I yelled. "At least mine are ones I willingly agreed to, not something I do out of misdirected guilt!"

As soon as the words were out of my mouth, I regretted them. She stepped back as if I had slapped her. I reached out, yanking her to my chest. She fought against me, but I refused to let her go. "I'm sorry, baby. I didn't mean that. I can't do this with you. Not right now. I have to go. I need to know you understand, and when I come back, that's it. I *won't* leave you again." I held her tighter. "Tell me you know that, please."

Sadness saturated her statement. "I don't know if I'm strong enough to keep doing this anymore."

My heart hammered in my chest at her words. It felt as if she was giving up on us.

"Don't do this to me, *to us*," I pleaded. "I can't leave you like this."

She pulled back. "But you'll leave me anyway."

"And you'll see Bradley."

"Not to get back at you. As a friend. Just a friend I can visit with so I'm not alone all the time."

We stared at each other, frozen at an impasse. She was pale, and I saw the vulnerability and apprehension she was trying to cover. Elena's death had made her fears of me getting hurt even stronger. My anger subsided, and I chose my next words carefully.

"Are you really going to do this? After everything we've been through? You're going to make me choose? Force me to tell Sean I won't follow through on my commitment and stay here because you don't believe me anymore? Because you're doubting *us*?"

She blanched, her eyes filling with tears. I gazed at her drawn face and made a decision, reaching behind her for my phone.

"If that's what you need—if that's what I have to do to prove this to you, then I will. I'll call Sean and resign right now. You win."

All the fight went out of her. Her shoulders slumped and her head dropped. Her emotions were all over the place, making me apprehensive. I needed her to talk to me, but she was shutting down.

"No," she whispered. "I'm sorry, Adam." She turned away. "I'm so sorry." Her next words hit me like a Mack truck. "You're leaving, and I'm so afraid you won't come back."

I caught her, spinning and dragging her into my arms, now understanding. Her anxiety was palpable. She was near her breaking point with all this. *With me.* My own trepidation increased. I couldn't lose her. We were so close to the end of these long separations.

"I know, Ally. I understand," I soothed. "It's almost done. I need you to be strong for a little while longer. Don't give up on me. You can do this. One last time. For me, please?"

Her fists gripped my shirt, her voice desperate. "You promise?"

"Yes."

She nodded, her head resting on my chest. "I won't see Bradley. I was just being a bitch."

"You're never a bitch," I assured her, feeling relieved. I really didn't want her seeing him. I didn't trust him as far as I could throw him. "You're not yourself. But I understand, baby. I really do."

"Okay," she replied. "We need to get you packed."

I pressed my lips to her head. "That's my girl."

———

She didn't hide her tears when I left. They ran down her face unheeded as we stood by the car. The harsh words we'd exchanged still hung between us. I wanted to leave on a good note—I had to see her smile before I left. I wrapped my arms around her.

"Your ring will be ready this week. You can go pick it up. Show it off."

She nodded into my chest, tilting her head back and offering me a watery smile.

"Take a picture of it and send it to me. Let me see it on your finger."

After Elena died, Ally had tucked her ring away, too sad

to think about it. Finally, I had pulled it out and taken her with me to see about having it sized. It was time to move on. The rose gold and the intricate pattern on the ring made it a job for a true artist to size it down to fit her tiny finger, and it took longer than we expected. The jeweler located on the main floor of my building had found the same antique rose gold and had been occupied with the careful work to make it flawless. We had been waiting for it to be done. Now I wanted it on her finger.

"I added something," I whispered to her.

"What?"

"An inscription."

"What does it say?"

Always. Forever. Yours.

"Am I?"

"Yes." I kissed her damp cheek. "A fight doesn't change that, Nightingale."

"Adam!" I looked around to see Chris heading toward us. "You ready to go, man? I've been waiting!"

I stifled a curse, knowing I had to leave her. I wanted to make sure she knew we were going to be fine. But more than that, I needed to know *she* was going to be fine.

She leaned up, brushing my cheek with her lips. "I'll pick up my ring, but I'm waiting until you come home to wear it. I want you to put it on my finger."

I slid my hand up her neck and pulled her to me, crashing my mouth to hers. I kissed her with everything I had. Hard, deep, and filled with words we didn't have time to exchange. I moved back, breathing hard, my chest tight. "Once I put it on, you can't ever take it off again."

"Come home safe to me."

I nodded. "Always."

She stepped away. I grabbed my bags, backing from her slowly. It took everything in me to turn and walk away from her. It still felt as though things were unresolved, even with her sweet words of farewell. I turned back to say something to her, surprised to see she was already moving toward me. I dropped my bags and caught her in my arms.

"This is the last time I leave you. I promise."

She nodded and released the grip she had on my neck. I lowered her to her feet, cupping her cheek.

"Come on, Adam!" Chris yelled.

I picked up my bags again, never breaking eye contact with her.

"I'll be here," she vowed shakily.

I held on to those words as I boarded a plane to Africa, once again leaving her behind.

SEVENTEEN

WEEKS LATER, I let my head fall back against the ripped material of the headrest while my body jarred and shifted as the Jeep hurtled down the torn-up road toward the small airstrip in the center of Africa. I ached all over, my body thin and weak. My tattered clothes were covered in stains of dirt, blood, and all manner of fluids. I was beyond exhausted, and after what I'd witnessed and been through the last while, it felt as though every nerve in my body was sitting on the top of my skin, burning and humming with anxiety. I repeatedly traced over the cracked screen of my iPhone with my thumb, the battery long since dead. There had been no point in plugging it in. The generator was needed for other things, and we had no cellular reception.

Two more hours.

Two more hours and I'd be in a small plane that would

take me back to something resembling civilization. A few hours after that, I could plug in my phone and let it charge.

But most important, I would use the landline at the hotel and call my Nightingale.

I hadn't heard her voice in what felt like forever, despite that it was only a few weeks.

I shut my eyes as my chest swelled with longing to hear her voice.

Even if she was still upset with me, I needed to hear her voice.

She would calm me, help me find my center, and regain enough strength to get home.

To her.

Because where she was, that was home. Then I would never leave her again. I never should have left her this time.

I glanced down at my phone again and wondered if, when it came to life, it would be filled with her sweet messages of love.

Or, if she was upset enough, it would be empty.

I prayed it was the former.

A deep shuddering exhale of air escaped my lungs.

I needed it to be the former.

———

When we had arrived in Africa, and we flew low over the terrain, I was shocked at the devastation below us. None of the news reports had shown the true, massive destruction the wildfires had caused. Tommy was going ahead with Larry, the journalist, to the clinic. After we separated, Chris and I hit the ground running, constantly moving as we filled memory cards with the horrific photographs. Our guide was amazing, taking us places most people would never see. Image after image filled my camera of destroyed villages, dead and displaced animals, and land that would take years and years to regrow and replenish. By the time I was shaking Chris's hand goodbye, I was drained. He would now finish on his own, while I headed farther inland to meet up with Larry and Tommy and complete this assignment. Chris would be home before I would, and I made him promise to call Ally and tell her I was fine. I had only gotten one brief message to her, and I knew she would worry. Larry had the satellite phone, so I could use that to contact her.

"Good luck, Adam."

"You too. I'm not around to pull you away from a crumbling precipice, so be careful."

He grinned widely. "But what a fucking shot I got—am I right?"

I shook my head. Ten years ago, I would have said the same thing. I snorted—ten months ago, I would have said it as well.

I climbed into the Jeep with my new guide, waving Chris off. I still had a long journey, both by Jeep and plane, to get where I was going.

I thought about Ally the whole time.

Nothing prepared me for what I walked into. A village close to the clinic had fallen victim to the fires, and now the clinic was filled with the wounded and dying. In the blink of an eye, I became a medic, tamping down my revulsion of blood and doing what I could. Dr. Conrad and his wife worked tirelessly, Larry and Tommy pitching in as well. I dressed wounds, cleaned cuts and gashes, washed and tended *burns. Peter, as he insisted I call him, and his wife Edwina handled the far worse cases. For two days, I did nothing but work, until finally, there was no one left to help—at least for the moment. As I sat surveying the wounded, watching families cry and mourn their dead, and the fires still raging, I realized I was in far graver danger than I had ever exposed myself to in the past. I would have to work harder than ever to keep my promise to my girl.*

When I finally got to hear Ally's voice and told her what had happened, she immediately realized the serious situation I was in.

"Come home," she pleaded through the very bad connection. I covered my ear in a vain attempt to hear her better. All around me, a storm was bearing down on us, the rain and thunder moving in rapidly, almost drowning out the sound of her voice. Every room in the building was full, so I had come outside to call her, desperate to hear her voice. I paced up and down the riverbank, wishing more than ever, I was on my way home to her.

"Soon."

I could hear the tears of worry in her voice. "What if the fires spread and the clinic is caught?"

"It's fine. We're fine."

"You can't say that, Adam! You don't know what will happen!"

"The fires are starting to burn out—it's raining right now. It'll be okay," I soothed, wishing I'd kept my mouth shut. I didn't want her upset again, and now I'd added to her stress. The fires had come dangerously close to us here, but we were sure the hazard was past now. The sound of the heavy rain approaching was a welcome relief to us all.

"I want you home."

"As soon as this is done."

"No," she sobbed. "Now. I can't lose you."

"You won't—"

"Don't make me promises you can't keep!" she yelled. "You're not safe there!"

I pulled on my neck in frustration. "Ally, I'm—"

A scream behind me, the sudden rush of footsteps, and a small body crashing into my legs startled me so badly I swung around, causing the phone to fly from my hand, arcing high and landing in the swirling, rushing water.

I cursed, shouting profanities into the air, wading into the water, though I knew I would never recover the phone.

Peter's equipment had died only days before we'd arrived. I stared at the murky water, realizing what I had done.

I'd lost our satellite phone, and now I had no way to get hold of her again. None of our cell phones worked here. I had no way to contact Ally.

Time passed in a haze of activities. I was a part-time medic as more people showed up from other places affected by the fires; I worked with Peter on the story, photographing him working and interacting with the people who adored the "pale healer," as he was known. With his snow-white hair and quiet demeanor, he was a calming presence, no matter what was occurring. His wife was a small, sturdy woman, with dark, flashing eyes and a no-nonsense attitude that was a cover for a gentle, empathetic heart. They gave everything they had to their cause. I pitched in and helped repair broken items, roofs, anything that had been damaged by the huge storms and subsequent wildfires that were ignited by the violent lightning. I helped Edwina with the children, my heart breaking at the sadness I witnessed daily. It was nonstop.

Seeing the desperate need, I sent Tommy with the guide to the closest center to get what supplies he could. I also gave him the information to contact my business manager, John, so he could have more supplies purchased and shipped here. Tommy was gone for three days. When he got back, he told me he had left messages on Ally's cell phone, explaining about the satellite phone and that we were fine. He also spoke with Sean, who promised to try to get in touch with her. It was the best I could do, although I hated that he hadn't spoken to her directly. He had been unable to purchase another satellite phone, and I still had no way to contact her myself.

The story Larry was writing would be powerful and moving, and I hoped it meant help for Peter's work. The pictures I had taken would add so much to it. I swore I would do whatever it took to bring attention to him and this place. I had quickly become fond of him and his wife, admiring their strength and generous, loving spirit. I promised more supplies would be shipped as soon as I could make the arrangements back home. Plans were set for me to leave the next day.

But that night, I became ill, which pushed back our leaving. A cut I'd ignored had become infected, and I fell, ravaged with a fever that racked my body for days, leaving me weak and unable to travel. Larry and Tommy stayed, refusing to leave without me. Peter wasn't happy when I insisted on departing before he felt I was ready, but I needed to get home. I needed to get to Ally.

I shook Peter's hand and hugged Edwina.

Then I got into the Jeep and headed toward home, allowing the part of me I'd kept at bay to leak out. I had missed her so much. My body shook with the force of my need.

I needed to get to her.

————

The room was small and sparse. A bed, a chair, and a small dresser. The bathroom had a shower, a chipped sink, and a toilet. The towels were thin and rough.

After the past few weeks, it was a palace.

I dropped my bag and gear and took a much-needed shower. The phone in the lobby was busy, so I'd have to wait anyway. I found the charger and plugged in my phone. I hoped it would work, having been dropped, cracking the screen and shutting down.

The shower was small, but the water was hot and felt great on my tense shoulders. Days of dirt and pain rolled off my skin. There was no shampoo, but the hard soap was fine on my hair. At least it was clean. I had buzzed it off two days after we arrived, and it was beginning to grow back. I didn't bother shaving.

I dug through my bag, finding the one semi-clean set of clothes I had left in the bottom. I pulled them on, not caring how wrinkled they were. I wasn't flying out until the morning, so I decided I'd find another pair of shorts and a shirt in one of the small shops and then throw out the rest of what I had left. I'd given most of it away to people in desperate need, so my bag was almost empty.

Downstairs, the phone was still in use. Larry was sitting, waiting for his turn, and I sat with him. Neither of us spoke much, other than Larry assuring me he'd looked after our travel arrangements.

"We'll probably have to stay the night in Nairobi and fly home the next day."

I nodded. As long as we were on the way back and I could talk to Ally soon, I could hang on.

"You okay, Adam?"

I looked up, not realizing I'd been grabbing at the legs of my shorts, twisting the material. I relaxed my hands, flexing them. "Yeah. It's been rough."

"I know. I'm taking some time off once this is done."

"I'm done. For good," I replied.

He nodded in understanding.

Once I was home, I would never leave Ally behind again.

———

When I finally got to the phone, the line just rang and rang. When her voice mail picked up, it was an automated greeting, so I didn't get to hear her voice. I frowned, wondering when she'd changed that. I called her home line, becoming more confused when a recording came on, saying the number was no longer in service. I hung up, redialing, convinced in my exhaustion I'd dialed incorrectly, but I got the same recording. I tried the cell number again, but the automated voice picked up. This time, I left a brief message, telling her I was safe, on the way home, and to please call my cell. I paused before adding, "I love you, Ally. Please, *please* call me."

We waited for Tommy, and we went out, seeking food. I wasn't overly hungry, but I knew I needed to eat. When we arrived back at the hotel, I headed upstairs, hoping the charge would be restored and there'd be a message from Ally.

The screen came to life, and I scrolled through the messages, past the ones from John and various other people, frowning at the lack of ones from Ally. I finally found four and hit the earliest one first.

It was short.

I'm sorry. I love you. Please be safe.

I shook my head. Was she still apologizing for the fight we had before I left? Or the phone call? I was the one who owed her an apology.

The next one made me frown.

This is too hard. I didn't mean to yell—I was just so scared. Why did you hang up? I don't know if you're okay or when you're coming back.

My head dropped. She thought I'd hung up on her and hadn't called her back. I needed to get hold of her fast. The third one made my worry increase.

I need you. Where are you? Please tell me you're safe. Just tell me that.

There was a time lapse leading to the fourth one. Over

ten days. It made me fall to my knees as my legs buckled under me.

I can't do this anymore. This isn't the life I want. I'm sorry, but I don't want to see you again. Don't contact me—it's over. Leave me alone, Adam. Move on with your life. I plan on doing the same. I wish you the best, but we're done. Be happy.

———

The plane touched down, gliding to the gate. I let everyone go ahead of me since I wasn't in any rush. I was completely calm as I gathered my bags and headed for the door. I hailed a cab after refusing Larry's offer of a lift home. I was motionless in the car, not speaking at all.

I walked into the loft, feeling detached. It was dusty and unused.

Ally wasn't here.

I didn't bother picking up my phone to check. I'd done that from the road several times. I had no missed calls from her. No other texts.

When someone finally answered the cell phone, it wasn't Ally. They'd only gotten that number a few days prior, they explained. They had no idea who Ally was.

Waiting for our flight home, I'd called the hospital. It took several attempts before I was finally able to get Vivian on the line. She was sad when she told me Ally had quit abruptly. Her attempts to reach her had failed as well.

I looked around the loft, realizing Ally must have been here at some point. Her shoes were missing from the floor. Her sweater that always hung by the door was gone. Walking around, I saw *all* her things were gone. I noticed a small item on the edge of my desk, and walking over, I picked it up, my hand shaking.

Her keys.

She'd taken her things and left her keys.

I closed my fist around them, holding so tightly, I felt the plastic on the little camera break and the edge of a key cut into my skin. Anger began to simmer, and with a roar of rage, I flung the keys away so hard they became embedded in the wall. I grabbed my coat and the keys to my motorcycle—I wasn't done with this.

Not by a long shot.

———

The key code didn't work as I punched it into the door of her building. The red light remained steady. As I was glaring at it, another tenant exited, and I grabbed the door, hurrying inside before he could stop me. I took the stairs two at a time, too impatient to wait for the elevator.

Her door was ajar, and I pushed it open, gaping at the room. The apartment was empty, except for a woman standing in the middle of the room, making notes on a thick pad. She glanced up with a frown. "The showing isn't for another twenty minutes. How did you get upstairs?"

"Showing?"

"The apartment. It's up for sale. I assume that's why you are here?"

"I don't have an appointment. I hoped I could walk through," I said, improvising.

"Fine," she huffed.

I looked around—for what, I had no idea—but the place was empty. I stood in the doorway of Ally's bedroom, staring. The indents of her furniture were still in the carpet. I shook my head in confusion and turned, a glint catching my eye. I crossed the room and bent, picking up a thin gold chain in the corner—somehow overlooked. A twisted, broken nightingale hung from it, but I recognized it. It was one of many I had given to her. A burning began in my chest, and I returned to the main area after shoving the mangled metal into my pocket.

"How long has it been up for sale?"

"I got the listing last week."

"Did you meet the woman who lived here?"

"No. I dealt with the owner. Why?"

I shrugged.

"Are you interested?"

I took her card. "I'll let you know."

I drove to the hospital, parking my bike on the sidewalk. I knew I'd get a ticket, but I didn't give a flying fuck.

I found Vivian in the busy ER. When she saw me, she waved me to an empty room.

"Have you heard from her?" I asked, not bothering with greetings.

"Only one email."

"What did it say?"

"Not much, really. She said she couldn't stay here anymore—that she broke it off with you and needed a fresh start." She paused, squeezing my arm in sympathy. "She told me she'd moved out of the city, Adam. I'm sorry."

"Did you reply?" I choked out. I'd beg her for the email address.

"I tried—several times. It bounced back. I can't help you get in touch with her. I'm sorry."

I blinked at her as numbness crept in.

Ally was gone.

She was really and truly gone. In fact, she'd run from me. Left her life and disappeared.

Wordlessly, I turned and left.

———

"Mrs. Givens will see you."

I paced as I waited. It had taken me ten minutes of talking to get in the building. The only reason I was allowed in was I threatened to cause a huge scene.

Now I was waiting in the drawing room.

A few minutes later, Sarah swept in, looking as unwelcoming and indifferent as I remembered.

"Where's Ally?" I demanded.

"My daughter's whereabouts don't concern you anymore."

"I need to talk to her."

Sarah shook her head. "She doesn't want to talk to you. She wants nothing to do with you. I believe she informed you of that decision."

"Via text," I spat out. "That isn't like Ally."

"My daughter's name is Alexandra. And I don't believe you left her any other recourse *but* to send you a text while you were off taking your pictures, leaving her alone once again, without any communication." She narrowed her eyes. "Even after she begged you not to go."

I stepped back in shock. She knew about that?

Sarah smiled. An emotionless, calculated smile. "Yes, Mr. Kincaid. She told me. I know you had a disagreement before you left. She told me everything, including how unhappy she has been." She raised a hand and patted her already perfect hair back into place. "After much thought, she decided she couldn't live this way any longer. She knew she would always be second place for you. She spoke with Ronald and me at length and decided she wanted to move —she needed a fresh start."

I barked out a humorless laugh. "A move I'm sure you strongly supported."

She studied me impassively. "Regardless of what she may have told you, I have always had my daughter's best interest at heart. Ronald and I agreed it was the best thing for her. She felt she didn't need to be reminded of her little error in judgment all the time."

I recoiled. Was that how she thought of me? *An error in judgment?*

"Where is she?"

"None of your business."

"Tell me. I need to get in touch with her."

With a roll of her eyes, she pulled out her phone and tapped on the screen. Only seconds passed before a return text came. She held out her phone, showing me the screen.

Alexandra, Mr. Kincaid is here. What shall I say?

The reply was short.

Tell him to leave. I don't want to see him.

I grabbed the back of the chair, unable to believe what I had read. I reached for the phone, but she pulled it back.

"I need to speak to her. I just need—"

"I don't care what you need. You can't have it. Leave my home, Mr. Kincaid. Leave my daughter alone." She held up her phone, her expression aloof. "She's made it clear—she wants nothing to do with you. Accept it and move on with your life."

She began to leave, and in desperation, I shot out my hand, stopping her.

"Please," I beseeched her. "Give me her new number."

I wasn't above begging—not for Ally.

She shook off my grip, wiping her sleeve with disdain. "I understand you're upset. But it's for the best. Alexandra is doing so much better now. She's happy." She fixed me with an all-knowing stare. "Even you must admit she hadn't been happy for a while, Mr. Kincaid. Leave her alone and let her live the life she wants to live. Go and live yours."

She left the room, calling for her butler to show me out.

I went without protest.

I didn't have the strength to fight.

THREE DAYS PASSED while I tried to find her. It was as if she had vanished off the face of the earth. With Elena dead, the only other person I could reach out to was Emma, and I had no contact information for her. Ally had it in her phone. I found Emma's design page online, and I left my information under *Contact Us*, but I had a feeling my attempt would fail. In desperation, I went to see Bradley, but his office informed me he was away on holidays.

It struck me then how small the circle around us had been. Losing Elena had been a blow to each of us. With the life I led, I had few people I considered true friends, and Ally's life was so isolated, I knew no one other than Vivian and Emma, and I didn't have a close relationship with either. I had only met Emma once since our schedules never seemed to line up. Vivian didn't have a new number for Ally, and when she checked with the other nursing staff, no one had heard from her either. I tried Emma again, but the messages I left on her social media pages were ignored. There were a lot of people with the same surname of Jones in the Ottawa area, but none of the ones I tried were right.

I hired a private investigator. I gave him the information I had, and he came up with nothing. All he could tell me was her phone had been canceled, her credit card not used. There were no plane or train tickets issued in her name, and no record of her being admitted to the local hospitals. It was as if she had disappeared.

"Give me some more time, Adam. I'll keep searching. You've given me so little information, it's going to take longer. I'll start checking into her parents next."

I felt numb. It was as if my brain and my heart were in two separate places. My brain screamed at me to react, to do something, but my heart felt sluggish and empty. I paced a lot. Drank too much scotch. My refrigerator was still empty, and I had no desire to put anything in it. I dozed in my old chair, restless and unable to relax.

I kept hoping the phone would ring. That she'd show up at the door and tell me it was all a mistake. I waited for that to happen.

I waited in vain.

A knock at the door roused me, and I raced to it, flinging the door open, startling the person on the other side. Mr. Freedman from the jewelry store downstairs stood there, smiling at me.

"Ah, Mr. Kincaid, you're home. I thought I saw you earlier. Excellent."

"What can I do for you?" I rasped out.

He held out his hand. "I was waiting for Ms. Robbins to pick this up. Since she hadn't come in, I thought I would drop it by for you."

Wordlessly, I stretched out my hand and accepted the small box.

"Come see me when you're ready for your band."

I cleared my throat. "Thank you for bringing it by."

"No problem." He paused. "Mr. Kincaid, are you all right?"

I looked at him, shaking my head. "No."

I shut the door.

An hour later, I was still holding the box in one hand, the bottle of scotch in the other. Finally, I raised the lid on the box and looked at Ally's ring.

Small, delicate, and perfect.

Just like her.

The diamonds glittered under the light, the white and rose gold seamlessly entwined, the design still as lovely as the day I saw it in the window of the antique shop in London. He had done an amazing job, the work on it perfect. You would never know it hadn't always been this petite. The inscription mocked me, the tiny words blazing in my eyes. Words that no longer held any meaning—at least not to Ally.

I remembered the day we finally went to see him. She

had asked him about a band for me, and he quickly sketched a simple design—far more masculine for me. He was going to make it up for us when we were ready and ensured he had ordered enough of the same gold so it would match.

I shut the lid with a loud snap.

I guessed we'd never be ready.

We'd never be getting married.

I hadn't listened to my gut, to the feeling that she needed me more than anything else. I'd shoved down the worries, the thoughts in my head that I needed to stay. I didn't listen to the voice in my head telling me to take her with me. I could have protected her in Africa. The jackals I left her to cope with on her own were far more vicious.

I lurched to my feet as the burn started. My legs began shaking, my stomach tightening. My chest was on fire as a sudden wave of blistering-hot pain coursed through me. My sluggish heart began racing, my breath coming out in gasps.

She was gone.

My Nightingale was gone, and she wasn't coming back. None of her smiles. Her pink notes. Her laughter. Her cinnamon-flavored kisses. No more of her love, her touch, or her sweet words.

I'd lost the one thing in my life that was good. By insisting on fulfilling my professional obligations, I had abandoned my personal ones and caused the woman I loved to walk away.

I was a fucking idiot.

I gripped the edge of the counter, a slow rage filling me, chasing away the numbness. With a roar, I flung the small box away. It bounced off the wall, hitting the counter and rolling to the floor.

Suddenly, I wanted everything gone. Destroyed. Nothing was safe. The dishes we bought together shattered against the wall, the shards hitting my skin. Blood dripped from the tiny cuts. Her favorite mug hit the floor, exploding in a fury of ceramic slivers. Small items she'd picked out were destroyed. Her favorite blanket, I tore, the material shredding under my angry hands.

Lenses and a few cameras were tossed across the room as I raged. My phone hit the wall, the repaired screen cracking again and going black. Everything that sat on top of my desk was decimated with a sweep of my arm. Gasping for air, I glanced up and froze. The photo, *my* photo of her, hung over my desk, where I could see it every time I sat there. Stalking over, I gripped the edges, tearing it away from the wall, raising it over my head, intent on destroying it as well.

Except I couldn't. My arms locked in place, and slowly I lowered them, the picture resting along the top of the desk. I traced the outline of her freckles with the tip of my shaking finger.

Enchanting, I had called them.

Freckles I had touched, kissed, teased with my tongue.

Freckles I wouldn't ever see again.

Hot, burning tears coursed down my cheeks, dripping

onto the glass. They mixed with the blood, splashing red on the image.

My heart's blood.

Rage left and agony moved in. I stumbled back, gripping my hair, one word leaving my mouth.

"*Ally.*"

I collapsed on the bed, shattered and drained. I buried my face in the pillow—the pillow that still smelled of her. I thundered in agony, no longer able to contain the pain.

I screamed until my voice was gone.

Until the physical pain overrode the pain in my heart.

Until the darkness inside became the darkness that drowned me.

Sean looked at me, shocked. "Adam, please—"

I shook my head. "No. I'm resigning. Effective immediately. I don't want to do this anymore—any of it."

"Look, I know the last trip was rough. I had no idea what you'd be going into would be so intense. Larry is taking a leave for a while. Take Ally and go away. At least think about it."

I swallowed at his mention of Ally. No one knew what had occurred. I didn't plan on sharing.

"No, Sean. I'm done. The last trip wasn't just rough. The suffering and death I saw—it was devastating. I don't know how Peter and Edwina cope with it."

"The satellite phones you ordered for Peter arrived, and he told me how invaluable you were—and how generous. He said he wasn't sure he would have made it through without your help." His voice dropped. "He told me it was pretty bad. He was worried about your health. I am as well. You look awful."

I didn't want to discuss my health or anything else. Only the fact that I was done.

"What are you going to do?"

"Actually, I'm going back. The clinic needs hands—any kinds of hands to help. I'm going to go and do some good for a change, and then I'm going to get lost for a while. Take pictures of beautiful things and try to remember a world that doesn't just contain death and devastation."

"I'll take your pictures. We'll use them in the travel section. Don't quit on me. You're one of my best." His voice was rough. "I was sure you'd change your mind about leaving. I had no idea this trip would push you further away."

I hesitated.

I knew I needed to get out of this city. Away from the memories that now haunted me at every turn. Ally was everywhere.

When I woke up after my breakdown, I spent hours cleaning the loft. Sweeping and scrubbing up the mess I had created with my whirlwind temper. The last thing I did was tuck her ring away into the back of my file cabinet, along with the pieces of her broken necklace. Then I sat down and thought of my options. The investigator had nothing still—he wanted more time. I could wait and see if he found anything and go see her. Make her say the words to my face. Except, I kept remembering her texts. She knew I was here since she'd responded to her mother's text, but she hadn't tried to get in touch. Her silence said more than any words she could have screamed at me.

She had run away because of me. I thought of how much she loved working at the hospital. Her quiet life, outside the world of Sarah and Ronald. I had only lived here a few years, and aside from people at the magazine, I had very little holding me here. And the memories that were here were too much to handle.

I should be the one to leave. She should be free to come back and live her life. If I wasn't here, she could return. My presence had to be keeping her away.

I looked at Sean, his expression hopeful.

"I'll make you a deal."

"Name it."

"I'm still resigning. And I want a press release issued stating that fact, as well as the fact that I have left the country. If anyone inquires, I am no longer under contract here."

"Doesn't sound like much of a deal to me."

I held up my hand. "When I'm ready and I start taking photos again, I'll think about coming back. But that information stays strictly between us. Not a word goes out I might return."

"You're really leaving?"

"Yes."

"What about Al—"

I shook my head before he could finish.

His face changed, his expression saddening. "I'm sorry," he said.

"I have to go."

He sighed. "Why do I have a feeling you might never return?"

"There's that chance. But if it happens, I'll let you know."

"I bought your photos before you lived here, you know. We can do that again."

"If I begin to work again, you'll be the first to know."

"When do you want the press release out?"

I wanted to leave fast. To escape and leave the memories behind. "Larry and I will finish the piece today. I need a few days to get my affairs in order."

"So, Friday?"

"Yes. Release it once I'm gone."

He stood, extending his hand. "I hope to see you back in that chair again, Adam." He drew in a deep breath. "And without that haunted look on your face."

I shook his hand without replying. I wasn't sure that look would ever leave.

Friday night, I looked around the loft, gazing at the space impassively. My bag was by the door, the case with my new equipment beside it.

I had arranged for the loft to be checked on and cleaned. John would handle my business affairs, and I would contact him when I could.

On the counter was my new phone. The other one still worked, despite the shattered screen, but with the way I was traveling, I changed plans and numbers. Only a few people had the old number, but I had passed on the new one to them anyway, and to a couple others as well.

The only contact who didn't have it was Ally.

I picked up the cracked phone, which hadn't rung in days. Now, unless it was a wrong number, the only person who would ever call it was her. I ran my finger over the broken screen and tapped the keys. I hesitated, then cleared my throat and hit voice mail.

"You've reached Adam Kincaid. I'm no longer at this number. If it is urgent, contact John Reynolds." I gave his phone number, then I paused, my voice dropping. "If this is you, Ally, come home. John can find me if you want that. I love you. I'll always love you."

I hit *save* and turned off the power. Opening the file cabinet, I tucked it in beside her ring.

I picked up my bags and walked out.

PART TWO—

SIX MONTHS LATER

CHAPTER
NINETEEN

ADAM

I STARED *at her hand and then her beautiful face.*

The woman I had loved passionately—desperately—and still loved to this day.

My former fiancée…who was looking at me with no recognition.

As if I were a stranger to her.

And then it hit me as I took in the emptiness in her eyes.

I was.

————

I paced the floor restlessly, stopping only to slam back another shot of scotch or run my hands through my hair in vexation. I didn't have any answers. I only had more questions.

What the fuck had happened to Ally?

I made many trips to the windows, looking for her car,

but Emma still hadn't shown up.

It had been two hours since Emma had pulled me back into the shadows, her face as shocked as my own senses.

"What the fuck is going on, Emma?" I hissed. *"Why is Ally looking at me as though she doesn't know me? What happened to her?"*

Her eyes searched my face, trying to determine if I was telling the truth. "You really don't know?"

"What the hell am I supposed to know?"

She shook her head, her hand covering her mouth. Her gaze was wild as she scanned the room. Then she gripped my arm, tugging on it. "Adam, you have to go. Now."

I wrenched my arm free. "I'm not fucking going anywhere until I get some answers."

"I'll come to you. As soon as I can. You have to leave."

"Right," I scoffed. "I'll leave and never hear from you again. You'll make sure I don't get back in."

"No, I will come to you. I promise." She held out her hand. "Give me your phone."

Wordlessly, I did, and she tapped in her number. "What's your address?"

"It's the same. You dropped Ally off after lunch."

Her fingers faltered. "You didn't move?"

"Move? No, I didn't move."

"Go home, Adam. Wait for me."

I looked past her, trying to find Ally, who, after shaking my hand, had turned and fled, leaving me gaping after her. It was only Emma's hand pressing on my chest that stopped me from storming after her and demanding to know what the fuck was going on.

"Do it for her," she pleaded.

"You'll come? You give me your word?"

"I gave you my cell phone number. So, yes. I'll be there as soon as I can." She stepped closer. "Don't let anyone see you, or I can't help you."

I left as she requested, hugging the shadows, slipping out the employee entrance.

Now, I was waiting.

I groaned, rolling my neck. I felt as if I was going to burst out of my skin. I had shed my jacket, tugged off my tie, and pulled my shirt out of my pants, leaving it loose. It still felt as if I was choking. The loft felt confining and small, my thoughts rampant. My gaze swept the unused space that, for a brief time, had felt like a home because of her. Pivoting, I stared out the window, recalling the past six months.

I had returned to Africa. I had a burning need to forget, bury myself in a project that would distract me, to escape the pain. When I showed back up at the clinic with trucks of supplies and looking like a ghost, Peter and Edwina were surprised but welcoming. When they'd found out I had no determined time frame for staying, they allowed me my privacy until I was ready to talk. Then they offered only their support and comfort. We grew closer as the weeks passed.

Over the next while, the Elena Ames Center was built. It was a rough wooden structure that would service this small area. I also set up a fund that would ensure the clinic had supplies whenever they were required. Elena had been right, as usual. I knew when and where to use her money. These people would benefit from her generosity for years to come. I spent my days building and working with Peter and

Edwina, and my nights fighting the memories and pain that never seemed to stop.

Finally, I came to understand they never would for me. I packed my bags and sat staring at the stars one last night. Peter joined me, sitting down with a sigh.

"Ready?"

I nodded in the darkness. "It's time, Peter."

"I'm grateful for every day you gave us."

"I've arranged for supplies to be delivered monthly. If there's something you need, all you have to do is call. Me or John. Whatever you need will be sent."

"That's incredibly generous."

I barked out a laugh. "No, Peter, what you do is incredibly generous. You devote your life to these people. The clinic, the people, and the kids—this orphanage. You and Edwina. If I can make your life a little easier by sending food, necessities, and medical supplies, it's the least I can do."

"You've given months of your time to me—to these people. You'll be missed."

"Thank you."

"Where are you going?"

"I need to take some pictures. Happy ones. I'm going to work my way back to Toronto."

"Will you try to contact her?"

His words hung in the air, heavy between us. I had finally broken down and talked about Ally to Peter and Edwina. Talking about her helped, but it didn't take away my pain.

"I don't know. I check my old phone and with Sean. She hasn't

tried contacting me. I think—I think maybe it's over. I wasn't what she needed."

She was what I needed, though—then and now.

"You need to talk to her, Adam. Find some closure."

I didn't reply.

His voice was filled with understanding. "There isn't any closure for you, though, is there? You still love her."

"I always will."

"Then find her. Open a dialogue with her."

"I don't know how to find her. I still don't understand what the hell happened. What her parents did or said to take her away. I thought she was getting stronger. I thought she had finally figured it out, but…"

"You still think they were involved in some way?"

"Yes. I know that as surely as I know she loved me. She just wasn't strong enough without me beside her. They knew how to get to her— wear her down. I never should have left." I sighed as I scrubbed a weary hand over my face. Elena had been so right on that subject. Ally's parents' cruelty knew no bounds.

"Are you planning on returning to your old life? Flying around the world and never putting down roots?"

"She became my roots. She was the only home I had ever truly known since I lost my parents."

"Then find her. Once and for all, sit down and talk to her. Ask her what happened. Try to fix it."

"I don't know where she is."

"Hire someone again—find her."

I had been thinking along those lines—deciding it was time to try again. Hire new private investigators and look into her parents as well.

Track down Emma. Not stop this time until I found her. I hadn't been in my right mind when I left—I was too broken and weak from my recent illness. I had given up too easily. My head was clearer now, and Peter was right. I needed closure.

"Then what will you do?"

"I'll go back and decide. Maybe take Sean up on his offer to take destination photos. Or maybe I'll do some of both. I'm not sure I'll stay in Toronto. I may sell the building and go elsewhere."

He stood, extending his hand. "Whatever you decide. If you need me, I'm here."

I looked at him curiously as I shook his hand. "Will you ever leave?"

"Yes. In a few years, I will. But this is where I have to be now." He smiled at me and clapped me on the shoulder. "You, my friend, need to be somewhere else. Go and find your life. Don't give up if she's where you have to be. Fight for her."

Then he turned and walked away, his form swallowed up by the dark.

A knock startled me from my memories, and I rushed to the door, wrenching it open. Emma and her husband, Alan, were there. I had never met him until now. His expression was as grim as Emma's.

I stepped back to allow them inside, offering them a drink. Emma shook her head. "Thanks, Adam, but I have a feeling you've drunk enough for all of us tonight."

"I'm fine. Confused as fuck, but I'm fine." My head was clear. I'd burned off the effects of the alcohol with the slow, simmering anger that coursed through my veins.

We sat down, and I didn't bother wasting any time. I'd wasted enough.

"Why doesn't Ally know me, Emma?"

She held up her hand. "First off, Adam, how did you find out about the party? I thought you left town."

"I did. When I returned the first time and found out Ally had broken things off with me, I couldn't stay. I thought if I left, she could come back to her life here. So, I returned to Africa." I huffed in disgust. "I've only been back a few days. I saw the announcement in the paper the day I got back."

I remembered my reaction to it.

I'd been skimming through a stack of newspapers left on the counter by the woman who came in and kept the place tidy. I had obviously forgotten to cancel my delivery. I didn't see much of interest until a familiar name caught my eye.

Bradley Bennett.

I unfolded the paper and read the announcement.

My hands tightened on my paper, fisting it so hard it tore under my fingers.

The good doctor was engaged and getting married in a few weeks.

He and his wife would be moving to Calgary, where he had accepted a new job at the hospital.

And there was a private party to celebrate two days from now.

My eyes were riveted to the picture of him and his bride-to-be.

Alexandra Robbins.

The glass of the beer bottle shattered as it hit the wall.

"You've been gone all this time?"

"I came back after my last assignment. But I had

nothing here without her. She was gone—it was as if she disappeared."

"But the first time, after you finished your assignment—you came home—you returned to her?"

"Of course I did. Why would you think otherwise? She left *me*, Emma. I didn't leave her." I snarled, then exhaled a long breath. I was beginning to lose my temper, and I needed to stay in control. Emma had the answers I needed.

She exchanged glances with Alan, then bent forward, her voice patient. "When you left for your assignment, Alex was terribly upset, and I came to town to see her. She was so worried about your safety. The news was full of what was happening where you were."

"I hated leaving." I rubbed my eyes. "It was a mistake. I never should have gone."

She pursed her lips in agreement. "After she finally spoke with you, and she thought you'd hung up on her, she was so despondent. I had never seen her that way. I suggested she come with me to Calgary—just to get her away from here. I had a meeting with a potential buyer of my designs."

I frowned. "I hired a PI. He never found airline tickets issued in her name."

She shook her head. "They flew me out in a private plane. Ally came as my guest."

I'd never considered that possibility. I rubbed the back of my neck. "I know she was upset. We'd argued the day I left about my leaving, my work—she wasn't herself. I was so worried about her." I exhaled hard. "But I didn't hang up. I accidentally dropped the phone in the river. I was in the middle of nowhere, and it was the only satellite phone we had. There was no Wi-Fi where we were—we lost all communication."

Emma nodded. "She told me about your argument. How terrible she felt. She was so conflicted about so many things. I suggested there had been some sort of mishap while you were talking since it made the most sense. I thought you'd call back as soon as you could."

"I tried. I sent Tommy to get supplies and he left her messages, but she didn't respond. Sean tried to get in touch with her, too. When I finally got my phone to turn on, I saw a few earlier texts from her, but then nothing for ten days." I swallowed the thickness in my throat. "Then the next text I got, she told me she never wanted to see me again."

Emma and Alan exchanged a look. Emma leaned forward, clasping my hand. "I don't think she got the messages. And she couldn't have sent you those texts. At that time, Alex was in the hospital, recovering from a head injury —caused by an accident. She had no memory of you or your relationship."

I blinked. *"What?"*

"She suffered a partial memory loss. She can only recall bits and pieces of the past year, and a large chunk is gone completely. Starting *before* the time you were together. The last clear memory she has is when she was dating Bradley."

I gaped at her, stunned by her words.

She stood. "I need that drink now."

I felt numb, unable to even move. "The liquor's in the cabinet."

Alan stood as well, and a few minutes later, a glass was pressed into my hand. "I think you need this, Adam."

I tossed back the shot, allowing the burn to settle through my chest before I spoke once more.

"When? What kind of accident?"

"Two days after your call got cut off, Ally flew to Calgary with me, and we were going to get coffee before my meeting. We were crossing the street, and a car came around the corner—the driver never stopped. He was drunk, and he hit us both."

My stomach lurched. "Oh God."

"Alex was in front of me. She took the brunt of the hit— she went forward, I was knocked backward."

"How bad were her injuries?"

"Her ankle was badly broken, and she needed a rod and pins in her upper leg. She was covered in bruises and cuts. The worst part was that she hit her head after she rolled across the car and was in a coma for ten days. They operated on her leg, and she had to have a lot of therapy on it."

That explained the limp I had seen. It also clarified Emma's statement that Ally hadn't sent me any texts. She couldn't have if she'd been unconscious. I had to clench my hands into tight fists to stop from grabbing something.

"What happened to the driver?"

"It wasn't his first offense. He went to jail."

"I hope he rots." I inhaled a calming breath. "And your injuries?"

Alan clasped her hand, his face filled with sorrow. "I recovered," she replied in a low voice. "I wasn't as badly injured as Alex—physically. I was released from the hospital after a few days."

I had a feeling there was more to her story than she was telling me, but I left it for now.

"Why didn't anyone try to contact me? Or even Sean? He would have sent someone to me and let me know what was going on."

Emma sighed. "Sarah told me she did contact you—right away. When I asked about your lost call to Ally, she said that your communication problem had been resolved. She certainly wasn't pleased, but she said she spoke to you."

"She lied. I never spoke to her. I had no missed calls or messages from her. The only thing I had were the texts from Ally's number." I growled in frustration. "If I'd known, I would have come back right away. Chartered a plane to get to her, Emma." I stood, unable to stay still any longer. "*Fuck.* I love her! You think I wouldn't be here for her? Even if it was days later? I would have come home immediately."

"Love?" she repeated. "You still love her?"

"I will always love her. That is never going to change."

Emma sighed, rubbing her head. "Sarah said you asked to be kept updated, but you refused to come back. She told me she spoke with you directly. I had no way to contact you to verify it, and I really had no reason to disbelieve her."

"She fucking lied. I spoke with no one."

I paced, a feeling of nausea bubbling in my stomach. The whole time I was working on assignment, *a stupid job*, Ally had been in the hospital. Alone. Needing me. And I had no idea. I had left her with promises of coming back and starting our life together, when I should never have left her in the first place.

Alan lifted his glass as he looked at Emma. "I think Sarah lied about many things. You'd better tell Adam the whole story."

"Yes. Tell me everything."

"Sarah and Ronald were contacted and they flew to Calgary, and Sarah basically took over. Ronald didn't stay long. Once I was discharged, I was lucky if I was allowed to go into her room." She paused and eyed me warily. "Even Bradley flew in."

I couldn't help the hiss that came out of my mouth. "But no one fucking called me."

"I didn't have your number. Looking back, I should have insisted that she give it to me, but I wasn't thinking clearly. I was too worried about Alex. Sarah had her cell phone and tablet—and she assured me she was keeping you updated when she could get hold of you."

"You didn't question the fact that I wasn't there?"

"No, I didn't. I'm sorry, Adam. I didn't know you very

well, having only met you once. I knew Alex was in love with you, but she was pretty private about things."

"We tried to stay private because of the hassles Sarah and Ronald gave her all the time. They didn't like me."

"They don't like anyone. They've always been very controlling." She shook her head. "I had no idea how controlling until right now."

"Continue, please."

"Alex finally woke up, and right away, it was obvious something was wrong. She was confused and agitated. She didn't know the proper date or why my hair was longer. They did a lot of cognitive tests and realized a big chunk of her life was missing."

"What happened next?"

Emma frowned. "You have to remember who was in charge. Once Sarah was involved, I was shoved aside. When I was able to see Alex, it was only for brief visits, and I was never alone with her. Sarah was given power of attorney for Alex for decision-making—and that continued after she woke up with so much of her memory gone."

They took over her life again, this time with full control. I shuddered at the thought. "How convenient."

"When she woke up and we realized what had happened, Sarah came to me and said she would be staying with Alex through her recovery. She told me it was time to get back to my life now that the danger had passed. She would handle things from there." Emma paused, fidgeting a little. "I asked her about you, Adam. She told me when she spoke with you and told you of Alex's memory loss and condition, you informed her you didn't have time to play nursemaid to someone who didn't know you. She said—" Emma swallowed and cleared her throat "—she said you wished Alex a good life, but you weren't going to be part of it anymore."

Rage raced through me at her words. "I. Never. Fucking. Said. That."

"I may not have known you very well, but I did question Sarah about it. It seemed so contradictory to the way Alex described you, or the feeling I got when I saw the two of you together."

"I would never have deserted her." I frowned at Emma. "When I came back, I looked for Ally. I hired a PI who got nowhere. I even went to see Sarah. I begged her to tell me where Ally was, and she refused." I looked down at my hands that were twisting and grasping my pant legs in agitation. "She threw it in my face that Ally had been unhappy with all the traveling I'd been doing and had begged me not to go. She knew about the fight we'd had and told me Ally decided I wasn't worth the hassle and decided to move on. I was so shocked that she had confided in her, and at the way she had broken up with me. It totally threw me."

Emma's cheeks colored, and Alan reached over to take her hand. "That's my fault."

"What do you mean?"

"When Sarah told me what you had supposedly said, I,

um, well, I called you a bunch of names and said I couldn't believe you'd do this, just because the two of you had a fight." She shook her head. "Sarah sort of played along as if she knew what I was talking about, and I told her everything Alex had told me—about your fight and the phone call and how distressed she was she couldn't get hold of you to apologize." She sighed. "Alex was so upset with herself. All she wanted was to hear your voice and know you were all right."

I sat back in shock.

Ally hadn't told her mother.

I wasn't an unfortunate *error in judgment.*

"She texted Ally while I was at her place," I frowned. "She showed me her reply."

Emma raised her eyebrow. "I don't think it was Alex who replied. None of what happened was Alex."

Sarah lied. It had all been lies.

When the accident happened, Ally still loved me. I should have stayed and pushed more, gave the PI time and let him do his job. Instead, I had let Sarah win and left. I'd deserted Ally—again.

I drew in a deep breath.

"Tell me everything, Emma. Don't leave out a single detail. Especially the part about how Bradley Bennett ended up engaged to my fiancée. Then I can make a plan."

Her eyes widened. "Your fiancée?"

I nodded emphatically. "I asked her to marry me before Elena died. She said yes. And I gave her a ring she loved, but we had to have it sized. With everything that happened, though…" I cleared my throat. "We hadn't told many people. But Sarah knew. She fucking knew."

"What are you going to do?"

"Fight for her. Get her back."

"She doesn't remember you, Adam."

"Then I'll get her to fall in love with me again until she does remember. Now, start talking."

I sat back, angry.

Sarah and Ronald had taken her away.

I was going to get her back.

———

I found out quickly that when Emma was upset, she tended to talk too much. Her hands waved, and she was emotional. After about ten minutes of her ramblings, I realized the best way to get information would be to ask her questions.

"Why was Sarah here when Ally was in the hospital? She was still in recovery then, wasn't she?"

"Yes. Sarah went between here and Calgary a lot." She blew out a big breath. "She had obligations here as well, she informed me."

"Her only fucking obligation should have been her daughter," I snapped, then paused to collect my thoughts. "Why didn't you return my messages?"

"I didn't get them." She sighed. "I wish I had." She met my stare, her face earnest. "I did call the magazine, trying to find you. They told me you no longer worked there and were out of the country indefinitely. I came by here to check, and I ran into one of the tenants. He told me you had moved. I thought Sarah was telling the truth and you had deserted Alex. Moved on with your life."

I shook my head. "I thought she had gone because of me. I left so she could return to her life *here*. There seemed to be no point in staying, so I disappeared." I swallowed the pain in my throat. "I couldn't be here without her. It hurt too much."

I ran a hand through my hair. "I made a huge mistake not keeping the PI on her parents. I let Sarah mess with my head. I should never have left. Or believed a word that came from that woman's mouth."

She nodded in sympathy. "We both believed the wrong thing."

"Tell me about her recovery."

Emma sighed. "I can't tell you everything. Like I said, Sarah and Ronald took control of Alex and her life. I saw her only rarely—she remained in Calgary to do her therapy, so I was farther away. And I was blocked from much contact."

My voice was quiet. "Was she in a lot of pain?"

"Yes—at times, she still is. Her headaches still trouble her. When she's upset, she gets confused and forgets things. They aren't sure if that's irreversible or if it will go away. The accident left her with a permanent limp."

I hated the thought of her in pain. "She hasn't

remembered anything?" It had been months. "This whole time?"

"No."

"Vivian told me she had an email with Ally's resignation."

"Alex doesn't remember Vivian either. She came to work at the hospital around the time Alex's memory is gone. Sarah sent the emails, I think. If she was responsible for the texts to you, I assume she did the emails. She told Alex the hospital felt she was too great a risk to have working there, so she'd been let go. She had Alex's tablet and phone the whole time."

I snorted. "Sarah tied up all the loose ends, didn't she? How very methodical of her." I flexed my hands, my fingers aching from being held in a tight fist for so long. "Why does nobody here know what happened? Why the secrecy?"

Emma and Alan exchanged a look. Alan spoke this time. "Emma and I were talking about that. This is conjecturing on my part, but I think they saw this as the perfect opportunity to get rid of you. If no one knew what happened to Alex and she simply moved, you couldn't find her if you came looking. No one would ask many questions if they thought it was a decision made by Alex. She was such a private person, it wouldn't seem out of character. They got control of her life again, and they could push her in the direction they wanted her to go."

I arched my eyebrow. "Big risk, considering her memory could come back."

Alan nodded. "I think they thought it was a risk worth taking."

Emma broke in. "She hasn't remembered anything, and now I wonder if that's why they kept her in Calgary. No memories of you or her life here with you. Although…"

"What?" I prompted.

"Alex showed me her tattoo and asked me when she got it. I told her I didn't know since I'd never seen it before. I knew the camera had to do with you, and I tried to ask her a few things, wondering if maybe it would jog her memory." She frowned. "Did you give her a leather band she wore around her ankle?"

A memory of the day I gave it to her flashed through my mind. "Yes."

"It was in her things from the hospital. She put it on—Sarah hated it, but Alex refused to take it off her ankle. She said it belonged there. She didn't know how, but it did. I brought it up, hoping to stir something in her head."

"It didn't, obviously."

"I think it did. She became upset and agitated. She got a terrible headache, and Sarah was furious with me. She pulled me out of the room and told me if I tried to talk about you again, she wouldn't let me see her anymore."

My heart sped up. Somewhere, lost inside Ally's head, there had to be memories of me. *Of us.*

She and Alan exchanged another glance, and Emma's eyes filled with tears. She excused herself, and I looked at Alan. "Is there something I should know?"

He shifted in his seat. "The accident…Emma was pregnant when it happened, Adam. She lost the baby because of it."

"I'm so sorry."

He swallowed before he spoke. "We'd been trying for a while, and she finally got pregnant—we found out just before the trip. But…" His voice trailed off, and he had to clear his throat before continuing. "She's been struggling ever since. Only our families know. But it affected her deeply, and she hasn't been herself. She didn't consciously give up on Alex, but she's been coping with her own issues."

"Ally doesn't know?"

He shook his head. "Emma didn't want to burden her, with everything else she was struggling with."

"I'm sorry for your loss," I murmured. "You must have been devastated. Is she going to be all right?"

"I'll make sure of it."

We shared a look, one that we understood—the knowledge of how much we loved the women in our life.

Emma slipped back into the room, and without a thought, I pulled her into my arms and hugged her. I knew she and Ally had drifted apart a little—life did that to even the closest of friends at times—but I also knew how much Ally loved her. She would want to comfort her friend. I offered the only thing I could.

"I don't blame you in any of this, Emma. The fault is mine. Please know that."

"Looking back, I know I should have pushed more."

I huffed a deep sigh. "Looking back, I should have done so many things differently. I shouldn't have gone on assignment, and I should never have left again until I found her. Let's not do the whole blame thing and just figure this out, okay?" I asked.

She smiled at me, her eyes damp. "Okay."

I sat down, tapping out an uneven rhythm on the arm of my chair. I drew in a deep breath and asked the question that was burning in my brain. "How did Bradley Bennett get involved in all this?"

"Alex could remember him. In her mind, they were dating. He was in Calgary all the time, visiting her. I assume he managed to convince her they were more than they actually ever were." Emma shook her head. "He's been in love with her from the start. Alex never saw it."

"Hardly news." I ran my finger over my chin. "So, when he saw his chance to get her back, he moved in, I'm guessing."

Emma and Alan nodded.

"I imagine," I mused, "between them all, they filled her head with lies and stories and made her think she and Bradley were deeply involved. And knowing Ally's need to make people happy, she went with it, thinking she must have been in love with him. She's never been able to stand up to them." I barked out a laugh. "Once she was married to him, they had her. She's so easily manipulated by them."

"I think Bradley is safe for her. He's been there this whole time, and he's something solid she can hold on to.

She's so lost, she needs that. But I don't think she's in love with him."

"You didn't question their engagement?"

"I asked her if this was what she wanted and she said yes, but she had to think about it before she answered me. Given our limited contact these days, I had to take her at her word. I didn't want to drive her further away or confuse her even more."

I thought about what Ally had said to me one time, about if she was married and gone, she would no longer be their responsibility. "This worked out so well for them, didn't it? They marry her off to the man they chose, he gets the girl he wants, and fuck the rest of the world. Fuck the man who would give up his life for her," I snarled. "They don't give a shit if she's happy, as long as they get what they want." I stood. "Well, they aren't going to get it. Neither them nor that bastard."

I paced the room, trying to figure out my next move. "Is she happy, Emma?"

"I don't know if she knows what she is, Adam. She's been *told* she's happy." She sighed and gave me a small smile. "But she doesn't glow the way she did when she was with you. She seems confused most of the time. It's almost as if, like you say, she is just doing this because she feels she has no choice." She closed her eyes for a moment, a sad expression on her face. "She's also trying to come to terms with Elena's death. It hit her hard all over again."

I swallowed the lump in my throat. My girl was confused, sad, and suffering. And she was doing it all alone.

"Why did they have a party here in Toronto?"

"Sarah, Ronald, and his father wanted it. They made all the arrangements—Alex came to town a couple of days ago, and she's only here until the wedding. The plan was for them to marry here where their families are and then go back to Calgary. I'm not sure you noticed, but no one from *her* life, aside from me, was there tonight. It was all for them."

I snorted. "All about image."

"Just like the fancy wedding," Emma agreed. "Alex has never wanted one, but that's what's happening."

I shook my head, gritting my teeth. "There isn't going to be a fucking wedding, trust me. And she isn't going anywhere."

Alan grinned. "You got a plan?"

"When is this supposed wedding taking place?"

"Three weeks from now," Emma replied.

I frowned. I didn't have much time. But I had to make it work.

"Okay. And she is staying here until then?"

"Yes."

"I assume at her parents' condo since they sold her place?"

"Yes."

I sat down. "How was she after I left tonight—was she okay? Did seeing me do anything?"

Emma shook her head. "She was upset. She tried to hide it, but I could see it. She was very quiet, and I heard her tell Bradley she had a terrible headache. He took her home early. But after you left…"

"What? What happened?"

"She kept looking around. She'd walk around the room, not talking to people, just walking. I think maybe…"

"…she was looking for me." I finished for her.

"I think so."

"I know she was. We've always had an intense connection—it was that way from the moment I met her. If I was close, she needed me touching her. Holding her hand or sitting near her." I slammed my hand down on the table in anger, hitting it so hard the glasses shook. "She fucking needs me, Emma. She needs me as much as I need her—even more."

"What are you going to do? Can I help?" She clasped my hand. "Let me help. I believed Sarah, and I shouldn't have. I should have known better. I want to make up for it. Please."

I studied her honest expression. We'd been deceived. Sarah removed us from Ally's life. It was time to change that.

"Are you in town for a few days?" I asked.

"Yes. I'll be back and forth until the wedding. Alan leaves in the morning."

"Then I think you're going to meet her for a walk tomorrow."

She tilted her head. "Will I be showing up for this walk?"

I paused, pursing my lips. "Maybe I need to run into you while you're out for your walk. You could get called away. Ally might be more comfortable if she sees you know me."

"Okay, that works. But if she's upset…"

"I'll ease off. I don't want to cause her any pain. I'll try again the next day. And the day after if I have to."

"Be sure to stay clear of Sarah. That woman is capable of more than we realized."

"I know, and I intend to."

"Be gentle with her, Adam. Alex is very fragile."

"I will. But today is the last day she's ever going to be without me again. She belongs with me."

Emma squeezed my hand. "Yes, she does."

"I made too many mistakes. I should have told Sean I wasn't going to Africa. I never should have left without her —then I should have stayed and fought when I got back. I should have given the PI company more time. My head said she left here because of me, even when my heart said she would never leave me the way she did. I let Sarah fuck with my head when she taunted me. Every time I thought I was doing the right thing, it was wrong. It was all wrong." I shook my head. "But not this time. Help me get my girl back, Emma." My voice caught. "I need her."

"She needs you too."

Deep down, I already knew that.

CHAPTER
TWENTY

I WAITED ANXIOUSLY in the park where I'd arranged to "bump into" Emma and Ally. Although it was only a few blocks away from Sarah and Ronald's place, I knew we'd be safe there. Ally told me once Sarah didn't like to walk anywhere, so she'd never go for a stroll. Limos were her choice of transportation. Bradley had returned to Calgary this morning, so we were safe.

The day was overcast and the park deserted. I prayed the rain stayed away long enough that I could pull this off. My camera hung around my neck as a prop once again—an excuse to be in the park. I paced up and down the path, too tense to sit. When I heard the murmur of voices, I ducked behind the trees. Emma and Ally came into view. My breath caught at the sight of her. She was beyond tiny—far too thin, in my opinion—which gave her the air of being fragile. Her steps were slow, the limp evident. Her hair was loose today, cut shorter, barely brushing her shoulders. She looked weary as she spoke with Emma, the two of them walking arm in arm.

She was still the most beautiful woman I had ever seen, though. They sat down on the bench, and I slipped farther into the trees, coming out onto the path around the bend. I took in a deep breath and paused, aiming my camera blindly at the tree line.

"Adam?"

Showtime.

I lowered my camera and turned with a surprised expression. "Hey, Emma."

She came over, giving me a hug. "What are you doing here?"

I held up the camera. "Just taking some shots. I like the muted light today." Glancing over, I saw Ally watching us, her brow furrowed.

I smiled, trying to keep it polite and easy. "Hello, *Alex,*" I swallowed as I spoke, the name sounding so wrong when I said it. "How nice to see you again." I extended my hand. She hesitated, then placed her palm in my hand.

"Hello," she murmured, her eyes showing her uncertainty.

My fingers closed around hers, my heart soaring at the contact, then skipping a beat when I realized she was wearing the earrings I had sent her. "You look lovely today." I paused, drinking in the sight of her, trying not to appear too anxious. "Your earrings are very pretty."

Instantly, color flooded her cheeks, and it took everything in me not to stroke the soft skin. I had missed her blush.

She withdrew her hand, touching her ear. "Thank you. They're my favorite pair. I'm not sure where I got them, but I love them."

Her favorite pair. I liked that. Even if she didn't know I gave them to her, they still meant something to her. It was a start.

Emma made a frustrated sound and pulled her phone out of her pocket. "Excuse me, I have to take this." She walked away, muttering into the phone. I hid my grin, knowing it was Alan on the line as we had arranged.

I indicated the bench. "May I sit?"

"Oh yes, please do."

I tried not to let her formality bother me. I tilted my head in Emma's direction. "Business, no doubt."

"You know Emma well?"

"Well enough."

She crossed her legs, her pants riding up. On her ankle was my band. My determination grew. "Nice anklet."

"Thank you."

She hesitated. "I'm sorry, have we met before the other night? My mind is a little fuzzy these days." She leaned closer, her voice lowering. "I hit my head, and sometimes I forget things."

She was near enough I could smell her familiar floral

scent. I gave her a gentle smile. "I'm sorry to hear that. Yes, we've met—several times."

She frowned, chewing on her lip again. "I don't remember, I'm sorry."

I wanted to yank her into my arms and tell her exactly how close we were. But I forced myself to remain calm. "That's all right. We can get to know each other again, like old friends, catching up."

"Is that what we were—friends?"

"Yes, we were friends. Good friends, I think."

Emma came back. "I'm sorry, Alex. I have something I have to take care of. Do you need me to walk with you back to the apartment?"

Before she could answer, I interrupted. "Actually, I was going to invite you for coffee. But maybe Alex and I can still go—get reacquainted. I'll walk her home afterward." I looked over at Ally. "If that's okay with you?"

I breathed out a sigh of relief when she nodded. "Yes, that's fine, Adam. Emma, call me later?"

Emma bent down and hugged Ally. "For sure." She shot me a glance. "Nice to see you, Adam. I hope we meet again soon."

I winked. "Count on it."

Emma headed out of the park, and we walked to the coffee shop in silence. Ally sat at a table while I grabbed our coffees. I slid a latte to her since she always loved one when we went out. She took a sip and frowned.

"You don't like it?"

"It's perfect. How did you know I liked lattes?"

"I know you."

She shut her eyes and rubbed her temples.

"Do you have a headache, Ally?" I asked, her name slipping out before I could stop it.

"No." She shook her head. "Why do you call me that?"

I took a sip of my coffee. I wanted to hold her and tell her I called her that because she was mine. Because I gave her that name so she'd know she was special to me. Instead, I shrugged. "I always have."

"No one else does."

"No, I gave you that name." I met her gaze directly. "I also called you Nightingale."

Her eyes widened, and a small spark of something passed through them. "Because I used to be a nurse?"

"Yes." Now it was my turn to frown. "Used to be?"

She shook her head, twisting the engagement ring around on her finger. I studied it briefly, hating it, not only because it wasn't my ring, but because it didn't suit her at all. Large and showy, it was far too big for her delicate finger. It was a statement, not a token of love.

"My fiancé is a doctor. I used to work here at Toronto General."

I tamped down my anger at her use of the word fiancé. "I know. That's where I met you."

Her gaze flew around the shop, her nervousness evident. "Do you, ah, know Bradley? Is that how we met?"

"Not as well as I know you, and no. I had an accident, and you were my nurse. We became friends after that."

Her voice grew upset. "I'm sorry. I can't remember that."

Without thinking, I clasped her hand in mine. "It's okay. Don't worry about it. Maybe one day you will."

She relaxed, leaving her hand in mine. I stroked my thumb over her skin gently.

"Can you tell me something about our friendship?"

I sucked in a fast breath, knowing I would have to tread carefully. "We were close. You liked to come for rides on my motorcycle, and we'd have picnics."

Her eyes widened. "Really? On a motorcycle?"

"You loved it."

"What else?" she asked eagerly.

"You helped me make my place homier. It was pretty sparse when I met you. You—" I stumbled over my words— "you helped make it a home, Ally."

"I like it when you call me Ally," she whispered.

I smiled and lifted her hand, dropping a kiss on the smooth surface. "Good."

She pulled her hand away and picked up her latte.

But she had a small smile on her face.

Was there a chance my words stirred something in her?

"What else?" she asked.

"You always called me out on my swearing." I grinned. "And you always had grape suckers in your purse for me."

She smiled back, and I reveled in the sight of her lips turned upward for me.

I kept the conversation light and relaxed, wanting her to be comfortable with me. It seemed to work, the tension easing from her shoulders as we chatted. I dropped hints in our conversation. How she loved to burrow under the blankets. How often she stole my coffee. Her love of honey on toast. Small pieces of information to help jog her memory.

When she was ready to go, I walked her back to the building her parents lived in. As we approached it, I was desperate. Our time was coming to an end, and I didn't want to leave her. Time was against me, yet I had to make sure Sarah and Ronald didn't know I was back.

I was anxious now that we would be separated. I glanced around, making sure we weren't seen, and stopped a couple of buildings away, stepping into the doorway. Cupping her elbow, I drew her in with me, forcing myself not to pull her into my arms. "I need to leave you here."

"Why?"

I decided to be honest. "Your mother doesn't like me. She wouldn't approve of us having coffee together." I brushed a stray curl back from her forehead, my fingers lingering, using the time to feel the silkiness of her hair. "Bradley doesn't like me much either. You might not want to mention we saw each other."

I knew if they found out, she'd disappear. I'd find her again, but I didn't want to take the chance.

"Oh. They didn't like you…before?"

"No."

"Oh," she repeated.

"We used to meet away from them." I sucked in a deep lungful of air. "Often with Elena."

Her eyes widened. "You knew Elena?" she breathed.

"Very well. I adored her." I sighed and spoke in a tender voice. "She loved you very much."

Tears filled her eyes, and her lips started to quiver. "I miss her."

"I do too."

"I don't remember her dying, I just know she's gone."

One lone tear dripped down her cheek, and I couldn't stop myself. I wrapped my arms around her, pulling her to my chest. She melted into me with a small sob, and for the first time since the night at the airport months ago, I held my girl. I breathed her in, feeling that intense satisfaction I got only when I was close to her.

I let her cry, holding and rocking her. It was only for a minute, but it was exactly what I needed. The way she clung to me, I knew she still needed me. Her love for me was still in there somewhere. I had to find the key to let it out.

When she drew back, I wiped the tears away with my thumb.

"Will you go for a walk with me again tomorrow?"

She didn't hesitate. "Yes."

This time, my smile couldn't be contained. It was wide

and joyful and grew bigger when she returned it. For one brief second, *my* Ally was in front of me.

"I have to go."

I stepped back, fighting the urge to kiss her. To beg her to remember me. "I'll see you tomorrow. Meet me in the coffee shop around ten?"

She nodded and began to walk away, then turned back. "Adam?"

"Yes?"

"I won't tell them. I don't know why they don't like you, but I do. I'll see you tomorrow."

"I like you too, Ally."

Then she was gone.

———

I was tense all night, apprehensive that something would happen. I wondered what she was thinking. Feeling. If our conversation had sparked any memories. I worried that she would slip up and her mother would find out I was back in town. I had spoken with Sean, who informed me that, yes, he had received a few calls regarding my whereabouts—one especially sticking out in his mind since it was a man and he asked a lot of questions. Sean told me he did exactly as I instructed, stating I was no longer employed there and had left the country indefinitely. While I regretted not leaving him Emma's name in case she called, it also told me this was a joint effort. I had a feeling the man who called was

Bradley—he would have wanted assurances I was out of the picture. If my being gone meant they relaxed enough to bring Ally back here, then I could still do this.

She wasn't lost to me yet.

I was waiting in the coffee shop when she walked in the next morning. She looked a little better and offered me a sad smile as she sat down. "I can't stay long, I'm afraid. My mother has things she needs me to do for the wedding."

I nodded, knowing I had to tread carefully. "You can make it up to me tomorrow."

She didn't say no.

"You look more rested today."

"I slept better last night," she confessed. "I haven't been sleeping well since we arrived. I keep feeling like…"

"Like?"

"Like I'm missing something. Silly, isn't it?" She took a sip of her coffee. "I don't know why I feel like that. I can't put my finger on it."

I shook my head, hope growing inside me. "Not silly at all. I'm sure you have lots on your mind. Trying to recall your past must be difficult."

She sighed. "My mother and Bradley tell me I know all the important things and to let the rest go. To move forward with my life."

I tightened my hand on my coffee cup. I bet they fucking did.

"You should do what is right for you, Ally. Not them."

She blinked at my words but didn't say anything.

I showed her some pictures I had taken of her and Elena. I taught her how to go forward on the screen and sat back, watching as she looked at the photos. When she frowned and her fingers flew to her head, I sat forward. I already knew that meant something was upsetting her and causing her pain. "What's wrong?"

She held up the camera to show me. It was a picture I'd taken of her and me—the camera turned toward us, held out at arm's length. Her head was nestled into my neck, a warm smile lighting her eyes. I was nuzzling her hair with the silliest grin on my face. We had just made love, and I'd grabbed the camera to capture the look of pleasure she was wearing.

"What is this?"

"We were goofing around."

She studied the picture for a minute and then handed me back my camera, looking down at the table. Once again, she began to massage her temples, and I lifted the camera, calling her name quietly. When she glanced up, I kept my finger pressed, letting the camera take shot after shot until the frown left her face and she smiled. "What are you doing?"

"Goofing around again."

She shook her head, still smiling. "Stop it."

I grinned. "Yes, ma'am."

———

Every day I could, I saw her. Coffee. A walk. I talked her into lunch one day and took her to the pizza place she liked so much—where I taught her how to really eat pizza. I hated watching her eat with utensils again, but at least I got her to eat more than one piece. She looked around more than once, frowning, but I didn't push her.

Some days she was shy and tentative. Other days her smile was easier. I tried pressing a little more each day. I would drop a hint or a memory and see what happened. It always hit me like a fist to the gut when she didn't show a flicker of recognition when I spoke. Other times I saw the smallest of sparks. Often what followed were her fingers pressed to her head. I always knew when to stop since I hated seeing her in pain. But I had to keep pushing. I had too much to lose otherwise.

I took her for a picnic to the park we'd been to before. She sat on the blanket, looking around, quiet.

"Have I been here before?"

"Yes."

"With you?"

"Yes."

She ran her fingers over the bark of the tree, frowning, then rubbed her head.

"You liked picnics, Ally. Especially with me. You could be yourself."

She nodded, confused. "I get the feeling I could always be myself with you, Adam."

"Always."

I left it at that, hoping the memories would stir in her head when she was alone.

The days I didn't see her were endless. I worried constantly. Emma helped when she was in town, and we kept in touch. Bradley was in Calgary most of the time, although he texted a lot. Sarah was busy with wedding details and her other activities. Ronald was never around, it seemed, so I managed to see Ally most days. But when I didn't, I was on edge somehow, worried they would figure out I was back and do something drastic. One day while she went to the washroom, I grabbed her cell phone off the table and got her number. I didn't dare put mine in hers, but at least I now had her information. I remained vigilant and staggered the times I saw her so our meetings didn't cause any suspicion. Sarah didn't seem to care that Ally went out for a walk to the park every day. She thought she had full control over Ally and wasn't worried. I loved every moment I had with my girl—often they were far too short, but I lived for each of them.

She no longer pulled back when I touched her hand. Instead, she often reached out to me. She leaned into my caress when I would bend down to kiss her goodbye, a small sigh escaping her lips when my mouth touched her cheek. I longed for the day I would feel her mouth underneath mine again. I never pushed the physical aspect, allowing her to feel safe.

I loved making her laugh. Some of the sadness that seemed etched into her skin disappeared when she would see me. I watched it creep back every time we parted. My heart ached when I had to stand and see her walk away. She started asking questions, and I always answered honestly, hoping and praying she would finally ask the one question I was waiting for the most.

I needed her to ask me what we were to each other. Sometimes the way she looked at me made me think she suspected there was something.

I wanted to tell her.

I remained patient, but time was running out. There were only five days to the planned nuptials, and I knew I had to make something happen.

I was quiet when she arrived for coffee that morning. She seemed nervous and tense.

"Something wrong, Ally?"

"Bradley arrives back tomorrow night."

I stiffened but kept my voice neutral. His visits had been rare and short. "For how long?"

She didn't meet my eyes. "Until the wedding."

"I see."

"I'm not sure how much I can see you now, Adam. There's a lot of wedding stuff I have to do, my mother tells me." Sadness filled her voice. "And then I'm moving."

I wanted to snort and tell her not to bother since there wasn't going to be a wedding. At least not between her and Bradley. And she wasn't going anywhere without me.

Her next words hit me like a Mack truck. "I have to go

for my dress fitting the day after tomorrow. The last one—thank goodness."

I struggled to remain calm. The dress she was supposed to be marrying *him* in.

It wasn't happening. No *fucking* way was that happening.

"I thought women liked that sort of thing."

She shrugged. "This whole *spectacle* is for my parents and Bradley. I'm not much for events."

I cleared my throat. "No, I imagine you would like a simple ceremony." I watched her reaction carefully. "Maybe on a beach in Greece? Or a private ceremony in some tiny chapel in England?"

Her hand flew to her head, and she shut her eyes, not saying a word, only nodding. When she opened her eyes, they were tormented and upset. "How did you know that?"

"I told you, I know you." I bent closer, deciding to push a little more. "I know you very well."

Her eyes searched mine. "How?"

My time was up, and I knew I needed to act. I stood, offering her my hand. "I need you to come with me."

"Where?" she asked, tentative but curious.

I shook my head but smiled. "I need you to trust me and come with me. *Please.*"

She stood, slipping her hand into mine.

———

She was silent as we stood by Elena's grave. Kneeling, she traced her finger over the headstone. "I don't remember this."

I helped her to her feet and tugged her over to the bench we'd sat on the day we'd buried the woman we loved. "We sat here together and said goodbye."

She shook her head, but I saw the telltale signs of distress creeping up as her fingers moved restlessly over her head. I kept talking. "She loved you like a daughter, Ally. Her happiest times were spent with you. With us. We played cards and talked. Elena and I drank scotch, and you laughed at us. We laughed a lot. She loved seeing you happy."

"Why are you the only person who will talk about her with me? Bradley shuts me down, and my mother brushes me off. No one wants to talk about her."

"They didn't like us spending time with her."

And they don't want you to remember how she supported us.

She furrowed her brow, her eyes dulling with pain. "But I want to remember those months before she died. I can *feel* they were good memories. I want *all* my memories back."

"I want that for you as well."

Her next comment was the simple truth.

"I have the feeling you may be the only one who does," she whispered.

I wrapped my arm around her, pulling her close. She leaned into my side, and for a few minutes, we sat in silence. She shivered a bit, and I pulled off my jacket and draped it around her shoulders. She rested into me, and I felt her sudden tension.

"What's wrong?"

I followed her gaze to my bare arms. Lately I'd been wearing long sleeves, but today, I was only wearing a T-shirt, and for the first time, she saw all my ink.

"You have tattoos."

"Yes."

Just like the first day, she reached out with her fingers and traced the designs. Around and again, her fingers swirled on my skin, igniting my need for her. I wanted to feel her hands all over me. I wanted to feel her lips tracing the images of ink the way they used to. I swallowed the thick lump in my throat.

"You always liked my ink," I murmured.

"It's beautiful," she whispered, moving her hand. "Your bracelet—it's like the one I wear around my ankle."

"*Band*, Ally. I explained that to you. It's a wristband."

She laughed, almost as if she remembered. As if somewhere in her mind, the words were familiar.

This was it. My gaze strayed to Elena's grave as I silently cast out a prayer to her for help one last time. I was about to do something that would either push Ally into my arms or send her away forever. With Bradley's imminent arrival, my time was running out.

I stood, taking her with me. "I have something else to show you."

———

She turned around, her gaze flying everywhere. Standing in the middle of the loft, she looked shell-shocked.

"You live here."

"Yes."

"I've been here before."

"Yes, you have."

"With you."

"Usually. Sometimes you stayed here when I went away."

Her hand flew to her head at those words. We hadn't talked much about my career; she knew I was a photographer, but I didn't expound on it very much.

"I stayed here without you?"

"Yes. You liked it here."

"You went away a lot?"

"Far too much."

"But not now?"

I inched toward her. "No. I don't want to travel like that anymore. I made that mistake once, and I'll never make it again. I found my home, and it's right here."

"This loft?"

"No. Not the loft."

"I don't understand."

We were so close I could feel the heat of her body. Hear the air escaping her lungs in small gasps. Small tremors shook her frame.

"The person standing in the loft with me."

Her eyes became huge. Panicked. The tremors became shudders.

"W—what?"

Slowly, I slipped my hands up her arms, tracing the smooth skin with my thumbs. I slid them over her shaking shoulders and up her neck until they cupped her face. "You, Ally. *You* are my home."

She shook her head furiously. "No. I don't know you like that."

"You do. You know me. I know *you* better than anyone else does." I moved closer. "*Anyone.*"

"No," she whimpered.

"I know you sleep on your right side, always curled up. You can't function in the morning without at least two cups of coffee. I know how much you loved being a nurse and helping people. I understand the pain and sadness you experienced growing up and how much you hate the restrictions you're living with. I know all about the emotional blackmail your parents have used on you. I know nothing makes you happier than a warm blanket and a good book." I paused and looked directly into her eyes. "And me —I made you happy."

"How—how do you know all these things?"

I drew in a deep breath. "When you love someone, you know them. You know all about them."

"I'm engaged. To someone else."

I shook my head. "No, Ally. You were mine first. You just don't remember it yet."

Her eyes widened more as I slipped my hand down and tapped her hip bone. "I know you have a small tattoo right here of a camera. If you look at the swirls, you'll find my initials there. You marked yourself as mine. You belong to me."

I tore my T-shirt over my head, letting her see the nightingale carved into my skin, right over my heart, her name woven into the feathers. I'd had it done while I was traveling, giving in one night to the desire of etching her on my skin. I had taken Rod's design and went to an artist he recommended when I called him. I needed to mark myself with her—to carry her with me the rest of my days—even if I thought she was lost to me forever.

"Just like I belong to you."

A small whimper escaped her lips.

"The band around your ankle *was* mine. I gave it to you. I gave you my heart."

The next second, my mouth was on hers.

I held her tight, molding her body to mine. I kissed her with everything I had. All the months of pain and torment, love and longing, went into that kiss. I drowned in the taste and feel of her. I groaned her name, pulling her closer. Her response was instant and passionate. It was perfect.

Until she pulled away.

Our eyes met. Panicked, pain-filled blue meeting pleading, terrified brown.

I reached out to touch her, and she stepped back.

"Ally, it's me." My voice broke. "*Please*, baby. *Please* don't leave. Stay with me. You're *my* Nightingale."

The last thing I saw on her face, before she turned and ran away from me, was shock.

She ignored all my pleas, and she left me—again.

The sound of the door slamming behind her echoed in my head for hours.

TWENTY-ONE

ALLY

THE RAIN BEAT INCESSANTLY on the windows, the wind blowing so hard tree limbs were bent over, almost touching the thick, sodden ground in places. The sky lit up with jagged, violent flashes of light. The thunder was so loud and forceful, the windows shook in their frames.

The weather outside echoed the turbulent maelstrom in my head.

When I had arrived back to the condo, my mother was furious, demanding to know where I had been. She became angrier when I told her the partial truth of visiting Elena's grave, telling me I needed to stop these useless bouts of emotion and concentrate on going forward with my life.

"Stop trying to live in the past, Alexandra. Nothing good comes from the past. Bradley, and your life with *him*, is your future."

I didn't understand why she was so upset, but the more I

tried to explain myself to her, the more agitated she became. Finally, when I pleaded a terrible headache, she relented and told me to go and lie down. She reminded me Bradley would be home tomorrow and I needed to be rested and ready for the busy week ahead.

Which would end with our wedding.

"Take some of your medication," she called after me.

I hated the medication. It made me groggy, and I only used it when I absolutely needed it.

I tried to rest, but I couldn't relax. There was so much happening in my head. Thoughts. Images. Voices. Things I wasn't sure were real, and others that were all too genuine to ignore.

I paced my room, back and forth, clawing my fingers through my hair, pushing them into my temples in a desperate attempt to stop some of the thoughts and images that kept appearing, only to fade away before I could fully grasp what they were. It had been happening more frequently now. Small bursts of thoughts, snippets of conversations. Flitting glimpses of things I didn't understand.

Dull pain centered behind my eyes as Adam's words —*his pleas*—echoed in my head.

Why did he say all those things? How did he know them?

If they were true, why couldn't I remember?

Then he called me *his* Nightingale.

Was it true? Was I his? And why did that name sound —*feel*—so familiar and right?

I traced my lips, still feeling the power of Adam's kiss from earlier—before I ran from him.

How had being in his arms felt so right? Why had his mouth on mine been so natural, as if it had claimed me long ago and was finally reasserting its ownership?

I didn't understand this tie I had to Adam. From the moment I saw him in the ballroom, I had been drawn to him. He was speaking with Emma, and I had to go over and be close to him. When his hand had wrapped around mine, the strangest feeling flooded my body—a sense of peace I hadn't felt in months. When we ran into him at the park and he told me we were friends, then took me for coffee, I silently rejoiced at the comforting feelings he evoked in me. There was a gentleness about him I so longed for in my life —something no one offered me but him. Every time I saw him, my body relaxed with his closeness. When he'd leave, I ached with a pain I didn't understand—an ache that dissolved as soon as I'd see him again.

I thought of him constantly, even though I tried not to. His eyes were a deep, rich golden brown, and when he moved in close to say something only for me to hear, I could see starbursts of lighter gold and green around the pupils. My fingers itched to bury themselves in his long, thick hair. I loved how the light picked up the strands of silver interwoven into the chocolate brown and the touches of silver that ran along his temple. A few times, he hadn't shaved, and the dusting of stubble along his strong jawline glinted with the same color. He often wore his hair pulled back, but some days, it fell well below his ears, a mass of crazy waves and curls. He towered over me, making me feel small and delicate. He never said a word about my limp, but his large hand was right there, steadying me when I stepped off a curb or engulfing my palm with gentle pressure when we spoke and he reached out in comfort. I felt safe and protected with him. As if I was meant to be beside him. It was the strangest sensation.

Normally an honest person, I didn't hesitate when he requested I not tell anyone we were meeting almost daily. I lived for those moments spent in his company.

Today when he kissed me, my entire body had eased, and for the first time since I woke up in the hospital, my soul was at peace. I had gasped when I pulled away and saw the fierceness in his expression, felt the possession in his grip. I knew we had crossed a line we could never step back from, and the most frightening part was that I wasn't sure if I wanted to.

Then the light had caught the ring on my left hand, and reality had set in, panic flooding my body.

I was wearing another man's ring—I was promised to someone else.

Terrified at my insolent behavior, I had turned and run, ignoring Adam's tortured voice calling my name.

Ignoring the fact that when Bradley kissed me, I never felt a fraction of what Adam stirred within me.

Adam.

The words he'd said to me—that I belonged to him, that we belonged to each other—replayed in my head. The things he knew about me.

How did he know so much?

He was right; the band around my ankle matched the one around his thick wrist, and my tattoo had his initials swirled in the design, the AMK curved around the camera more than once.

Why would I do that unless what he said was true?

Why did he stir something inside me no one else could? Why did his mere presence soothe me so much?

Thunder crashed loudly, startling me. I disliked thunderstorms—I always had.

I paced around the room again, restless, edgy, and confused.

Had Adam and I been secret lovers? Is that why he told me not to tell anyone I had seen him?

I stopped short, realizing if we had, then I had been cheating on Bradley.

But that made no sense to me. If we were in love the way Bradley and my mother kept telling me we were, and as happy as they said, why would I be cheating on him? Why would I marry him?

I rubbed my throbbing temples. I was missing something. Someone was lying to me—they had to be.

I grabbed my phone to call Emma. She was my best friend, and if anyone would know, it was her. She appeared to know Adam. I must have confided in her. The call went straight to voice mail, and when I glanced at the clock, I saw it was past two o'clock. She would be asleep, and I knew she turned her cell phone off overnight. I hung up, not wanting to leave a voice mail about this subject. I lay down again, trying to calm my mind and body, but neither could relax. I closed my eyes and took in some deep breaths.

Images—the edges of dreams, perhaps—flickered in my mind.

I was in a bed…a comfortable bed, surrounded by soft sheets and strong arms. The room was dark, lightning and thunder raging outside. Tender lips lingered on my head. Quiet whispers were dropped in my ear. Comforting, calming words of love were spoken. Promises of being safe and never alone. Of love so deep it would never end.

I saw a blanket on the floor of a large open space with huge windows all around me, a picnic spread out in front of me. Long fingers touched a strawberry to my lips.

I felt the curve of a deep chair, the warmth of a blanket draped around my knees. Warm lips grazed my head as a cup of coffee was set beside me.

A steamy room, a hard body unyielding against mine, hot, sexy curses filling the air as my back pressed into cold tile and I screamed my release into a strong, thick neck.

I opened my eyes, and the images were gone. I had no idea if they were real, but my eyes stung with unshed tears, and I felt as if I'd lost something precious.

Were they dreams? Something I had experienced? The

windows reminded me of the ones that lined the walls of Adam's loft… Had I been there with him?

I shivered, my entire body feeling cold. I needed to warm up. Getting out of bed, I pulled open my dresser drawer, searching for some thick socks to put on my feet. I only found some cotton ones, which offered no comfort.

My glance fell on the box sitting on the floor. My mother had brought my things to Calgary but had missed this one, and I planned to take it with me when I left. It was labeled clothes, and I wondered if perhaps there was a pair of thicker socks inside. Deciding it was worth a shot, I sat down on the floor and pulled it close, opening the lid and looking inside. I was rewarded instantly when I saw small piles of brightly colored wool. I slipped a pair on my feet, wiggling my toes in gratitude at the immediate warmth. Wanting to occupy my mind and hands, I decided to go through the contents. I dug through the rest of the box, creating piles around me. More socks, some pajamas, a couple of sweaters, a few trinkets, and books were wrapped in paper. I pulled out two T-shirts, holding them up and frowning. They were huge. Maybe they were Bradley's. He probably stayed the night, so it would make sense. I rubbed the material of the gray one between my fingers. It was soft from being laundered so often, the seams showing wear and the material pulling away around the neckline.

The ghost of a loving, playful voice resonated in my brain.

"You ever gonna give me back that shirt, Ally? I might want to wear it myself one day."

I shook my head. Bradley never called me Ally.

The only person who ever called me that was Adam.

I must be getting things mixed up in my head again. That had been happening a lot lately. The neurologist I had been seeing in Calgary told me it was normal to be confused at times. Bits and pieces of memories sometimes blended together. I had to work at separating them. The doctor had been kind when he informed me I needed to keep trying to recover the missing months, but there was a chance I never would.

"Nothing is for certain," he told me with a small smile. "The brain is a mystery we have not yet solved."

I lifted the shirt to my nose and inhaled. It was faint, but I could smell something familiar—a scent that wrapped around my heart and made my eyes sting. I inhaled again. It smelled like home.

It *didn't* smell like Bradley. His cologne was strong and musky. I never told him, but at times, it made my nose tingle and I had to repress a sneeze or two when he was too close.

I frowned, feeling a strong headache coming on.

Maybe Bradley had changed cologne. I was missing months of my memory. Perhaps at some point he had changed the brand he wore.

I pulled out another worn shirt, one I recognized as my favorite shirt to sleep in. It had been my dad's, and I'd kept it all these years. I lifted it up, startled when a small box fell out of the rolled material.

I picked up the wooden box, turning it over in my hands. It well-made, and as I rotated it, I heard small thumps as the contents moved inside. Reaching behind me, I turned on another light and studied the box. A beautiful bird was carved on the lid, sitting on the branch of a tree, the image familiar. My heart started pounding as I realized it was the same image as Adam wore on his chest. The one he said was for me. I looked down at the box again, my hands shaking as I stared. The wood gleamed in the light, the hinges glinting on the back. I lifted the lid and pulled out a necklace. On the end of a set of heavy silver links hung another bird, its wings spread out, a small jewel embedded on its breast. My hand shook as I held it up to the light, the feeling it evoked in me overwhelming. A sapphire glittered in the light—vibrant blue—and again, I heard the ghost of a whisper.

"Your eyes fascinate me, Ally. So blue and deep. I love how they look at me."

I looked inside the box, seeing another smaller case was tucked in the corner, the dull gold and lacquer gleaming. I ran my finger over the painting on the lid. It was the same bird as the larger wooden box. Opening the lid, I found another necklace. This one was a flat disk, the bird motif etched out of the silver. I laid the necklaces out on the floor. They were beautiful and unique and, like the boxes, the craftsmanship undeniable.

Why did I have them rolled up in my dad's old T-shirt?

There was one last item in the box, and I lifted it out, opening the small velvet pouch and spilling it into my palm —another necklace, this time gold. A small bird set in a tree branch, tiny gemstones surrounding it. It glinted and shone in the light, the artistry exquisite.

The bird was a common theme on all the pieces. A nightingale.

I stroked over the gold, wondering when I had collected all these pieces. They looked foreign. They were exotic, as if they had come from somewhere other than Canada. I had never been off this continent.

I looked at the pieces again. My gaze drifted to the small painted tile I kept on my bedside table. It had been tossed into one of my boxes and the frame was damaged, but I still loved it. I had no idea where it came from either, but I looked at it every day, even bringing it with me, and I would trace the small frame and look at the pretty image of the bird, wondering why it meant so much to me.

Never thinking of the type of bird it was—or why I had it.

Until now.

Nightingale.

An old-fashioned term often used for a nurse. And Adam had said he called me that as well as Ally.

I gasped out loud, the necklace slipping from my fingers as the earth stopped spinning on its axis.

Time stopped.

Images came, hard and fast.

A patient with warm, golden-brown eyes. Eyes that saw *me*.

A tender, melodic voice that wrapped around a new name…a name given only to me.

His Nightingale. His Ally.

Packages arriving from faraway places.

Sweet words of love on small notes.

Wait for me, my Nightingale.

Wear this and think of me, Ally. I think of you every day.

Days of laughter, nights of passion, filled my head. Memories of his laugh, his smile, *his love*, ran through my mind, playing over and again, once more becoming real and solid.

The feel of his mouth against mine as we kissed—gentle and loving, hard and demanding. His warm touch and strong arms that protected and soothed, loved, and caressed. His whispered promises echoed, drenching my parched soul with the truth behind the sweet words.

"You're mine, Nightingale. Nothing will ever change that fact. We belong together."

I shut my eyes as a sob burst out of my chest and the missing months of my life returned. One incredible and affecting image at a time.

All those months summed up in one beautiful, frightening word.

Adam.

CHAPTER
TWENTY-TWO

ADAM

THE COFFEE MACHINE gurgled on the counter. My gaze was fixed on the windows—the foggy darkness deeper than usual due to the ongoing storm. I rubbed my tired eyes; another night of restless slumber was catching up with me.

I couldn't sleep, no matter how hard I tried, so I gave up, made coffee, and started sorting through some of the pictures I'd taken the past days I'd spent with Ally. All I could see when I closed my eyes was the expression on her face when she pulled away and ran from me. All I could feel was the fullness of her lips as they pressed to mine. Her scent and taste lingered—no longer distant memories, but sharper—clearer.

They were even more painful than they had been. It made me even more determined to make her mine again.

I tried calling her, but all I got was voice mail. I went by her parents' building, but the lights on the top floor were out, and I knew I wouldn't be welcomed by the doorman.

I grabbed my mug from the cupboard, filling it with the fragrant liquid. I added some cream, shaking my head. Another habit I got from Ally. Before I met her, I drank it black, but she so often sipped from my cup, I started adding it so she could drink it anytime she wanted. I liked knowing her lips had lingered where my mouth touched. I got used to the taste, and now I liked it.

My gaze drifted back to the windows. Rivulets of rain ran down the large glass panes in a constant stream. Lightning lit up the sky, thunder rolled behind the bright strikes in long, slow rumbles. I set my mug on the table beside me and relaxed back in the chair.

Ally loved this chair. She always looked so good, snuggled in the corner, reading. She looked even better curled up on my lap as we watched a movie or when she nestled into me as a storm, much like this one, would rage outside. She hated storms and would burrow herself as close to me as possible. The very best moments, though, were when we would make love in this chair, slow and sensual or fast and furious—pressed together, wrapped in each other. Nothing else mattered in those moments—nothing but us.

I looked around the loft, thinking how it had changed since the day she entered my life. The thick, padded stools were in place at the counter—the spot we would sit and eat together, exchanging news of our days. The bed, adorned with the softest sheets and warmest duvet in a golden brown that she picked to match the leather. She said the color reminded her of my eyes.

Long white curtains hung in the windows, along with the blinds I'd added that ensured our privacy. Bright artwork and thick throw rugs made it a welcoming space. Or at least it had been when she was with me.

Now, the sheets remained cold, the bed rarely used. The blinds were dusty from misuse, and the stools were barely sat on. I hadn't been here in months, and since I'd gotten back, I was rarely in the loft. It felt like home when she was with me. Now it felt like an empty memory, and I disliked being here.

Rapid, furious knocking interrupted my thoughts. With a frown, I pulled myself out of the chair and walked over to the door, wondering who the hell would be at my door at five a.m. Very few people had the access code to the elevator.

I looked through the peephole and, with a curse, flung open the door.

Ally stood there, dripping wet. Her hair clung to her head and shoulders—a dark-red ribbon of wet silk. Against the ghostly pallor of her skin, her eyes were wild, the vivid blue standing out. She gazed at me frantically, those startling eyes red-rimmed and watery. Her chest heaved, and she shook from head to toe, her teeth chattering as she tried to speak. She clutched one arm to her torso, her hand a tight fist, a small bag held in her other hand. I dragged her frozen body into the loft, half carrying her to the chair I had just vacated. Pulling off her wet coat, I snagged the blanket from the back of the chair, wrapping it around her. I lifted my mug to her trembling lips and cupped the back of her head. "Drink, baby. It'll warm you up."

She took a deep swallow, a shudder running through her. Her panicked eyes focused on my face. "I was so afraid—" she gasped.

"What? Afraid of what, Ally?"

Tears poured down her face, and her shaking increased. I used the blanket to rub her hair, yanked off my sweatshirt, and pulled it over her head.

"Tell me."

"I was afraid you'd be gone."

I rubbed her back, desperate to warm her. Her skin was frozen.

"I'm right here." I pulled her close, dropping a heavy kiss onto her forehead. "Why are you out in this storm? You hate storms."

"You *know* that," she sobbed.

"Yes."

Her voice was incredulous. "You know *me*."

"Yes."

She cupped my face. "I know *you*," she breathed.

My heart hammered in my chest. "What?"

She opened her clenched hand, and light glinted on the silver chain she was holding. Attached was the nightingale pendant—the first gift I'd sent her.

"I remember you." Another sob escaped her lips. "I remember *us*."

Thunder rumbled as I stared at her. "Say that again."

"You. Me. Us. I remember us, Adam."

My throat was so constricted, only one word came out. I tightened my hands on her skin, frantic to know this was real. I had to know I was awake and not dreaming this moment. "How?"

"After you kissed me and I ran, I was so upset…"

"I'm sorry," I murmured. "I didn't mean to upset you."

She shook her head furiously. "No. You don't understand. I wasn't upset that you kissed me. I was upset because how it made me feel. I was so guilty."

"Why?"

"I should have been angry with you. I should have pushed you away and told you off. I'm engaged. I belong to someone else—"

It was my turn to shake my head. "No," I growled, interrupting her. "You belong to me."

"I'm so confused," she whispered. "You left me. You never came back…"

"No, I did. I came back. You were taken from me." I drew in a deep breath. "I don't understand everything that happened, but somehow, someone split us up. I didn't think you wanted me anymore."

"I don't understand." She gripped her hair and shook her head. "There was an accident…"

"I know. And we'll figure everything out. Together, we'll put the pieces together, and we'll find the answers."

"My mother and Ronald—were they…?" She left the question in midair.

"Yes. I'm certain they had something—" I drew in a deep breath "—*everything*, to do with this."

"I'm sorry." She clasped my hand. "I remember they didn't like you. But I never thought—" Her eyes met mine. "Bradley?"

"He's involved too. And we'll get to the bottom of it. But this isn't your fault," I insisted. "Tell me what happened tonight."

"My head kept aching. I couldn't relax, and the storm was bothering me. Little things kept coming into my head. Flashes, I guess. I kept seeing this place, but different. I saw you taking my picture. I heard your voice telling me you loved me and calling me your Nightingale. I saw picnics on the floor over there." She pointed to the middle of the room. "I remembered being in your bed." She rubbed her temples. "I thought I was going crazy—I didn't know if the flashes were real or if they were something I was dreaming up. I had this feeling I was standing at the edge of a cliff and my next step would either send me over or save me."

I pressed the mug to her lips. "Another sip." When I had gotten more hot liquid in her, I set it down and clasped my hands around hers. "Keep going."

"I needed to do something—concentrate on anything but the pain in my head and the thoughts I kept having. My feet were cold, and I found a pair of socks in a box that was overlooked. I decided to empty it out and see what was inside. My mother had told me it was just some clothes, so I hadn't bothered to look before now. But at the bottom of it, I found this little box, wrapped in my dad's T-shirt. I remember wrapping it up before I went away and tucking it into the drawer for safekeeping." Her forehead furrowed. "It was a carved, wooden one—with a nightingale on it."

"Yes." I nodded in encouragement. "I sent that to you."

She nodded. "I kept looking at it, and I started to remember things. I opened the box, and inside was everything. The necklaces, the small, lacquered case. I even had the little painted tile on my bedside table. I took it with me everywhere—it meant something special, I just didn't know what. Things you had sent or given me." She touched her earlobes, where the diamonds I had given her still glimmered. "I could never take these out. I had no idea why they were so important, but they were." A tear ran down her face. "And it all came back. All the months I was missing. The memories." Her voice started to quiver. "And every single one of those missing moments was filled with you."

Our gazes locked, and I saw it all. Her beautiful eyes were swimming with feelings—the ones I had missed seeing all these months: understanding, acceptance, and love.

Her love for me.

It was right there again.

Our history, our story, was reborn in her eyes, and the emotion of the moment hit us both.

"*Ally*."

"You asked me to marry you."

I wanted to reach out and grab her. Hold her hard so she couldn't leave again. But I didn't want to frighten her. Instead, I simply said, "Yes, I did."

"You gave me a beautiful ring I couldn't wear because it was getting sized."

"That's right."

"I belong to *you*."

I groaned at those words. "Yes, my Nightingale. You always have."

A wild sob escaped her mouth, and I dragged her into my arms, enfolding myself around her. Lifting her, I settled her on my lap as she wrapped her arms around my neck, holding me tight. I pulled her as close as I could, allowing our emotions to escape. Her tiny frame shook with the force of her sobs, and I let her cry. My own tears soaked into her hair. I rocked us, running my hands up and down her back, her arms—anywhere I could touch to soothe her and let her know I was right here. She was exactly where she belonged, and I wasn't letting her go again.

A shudder raced through her, and I realized how cold she still was. Her clothes were damp, her hair wet, and the blanket wasn't helping her. I stood, striding to the bathroom, keeping her close to my chest. I sat her on the counter, gently tugging on her arms. Her grip tightened, and I lowered my mouth to her ear. "I'm not going anywhere. I promise. I need to warm you up. Let me do that, baby. Please."

She loosened her grip, and I slid her hands down from my neck, kissing the knuckles as I laid them in her lap. Her shoulders were still shaking with her emotions, and I hurried to turn on the water, letting the air fill with steam. I lifted her face, carefully wiping away the tears. Her eyes were shut, long lashes fluttering across the tips of my fingers. Dark circles were bruised into her pale skin, and her face was drawn and exhausted. "Open your eyes, Ally," I whispered.

Blue irises, all at once so lovely but tormented, met mine. Questions, pain, doubt, and fear filled them. I wanted all of that gone. Once she was dry and rested, we would talk more so I could erase the pain and fear. I was worried about the sudden onslaught of emotions and how she was coping, and if this affected her medically.

"Is there a doctor or someone we should call? Are you under medical supervision?"

"No, I only see the neurologist for checkups. There wasn't much he could do but monitor me."

"Maybe you should check in later, okay? You can tell him what has happened and get him to recommend someone here. I need to make sure you're all right."

"I'll call him later."

She smiled, her bottom lip still quivering. I felt our connection reforming, already growing stronger. I pressed a gentle kiss to her mouth.

Standing her up, I drew the blanket from her shoulders and tugged off my sweatshirt and her wet clothes, leaving her in her underwear. Her skin was pebbled with goose bumps with a slight bluish tinge. Muttering a curse, I opened the door and tugged her inside, holding her under the warm spray. Long tremors rushed through her until, at last, she relaxed and, with a sigh, melted into my chest. Her hand fisted my T-shirt, her head resting over my heart. I let the water run over us until I knew she was no longer cold. I turned her to the water and helped wash her hair, remembering all the times this exact scene had played out right here. As I reached out to shut off the water, she covered my hand with hers. "My turn," she said quietly.

"Ally…"

"Now, Adam."

I smirked at her tone as I hunched low enough for her to reach. "Here we go with you being bossy again," I teased her.

She pressed her lips into my skin. "Get used to it."

I lifted my face, the water running over my skin nowhere near as warm as her touch. "Happily."

After the shower, I dried her off and slipped a shirt over her head. "My favorite," she whispered, rubbing the thin cotton of my shirt between her fingers. I grinned as her wet, lacy brassiere hit the floor. Another patented Ally move and I knew her underwear would follow, so I handed her a pair of my boxers. "It's been waiting for you," I told her, running my hand over her shoulder and smoothing the fabric. "Just like I have."

"Adam—"

I shook my head. "Later. I want you to rest." I stroked her temple. "How's your head?"

"Better."

"Do you need some pain meds?"

"I only need you."

"You have me."

I tucked her into our bed and pulled on a fresh T-shirt and boxers before slipping in beside her. Her entire body loosened as I drew her close and felt the warmth settle inside me that could only be from her touch. I breathed in deep lungfuls of her scent, and I calmed—finally feeling some semblance of peace. Her hands clutched my shirt, fisted even in sleep, as if she was afraid I would slip away. My arms held her equally as tight, the same fear etched in my head. I couldn't close my eyes, too worried this was all a very real dream and I would wake up, once again alone and empty.

I had her back, and I wasn't letting her go again. We were both exhausted, and I wanted her to rest. When she woke up, we could talk and reconnect. Figure out where we went from here.

Slowly, I relaxed, letting sleep pull me under.

———

Hours later, I woke up feeling different. Lighter.

Warmer.

My arms felt the weight of another person, and I opened my eyes. The room was dim, but I focused on the woman I was holding. Ally's eyes were open, and she was staring at me.

"I'm not dreaming, am I?"

Gently, I stroked her cheek. "No, you're not dreaming. The nightmare is over—for both of us."

"We need to talk. There's so much I don't understand." She frowned. "And I need to understand to move forward."

Her strength and determination made me proud. I loved her for both those traits.

"I know. Are you up to it? How's your head?"

"Clearer today. My brain is so full of memories, I'm trying to them sort out." She worried her bottom lip. "It's like…"

"Like what?" I prompted.

Her wondrous eyes lifted to mine. "It's like my mind found what it was looking for and it doesn't have to work so hard anymore. Does that make sense?"

I was feeling my own anxiety subside, so it made perfect sense.

She continued. "I missed you—every single day, even when I didn't understand what I was feeling."

I brushed her cheek, agreeing. "I missed you too. I felt empty without you, Ally."

"You must have hated me," she whispered, pressing a tender kiss to my jaw.

"No. I never hated you. I could *never* hate you. I was hurt and I didn't understand. But I never stopped loving you. And I'm not letting you go."

She gripped my hand. "I don't want you to."

I brought her tight to my chest, her head over my heart. "You're home, and we'll figure this out. Today is for us to reconnect and talk."

She looked up. "Together?"

I knew we had a difficult discussion ahead of us. I had to hear about her accident, find out from her about our time apart—about her parents' manipulation. Hear what had transpired between her and Bradley, even though I cringed at what she might say. She needed to know I would really listen, though—and, if needed, forgive.

Except she wasn't the one who needed forgiving.

The people around her, her so-called family, they were the ones responsible. I held them accountable, not her.

And I needed her to forgive me for not being the man I promised her I'd be. I should never have left her.

I brushed a kiss to her forehead.

"Together."

CHAPTER
TWENTY-THREE

ALLY

EVER SINCE THE ACCIDENT, my days had started the same way. It was as if my body was set on repeat. I would jar awake, every nerve twitching, my body tense and my chest aching.

I never knew what it was aching for.

This morning, awareness came softly, slowly. I woke up, warm and content, relaxed and peaceful. There was no feeling of loss, no tension and no ache.

There was just…

Adam.

Surrounding me with his strong body. Holding me in his arms and keeping me safe. Making me feel as though I was loved.

And home.

His quiet assurances of no matter what, only made me feel safer. His sincere golden-brown eyes were filled with so much emotion when he spoke. He would love me, regardless of what I told him.

I wanted to ease his mind—the way he had eased my soul.

When I had first woken up, he was asleep. I stared at him, seeing the subtle changes to his appearance. His wild hair was a little longer. Shot with more silver. His scruff was thicker, and more silver was laced through the wiry strands. His face was thinner, and there were a few more lines around his eyes. And until now, there had been a haunted look in his eyes. I had wondered where it came from, and now I knew. He had been suffering the same way I had—missing the person he loved.

Only he knew who I was. Until a few hours ago, I couldn't remember who it was my heart and soul longed for.

Meeting him had changed my life. He had been a force unto himself from the moment he was wheeled into the ER and woke up, grumpy and demanding. Yet somehow vulnerable and sweet at the same time. He had exploded into my world like a tsunami slamming into land. He obliterated everything I thought to be true. He questioned every negative thought. Struck down all the guilt I carried. He made me stronger; although every time he left, my parents tried to drag me back into that world.

He listened to me. Challenged me. He made me feel beautiful. Sexy. Wanted. Loved. So deeply loved. It was as if his adoration wrapped around me, defeating the negative and bolstering the good.

His gifts always made me smile with his thoughtfulness. Making sure I knew even if he wasn't with me, his thoughts were. The best gift was always when he returned safe and sound, though.

And now, he assured me he wasn't ever leaving me again. No one would separate us. We would talk and figure everything out. Together.

My phone rang, my mother's ring tone loud and obnoxious in the quiet of the room. When it fell silent, I looked at Adam. "She'll call back until I answer."

"Yeah, I remember her insistence. You should answer it. Let her know you're safe and be done with it."

I wasn't sure I could talk to her without screaming. "I don't want to talk to her."

"Then send her a text. You left their condo in the middle of the night. Even your mother would be concerned. And you have to face her when you go back for your things."

I shook my head. "I don't want to go back there!"

Adam captured my hand that was rubbing my forehead. "Okay, Nightingale. Calm down. Are you in pain?"

"No. Sometimes when I get upset, my head aches. It'll go away." I snuggled closer. "This helps. I don't ever want to wake up without it again."

His lips were warm on my temple. "Not happening. Ever. I'm never letting you go."

My phone beeped, and I shut my eyes.

Adam rolled out of bed and got my bag, fishing out my phone. "Is Emma in town?"

"Yes. She's in meetings all day about her new designs."

"Does Sarah know that?"

"No."

"Where's Ronald?"

"Away on a business trip. He's away a lot these days."

"Good. That's one less asshole to deal with today." He grunted as his fingers moved over the keypad quickly. "That'll buy us some time."

"What did you say?"

"She now thinks you couldn't sleep with all the wedding excitement, and you went to Emma's early to have a spa day so you'd look nice for Bradley."

The phone beeped, and he shook his head after reading the screen then tossing my phone back into my bag. "She's reminding you she's out this evening and that you have a final dress fitting." Then he arched his eyebrow. "You won't need that fitting. You aren't going to need that dress."

I met his steady gaze. "No, I won't."

The sunlight coming in the window glinted off the large diamond on my finger.

"Or that ring," he added.

Nodding, I slid it off. Adam handed me my bag, and I tucked it into the side pouch. "I have to give it back and tell them all the wedding is off." I hesitated, pleading with my eyes. "Will you come with me?"

"Absolutely."

"Bradley's going to be upset. I don't think he's totally innocent in all this, but I don't know how much he knows."

"I think he knows quite a bit." He bent down close, meeting my eyes, his expression intense. "I've been in hell for months, aching for you. I've been without you, and that bastard kept you away from me. I woke up every day thinking you didn't love me anymore. So frankly, I don't give a fuck how upset he is. I owe him some pain."

"I'm so sorry. I can't believe all this has happened."

He shook his head. "This isn't on you. He and your mother kept you away and let me think you didn't love me. I'm sure of it."

I stroked along his jaw, feeling his rough scruff under my fingers. "It's amazing how the mind works, because I did love you. Even when I didn't know it." My voice caught. "My soul missed you every day."

His face softened. "I know that now."

"I have to face them all, don't I?" I asked, the dread in my voice evident.

"Yes, but I'm not risking you being near them alone. We'll face it together. Bradley, Ronald, your mother— whatever shitstorm it causes. They have to answer for their actions—not you."

"I need you there. I need them to see they failed."

He brushed his lips over my temple. "I'm not letting you out of my sight. It's my turn to tell them what to do. They'll never get close to you again."

I let him surround me. I hated it had come to this. But there was no decision to be made—Adam would always come first. What they had done had proven how little I meant to them.

———

ADAM

Ally hung up the phone and smiled reassuringly at me. "My neurologist is amazed how much I can remember. He's going to have me see a colleague of his in the next couple of days, just to make sure everything is okay. Now, will you stop worrying?"

I trailed my fingers down her cheek. "Not sure I will ever be able to stop worrying about you." I tucked the blanket higher around her shoulders and settled back into the chair. I studied her face—she looked tired, but her eyes were clear. "Are you ready to talk? Just pick somewhere to start, and we'll figure it out."

She thought about it a moment, then spoke. "I was so upset after we got disconnected—"

"I didn't hang up on you," I interjected. I had to make sure she understood that. "I was startled by a couple of the children from the village. They broke through the bushes and ran into me. I dropped the only sat phone we had into the river. It was an accident. We were in the middle of nowhere and had no communications for days. When I sent Tommy for supplies, he called and left you a message, but I don't think you ever got it."

She shook her head, putting the pieces together. "I was already in the hospital. My mother had my tablet and phone. I'm sure she deleted everything to do with you. She gave me new ones with new accounts—she said they were a get-well gift. I'd been carrying the other ones in my bag when I was hit, and she said they were damaged beyond repair. I should have known better than to believe her."

"Don't blame yourself. The bitch and her fucking sidekick thought of everything."

I ran my hand down her thick hair, stroking the silky curls. "Emma told me about the accident. I wish I had been there for you."

"I don't remember much about it—even now. Only bits and pieces." She rubbed her head. "When I woke up, I was in the hospital, and things were so confusing. I was in pain, scared. I had no idea why, and not being able to remember such a huge part of my life was so frightening."

"Emma said you were in pretty bad shape."

"There was so much I couldn't remember. Emma looked different than I thought she should. It was the wrong time of year. My head ached all the time, my leg was in a cast, and I had bruises everywhere. My entire body hurt. They told me I'd been hit by a car, but I couldn't remember that. The last things I could remember clearly were going out with Bradley to dinner and being at work. I couldn't remember going to Calgary or anything in between." She shook her head. "Emma was hurt, and when I finally saw her, she seemed withdrawn. And my mother was always around, hovering, and kept her from saying too much, and then Emma stopped coming to see me."

"She didn't want Emma saying too much. She was afraid it would trigger your memory." My anger started to build as I thought of the lengths they had gone to in order to separate us.

"I know that now."

I kissed her head. "Emma was injured too, and I know you two aren't as close as you had been, but I think you can rebuild your friendship."

"I want to." She looked sad. "When she was here last week, she told me she'd had a miscarriage because of the accident. I wish I had known and could have been there for her. We cried together when she shared."

"I'm glad you're reconnecting." I pushed a lock of hair behind her ear. "I think with Emma out of the picture, your mother and Bradley were more than happy to fill in the missing details—at least, their version of the details."

She became quiet, playing with my bands and thinking. When she spoke, her voice was forlorn as she processed thoughts in her head.

"They didn't tell me very much, and the times I was alone, I tried to remember on my own, to try to fill in more of the empty spaces, but nothing ever came."

"How often were you alone?"

"A lot," she admitted. "My mother left often to come here for her *obligations*, and Bradley flew in and out. Ronald never came, not that I wanted him to." Her voice was wistful. "I spent a lot of time in the hospital room alone." She paused. "I cried a lot at times. I didn't know what I was crying for, but I couldn't stop. I think—I think maybe I was crying for you."

I swallowed the thick feeling in my throat. I hated knowing that. The fact that she was alone in a strange place, with no one to comfort or care for her the way she should have been cared for, made me angry. The fact that she needed me and I wasn't there upset me. I pulled her head to my chest, stroking over her skin gently.

"I'm sorry I wasn't there for you."

Her voice was muffled in my shirt. "You didn't know."

"No, I didn't. If I did, I would have moved heaven and earth to get to you." Tilting up her head, I laid my forehead on hers. "It kills me to know you were hurt and alone." I brushed my lips on her temple. "I will never fucking forgive your mother for that."

She looked up at me, determined. "I won't either."

"I should never have left you. I should have stayed when you asked. I did so many things wrong. I'm not sure I can ever forgive myself."

"I forgive you," she whispered. "We made mistakes. What my mother did wasn't a mistake. She was being cruel."

"They kept me away from you, Nightingale. When I got back to a place where I could get my messages, I found four from you—the last one telling me you didn't want to see me again."

"I didn't send that." Her voice was emphatic.

"I know that now. I came home and tried to find you. Vivian told me you quit your job, your place was up for sale, I couldn't get hold of Emma, and your mother…" My voice trailed off, and I clenched my hands, thinking about her words and the almost sick enjoyment she got out of my pain.

"What did she say?"

I repeated the words her mother flung at me and the fake text I fell for. Ally's eyes filled with tears and anger as she shook her head rapidly. I took her face in my hands, cupping her cheeks. "I know it was all lies now. She wanted me gone, and she got her wish. I let her defeat me, and I packed up and went back to Africa and helped build a new clinic. I thought, with time and distance, I could get over you. I hoped you could come back and pick up your life here, without me interfering."

"But you left me a message before you left."

I brushed the tears from her face. "You heard that?"

She nodded. "Last night, when everything came back, I called your number—I could remember it, and I wanted to hear your voice. I heard what you said. That's when I knew there was so much more to this than I could handle myself and I had to come to you. I grabbed my things and left." She covered my hand with hers, stroking the rough skin gently. "You thought I'd left you, and you still loved me?"

"I'll always love you. Nothing can change that. Your mother and Bradley failed. I came back to find you."

"I can't believe Bradley did this. I don't understand why or how they thought they'd get away with it."

"I think when they found out how much of your memory was missing, they decided to make sure they got what they'd wanted all along. I know you could never see it, but Bradley wanted more than friendship from you—even Emma could see how he felt. This was his chance. Bradley got you, and your mother got rid of me. Your mother kept you in Calgary, supposedly for you to heal. He accepted a job there. I think once you married Bradley and left Toronto for good, even if you got your memory back, they'd convince you I'd been the one to walk away from you, not the other way around—and probably tell you I never came back when they got word to me that you'd been hurt. I'm sure they had all their bases covered."

She shook her head in disbelief. "I can't even fathom—"

"It doesn't matter now. They failed. They were overconfident, and they made a big mistake."

"Coming back here?"

I nodded. "Fucking big mistake. I know they checked and thought I was gone indefinitely. Your mother wanted the big social aspect—to show off you marrying the right, *acceptable*, kind of man. One she and Ronald approved of. So, they had the party here, for their circle. They had no idea I would show up." I breathed out a huge sigh. "Thank God I came back."

Ally ran her hand over her temple.

"Is your head hurting?" I asked, concerned. "We can stop and talk more later."

"It still hurts sometimes, but not as much," she admitted. For a minute, she worried her lip, looking anxious. "I'm not–I'm not the same as before, Adam."

"What do you mean?"

"I get headaches, and sometimes I'm confused and forgetful. I don't know if that'll get better or not. I tire easily. I have a limp, which makes me a little clumsy at times. I'm not quite *me* anymore, so I've been told."

"Is that what they've been telling you?" I asked, keeping my voice low.

"My mother told me time and again I was lucky Bradley was so in love with me, that he would overlook my, ah, drawbacks. Even Bradley said things—he'd say he was teasing, but it hurt. My mother, though, especially likes to tell me how, ah, diminished I am now."

Deep, clawing rage filled me. How fucking *dare* they say that to her? I closed my eyes. "I don't believe in hitting women, but I'd really like to slap your mother. And then beat the living shit out of Bradley."

"Adam—"

I leaned forward, speaking slowly so she understood what they'd been telling her was bullshit. "Listen to me, Ally. You are *in no way* diminished. You're still *you*—the woman I love. I don't care if you walk with a limp. I'll carry you if that's what you need. If you forget something, I'll remind you. If you're confused, tell me, and I'll explain it to you until you aren't confused anymore. When you're tired, I'll watch over while you sleep. I'll do all that happily until we're old and gray if that's how it is. I don't care. You're still nothing but perfect in my eyes. You always will be." I paused to brush my lips across hers. "I love you. I will *always* love you. No matter what."

"I love you," she whispered.

"We have each other, and we'll deal with everything else."

"I didn't sleep with Bradley," she burst out.

Relief coursed through me at her words, and I struggled not to show it on my face. "Why?"

She eased off my lap and paced in front of the windows, the blanket still draped around her shoulders. Her bare legs showed the scar that ran down her leg to her ankle, still vivid against her pale skin. She was so thin and wan-looking, it made me want to pull her into my arms and keep her safe. Make her strong again.

"I couldn't," she said simply. "His touch—it felt so wrong."

"Did he try?"

"Yes. A few times." Her hands fluttered nervously, the blanket falling from her shoulders as she kept pacing. "I could never feel completely comfortable with him. I kept telling myself it was because I couldn't remember and I'd get over it. Except it never got any better."

"How did he handle it?"

She shrugged, not looking at me.

"Ally."

"He was fine at first, telling me he would wait until I was better. The last couple of times, he got impatient. He said I was stalling." She paused. "He was right."

"Why? You were engaged. It would be natural to explore that with the man you were supposed to be in love with."

"That's just it! It didn't feel right. I didn't like it. I was so confused all the time." She stopped her pacing, standing in front of me. She clenched her hands, wrapping them around the bottom of my shirt. "My mother and Bradley kept telling me how in love we were and how happy I *should* be. No matter how hard I tried, though, I was never very happy. I wasn't even sure why I said yes when he asked, except it seemed to be what I was *supposed* to do. He'd been so good, coming to see me all the time and being kind." She twisted her hands some more. "I kept telling myself if I loved him so much, it would come back. One day, I'd feel it. Except the only thing I felt all the time was bewilderment and worry. Like I was doing something wrong."

Tears filled her eyes. "I was so lost, Adam. I missed you. I missed you so much, and I didn't know that was what I was feeling."

I opened my arms, engulfing her small, shaking frame as she launched herself at me. "I missed you too. It felt as if all the color had drained from my world without you, Ally. Everything was black-and-white. I was barely existing. But not anymore. I feel as if everything is bright again. I'm not letting you go. Ever."

We sat wrapped around each other in silence. "What do we do now?"

"We're going to confront them. Tell them it's done. We'll

have the power of attorney removed. You need to have control over your own life again." I ran my finger over her pale cheek. "We'll have you checked by the doctor, and then we're going to move forward with our plans. The ones they took away from us."

"I'm worried," she admitted quietly.

"Tell me why."

"I'm not sure I've ever felt so angry toward someone. I don't know how I'll react when I see my mother or Bradley. And all of this seems so overwhelming, I'm not sure how to handle it."

"I know it's a lot. We'll figure it out a step at a time. You don't have to hide how you feel, Ally. You've been hiding long enough. Speak your mind to them. I'll be beside you the whole time. No one will touch you, and nothing is coming between us."

"I never want to see my mother again—or Ronald. And I'm not sure I can forgive Bradley if he's as involved as I'm afraid he is. I can't believe he'd stoop so low."

"Then don't. It's time to get your life back. Ask your questions, say what you think. It's time to finally be free of them."

A look of determination crossed her face.

"All right."

CHAPTER
TWENTY-FOUR

ADAM

"ADAM," Ally called as she searched the cupboard a short time later. "Where's my mug—the one you brought me from London?"

"Oh. It, ah, got broken."

"What a shame! I liked that mug—it was my favorite." I heard her rummaging a little more. "Where are the other mugs? The ones that went with our dishes? In fact…"

I shut my eyes, knowing what was next. I was ashamed when I thought of my tantrum that day, but I couldn't take it back.

"…where *are* the dishes?" She turned around. "All that's in the cupboards are a bowl and a couple of plastic containers. The only mug is the one we've been sharing. Where are the rest of them?"

I tried stalling. "You don't like sharing a mug with me anymore?"

"Adam." Her voice held a warning.

I sighed heavily. "I was angry."

"And?"

"I threw things. Lots of things."

"You broke *all* our dishes?"

"Yes."

"*And* my mug?"

"I was angry," I repeated. "I thought you'd left me—left our life behind. I didn't want any reminders. So I destroyed anything that reminded me of us."

"Did it make you feel better?"

I shrugged. "Not really."

She walked around, running her fingers over the walls. "Here?" she asked quietly, tracing a deep hole. "Was this my mug?"

"I think so. Or your keys."

"Adam …"

"They were on the desk. All your things were gone. I thought you were gone too," I added, trying to explain my pain and anger.

"I didn't take them," she replied.

"No. I assume your mother did. Was my information in your phone?" I asked, more pieces of the puzzle coming together.

"Yes."

"That explains how she got the address. I guess she decided to make it look like you took your things. Made sure I got the message. Bitch."

"I'm sorry. She certainly thought of everything." She tilted her head. "You were hurting."

"I was. I thought I was going to explode. I didn't know how to deal with the pain and frustration."

"So my mug had to suffer."

I knew she was trying to make me smile.

"It was an honorable death."

She rested her hand on her hip, a stern expression on her face.

"I expect you'll be replacing my mug," she huffed. "And my key chain."

I nodded, trying not to laugh at her stern tone. I had missed how adorable she was when she was trying to be tough.

"I guess we need to pick up some new dishes. Eating off paper plates is more your style than mine," she teased.

"Saves on dish soap."

"Nope. New ones."

I grinned. "Bossy."

"You love me bossy."

I yanked her to me. "I love you *any* way—as long as I have you."

She pulled my mouth down to hers, her breath drifting over my skin.

"I know."

————

The day was filled with ups and downs. Some moments of sharing were easier and lighter—like the mug and dishes. Later, however, I heard her crying in the shower, and I went in to find her on the floor of the stall, weeping over her silly mug and the pain it symbolized for me. Fully dressed, I sank down beside her and held her, letting the water wash away her tears.

I left her in the loft, running to the Chinese place to get some food. The order took longer than usual, and I became agitated, a gnawing feeling clawing at my gut at being away from her. I grabbed the bag from Chang and tore back home, only to find her waiting anxiously for me by the door. I wrapped my arm around her and lifted her, carrying her and the food to the counter, setting them on the hard surface. Cupping her face, I stared at her. "I don't think we can be apart for a while," I admitted. "I can't be away from you right now."

"Me either. I feel better when you're close."

"Good."

We ate, then she curled up in the chair, and I sat in front of her, holding her hands, wanting to hear more about our time apart.

I asked the questions I hated hearing the answers to. She told me about her recovery, trying to come to grips with the missing pieces of her life, and the therapy on her leg. I disliked hearing about her being in physical pain, and even more, I loathed hearing about her emotional pain. How she worried about her memory and what the future held for her.

I gripped her hand tighter as she whispered some days she cried when the pain was too much to handle.

She asked me questions about Peter and Edwina and what I had done during the months we'd been apart. I explained about the clinic I used Elena's money to build, and how the trust fund would ensure continued care for the people there. I shared memories as we went through the images I had captured on my laptop. She loved the ones I took of the remote area and the clear horizons that surrounded us.

"The stars at night, Ally. They're like diamonds thrown into the inky blackness. I had never seen skies like the ones I saw there," I explained.

She touched my hand that was on the mouse, stopping me from going forward as she gazed at my face on the screen, her finger tracing the image. For a change, I was staring into the camera while Edwina snapped the shutter. My face was impassive, but my eyes and expression said it all. Weary and lost. That was how I looked.

"I remember that day," I murmured. "It had been a bad night."

"Tell me," she urged.

I set down the laptop, needing to hold her. "I'd dream of you. You'd be with me…then I'd wake up, and you weren't there. I wasn't here. I was alone in a strange place and missing you so much."

"Just like me."

I nodded against her neck, burrowing my face into her

fragrant skin. "Never again," I vowed. She was mine, and I wasn't letting her go.

"No. Never again." She agreed.

———

Her phone buzzed a short while later. She looked up from the screen. "Bradley's returning early."

I couldn't keep the loathing from my voice. "How awesome."

Her eyes filled with trepidation. "What should I say to him?"

"The sooner we do this, the sooner we can move on."

"The thought of seeing him makes me anxious."

"*He* should be anxious facing you after what he's done. I'll fucking make sure he is." I felt a tremor go through her, and I regretted adding to her worry. "Everything's going to be okay, Nightingale. I won't leave your side."

"My mother…"

We needed to develop a plan. "What time will she be home this evening?"

"Probably about nine."

"Why don't we tell Bradley to be at her place tonight, too? Face them both at once."

Her already pale face became ashen.

"Ally, don't. I'll be right there. Nothing is going to happen, and we're going to walk out of there together. I promise."

"Okay," she whispered. She picked up her phone and sent off the texts.

"Your mother has become lax about checking up on you," I said, grateful for the fact. "She's so confident she's won, she hasn't seen what happened right in front of her. She never suspected that I was here, or that you had been seeing me."

"She's been distracted, and Ronald's been away so much. I told her the walks I took every day made me glad I was moving to Calgary since nothing felt familiar here. She thinks I sat in the park and read and never spoke to anyone."

I grinned. "You played her."

"She's so busy today with appointments that she hasn't even checked up on me." She huffed a sigh. "She's been enjoying all the wedding nonsense."

"Of course. She loves the attention." It was another thing I loathed about that woman.

"I asked Bradley to come to my mother's place at eight-thirty. I told my mother I'd be home when she got there."

"Good. We'll go a little early, and you can grab anything you may have left behind." I grinned. "Not that I mind you wearing my stuff all the time, but you must want a few of your own pieces of clothing to tide you over until we go shopping."

"Okay. I probably should make sure I have everything." She lifted her chin. "After today, I'm not going back."

"Nope."

Slipping my arms under her legs, I lifted her, carrying her to the bed. "You look exhausted. I want you to rest."

"I don't think I can."

"What if you just lie down and I'll stay beside you?"

"Will you tell me more about Africa? I want to know all about the clinic and the fund you started with Elena's money."

I smiled at her. It was a cause close to my heart because of the memory of the person it represented and the couple who had been there for me. I had the best people overseeing the project—Elena would be pleased. And I'd tell Ally anything she wanted if it meant she rested. "Yes."

She curled up on her side, tucking her pillow under her head. I slipped in beside her, pulling her close, nuzzling her hair. I had missed her soft, feminine scent. I spoke quietly, hoping to lull her into sleep. I talked about the heat that bounced off the dirt, some days so hot you could see the shimmer of it in the air around you. I told her how I had finally confided in Peter and Edwina, and it was they who convinced me to come home and find her. They told me I couldn't move forward until I had some closure, and they had been correct.

"I came back to put you behind me, but instead, I have my whole life ahead of me with you in it," I murmured against her skin. "I have them to thank for that."

I kept talking, keeping my voice low, until I felt her relax, her body easing farther into me as she slept. I looked down at her, hardly able to believe she was with me once again. Safe in my arms.

Gently, I stroked her hair back, frowning at the edge of the scar I could see. I knew it went under her hairline, and if I ran my finger over her scalp, I would feel it, along with the shorter hair that was there when they had to shave around the injury. A scar she would carry the rest of her life. One that would remind us of a time we thought we'd lost the most important thing in our lives.

However, I was determined it would only make us stronger.

———

ALLY

Wrapped in Adam's arms, I slept. He was beside me when I woke up, one hand busy on his laptop, while the other one rested on my arm.

"Hi," I whispered.

His gaze flew to mine, and he shoved his laptop to the side. "Hey."

"Don't stop what you're doing."

"It's fine. I just finished getting some documents from my lawyer. I'll print them in a while."

"What time is it?"

"Seven."

I sat up, feeling more alert. "I slept that long?"

He nodded, smiling. "It did you good. Feel better?"

"Yes. Thank you for staying beside me."

"There isn't anywhere else I want to be." He paused. "Are you up for this? We'll leave soon."

I drew in a deep breath. The truth was, I never wanted to see my mother again. Especially knowing the depths of her deception. Bradley either. He had lied to my face for months. But I knew I had to face them. Show them I knew the truth and they had lost. With Adam beside me, I could do it. "I have to be. With you there, I can be brave and do this."

"You are brave. You always have been." He tilted his head, his voice becoming low and soothing. "I have something that might help." He furrowed his brow. "I think, anyway."

"Oh?"

He pressed a small box into my hand. "This has been waiting for you."

I stared at the tiny leather box. My hands shook as I opened it. The light caught the delicate diamonds that were scattered around the intricately designed ring. "How?" I gasped.

"Mr. Freedman dropped it off. I kept it for you."

Tears filled my eyes. "You kept it?"

"Of course I did. I gave it to you the same way I gave you my heart. It's yours. Forever." He assured me.

"You still—" I swallowed "—you still want to marry me?"

He nodded firmly. "As soon as we can. I'd marry you tonight if I could." He hesitated. "If that's what you want. If you want to marry me."

"I do, Adam. More than ever."

He tugged on my hand and slipped the ring on to my finger. "Then wear this. We'll face them together with you wearing my ring."

We looked down at the shining symbol of his love. "It's perfect," I whispered.

"It's not as, ah, showy as…" Adam's voice trailed off.

"I don't want showy. I was never comfortable with that one." I rubbed my finger over the surface of the gold. "I would pick this ring over any other ring in the world."

"Ally." His voice was nervous—a tone I wasn't used to hearing from Adam. I looked up into his anxious gaze.

"Did you know, hundreds of years ago—even longer—a marriage was a simple exchange of vows between two people? No pomp or ceremony. No other guests. It was a private moment."

My breath caught in my throat. "No."

He nodded. "I'll marry you anywhere you want. Maybe, though, you'd like to start with us? Today?"

My heart soared with his words. "Yes," I whispered. "Us."

He sat up straighter and gathered my hands between his. "Alexandra Robbins, I promise to love and honor you every day for the rest of my life. I will protect and cherish you and put you above all else. I give you my heart, my soul, and my life. I take you as my wife. Right here, right now, for as long as we live."

My voice shook. "Adam Martin Kincaid, I promise to love you all my days. Nothing will separate us again. I give you my heart and my love. I give you me." I swallowed as a tear ran down his cheek, my own spilling. "I take you as my beloved husband. Always."

Our lips met in the sweetest of kisses. Love, adoration, and a promise of forever were in our shared caress. He crushed me to him as he kissed me, his mouth possessive and gentle at the same time. When we pulled back, his smile was brilliant, his eyes filled with love.

"You're mine."

"Yes."

"We'll do this in a more traditional way as soon as we can. But as of now, we're married."

Married. I belonged to him. With him. And he belonged to me.

"No one can take me away now," I murmured.

"No."

I looked down, frowning. "You don't have a ring."

He grinned. "You want to mark me as taken?"

I nodded, then gasped. "Wait!" I scrambled off the bed. "Don't go anywhere!"

Adam chuckled. "Already issuing orders."

I grabbed my bag and found my nightingale box, bringing it back to the bed where he sat, looking mystified. I opened the small pouch I had added and held up a thick silver band carved with Celtic symbols. At his quizzical look, I explained. "It was Theo's. Aside from his wedding ring, it was the only piece of jewelry he ever wore. Elena wore his wedding ring around her neck, but she gave this to me and I tucked it away—it was in the box. She said I might need it one day."

Adam laughed low. "Crafty old bat. She always knew."

He held out his hand and I slipped on the ring, and we grinned when he declared it a perfect fit. "I'll wear it until Mr. Freedman has the other one ready, and then I'll wear it on my right hand, like Theo did." His voice caught. "I'm proud to wear something that meant so much to Elena. To carry a piece of her life with me."

"She'd love knowing you had it and used it for a wedding band—even if it's temporary."

He pulled me close. "She would."

We were quiet for a minute.

"You feeling brave enough to do this now, my wife?"

His words filled me with joy. "Yes. Let's do this and move on."

———

The slightest hope that somehow Bradley had been an unknowing part of this entire mess died the instant I opened the door.

"Jesus, Alexandra. What the hell is this all about? You're not answering your phone, you tell me to come here…" His voice trailed off as he saw Adam standing behind me.

"*Fuck.*"

"Fuck *you*, asshole." Adam mocked him, his grip tightening. I knew he wanted to hit Bradley, but that would get us nowhere, and I wanted some answers.

Bradley's shoulders dropped, and without another word, he walked in. We stood in the living room, all staring and silent. Adam was tense, his hands holding me close as if he was afraid I would disappear. Bradley's normally easy confidence was shaken, and he fidgeted and shifted his weight.

Finally, I spoke up. "Why, Bradley?"

He stared at me as if I was dense. "I've been in love with you since the day I met you, Alexandra."

I shook my head at his matter-of-fact tone. As if that made everything he did all right.

"I didn't love you, though. I told you that over and again. You knew I was in love with Adam. Why would you do this? It's almost criminal!"

"I tried everything else. I thought if I gave you time and space, you'd come to your senses. I even pretended to date other women to get you to agree to my idea. When I convinced you to pretend in front of Sarah and Ronald, I thought we were finally on our way to being a couple." He sneered at Adam. "Until you met *him*."

"So sorry to have fucked up all your plans," jeered Adam. "How inconvenient for you. When you couldn't have her, you decided to manipulate her? That's how you think love works?"

"You're such a smug bastard, aren't you?" Bradley spat.

Adam shrugged. "Think what you want. Your opinion doesn't matter to me. Only hers does."

Bradley glowered at us. "I'm not so sure her opinion is exactly reliable these days."

"*Bastard*," Adam roared, and he moved so fast, I had no time to react. His fist shot out, slamming into Bradley's jaw, while he rammed his other hand into his stomach. Bradley fell to the floor, gasping.

Adam stood over him, panting. "Don't you *dare* say another derogatory word about her. Not one fucking word, you hear me?"

"Adam!" I pleaded, clutching at my head. "Stop!"

He looked up, his stance relaxing, and he stepped away from Bradley. "Don't you say shit about her. You haven't helped the situation with her memory—feeding her lies all the time."

Bradley slowly got to his feet, holding his stomach. "I guess I can't argue with that." He rubbed his jaw. "That's gonna leave a mark."

Adam huffed. "You deserve worse."

Bradley eased himself down onto the sofa, his gaze finding mine. "I'm sorry, Alexandra."

"Did you think this was going to work, Bradley? That we'd get married, I'd never remember, and we'd—what—

live happily ever after? Do you have any real remorse for tricking me?"

"I thought it would work. You'd marry me, and I could make you happy. Our parents would be happy too."

I was shocked at his words. "You think our marriage would have worked? A relationship based on a lie?"

"You could have loved me. Once we were settled and away from here, you would have loved me. I knew even if you remembered him—" he indicated Adam with a jerk of his chin "—you would have realized I was a much better man for you."

"Because you would have let me think he walked away from me. You would have added yet another lie."

"I would have done whatever it took to keep you."

"Are you out of your mind? That isn't *love*. That's twisted and sick. I'm not a possession—something you bought and have the right to *keep*."

"I was protecting you."

I shook my head in disbelief. He acted as if he was doing me a favor. Behind me, Adam cursed, and I held up my hand. I didn't want him to start beating on Bradley again. "Explain that to me."

"You were swept away by him. Not thinking straight. He's not the man you need. I can give you stability and take care of you."

I shook my head, feeling the anger build. "No, Bradley. For the first time in my life, I *was* thinking straight. And I am *not* a child. I do not need to be 'taken care of,' or at least your version of what that means."

He stared at me, frowning, as if he was trying to understand what I had said. He stood. "Well, I guess that's it then, isn't it? You've obviously made up your mind."

"It's over, Bradley. Not that there was anything real about it." With a shaking hand, I held out his ring. "This belongs to you. I don't want it."

With a muttered curse, he took the ring, looking at the large stone. His eyes fell on my left hand, growing wider as he took in the new ring on my finger. He glared at Adam. "You didn't waste any time, did you, asshole?"

"We were already engaged before this happened." Adam snapped. "Her ring was being sized."

Bradley stepped back, caught off guard. "*Engaged?* Your mother told me you had broken up. She said he'd walked away from you after the accident." His gaze flew back to Adam. "Your magazine said you'd left town. I checked. I thought you were out of the picture."

His words sounded almost true.

Adam shook his head, studying him. "You didn't check too hard, did you? And you didn't waste any time either. Sorry if I don't feel bad or even believe you."

"I had too much to lose." Bradley's shoulders dropped in defeat. "I guess I lost it all anyway."

"I'm sorry, Bradley. You deserve someone who loves you the way you love them. But it has to be real. You can't force someone to love you. I hope you find it."

He looked at me, almost with respect. "Always so generous and kind. You should be screaming. Calling me names. Instead, you wish me a good life." He looked behind me at Adam. "I guess you deserved those shots." He paused. "You're not, ah, gonna hit me again, are you?"

For a moment, Adam didn't say anything. Then he shook his head. "I want to. I want to beat the shit out of you for the pain you caused me. For the way you treated Ally, making her feel less than she is. I hate you for all that."

Adam tucked me into his side. "I have her, and I'm never letting her go again. We're going to build a life together. And you'll spend the rest of your life regretting the fact that you lost her. I think that pain is far greater than anything I could inflict with my fists."

Adam lowered his voice. "Know this, Bradley. Try to come between us or say anything bad about her, and I will come after you. You won't have her goodness to protect you next time. I promise you that."

Bradley only nodded.

Behind us, the door opened, and my mother called out to me, her voice impatient.

Bradley was one thing. I thought, in a small way, Adam felt sorry for him. My mother, however—Adam hated her. I wasn't sure how he would handle this confrontation.

How she would handle him.

Bradley spoke up. "I think I should leave."

Adam shook his head. "No, I think you should stay. Sarah has a lot to answer for to all of us."

Bradley sat back down on the sofa, his tone defeated. "Well, this should be interesting."

I drew in a deep breath. Adam pulled me closer.

"I have you. Remember that."

I held his hand tighter as we turned to face my mother.

CHAPTER
TWENTY-FIVE

SARAH SWEPT IN, her voice impatient. "What is going on, Alexandra? Why is there a bag by the door?"

She stopped dead, words drying up when she saw me standing with Ally. All the color drained from her face.

I couldn't resist. "Hey, *Mom*. Miss me?" I held out my arm. "How about a welcome-home hug?"

"What are you doing here?" she hissed, her gaze darting around the room. She was cornered, and she knew it.

I tilted my head to the side, studying her impassively. "I came home to get what's mine, Sarah. Did you honestly think you'd get away with this?"

She glared at Bradley. "What are you doing just sitting there? Do something!"

Bradley laughed, throwing her under the bus. "Oh, Sarah. I think we did enough. It's all done, and I'm not your lapdog anymore."

She took in the way I was holding Ally and reached toward her. "Take your hands off her. She's unwell and engaged to another man!"

"Don't. Touch. Her," I snarled as Ally shrank away from her touch. "She's perfectly fine. And she *isn't* engaged to Bradley. Not anymore."

She froze, lowering her arm. "I want an explanation, and I want it now!"

"Oh, you're going to get one." I smirked. "*Sit down.*"

"I don't take orders from you." Sarah turned around, heading back to the hall. She gasped when I blocked her path by throwing out my arm.

"I said, sit down. *Now.* You, lady, are going to listen. You owe us that, at least."

Her chin lifted haughtily. "I owe you nothing."

I dropped my voice to a dangerous, low tone and narrowed my eyes. "You owe more than you can *ever* account for—especially to your daughter. Now sit your fucking ass down before I help you do it."

Shooting me a look that could kill, she sat down, Bradley remaining silent.

Ally's legs were shaking so hard I wasn't sure how much longer she could stand. I kept my hands gentle as I tugged her into a chair beside me. "Everything is okay," I murmured into her ear. Her mother's presence reduced her to such an emotional low, I wanted this done and over with as fast as possible.

I turned back to them, keeping my hand on her

shoulder. They eyed me warily, and I gazed back at them without emotion. I would always dislike Bradley and would never forgive him for what he did, but my anger at him had waned. His pain at losing Ally was real, and he would have to live with it. He, too, had also been deceived by Sarah. And besides, his fucking jaw was like granite, and my hand was already aching like a bitch from the last punch, even though I enjoyed it.

"Tell me how the hell you thought this was going to end, Sarah. Did you think my feelings for Ally were so shallow, I wouldn't try to find her at some point? Did you actually think you'd get away with this charade? That you could control her forever?"

"I did what was best for my daughter."

I cocked my head in confusion. "Let me get this straight. What was *best* was taking away the person who truly loved her, who would have done anything for her, and instead, left her alone to face the pain and confusion of trying to heal from a horrific accident by herself?" I clenched my hand on Ally's shoulder. "What you thought was *best* for your *daughter*, for her peace of mind and well-being, was to lie to her and fill her head with ideas of what you thought was an acceptable path in her life?"

Sarah stared at me, refusing to answer.

"Does your daughter's happiness not mean a fucking thing to you?"

She waved her hand. "Do you honestly believe you're going to make her happy, Mr. Kincaid? The lifestyle you lead? Dropping everything and everyone whenever you hear of a new adventure to go on? At least married to Bradley, she had a chance at a stable, normal life. With you, she'll have nothing but heartache and regret."

"I made mistakes—yes, I admit that. But I gave up that life for her—for us. That was my last trip."

"So you say. You disappeared quickly again," she sneered. "Off somewhere, no doubt taking your little pictures. Making *that* your priority over her."

"I left because I thought the woman I loved no longer wanted me. I left town so she could come back to her life here without me interfering. I only wanted her to be happy, so my pain meant nothing. I put her first, unlike you."

Bradley frowned and looked over at Sarah. "You told me he dumped her when he heard about the accident. That he packed up and left town." He shook his head. "You showed me the box of her things he'd sent over, that he said he didn't care when you called him and told him Alexandra was hurt. You said it was time for me to move in and help Alexandra make the right choice. I went along with it because I thought she would come to love me. You lied to all of us."

I smirked, realizing how large her web of deception was. "Spreading lies everywhere, weren't you, Sarah? Busy little bee you were, while your daughter was lying in a hospital, alone and injured. As usual, your priorities were skewed."

"I don't have to answer to you."

"No, you should be answering to your daughter."

Ally spoke up. "I can't believe you did this to me, Mother. You lied and made things up. You took Adam away from me. You made me think I was no longer capable of trusting myself. I doubted myself all the time. How could you? Why would you—"

She cut Ally off, waving her hand dismissively. "Spare me the dramatics, Alexandra."

Ally sat forward. "I want you to tell me why. Why have I never been enough? Why did you let Ronald punish me for years? Why didn't you try to stop him?" She drew in a shuddering breath. "Why did you stop being my mom and become his possession?"

Sarah glared at her. "I owe you no explanations. I did what I had to do so we had a roof over our heads. Ronald was a savior for us. You were always in the way. So much trouble. I should have sent you away."

I felt Ally flinch, her mother's nasty words like arrows into her flesh.

"What you have done this time is unforgivable," Ally said, her voice quavering.

"I'm not asking forgiveness. I did what I thought was best."

"For whom?" Ally asked quietly, the simple words like gunshots in the room.

Sarah regarded her impassively, not a flicker of remorse or guilt on her face. She sighed and glanced down, flicking an imaginary piece of lint off her skirt, effectively dismissing Ally. Dismissing her pain.

Anger shot through me, burning hot and bright. I shook my head in disbelief at Sarah. She felt no remorse, no regrets for her actions. She sickened me.

"When did your heart die and forget to tell you, Sarah? Who the fuck decided you could play God with not one, but three people's lives?" My voice rose. "What gave you the right to fuck with me—with us?"

She stood, her posture straight and unrelenting.

"I don't have to answer to you—or to anyone," she repeated.

I laughed, a dry, low sound in the back of my throat. "Oh, you'll answer at some point."

"Not to the likes of you, you tattooed *nobody*."

Ally stood, and I felt the anger rolling off her. "Stop belittling him. Just *stop* it."

Sarah regarded her silently, and I wrapped my arm around Ally's waist, pressing a kiss to her head in silent thanks.

But I was truly curious. "Why do you hate me so much? It can't only be because I have some ink on my arms. You've never given me a chance. I can provide everything in life for your daughter, as well as the fact that I love her. Why doesn't that count with you?"

"You're just like my first husband. Full of promises. I didn't even want a child, but when I got pregnant, he swore he'd stop taking chances. Stop being the hero. I thought he'd get a desk job, but no, he had to keep being a cop. Keep the streets safe. And what happened? He died and left me with bills to pay, a child I never wanted to raise, and nothing to do it with. Our home was worth less than we paid for it, his insurance didn't begin to make a dent in the debt I owed. If I hadn't met Ronald, I don't know where we would have ended up. I owe him everything. He deserves my loyalty."

I felt Ally stiffen when she heard Sarah's vile words. She knew the why now. She hadn't been wanted from the start—at least not by Sarah. She truly believed she owed Ally nothing, and Ronald everything. She had no clue what she was going to lose.

"Our situations aren't similar. That isn't going to happen to Ally. I'm not leaving her again."

"Until the next time," Sarah fired back.

I shook my head. "Never." I frowned at her. "Where is your husband? I have a few things I want to say to him too."

For the first time, she looked unsure. "He is away. Not that he'd be interested in your words anyway."

I sneered. "Of course not. Neither of you is interested in the truth. You think you owe Ronald? What about what you owe Ally? What about what she deserves?"

"Stop calling her that! She was given every opportunity in life, thanks to Ronald. She had a home, a good education, and all she's ever done is cause me grief! She almost cost me my marriage!"

I narrowed my eyes. "*Every opportunity?* She had a roof over her head and you provided her the necessities, but I wouldn't call it a home. You never gave her the love she needed. You let Ronald blame her for something that wasn't her fault."

"She never should have called and asked Oliver to pick her up. If she hadn't, he never would have been in that convenience store. Because of her actions, Ronald lost his son. His heir. Someone had to pay. She owed him."

"She owed him *nothing*. The man who pulled the trigger killed Oliver—*not her*. You let Ronald control her life because of a debt she never owed. You denied her the one thing she wanted the most her entire life!" I roared, my anger cresting.

"She had everything she needed."

"Not your love—your affection," I spat. "You denied her that because you felt you owed Ronald. Because you were too scared to give up the lifestyle you enjoyed, you let him bully and control the life of your child. He lost his son because of the actions of someone else. But he used that accident to his advantage, didn't he? Capitalized on Ollie being the hero, while blaming Ally for it. He used Ollie's memory for his own gain. And you sacrificed your daughter knowingly. A child you should have protected and put above him or anyone else."

"You know nothing of my life or what I sacrificed."

I couldn't believe her. She would never accept it. She would never bend on this. "Was it worth it? You're about to lose your daughter for good. Are you prepared for that, Sarah?"

She crossed her arms, regarding me arrogantly. "If

you're finished with your self-righteous lectures, I'm already done. Now I have to clean up yet another mess you've made, Alexandra."

Beside me, Ally trembled, her shaky voice drenched in tears. "Mother…please."

Sarah remained rigid. "This is your last chance. Stop this bleeding-heart nonsense, and we'll forget this ever happened. You can marry Bradley as planned. If you leave here today, with him, you are no longer my daughter."

A long shudder went through Ally. She gripped my waist harder, her entire form shaking. I pulled her tighter to my side, silently cursing the coldhearted bitch who stared at her.

"I know now that I stopped being your daughter the day you married Ronald. It's just taken me a long time to see that."

Sarah's gaze never softened as she took in her daughter's distress.

"I'm not forgetting anything else, Mother. You took enough away from me already."

"Just like your father—you're far too sentimental for your own good."

Ally smiled sadly. "I realize you didn't mean it that way, but that is the nicest thing you've ever said to me."

Sarah rolled her eyes.

Ally's voice shook. "Someone did pay that day, Mother. *Ollie did*. He died trying to care for me. He put me first. Until Adam, he is the only one who ever did."

Sarah didn't even blink at those profound words.

I pulled an envelope from my pocket. "Sign this."

Sarah made no move to take it from my extended hand. "What is it?"

"It's a release form my lawyer drew up. Effective immediately, Ally no longer requires anyone to make her decisions. The power of attorney you had in place will be null and void." I pushed the paper forward. "Entirely voluntary, of course. But if you refuse to sign it, he'll start legal proceedings right away."

"Is that a threat?"

"If you sign it, no. It's a request."

She snatched the envelope away. "I'll have our lawyer look it over."

I shook my head. "You'll sign it now. It's very straightforward." I locked eyes with her. "I'm sure you want all of this kept as quiet as possible. It would be a damn shame for any of this *nasty business* to get out."

Her eyes narrowed.

I stepped forward, my voice shaking as I struggled to stay in control. "You're a piranha in a designer dress, lady. You are truly the coldest bitch I've ever had the displeasure to meet, and if I had my way, you'd be in jail. I want to go to the press and give them the story of the year—*the fucking decade*—and tell them exactly what you've done, blow your precious little world apart. I want you to suffer the way you've made Ally suffer."

She had the audacity to roll her eyes at me. "Is that your plan?" she demanded.

I smirked at the slight tremble in her voice.

"My plan is to get Ally as far away from you as possible. She is never going to be subjected to your unfeeling, joyless world again." I indicated the envelope she was gripping. "Sign the paper, Sarah. Your daughter, who is just like her father in that she *has* a heart, refuses to let me tell the world how ugly you truly are. Her massive capacity for forgiveness is what's keeping you from public humiliation. The *only* thing. However, if you don't sign it, *right fucking now*, all bets are off."

"I don't think I care for your tone, Mr. Kincaid."

"I don't give much of a toss what you care for. I *care* about your daughter and the damage you've done to her. That's all that matters. Now, sign the damn paper so I can take Ally home with me where she belongs."

She grabbed a pen, signing the papers with barely a glance. When she turned back, her frigid gaze went to Ally, and her voice was icy. "Marrying this man will be the ruin of you. You will regret it."

Ally shook her head. "No, I won't."

"Take your things and leave. When he's done with you, don't come crawling back."

I was tired of her ugly words. I wrapped my arm around Ally, lifted her hand, and kissed it. "How could you think I'd ever be done with this remarkable woman?" I smirked as I looked at her. "I would never walk away from my *wife*." I held Ally's hand so the light caught the diamonds glinting on her finger and the thick silver band on my finger was visible.

She gaped at us. "You're already married?"

"We are," I said firmly. "I assume you won't be hosting an event to welcome me to the family?"

She pointed a shaking finger to the door. "Get out." She drew in a deep breath. "*Get out!*"

I tugged Ally with me as I stepped back. Sarah was so livid, she was almost vibrating. Her carefully concealed emotions were on display, and they were ugly. I didn't want her even remotely close to my girl. If she struck out and tried to hurt her, I wouldn't be able to control myself.

I spoke softly. "Do you want to say goodbye to your mother?"

Ally shook her head, already turning to leave. "I don't have a mother."

Those words broke my heart.

———

The elevator ride down was quiet. I held Ally close, worried over her unnatural stillness. She hadn't said a word since her mother brushed past us, pausing only to open the door and indicate with a haughty wave of her arm we needed to leave. The quiet click of the door shutting behind us made Ally flinch.

Sarah had shown her true colors to us all. Her need for social standing and wealth was more important than her daughter—a child she never wanted in the first place. She allowed Ronald to take out his deep-seated bitterness on Ally like some twisted equal exchange. Her life for his. To him, Ally meant nothing, and Sarah allowed it. Because she was punishing Ally for being born.

I hoped one day she would rot in hell.

Bradley and I glanced at each other, no animosity in our eyes, united in a common worry. He cleared his throat.

"Alexandra."

She turned her head, gazing calmly at him.

"Are you all right?"

"I'm fine."

Our gazes locked again as the doors opened. We didn't speak as we crossed the lobby and went outside.

Bradley turned to us. "I'll handle the details of canceling everything. You don't have to think about it."

"We appreciate that. Thank you," I replied, surprised at his offer.

Ally dug into her purse, pulling out a small notebook. "This has all the information in it. You might want to start with Gretchen, the wedding planner. She can take it from there." A small grimace passed over her face. "I'm sure she'll be grateful she doesn't have to deal with my mother anymore. She isn't, ah, easy to handle." Then she smiled. A strange, vacant smile that made me shudder. "I guess neither of us has to deal with her after today."

"Ally—"

"I'm just stating the facts, Adam."

I didn't like the sound of her voice—controlled and removed.

"Alexandra—" Bradley started.

"Don't call me that. I always hated how formal it was."

"What would you like me to call you? Ally?"

"No," she said sharply. "That's Adam's name for me. You can call me Alex. My friends call me Alex."

"Are we still friends?"

I was shocked when she suddenly drew back her hand and slapped him. Once. Twice.

Bradley blinked but didn't move. He barely flinched. I had a feeling the impact of her hand hardly registered. His face *was* abnormally hard. I only hoped she didn't hurt her hand.

"That's for lying to me."

"I'm sorry."

"I don't want to see you again."

"I understand."

She turned and walked away, stopping after a few steps. She looked back. "Have a good life, Bradley. I hope Calgary is everything you want it to be. Don't call me." She paused and cleared her throat. "We're going away. Maybe we can talk after that. I'll think about it."

She hurried over to the car and slid in, slamming the door behind her.

We stared at each other.

"She's all over the place—she's gonna explode," he muttered. "Worse than a slap across the face."

"Did it hurt?"

"No."

"That's a shame."

He chuckled, then became serious. "Watch her, Adam. This is coming from the doctor in me. Tonight—the events leading up to tonight—it's all swirling in that head of hers. Add in the side effects she's still feeling from her head injury… I'm not sure what will happen when she lets it out."

"I know. I'll watch her." I hesitated. "So you'll look after everything?"

"Yeah, I will. It's the least I can do."

Fucking right it was.

"What are you going to tell people?"

"That we agreed to part as friends. Simple."

"And then?"

"I'll go to Calgary as planned." He rolled his shoulders. "I think it's time bachelor Bradley got to know the city and all its wonders."

I held out my hand, surprising myself with the gesture. "Good luck."

He took my hand. "Take care of her."

"With my life."

Then he grinned. A wide, evil grin. "And good luck— you're gonna need it."

I glared. "You think I need luck with Ally?"

He shook his head, his grin getting wider. "Nope. Not her. Sarah is now *your* mother-in-law." He chuckled. "Your headache, not mine anymore. And what a fucking headache she is."

He walked away.

I stared after him.

The bastard was right. No matter what happened, Sarah was still Ally's mother, and by marrying her, she was now a permanent part of my life—however limited our contact.

I stomped over to the car.

I should have fucking hit him harder.

CHAPTER
TWENTY-SIX

I SLID into the car and turned toward Ally. Her arms were wrapped around her torso, and she was as far away from me as she could get—tucked right to the door. She was tugging on her sleeves, and her feet were fidgeting. She stared straight ahead, and everything about her screamed *back off*.

I said only one thing. "Please put your seat belt on."

I waited until she complied before I started the car and headed toward home. This wasn't the place to push her. I desperately wanted to reach over and take her hand, touch her in some small way, but somehow I knew I needed to let her be.

My mind flipped through the events of the last couple of days, focusing on the scenes tonight. My reaction to Bradley had surprised me. Aside from the one episode, my desire to hurt him had dissipated when I saw the way his eyes looked when he gazed at Ally. I knew that pain—the pain of losing the person you loved. His case was different, however, because he was going to have to live without her—forever. I wasn't letting her go. I almost felt sorry for him. *Almost.*

But Sarah. My hands tightened on the steering wheel with the rage I was feeling. I would happily have pitched her out the window or hit her with my car for the callous way she'd cast her daughter aside. Ally's happiness meant nothing to her if it caused her the slightest inconvenience.

And I was a big one.

Ally didn't speak until I parked the car.

"Do you have any cereal?"

Cereal?

I wasn't sure I had any sort of edible food left in the cupboards. "Um, if I do, it's stale."

She got out of the car and started walking toward the open garage door. I scrambled out of my seat, slamming the door behind me.

"Where are you going?"

She looked at me as if I was crazy.

"I want some cereal," she stated slowly. "If you don't have any, I'll get some at the convenience store."

Then she kept walking, so I hurried to catch up. She glanced over her shoulder at my approaching footsteps and stopped.

"I'm perfectly capable of going to the store and getting some cereal." She paused, her voice becoming somewhat sarcastic. "I can remember how to get back now."

"You might want some milk, too. And besides, I'm rather hungry, except I don't want cereal. I'll get some chips or something."

She rolled her eyes but didn't order me away—not that I'd go if she did. I let her wander the store, filling her basket with more than highly overpriced cereal and milk. She threw in some chocolate bars and a package of pastries, studying the picture on the box. She paused by the freezer, looking at what I was sure were out-of-date frozen pizzas.

"We can order a pizza if you want," I offered.

She huffed at me with a glare and moved on, waiting for me by the display of chips. Obviously, I had displeased her with the offer of a fresh pizza instead of a freezer-burned one from the convenience store. Blindly, I grabbed a couple of bags and threw them into the basket.

"Do you have any beer?"

I had to look away so she didn't see my grin. Ally hated beer and never drank it. I wasn't sure why she suddenly wanted some. Bradley was right—she was all over the place.

"Yeah. A couple bottles."

I got another glare when I reached across her at the counter and paid for the items. I handed her one of the bags to carry, and we were silent until we got into the loft.

She went directly to the kitchen and grabbed the only bowl, sitting down at the counter and opening her Alpha-Bits. I sipped a beer and munched some chips while I watched her, fascinated. She ate an entire bowl and poured another one before she slowed down. I had never seen her eat so fast.

She turned to me, her eyes narrowed, her voice challenging. "You and Bradley were all buddy-buddy. Are you best friends now?"

I blinked. Was that what was upsetting her the most?

"No," I replied. "We'll never be friends. I thought he'd lost enough tonight," I explained. "He lost you, after all. That's one hell of a punishment."

"Hmph."

"Did you want me to beat him up, Nightingale? I can go find him and do that if you'd feel better."

"Don't be ridiculous."

"He's an asshole and took full advantage of the situation to keep you. I agree with that." I risked touching her shoulder. "I can't say, if the situations were reversed, I wouldn't have tried to keep you as well."

She glared at me. "You'd lie to me for months? Keep me away from the person I loved so you wouldn't be unhappy?"

I let out a long exhale. "No. I don't think I could do that to you." I caressed her arm. "As much as it would kill me, if I knew you loved someone else, I'd let you go. Your happiness is more important."

She softened a little under my touch. "It always is with you, isn't it?"

"Always."

"Because you love me."

"Yeah, Nightingale. I do."

Her lip started to quiver. "You're the only one who does."

"Ally, your mother—"

"Don't call her that!" she yelled, slamming her hand on the counter so hard that her bowl and spoon rattled.

"I—"

"She isn't my mother! She never has been!" Tears began to run down her face. "All I've ever been to her is a burden —she's never forgiven my father for dying! She never even wanted me! You heard her, Adam. I'm just like him! All these years, she's tried to make me like *her*, but it didn't work. I'm. Just. Like. Him!"

I had no idea what to say to soothe her. I wasn't sure if there was anything that would calm her right now.

"Why couldn't she love me? Why couldn't I ever be good enough?"

"You are good enough. The problem is with *her*, not you."

"She made it my problem, though, didn't she? And I let her. I let them rule my life." A sob escaped her lips. "All I ever wanted was for them to love me. Why couldn't they just love me?"

"I don't know, baby. I don't know if either of them knows how to love. You deserve nothing but love. Sarah…" I paused, not sure how to continue with this unpleasant subject.

"What?"

I drew in a deep breath. "She's an unhappy, uptight,

scared woman. She lost herself somewhere, and in doing so, she lost you too. You have to forgive her and move on."

Suddenly, she was furious. "Forgive her? You want me to *forgive* her? When did you get so fucking magnanimous? You shake hands with Bradley, you tell me to forgive my mother? Well, fuck that!

"Fuck it all!"

Her cereal bowl flew, hitting the wall and shattering into hundreds of shards, the wet mess dripping down the concrete surface. My half-full bottle of beer followed, the foamy liquid exploding as the glass smashed. The milk was next, the white spray hitting the counter, she threw it so hard—then the open bag of chips, the contents spilling everywhere. The one and only mug we had left met its demise in a blaze of curse words as she flung it, almost panting in her fury. I wasn't in time to stop her when the glass coffeepot sailed past me, the sound almost like a high-pitched shriek when it hit the wall, bursting into tiny fragments that flew far and wide.

I stared at the destruction she had caused in such a short period of time. It was impressive. So were the curse words she had shouted as she raged. I'd never heard her use language like that before in anger. I wasn't even aware she knew half those words. I was partially upset, more than amused, and somewhat turned on.

"Well," I drawled. "Guess I rubbed off on you more than I realized. The coffee shop will thank you for that tomorrow morning. I have a feeling we're gonna need a lot of caffeine, and they'll benefit from your little tantrum—spectacular as it was."

Her gaze flew to mine, and she crumpled. She dropped her face into her hands, sobbing. Her knees buckled, and I lunged forward, catching her before she hit the floor. Lifting her into the safety of my arms, I held her close. Hiccupping apologies and incoherent words were intermingled with her harsh cries. I carried her to the bed, cradling her face to my chest, letting her sob. The past few days had been one emotional upheaval after another for her, and the scene with her mother tonight had been the final straw. She needed to let it out. I ran my hands up and down her back in comforting passes and nuzzled her hair. Her hot tears soaked into my shirt, and as much as I hated hearing her crying, it was better than her holding in the pain.

Her sobs became gradual whimpers, and the horrible shudders eased off to shivers as she quieted. When she tilted her head back, I handed her some tissues, letting her wipe her eyes and nose. I dabbed at her cheeks when more tears slid down.

"I got your shirt wet."

I chuckled. "Snotty, too."

Her lips trembled, and I shook my head. "I'm teasing. It's fine." I shifted, sliding her forward a little, and tore my shirt over my head, tossing it away. "See? It's fine."

"I'm sorry. I made a mess."

"We'll clean it up." I ran my fingers through her knotted hair. "Do you feel better?"

"I feel confused and…torn."

"Understandable."

"They controlled me for years. I was never going to be enough. I accepted the blame for Ollie's death because they told me it was my fault. They drummed it into my head for years, and I believed them. But it wasn't my fault."

Hallelujah. She finally understood.

I caressed her cheek. "No, it wasn't."

"No more, Adam. It was an accident. I'm not going to be their scapegoat anymore."

"Good. You're done with them. With all that bullshit."

She looked toward the kitchen. "I shouldn't have done that, though."

"I must be a bad influence." I smirked down at her, trying to get her to smile. "It's okay. We'll get more bowls and stuff. You could have spared the coffeepot, though. It never did anything bad. I'd finally broken it in, so the java tasted good."

"Um, Adam, your coffee is like tar."

I was quite partial to my strong brew. "Exactly."

"I'll replace it. The coffeepot, I mean."

I shook my head. "We'll call it even over your mug. They died in acts of bravery." I kissed her nose. "We'll add a new one to the list, along with dishes."

"We'll pick out different ones."

"Damn right." I traced a finger down her damp skin. "New dishes, new coffeepot, and a new life—for both of us." I hesitated. "You have to forgive her to move on, baby. I do too. We need to. It doesn't mean what she did was right —Bradley, either. But that's how closure begins."

"I don't know if I'm ready to forgive."

I brushed a kiss to her forehead. "Okay, I can understand that. There isn't a time limit on any of this. I think maybe you should talk to someone—someone who can help you deal with all this. You've been through so much."

"I can't talk to you?"

I smiled ruefully. "You can always talk to me. But maybe someone who doesn't want to push your mother into an oncoming train. A professional who can help you sort through everything and come to terms with it."

"I'll think about it."

"Okay."

"But I want to go away—just get away from here—from all of it."

"We will. We'll sort everything out here, and we'll leave. We can start planning tomorrow." I brushed my lips across hers. "We'll get a legal marriage license, then I'll marry you, and we'll go."

"You want to get married here?"

"Here first, then anywhere you want. I'll marry you a hundred times over. We can renew our vows any place you like. Privately, in front of people, man, or God. I don't care. But when we leave here, I'll have a piece of paper that tells the world you're mine and nothing can come between us or take you away. All right?"

"Yes."

"Then we'll go."

"Where?"

"Fiji first—like we planned. I want you somewhere warm and peaceful. Us, a villa, and nothing but the ocean and sun. We'll recover from all this and then move forward. England and Scotland next."

"Ireland?" she asked eagerly, with a small spark in her eye. I had missed that spark.

"Yes. Then we'll head to mainland Europe."

I stroked her cheek with the back of my hand. She leaned into my caress with a small smile, then gasped as she pulled my hand down. "Adam! Your knuckles are all bruised!"

I grunted. "Bradley has an incredibly hard jaw. His abs weren't anything to sneeze at either." I inspected her palm. "How about you?"

She shook her head. "It's fine." She blushed. "I've never slapped anyone before. I don't think I did it right."

"You can try it again if you want—as long as it's Bradley you slap." I kissed her palm. "Although I don't want you to hurt yourself. So, if you feel the need, tell me, and I'll do it for you."

She giggled, the sound making me happy. I was glad the storm had passed—at least for now. I knew there was a chance I'd witness more outbursts as she dealt with everything she'd been through.

She looked at my hand again. "You need an ice pack."

She climbed off me and headed to the kitchen, stopping at the counter.

"Oh no," she breathed out. "I made a huge mess."

I joined her, nodding at the disastrous state the kitchen was currently in. I shoved my feet into my sneakers and picked my way through the glass and broken ceramic to grab the ice pack. "I got past the blood thing, but I still don't want you spilling yours, thank you." I handed the ice pack to her, and we lay on the bed. She wrapped the ice around my throbbing hand.

"It doesn't bother you anymore—the blood, I mean?"

I shrugged. "It was always seeing my own that was the worst, and with everything I did to help at the clinic, it doesn't faze me anymore." I tweaked her nose. "But stay out of the kitchen without shoes until we clean it up."

"Will you take me to meet Peter and Edwina one day?"

I smiled. "You'd like that?"

"Yes. I want to meet them and see the clinic that bears Elena's name."

"I'd like them to meet you as well. I talked Edwina's ear off about you." I chuckled. "Peter's too, I suppose. On the next trip. This one is all about us."

"Okay."

The ice felt good. Relaxing together also felt good. We were quiet for a while as the ice soothed my hand and the silence soothed Ally. I felt her relax more and more as I held her. She snuggled into my embrace, flattening herself against me. I held her as tight as I could.

She yawned, and a shiver of exhaustion went through her. I traced my finger under her weary eyes. "Can you sleep now, Nightingale?"

"If you keep holding me."

"Always."

———

Before my eyes had opened, I knew. She wasn't in bed with me. She wasn't even in the loft. I was out of bed in an instant, searching for my pants. I couldn't explain my panic, but I needed to know where she was. I dragged on a shirt and bent down to grab my sneakers, stopping only when I saw the piece of pink paper sticking out of one of them.

Relax, Adam. Giving the coffee shop some
business. I'll be back before you know it.
Keep the bed warm for me.
I love you. xx

I quirked my eyebrow and grinned.

She was on a coffee run, and she had left me a task.

I stood and looked over at the kitchen. Ally had obviously been busy while I slept. The floor was swept, a pile of glittering glass in the corner. She had wiped down the wall as well, although it was going to need some scrubbing. Little pieces of cereal were stuck in places, and some chip crumbs were scattered around. I traced some of the new scratches and nicks in the wall, remembering her breakdown last night. I hoped today would be a better day for her. For us.

I glanced behind me at the bed.

She wanted it warm when she got home.

I could do that.

A short time later, the door opened quietly, the telltale squeak of the bottom hinge giving away Ally's attempted stealth. I remained on my back, keeping my breathing steady as she approached the bed. She placed something on the table, then the mattress dipped as she settled beside me. She ran her fingers through my hair, light, gentle passes reminding me so much of the first time we met.

"Adam," she murmured. "Wake up for me."

I was enjoying her touches too much, so I kept my eyes shut and burrowed deeper into the warmth of the bed, rolling onto my side toward her. Her low laugh made me want to smile, but I didn't want her to know I was awake. She stroked the skin of my neck, her fingertips cool from being outside, making me shiver.

"I have coffee," she whispered. "I got you a breakfast sandwich at Alvin's too. The double bacon one you love so much."

I grunted a little but kept up the charade of being asleep, even though Alvin's sandwiches were awesome—and she did destroy my snack last night. But I had missed her playing with my hair and her sweet way of waking me up, so I decided to pretend a little more. She bent closer, the ends of her hair tickling my face.

"You, Adam, are the world's *worst* faker. I know you're awake."

I cracked open an eye, meeting her lovely blue gaze. "How?" I rasped.

"I just know you." She passed her hand along my hairline, tenderly ruffling the mess. "I know what you look like when you're really asleep as opposed to faking it for head rubs." She smirked. "I figured that out the first night I met you. You faked most of it then, too."

Reaching out, I pulled her down next to me, chuckling at her gasp. I hovered over her, grinning. "Think you have me all figured out, do you?"

"Yes."

"You know me?"

"Yes."

My voice became husky. "You know what's going to happen next?"

Her cheeks became pink, the color extending down her neck. "I know what I *hope*..." she breathed out.

My body responded to her blush. It always did. I felt my cock begin to harden with desire. It had been so long without her. I had been so long without her. "Tell me," I demanded, tracing a finger down her neck.

"I hope the coffee is going to get cold."

"And?"

"I hope you're naked under those sheets."

"And if I am?"

"I'll join you."

"Well, today is your lucky day. I kept the bed warm like you asked, I *am* naked," I murmured, grinding my hips against her, "and I am more—*more* than *happy* to have you join me."

"Adam," she moaned.

"Are you ready for this? For me to make you mine again?"

"Oh God…*yes.*"

I found the hem of her shirt. "Good."

Within seconds, we were pressed into each other, nothing between us but air. I groaned loudly at the feeling of having her skin flush with mine. "Like silk, baby," I murmured as I caressed the smoothness with my lips. The warmth of the blankets around us was nothing compared to the heat coursing through my body at being able to touch her again. I spent endless moments reacquainting myself with her. I traced every dip and hollow with my fingers and lips, tasted her everywhere with my tongue—reclaiming every inch of her as mine.

"So fucking beautiful." I ran my tongue over the freckles I had missed so much. "Mine, Ally, you're mine."

"Yes," she whimpered. "Yours," she vowed, dragging my mouth back to hers, infusing my senses with her cinnamon-scented breath.

"I love you," was murmured repeatedly as our mouths joined and separated, our skin sliding sensuously together as our bodies melded into one. The feeling of her hands on my skin, pressing and grabbing to keep me close, was grounding. Her soft pants of desire and the pleading way she whispered my name brought back memories of the times I'd longed to hear her say it. I blinked back the moisture in my eyes, looking down at her to see the same intense emotion reflected in her stare. Love blazed from her fierce gaze.

I couldn't get close enough; I couldn't feel her enough. Her touch was overwhelming, and yet still, I needed more. I cried out her name as she wrapped her hand around my erection, stroking and urging me closer. I settled between her thighs, feeling her readiness, desperate to be inside her.

"*Now*, Adam," she pleaded. "I need you now."

As I slipped inside her heat, my eyes shut. A long shudder rippled down my spine as I felt her surrounding me again—welcoming me back home. Cradled inside her body, I was finally complete.

I opened my eyes, our gazes locking. Fervent golden brown met adoring blue. I kissed the tear rolling down her cheek as she whispered my name, the one word saturated with so much love and tenderness my heart ached from it. I began moving, long, slow thrusts, as I showed her with my body how much she had been missed. How much I loved her.

I had fucked her. Made love to her. But nothing was like this—so powerful. It was coming home, being born again, and knowing how close I had been to losing her forever. It was overwhelming and emotional. It was painful and beautiful. It was agony and ecstasy all rolled into one.

It was perfect.

I buried my head into her neck, breathing her in, groaning her name. Ally clung to me, moving with me as we loved. Everything about her came back tenfold. The clutch and pull of her body entwined with mine, her sharp gasps of pleasure in my ear, the way her hands felt on my skin were all so new and yet so familiar. She cried out my name, coming hard around me, her muscles fluttering, my own release following in rapid response. It sparked and surged down my spine, piercing me with an intensity I had only ever experienced with her—as much an emotional release as a physical one. I gripped the pillow around her head, feeling the material give way under my hands as I roared her name and came inside her.

For a moment, there was nothing except the blissful peace as my body surrendered to the pleasure and I held my girl. She stroked my chest, her hair a heavy cloud around her face. I gathered the thick tresses, pulling her face up to mine and kissing her deeply.

Her voice caught. "I missed you so much, Adam."

I held her tightly. "I missed you. But it's behind us now."

Her voice was muffled. "I know."

I nuzzled her head. "Never again. We'll never be apart again."

"No."

"And no more leaving to get coffee. Wake me up."

"You were sleeping peacefully. You didn't even move while I was cleaning up. I wasn't gone that long."

"I didn't like it," I confessed. "As soon as I woke up, I knew you weren't here. It reminded me of all those mornings I woke up without you." I paused, clearing my throat of emotion. "I'm not ready to do that again."

She tightened her arms. "I didn't think—I'm sorry."

"I just need time, Nightingale."

She tilted her head back. "We both do. We'll figure it out."

I pressed a kiss to her head. "Okay."

———

I smirked at her as I sipped my coffee and ate my breakfast sandwich, sharing nibbles with her. They had been reheated in the microwave, tasting better because of the reason they had to be warmed. Ally was furiously writing out a list, her tongue sticking out as she concentrated. I had to resist throwing down the sandwich and taking her tongue into my mouth instead. It would taste even better.

She glanced up, color instantly staining her cheeks as she saw me watching her, knowing exactly what I was thinking. I winked at her with a grin.

"Keep writing, Nightingale. We have a lot of stuff to replace."

She chuckled, freezing as my phone rang out with a tone she recognized. Her panicked gaze met mine, and I shook my head with a mild curse. "No. That's *not* happening. I forgot I was supposed to have coffee with Sean this morning. I'm sure he's calling to give me shit for being late."

"Why were you having coffee?" she asked, her voice anxious.

"I gave him the pictures of my time in Africa. He wants to use some of them." I picked up her hand, kissing the palm. "That's all. I am *not* leaving you again. Not ever."

Her shoulders loosened. "Oh."

The phone fell silent, and she looked at it. "You should call him back and go meet with him."

I chewed the last bite of my sandwich, crumpling up the paper and tossing it into the bag. "What will you do?"

"I thought I would see if Vivian was working. She deserves to know the truth about what happened."

I nodded slowly. I knew it was stupid to be anxious about being apart. We had things we needed to do. I reached out my hand, grabbing hers. "How about I drop you off, and when I pick you up, we can go get our marriage license? Then we can go shopping. Are you up for that?"

"I'd like that."

"Is an hour enough?"

She shook her head. "Adam—"

"Okay. One and a half?"

"Yes."

"We need to go see my lawyer. He can file the papers, and I want to make sure everything is taken care of. I swear, if there is one mismanaged dollar, your mother is going to regret it."

"I don't care about the money."

"*I care.* They have taken so much away from you. We'll get everything transferred back to your name and under your power." I tilted my head in curiosity. "What have you been doing for money?"

"I had a debit card my mother gave me," she replied. "She told me that she paid the bills from my account. I imagine she's canceled the card by now. I guess I'm broke until this is resolved."

I shook my head and reached into the drawer, handing her an envelope. "I, ah, had ordered a second debit card for you before all this happened. It gives you access to my accounts. It's active, and you can use it now." I held up my hand to stop her protests. "Please, let me take care of you. We *are* married after all." I nudged her foot with mine. "We consummated it and everything."

She rolled her eyes, and I snickered, before becoming serious. "We'll let the lawyers straighten everything out. What's mine is yours."

"Then what's mine is yours as well," she insisted.

"I know that. You need to accept this—" I held up the card "—and use it for whatever you need. Clothes, shoes, girly shit…whatever. We'll figure it all out and get you cards with your married name on them. Assuming you want to change your name?"

"Yes, I do. I want to belong to you in every way."

I ran my finger down her cheek. "So do I. Alexandra Kincaid. It's got a nice ring to it."

She smiled. "Yes, it does."

"All right." I winked. "Maybe you'd like to stock up on some pretty lingerie, Mrs. Kincaid. You do have a long honeymoon coming up."

A mischievous smile curved her lips. "Is that the only thing…coming up, Mr. Kincaid?"

I dragged her onto my lap, laughing.

"Nope," I growled, covering her mouth with mine.

I'd show her what else was coming up.

Repeatedly.

CHAPTER
TWENTY-SEVEN

ALLY WRAPPED her hand around the door handle of the car, and she hesitated. "Maybe only an hour."

I nodded. "Okay."

She paused again. I ran my fingers along her neck. "You know, I'd like to see Vivian."

Her expression was filled with relief. "Yeah?"

"I know Sean would love to finally meet you."

"Are we being ridiculous?"

I shrugged. "I don't care. If we want to stay together, we can. We can try tomorrow or the next day to do things without each other—or next week. But for today, I'd feel better being beside you." I hesitated, my voice gruffer when I spoke again. "I was without you for too long to have to apologize for wanting to be with you now."

"Me too."

"Okay. Vivian first, Sean next. Then we'll do our errands—the lawyer and shopping."

"You forgot the license."

I shook my head, lifted her hand, and kissed it. "That isn't an errand. That's the highlight of my afternoon." I winked. "I don't think I have to tell you the highlight of the morning."

"Your sandwich?" she replied, smiling widely.

I laughed. "My Ally sandwich, yes. You were as tasty as I remembered."

Her cheeks flushed and I chuckled. "You go get Vivian. I'll park and be right behind you."

"Okay."

———

Vivian was shocked when Ally told her the story. She shook her head in disbelief.

"Oh Alex, how terrible." She clasped her hand. "I'm so glad you remembered. I wish I'd met you sooner. Been part of your memories and could have helped Adam find you."

Ally smiled. "It feels as if you've been in my life longer than you have, Vivian. You were my favorite boss. When you took over running the ER, it got so much better."

"Will you be back?" Vivian asked hopefully.

Ally shook her head, meeting my eyes. I lifted Ally's hand and kissed the knuckles.

"I'm taking her away, Vivian. For a long time. Any place

she wants to go, that's where we'll go. We need to get away from here for a while and heal. Both of us."

Vivian smiled. "I understand. But your job is there if you ever want it. I'd hire you in a heartbeat."

Ally grinned. "A good backup plan."

"One you won't need," I murmured.

She met my eyes, her expression soft. "No, I won't."

———

Ally's low laughter across the room made me pause in my discussion with Sean and look over. She was being entertained by not only Chris but Tommy as well. They were showing her some pictures and, no doubt, telling stories of me from the times we had worked together. She was in the same room and I could see her, so I was relaxed.

Sean grinned as he looked between us. "It's good to see you look like this, Adam."

"Feels good too."

"She's lovely."

I grinned. "I know."

"I can't believe all the shit her mother pulled."

My expression darkened. "She's a piece of work. I hope she pays."

He regarded me silently for a minute. "You know, I've heard rumors."

"Oh?"

"I was having dinner the other day with some friends. Ronald's name came up."

I moved forward, suddenly very interested. "Do tell."

"It seems Mr. Givens has been doing a bad job lately of managing his affairs—his business is in trouble."

I drew in a sharp breath. "Meaning?"

He shrugged. "Bad decisions and management, investments going south. The rumor is he is on the brink of disaster."

Ronald's absence and the strange look on Sarah's face last night suddenly made sense.

"Could just be that—rumors," I mused.

He shrugged. "My sources are well-connected. Rumors tend to have some truth behind them. I saw him a few weeks ago while I was out of town at some meetings. I went down to the bar to have a drink, and he was there." He sat back. "He didn't see me, but I saw him."

"And?"

"He wasn't alone. And it wasn't Sarah with him."

I let out a low whistle.

Sean smirked. "They were pretty...*cozy*. That might be part of the problem."

I stared at him. If this was true, Sarah had a whole new set of things to occupy her time. A possible failed marriage and no money would be two very hard, bitter pills for her to swallow.

"Your new mother-in-law may need a place to live, Adam."

I grinned. "I hear accommodations at the Y are excellent."

"You'd let that happen to her mother? You'd let her be thrown into the streets?"

"After what she did? Without another thought."

"What about your wife?"

I exhaled heavily. "I'm sure Ally would have different thoughts on the subject."

Despite what her mother had done, Ally would never allow her to suffer if she could help. I'd let her rot, but I wasn't sure how Ally would react.

"I'm not saying anything right now. Keep me posted, though." I shook my head. "What a two-faced, sanctimonious bastard he is."

"There's more."

"Oh?"

"He's sent me all sorts of investment opportunities over the years. I've never been interested, but the last one that came mentioned one name in particular that stood out."

"Oh?"

"Bradley Bennett." He raised his eyebrow in amusement. "I doubt that will happen now that the marriage is off. And if the other rumor I heard is true, he *needed* that deal."

Another piece clicked into the puzzle. The reason they pushed so hard for Ally to marry Bradley—it was more than just control. Ronald needed the money. Once again, he wanted to take from Ally.

"Too fucking bad for him, isn't it?" I grinned at Sean. "She doesn't owe him her life. If it's true, he made this mess. He can deal with it."

"You'll tell her?"

"Yes, but not today. I'm marrying her legally soon, and then I'm taking her away. We're going to spend time on us. Nothing else." I pulled my hand through my hair, tugging on the ends. "But she's been lied to enough, so I'll tell her if and when something concrete happens. I'm not jumping the gun on rumors. I'll support her no matter what she decides."

"Sarah may have suspected something. Maybe that was part of all her lies. She was desperate," Sean said, rubbing his chin.

I snorted. "She was stupid. If she had supported me, *us*, and this happened, I would have taken care of her. She would have been as protected as Ally. I would have made sure of it."

"You're a good man."

I shook my head. "Part of me is hoping shit happens and happens fast, and Sarah is screwed for a while. It would serve her right."

"But you'd help her if Ally asked."

"Yes."

"Like I said, good man."

I narrowed my eyes and glared. "Don't let that shit get out. I have a reputation as a hard-ass."

He laughed, and I had to join him.

Hard-ass for everyone—but my girl.

We both knew it.

————

As soon as we had the license, I married my Ally on Sean's boat at the marina. It was really where it all started for us— me taking pictures of his boat. Without that request, I would never have met Ally.

The sun was setting low in the sky, and the colors of the sunset shimmered on her hair, highlighting the red. She wore a pretty cream-colored dress that floated around her feet, and I donned her favorite suit and tie. When I slipped her ring back on to her finger, the glimmer of happy tears I saw were mirrored in mine. I liked the feel of the heavy band she placed on my finger. Theo's ring now rested on my right hand, and I didn't plan on removing it. The meaning of the Celtic symbols resonated with me, and I felt as if I had a part of Elena close.

Our gathering was small. Emma stood for Ally, while Sean was my best man. The people we cared about witnessed us become husband and wife. Sitting on the table beside us in the place of honor was a photograph of the woman we loved and missed—Elena. Amid flowers and candles, the air filled with soft music, we celebrated our love and our marriage.

The first time.

I married her again on the beach in Fiji, just us and the stars as we recited our vows to each other. We had been there six weeks, the time away helping us heal. Our days were spent in warm sunshine, our nights in each other's arms. We explored the island, visiting my favorite places, discovering new ones, always hand in hand. Ally rested by the shaded area of our back garden, often sleeping in my arms after we made love in the hammock or the heated water of the pool. We were rarely apart, and we were content to be that way.

I smiled all the time, and Ally was relaxed and happy, seldom a frown crossing her face, unless I hid her clothes again and called another naked day.

Those were my favorite days.

From Fiji, I took her to England. We spent another six weeks driving along narrow roads and exploring ancient ruins and castles.

There, we met a woman vicar, who, after hearing our story and Ally's desire to be married in a county chapel, did exactly that for us. Not, she explained, in any official capacity, but as with the beach in Fiji, for our own memories. Ally said she felt as if we'd been blessed that day. I knew I'd been blessed since the day she came into my life.

I whispered our vows to her while we stood looking over the craggy, foggy moors of Scotland, feeling as though we were the only two people on earth. Then one night, stumbling back to the hotel in the late hours, after an evening at the local pub in Ireland, our sloppy kisses and slurred words still meaningful. And once more in the early morning hours on a beach in Greece as the water lapped at our feet and the sun danced on the lazy waves. Her happiness reflected the warmth of the air around us.

Every chance I got, I recommitted myself to her.

On her right hand now resided a sapphire ring, the blue so deep and vivid it was a replica of her stunning eyes. I saw it in a jewelry store window in London, the remarkable blue catching my eye. The small diamonds around it shone like bright stars. I was like a kid on Christmas morning waiting for her to notice it on the napkin where I'd placed it, beside her breakfast plate.

Room service had to be reordered. She lunged my way, and the tray went the other. We made love among the crumpet crumbs and sheets damp with tea and sticky with marmalade. It was perfect.

Our extended honeymoon was the ideal start to our life together.

My bag held many SD cards filled with pictures. Thousands of images I had taken of the scenery around us, the memories we had made, the adventures we'd experienced. Many shots of the two of us showed us wrapped around each other, laughing and in love. There were a few that were quiet and reflective—deep in thought. Some Ally had snapped of me while I was unaware.

And, of course, *her*. I had thousands of images of her.

Smiling, joyful, sweet as she loved me.

Annoyed, exasperated, resigned as she argued with me.

Sleeping and content with a small smile curving her lips.

Excited and wide-eyed as she discovered a new adventure with me.

Sad as she left each place, holding the memory of our time there in her tears.

My wife.

————

I looked over at her, her expression reflective as she gazed outside into the dark sky surrounding the plane.

"What are you thinking?"

She smiled as she turned her head, resting her chin on my shoulder. I leaned my cheek on her head. "You look very serious."

"I'm thinking I'm glad to be going home. And yet," she sighed, the sound sad and quiet, "I don't want it to be over."

"It's not. We're just going to reconnect with our lives here. Check in on everyone and then decide our next step. We can go away again, stay here, move—whatever you want." Brushing my fingers along her cheek, I smiled. "Home isn't four walls anymore. It's where you are."

She snuggled closer. "I always thought I was a homebody, but I'm already longing for the next adventure."

"That's because your wings were clipped, Nightingale. I'll take you anywhere you want to go. Name it, and it's yours."

"Africa?"

I snickered into her hair. I knew she'd want that next.

She wanted to meet Peter and Edwina. She wanted to meet the children. To see the place I had spent all those months without her and visit the clinic Elena's money had founded.

"If that's what you want. You'll need some shots."

"I know. I already checked."

"Of course you did. How about we get home and settle in for a while, and we'll plan it, yeah?"

"I'm not sure I'm ready for real life again."

"Real life?"

"People…questions." She hesitated.

"We've been gone for six months—it's old news. People will have moved on to more important stories." I grinned. "Besides, the ex-groom has moved on as well."

Bradley had announced the cancelation of their wedding in a simple statement, then left town for his new life. He sent Ally a text about four months into our trip, telling her he had met a neurosurgeon and fallen—hard. They were already living together, and he now understood, more than ever, how wrong his actions had been. He expressed his apologies and hoped one day she would meet Jillian, to whom he had lost his heart. He also hoped one day to earn her forgiveness.

Ally was pleased for him. I was glad it was something she didn't feel bad about anymore and slightly disappointed there didn't seem to be any excuse to have to hit him again. He had moved on, so I had no reason to dislike him as strongly. I still did, though.

"You're right."

The announcement came over the speaker that we were beginning our final descent. I kissed her hand. "You ready?"

"As long as I have you, then I'm good."

"Then you're set for life."

———

The loft was clean and ready for us. We set down our bags and looked around. It was the same, and yet so different. The space was large and felt rather empty.

"We need more furniture," Ally mused.

I laughed. "Ten seconds and she's ready to shop." I grabbed my messenger bag and put it on the desk. "We can find you whatever you like. Maybe we want a different place."

She paused as she reached for her case. "A different place?"

"Maybe we should have a house, with a yard, for the kids."

"Kids?" she repeated.

I frowned at her and ran my hand along the back of my neck. "We've discussed having a family. Maybe we should think of a house instead of a warehouse loft in the middle of a business area."

A teasing grin curled up her lips. "Are you pregnant, Adam?"

I chuckled and waggled my eyebrows at her. "No. Not from lack of trying, though."

She laughed. "Well, I guess we'll have to try harder."

"Now you're talking, wild girl."

"What will you do with this place?"

"Keep it as a studio. The light is great." I leered at her. "We can use it for afternoon trysts when the kids become too much. Unload them on a nanny and come here and be naughty." I grinned, then thrust my hips. "Make more little buggers to drive us crazy."

She chuckled and walked toward the kitchen, checking out the cupboards and refrigerator. I knew she had asked the woman who came in to check and clean the loft to pick up a few things. I grinned when I saw her reach for the coffeepot. We had an unhealthy addiction to caffeine, and what they served on the plane barely passed as dark water, let alone coffee. It had been a long trip home, and I needed some coffee to stay awake.

We moved around, unpacking the necessities, and sitting at the counter with mugs of the steaming brew. Ally was quieter than I expected. I nudged her leg with my foot. "What's on your mind?"

Her gaze was honest and slightly apprehensive.

"I was wondering…"

"About?"

"Well, like you said, we've discussed children, but we never talked about when."

"Whenever you want them. We can travel now, later, with them, after them… We can settle here and never go anywhere else. I just want my life with you. Our children will only make life better." I tilted my head as I studied her. "Are you ready for them now?"

She furrowed her brow, then shook her head. "No. I don't want to wait a long time, though. I want to show our children everything. Be part of their life." Her expression grew wistful. "I'll make sure they know how much I love them—every day. They will never doubt what they mean to me."

I caught her hand with mine. "I know you will. You'll be an amazing mother. You have so much love inside you. Our children will know it—the same way I do."

She nodded, her eyes glimmering in the light. She still got emotional when she spoke of children or anything to do with her own childhood. Her mother would, I knew, remain a painful subject for a long time. I drew in a deep breath, thinking of the email I had received from Sean last week.

He let me know, only a couple weeks ago, Ronald's company had declared bankruptcy, and the gossip had been rampant. Reports of mismanagement and embezzling were persistent. More rumors of a mistress added to the whole distasteful package. I had almost taken Ally on another side trip to delay her having to hear about what was going on—and any chance of having to deal with it. But I knew she would be upset if she found out why I wanted to stay away longer.

Unable to hide the truth from her, I held her hand. "I have something to tell you."

"Okay."

I told her the truth Sean had shared with me, unsure as to her reaction. I was shocked when she nodded, not at all surprised at the news.

"I do know how to use Google," she informed me. "I saw something in the newsfeed."

"You've known all this time? You didn't say anything."

She arched her eyebrow at me. "Neither did you."

"I didn't want to upset you."

She stroked my cheek. "No, you wanted to protect me." She smiled in understanding. "I love you for that."

"I love you."

"What do you think will happen?"

"I think life for Sarah and Ronald is about to take a fast turn to reality. It's going to be a rude awakening."

She lowered her head. "I don't care about Ronald," she whispered. "He made his own decisions."

"Your mother?" I asked through tight lips.

I wanted the bitch to suffer. To see her haughty manner dissolve when she had to pay bills and forgo her designer shoes and lunch at the club. Her so-called friends would turn their backs once she was no longer "one of them," and she would find herself alone and an outcast. I wanted her to have to clean houses and scrub floors for a living, her perfectly manicured nails raw and bleeding from actually having to do some work.

"I'm struggling," she admitted.

"Why?"

"Does me turning my back if she needed help make me the same sort of person she is?"

"No, this is entirely different. She chose this life. She's the one who made the decision to align herself with Ronald."

She was quiet for a moment, then shocked me when she nodded. "You're right."

"What are you saying?"

She drew in a long breath. "You told me once I had to forgive her and move on. I did. But what I can't forgive her for is the cruelty she showed to you. The pain she put you, *us*, through. That was deliberate and malicious." She drew back her shoulders. "I will help her if she comes to me and asks forgiveness—from both of us. Otherwise, I'm not going to."

"You won't seek her out?"

"No. She never wanted me, and she cut me out of her life. If she wants my help, she'll have to abide by my rules this time."

"She won't. Because she'd have to swallow her pride."

Which I hoped she'd choke on, I added silently.

"Then she's on her own."

"And you're all right with your decision?"

"I've thought about it a lot, and yes. But if I do help her, I don't want her in our life. I'll help her financially because it's the right thing to do. That's all."

I set down my empty mug and pulled her into my arms. "You're still too good. I wouldn't even consider it."

She smiled up at me, shaking her head. "I'm the lucky one, Adam. I got my fairy tale. I got you. I can afford to be good."

I kissed her. Long and deep, tasting her sweetness, knowing how precious this woman was. How she had it wrong, because I was the lucky one. I chuckled when she yawned, trying to cover it up. It had been a long journey home. I was rather tired myself.

"You wanna nap, my girl? There's a bed over there that looks pretty inviting." I waggled my eyebrows, hoping to coax her into lying with me.

She burrowed into my chest. "Will you kiss me some more in bed?"

We stood, snuggling as we walked to the bed. "I'll kiss you until you fall asleep."

"And when I wake up?"

"I'll kiss you then, too. I plan on kissing you the rest of your life."

"I'll kiss you right back."

I pulled her tight to me as we sank into the deep mattress. "Now you're talking."

EPILOGUE

Three Years Later

THE FLASH WENT OFF AGAIN. And again. With a grin, I looked up from my laptop at my son, who had crawled over and was now using his chubby little finger to press the button on my camera I had left on the floor. Ally constantly told me not to leave things where Teddy could get them now that he was crawling, but I didn't care. I loved watching him explore.

I shoved the laptop off my knees and held out my arms, grinning. "What are you up to, little man? You wanna take some pictures with Daddy? Show Mommy what we did all afternoon while she was out?"

He giggled and chortled away as he crawled toward my

open arms. Scooping him up in my embrace, I nuzzled his downy head, breathing in his special scent. Ivory soap, baby shampoo, and little boy.

My little boy.

Theodore Oliver Kincaid was born eight months ago, completing my world. Ally and I had traveled some more, then bought a house we loved and settled into our life here. Our circle of friends was small but close. Emma and Alan were back in town, their daughter, Anna, almost a year old, and Ally saw lots of her best friend. Sean and his wife, Abby, were frequent visitors. And our closest friends, Peter and Edwina, lived near us, and we saw them almost daily. They were Teddy's godparents and, for all intents and purposes, his grandparents. They doted on him. And us.

As I promised, I took Ally to Africa, where we spent almost a month. A short while after we came home, Edwina and Peter decided it was time to return to Canada when Edwina's sister became ill. Peter flew back regularly, and the supplies I sent over still were well-used. The clinic was thriving, run by local doctors and those who volunteered weeks of their time after the article had come out in Sean's magazine.

In Africa, Ally's need to help overwhelmed her at times. When we came home, she threw herself into volunteering, raising awareness for suffering children everywhere. I supported her with anything she asked. Now that Edwina was back, the two of them made quite a team.

When Ally had told me she was pregnant, my life, which

I didn't think could get any better, expanded to contain joy I couldn't even imagine. She did it in perfect Ally fashion, handing me a small book of pictures she had taken, telling me she had a new project. I was confused as I looked at them.

A picture of a bread roll. One of the oven in the kitchen. One of her pointing to the roll inside the oven. And finally, a selfie of her grinning and holding a positive pregnancy test.

A bun in the oven.

My clever girl.

Teddy squirmed and kicked his feet, his tiny fingers grabbing at the two rings I wore. Theo's ring on my right hand, the heavy silver and black glinting in the light. My wedding ring was made of the same white and rose gold as Ally's. Inside, she included the same words engraved into the thick metal, along with one more.

Always Forever Yours ~ Ally.

I never took it off. Teddy loved to pull at it, grinning and babbling when the light caught it as he yanked on it with his eager hands.

I stood, glancing at the clock. "It's bottle time, isn't it?"

He cooed and made his little grabby hand motions as I heated the bottle, sitting down in the living room to feed him. He gripped the side of the bottle, sucking away as he stared up at me, his eyes blue and similar to Ally's. I ran my fingers through his hair, grinning at the mess of red curls on his head. He had my facial features, although his smile was more like my wife's, and he had her dimples. He was long and lean—a large baby when he was born, weighing in at almost ten pounds. Ally had been huge while she carried him.

When he began to squirm and make his grizzly noises, I lifted him to my shoulder, patting his back. I was soon rewarded with one of his loud burps, and he spit up on my shoulder. I chuckled as my shirt became wet. I always forgot the damn cloth.

"Nice job, buddy," I crooned, lifting him away. "Did you get the sofa again? Mommy will be *thrilled.*"

He beamed down at me, then spewed again. I glanced down at my shirt with a wry grin. Ally was right. I never learned. I held him with one arm and tugged the disgusting shirt over my head, tossing it to the floor. How something so fucking cute could make smells like he did was beyond me.

I grabbed a blanket and flung it over my chest then settled Teddy back down with his bottle. His eyes started to flutter, and I knew he'd be out soon. Our son loved to sleep, and when he did, he slept hard.

The nipple fell from his mouth, and I pulled it away, setting the bottle on the table. I was in no hurry to take him to his crib to lay him down, though. These moments were special. I loved being a dad, and I was surprised how good I was at it. I looked forward to watching him grow, teaching him about football and photography, and being with him. I never thought I would be a homebody, but he and Ally changed all that. The only traveling I was interested in now was when they were with me.

Today, we'd gone to the park and hung out with Peter. I got some great pictures to show Ally when she got home. She'd love them.

With another sigh, I turned and stretched out on the sofa, settling him close on my chest, keeping him safe in my arms. I'd lie here for a while, and then I'd put him down in his crib.

Just a little while.

Gentle fingers ran through my hair, while the voice I loved the most whispered my name close to my ear. "Adam."

Blinking at the light, I squinted up at my wife.

"I love coming home and finding my boys having a snuggle."

Teddy was still wrapped in my arms, his warm weight sunk into my chest. I smiled up at Ally. "We had a busy day."

"Take lots of pictures for me?"

"Always."

"How long have you been asleep?"

I glanced at my watch. "Only about an hour."

She rubbed Teddy's back in long, tender strokes. "Did he eat?"

"Some. He fell asleep pretty fast. Took me out with him too." I grinned.

"Okay, I'll feed him when he wakes up."

"How was the afternoon?"

"Good. We got a lot of interest."

"Of course you did. You and Edwina worked hard on the luncheon." I paused but had to ask, "Was Sarah there?"

A look of pain passed through her eyes, but she simply shook her head. Anger still simmered in my chest every time I thought of that woman. She hadn't been as blind to Ronald as we thought she was, and when the scandal broke, she distanced herself immediately, portraying herself as the victim. He ended up in jail, dying not long after of a massive heart attack. Sarah was like a phoenix and somehow rose from the ashes, marrying yet another wealthy man and carrying on with life. She never once attempted to reconcile with Ally.

Edwina more than made up as a mother figure for her, and I thanked God every day for the blessing of her in our life. She loved Ally like the daughter she never had, and it was returned fully by my wife.

Ally and Sarah did, on occasion, see each other in public. Polite nods were all that passed between them before Ally would turn and walk away, her head held high. Still, I knew it hurt her. It would always hurt her.

I cupped her cheek, stroking the silky skin. She leaned into my caress, our gazes locked as I silently showed her I understood.

She stood, lifting Teddy off my chest, snuggling him close. I missed his warmth immediately and sat up, pulling her down beside me and wrapping them in my arms. He gurgled and shifted but still didn't wake up.

"He sleeps so hard—just like you."

I chuckled. "Yeah, he does. He's safe and content, and he knows it."

She looked up at me, her eyes brilliant in the late afternoon light. "We're both safe and content. Because of you."

"Works both ways, Ally."

She snuggled closer. I brushed my lips over her head. "I was thinking…"

She looked up, already smiling, ready for whatever I had to say. "Yeah?"

"The villa is open next month in Fiji. I checked yesterday. Sean wants a few new pictures. You up for a trip, my girl?"

Excitement lit up her face. She loved it in Fiji. All the stress fell away, and we existed in a world of water and sand, sunshine, and warmth.

"I talked to Peter. He and Edwina would love to go as well. If we stay long enough, maybe Emma, Alan, and Anna could come down for a visit?"

"I'd love that," she breathed out.

"I'll take care of it."

She pressed her soft lips to my cheek. "Adam…"

"What?"

She drew in a deep breath. "I want something."

"It's yours."

"It's rather big."

I grinned in delight. She never asked for anything. Ever. If there was something she wanted, I would get it for her.

"Tell me."

"I want another child."

My eyes widened. "Now?"

She laughed. "Well, it takes a while, but I'd like to start trying. I'd like them to be close in age." She bit her lip. "How do you feel about that?"

Wrapping my hand around her neck, I drew her close and kissed her until I couldn't breathe. Until we were dizzy.

"I feel," I murmured against her lips, "as if I was just given a huge gift. I want more children with you. If you're ready, so am I."

"Yeah?"

"Absolutely."

Then I grinned and winked at her. "I'll make sure to add a couple weeks before and after our visitors at the villa, so we have lots of time to make sure the project is a success." I trailed my lips over her cheek. "Naked private time."

"I like naked private time."

I kissed her again. "I like you."

Her voice caught, and she touched my cheek. "I love you, Adam."

"Always, my Nightingale."

Teddy lifted his head, blinking and sleepy. Ally nuzzled his face, and his chubby cheeks lifted in a wide, toothless grin as he chortled and reached for her. I looked at my wonderful family—my wife and son—knowing that soon we could each be holding a child, and I smiled affectionately, already thinking of the photo I would take.

What an image that would be.

———

Thank you so much for reading THE IMAGE OF YOU. If you are so inclined, reviews are always welcome by me at your retailer.

This was original published by Random House under the Loveswept group. When the rights reverted back to me, I wanted to add back in scenes and expand on some that I felt would give a richer storytelling.

If you love a story that pulls are your heartstrings as the main characters find their way to a happily ever after, my soulmate's standalone, THE SUMMER OF US, should be on your TBR. You meet Sunny and Linc as high school sweethearts falling in love only to be separated by circumstances beyond their control. Finding their way back to one another is the journey I take you on.

Enjoy meeting other readers? Lots of fun, with upcoming book talk and giveaways! Check out Melanie Moreland's Minions on Facebook.

Join my newsletter for up-to-date news, sales, book announcements and excerpts (no spam). Click here to sign up Melanie Moreland's newsletter
or visit https://bit.ly/MMorelandNewsletter

Visit my website www.melaniemoreland.com

ACKNOWLEDGMENTS

This book has been a labor of love. From its first publication until now, many hands have contributed to it.

Stu Reardon, who not only is Adam on the cover, but took the beautiful pictures and captured the feeling of the book the way I described. Your work made me smile. You were a joy to work with and made Karen's year with your generosity and kindness. Thank you.

Lisa, thank you for your patience with a manuscript that proved to be more difficult than expected. Lots of love.

Carissa, thank you for your keen eyes.

Many thanks to my usual team who support and contribute to all my books. Beth, Carol, Deb, Trina, and Melissa—lots of hugs.

Kim, for all you do that I don't understand, and for all your assistance and patience—many thanks, tons of love, and lots of wine.

For Karen, my PA, my friend. You hit it out of the park on this one. Not only did you bring your vision of the cover to life, your beautiful work on the interior on the special edition made it a thing of beauty. Not to mention the hundreds of little ways you look after me and make my life easier. How or why I got so lucky as to have you, I don't know, but I will be eternally grateful that I did. Love you to the moon and back.

Nina (Valentine PR). Thank you—I'm glad to be working with you!

Stephanie, hugs my friend.

To all the bloggers, readers, and my promo team. Thank you for everything you do. Shouting your love of books—of my work, posting, sharing—your recommendations keep my TBR list full, and the support you have shown me is deeply appreciated.

My reader group, Melanie's Minions—love you all.

MLM—for all you do, I cannot say thank you enough. I wish I could hug you all.

Matthew—you are my world. Every book, I write a little of your wonderful soul into it. I am the luckiest woman to be able to call you my husband. Always yours. Forever.

ALSO AVAILABLE FROM MORELAND BOOKS

Titles published under M. Moreland

Insta-Spark Collection

It Started with a Kiss

Christmas Sugar

An Instant Connection

An Unexpected Gift

Harvest of Love

An Unexpected Chance

Following Maggie (Coming Home series)

Titles published under Melanie Moreland

The Contract Series

The Contract (Contract #1)

The Baby Clause (Contract #2)

The Amendment (Contract #3)

The Addendum (Contract #4)

Vested Interest Series

BAM - The Beginning (Prequel)

Bentley (Vested Interest #1)

Aiden (Vested Interest #2)

Maddox (Vested Interest #3)

Reid (Vested Interest #4)

Van (Vested Interest #5)

Halton (Vested Interest #6)

Sandy (Vested Interest #7)

Vested Interest/ABC Crossover

A Merry Vested Wedding

ABC Corp Series

My Saving Grace (Vested Interest: ABC Corp #1)

Finding Ronan's Heart (Vested Interest: ABC Corp #2)

Loved By Liam (Vested Interest: ABC Corp #3)

Age of Ava (Vested Interest: ABC Corp #4)

Sunshine & Sammy (Vested Interest: ABC Corp #5)

Unscripted With Mila (Vested Interest: ABC Corp #6)

Men of Hidden Justice

The Boss

Second-In-Command

The Commander

The Watcher

The Specialist

Reynolds Restorations

Revved to the Maxx

Breaking The Speed Limit

Shifting Gears

Under The Radar

Full Throttle

Mission Cove

The Summer of Us

Standalones

Into the Storm

Beneath the Scars

Over the Fence

The Image of You

Changing Roles

Happily Ever After Collection

Heart Strings

ABOUT THE AUTHOR

NYT/WSJ/USAT international bestselling author Melanie Moreland, lives a happy and content life in a quiet area of Ontario with her beloved husband of thirty-plus years and their rescue cat, Amber. Nothing means more to her than her friends and family, and she cherishes every moment spent with them.

While seriously addicted to coffee, and highly challenged with all things computer-related and technical, she relishes baking, cooking, and trying new recipes for people to sample. She loves to throw dinner parties, and enjoys traveling, here and abroad, but finds coming home is always the best part of any trip.

Melanie loves stories, especially paired with a good wine, and enjoys skydiving (free falling over a fleck of dust) extreme snowboarding (falling down stairs) and piloting her own helicopter (tripping over her own feet.) She's learned happily ever afters, even bumpy ones, are all in how you tell the story.

Melanie is represented by Flavia Viotti at Bookcase Literary Agency. For any questions regarding subsidiary or

translation rights please contact her at flavia@
bookcaseagency.com

facebook.com/authormoreland
twitter.com/morelandmelanie
instagram.com/morelandmelanie
bookbub.com/authors//melanie-moreland

www.ingramcontent.com/pod-product-compliance
Lightning Source LLC
Chambersburg PA
CBHW070230200726
48293CB00005B/1551